T0208669

GOSLING TWO

A Novel

Thomas Dale

authorHOUSE®

AuthorHouse™
1663 Liberty Drive
Bloomington, IN 47403
www.authorhouse.com
Phone: 1-800-839-8640

All characters appearing in this works are fictitious. Any resemblance
to real persons, living or dead is purely coincidental.

First published by AuthorHouse 11/04/2011

ISBN: 978-1-4567-3483-1 (sc)
ISBN: 978-1-4567-3653-8 (ebk)

Printed in the United States of America

Any people depicted in stock imagery provided by Thinkstock are models,
and such images are being used for illustrative purposes only.
Certain stock imagery © Thinkstock.

This book is printed on acid-free paper.

Special Thanks

To my wife, Patti, for patience and proof reading, and Judy Kelly and Rod Jermain for valuable resource material. I owe a great deal to Maralys Wills' critique group, a bottomless well of guidance from other writers who were generous with their time and talent. But to Michele Lack I owe the most, for her unflagging encouragement and assistance.

Contents

The Prologue   xiii

CHAPTER ONE   1

CHAPTER TWO   4

CHAPTER THREE   15

CHAPTER FOUR   27

CHAPTER FIVE   39

CHAPTER SIX   50

CHAPTER SEVEN   57

CHAPTER EIGHT   69

CHAPTER NINE   82

CHAPTER TEN   95

CHAPTER ELEVEN   116

CHAPTER TWELVE   130

CHAPTER THIRTEEN   143

CHAPTER FOURTEEN   160

CHAPTER FIFTEEN   169

CHAPTER SIXTEEN   178

CHAPTER SEVENTEEN   185

CHAPTER EIGHTEEN   192

CHAPTER NINETEEN   199

CHAPTER TWENTY   207

CHAPTER TWENTY-ONE   220

CHAPTER TWENTY-TWO   241

CHAPTER TWENTY-THREE   252

CHAPTER TWENTY-FOUR   261

CHAPTER TWENTY-FIVE   275

CHAPTER TWENTY-SIX   279

CHAPTER TWENTY-SEVEN   288

CHAPTER TWENTY-EIGHT   295

CHAPTER TWENTY-NINE   300

CHAPTER THIRTY   310

EPILOGUE   330

I CERTIFY THAT THE ENTRIES MADE BY ME ABOVE ARE TRUE, COMPLETE AND CORRECT TO THE BEST OF MY KNOWLEDGE AND BELIEF AND ARE MADE IN GOOD FAITH. I UNDERSTAND THAT A KNOWING AND WILLFUL FALSE STATEMENT ON THIS FORM CAN BE PUNISHED BY FINE OR IMPRISONMENT OR BOTH (Sec. U. S. Code, title 18, section 1001)

DATE	SIGNATURE OF PERSON COMPLETING FORM		
9 May 1959	James R. Donlin		
	TYPED NAME AND ADDRESS OF WITNESS		SIGNATURE OF WITNESS
	Lt. Donald W. Gare Tulsa, Oklahoma 714 E. 38th St. N.		Donald W. Gare

THIS SECTION TO BE COMPLETED BY AUTHORITY REQUESTING INVESTIGATION

BRIEF DESCRIPTION OF DUTY ASSIGNMENT AND DEGREE OF CLASSIFIED MATTER (top secret, secret, etc.) TO WHICH APPLICANT WILL REQUIRE ACCESS

Above is now assigned to duties of demolition specialist
in 400th Special Forces Det. Airborne ▮▮▮▮ and is
required to handle up to and including secret material.
D.O. Form 96 has been completed by James R. Donlin.

Anthony I Casson Jr.
40JG USAR
ASST ADJ OFFICER

RECORD OF PRIOR CLEARANCES			AGENCY THAT COMPLETED INVESTIGATION
DATE OF CLEARANCE	TYPE OF CLEARANCE		
REMARKS			

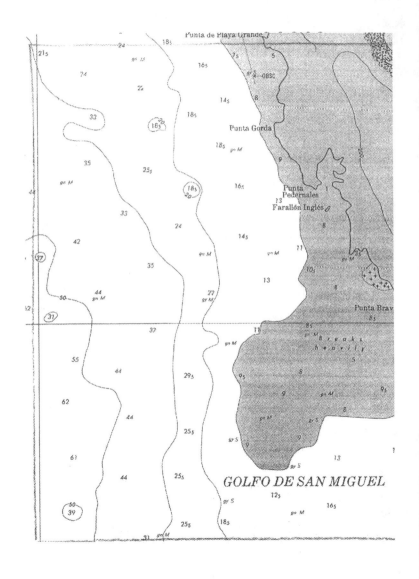

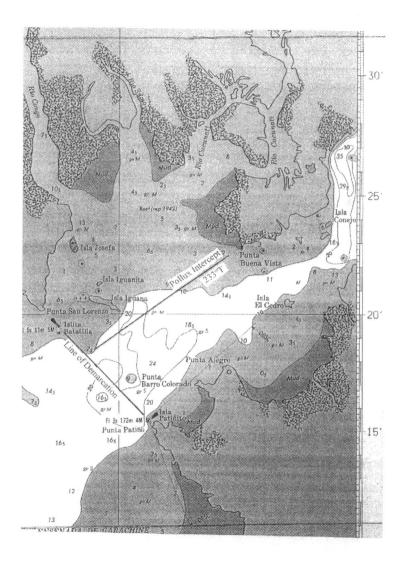

GOSLING TWO
The Prologue

Viva 26 de Julio!

In nineteen sixty-one the Cold War glowed red-hot. The world's spotlight fell on a captured U-2 pilot, Francis Gary Powers, and his trial in Moscow. Cuba, after fighting a bloody revolution to oust Fulgencio Batista Zaldivar, a corrupt US puppet dictator, declared itself Marxist. April 17, 1961, the world witnessed the tragic debacle of the Bay of Pigs Invasion. In August, an ugly wall partitioned East and West Berlin. In the fall, Russia detonated its first hydrogen bomb, with a yield of fifty mega-tons.

In the early fifties, American leadership still smarted from a Russian nose-twisting in the Berlin Airlift. They nervously watched developments in Europe, and the frustrating stagnation of peace talks in Korea, and the furious rantings of Senator Joseph McCarthy. Unfortunately, US intelligence paid little attention to incursions of organized crime into Cuban society and economics or the unscrupulous labor practices of American-owned fruit and sugar companies in Cuba and Central America.

American intelligence organizations were at last compelled to follow the activities of Fidel Castro, an upstart Havana attorney, the son of an exiled Spanish rebel. An inspirational leader, he challenged the status quo by arming rebels to oppose Batista.

Jose Ramon Fernandez and Fidel Castro had launched their crusade on 26 July 1953. They were soon arrested by the secret police and charged with plotting against the Batista regime.

After their release from prison in 1955, the revolution resumed and Fernandez became Castro's most valuable asset. In Europe, he shopped for arms and established contact with several nations involved with the manufacture and marketing of war materials Castro needed to pursue more intense and determined revolution.

Fernandez bought shiploads of Belgian FAL light automatic weapons, ammunition, hand grenades, and surplus American-made 105 howitzers and 81 mm mortars from Italy. Even Israel's Prime Minister, Golda Meir, wined and dined Fernandez, but ultimately he rejected Israel's proposed arms package. His most important acquisition was the goodwill and generosity of the USSR.

In the late spring of 1960, Castro declared himself a socialist and formal Cuban-American relations suffered a permanent breach. Three months later, the first shipments of arms from Czechoslovakia and the Soviet Union filled warehouses at Havana docks.

It had been to Castro's advantage to let America's political leaders indulge their Euro-centric paranoia, declaring himself a Marxist only after the revolution was all but totally won. American intelligence incorrectly assumed that all of Cuba's rebels were communist. From the start, ousting Batista was the primary, if not the singular objective of most Cuban rebels. At the close of the revolution, there were ten different factions which had assisted in the removal of Batista from power but opposed the leftist ambitions inherited from Fidel Castro's tough and obstinate Spanish father.

Disorganized and poorly led, non-leftist and stubbornly anti-Castro groups fought to reverse Cuba's course toward Marxism. With little possibility to consolidate resources and coordinate their efforts, these groups were eventually isolated and captured or, more often than not, simply wiped out. The summer of 1965 saw the last and largest anti-Communist enclave neutralized deep in the Escambray Mountains of central Cuba.

American intelligence groups had struggled with distractions for years, but Russia's launching of Sputnik, the first orbiting artificial satellite in October of nineteen fifty-seven, sparked hysteria.. Also advances in technology had made nuclear warhead delivery systems more reliable and increased their range. American leaders firmly believed that Russia had sprinted ahead in the arms/technology race.

A fearful America struggled to catch up. Terms such as inter-continental ballistic missile, DEW line, massive retaliation, kill radius and fall-out became household words. Bomb shelters were included as options in new home plans.

Forget Flower Children and Woodstock. This was the real nineteen-sixties.

CHAPTER ONE

In the dead vast and middle of the night.
Shakespeare

Eventually, good luck always runs out. In mid June, 1961, Eddy Rush and I struggled with our assignment of stringing field telephone wire across a marsh near the Rio Sucio estuary on the Pacific side of Panama, down coast of the canal.

Sssssh . . . POP!

Eddy and I froze. The noise and brilliant illumination of a parachute flare startled and confused us.

"Jimmy! Who the hell's playing with fireworks?"

"It came from the other side of the swamp, close to where we came in," I whispered, pointing toward a column of white smoke glowing above the brilliant light. I had never seen flares in our inventory. I doubted it could be one of our guys.

Above our corner of the Panamanian jungle, a tiny errant sun burned on a stainless steel leader. Particles of retina-searing white fire drifted over our tracks. It swayed in the faint breeze and slowly descended, filling our edge of the triple canopy rainforest with a harsh, surrealistic light.

A panicky voice shouted only a few yards away. "Javier! ¿Que coños esta pasando?"

In a clearing to our left, we saw two figures tumble from hammocks. Like us, they tried to comprehend a grotesque world etched in Prussian blue shadows and blinding light.

"Jimmy! You take the one on the right!" Eddy shouted and threw himself on the other Cuban sentry. I stood there, one hand filled with a roll of electrician's tape and the other held a pair of wire cutters. "Get him!" Eddy shouted as my man, shielding his eyes from the glare, stumbled toward an M-1 carbine propped against the tree at the foot of his hammock.

Eddy hammered his sentry with heavy blows and I heard the sickening smack of fists on flesh and bone. I stood transfixed as the other sentry reached for the carbine. The paralysis of surprise and fear fell away and I threw the heavy steel wire cutters, striking him behind his right ear. He recoiled in pain and I hit him with a body block coach Rowden would have been proud of, carrying us several yards, but the weapon was in his hands.

How the fuck did I get here?

* * * *

My name is James Brendan Donlin, and I've been looking over my shoulder for nearly fifty years.

It's unlikely that anyone can pinpoint the exact moment when they no longer view the world through the eyes of simple and idealistic youth. We cling to concepts of fair play as long as the unfolding events of history will allow, but ultimately witness the extinction of the flawless morality of childhood, the robust faith in our taught, preached, and coached perceptions of right and wrong. Now, across the dinner table, a television screen shows us decency and justice sacrificed to political expediency, in living color with a running commentary. Every night. Details at eleven.

In the end, adolescent illusions are betrayed by chance acquaintances. The demands and compromises of adulthood drag us into a dirty, cynical and complicated reality. My venture into the larger world began at 6 am, on a warm morning in early May, nineteen sixty-one.

CHAPTER TWO

It is by presence of mind in untried emergencies that the
native metal of a man is tested.
Abraham Lincoln

At eight o'clock on a muggy morning in early May, 1961,
both civilian and military men assembled in building
number T-23. The aging two-story wood structure, formerly
barracks, stood behind a triple curtain of chain link fences
topped with razor wire. It was one of eleven two-story
whitewashed converted barracks that housed the temporary
quarters of the Caribbean and Central American section of
the National Security Agency at Fort Meade, Maryland.

Shiny-faced Ivy League recruits with short hair and
long resumés quick-stepped at the elbows of their mentors,
older men with gray hair or balding heads, and tired, jaded
expressions. The thump and rattle of folding chairs echoed
in the dark interior as they randomly took their seats.
Uniformed men of all branches of the armed services, men
of quick minds and fearsome resources occupied the first two
rows. Representatives from a variety of intelligence-gathering

entities filled in behind them. Nervously, they awaited the first in a series of briefings on a very disturbing fragment of news to be detailed by a newcomer to the NSA.

A small and nervous speaker, Dr. Sidney Borden, leaned against a too-tall oak podium and tiptoed to speak into the microphone. Dr. Borden held credentials impressive enough to attract the attention of a think-tank centered at a prestigious eastern university, and win an appointment to the Caribbean and Central American section currently undergoing a drastic restructuring. The shake-up was so extreme that one of its members, while busily packing personal items into a cardboard box, declared, "The damned section isn't being reorganized, it's being turned into sausage."

A helpful figure walked from the wings to the podium and adjusted the mike to a lower position. Dr. Borden nodded his thanks and his heels settled to the floor.

Dr. Borden's recent papers established his credentials and brought him to the attention of the intelligence community. His grave shortcomming was a near-suicidal recklessness of political toes. In his recently published book, An Overview of the History of American Intelligence Service From the Civil War to the Present, he gave General Curtis LeMay credit for developing an efficient aerial intelligence-gathering service where none had existed before, did it well, and without spending enough money to draw attention to his project.

As Dr. Borden introduced himself in academic term in a voice that would have induced a coma in most college sophmores, two naval officers sat near the front and to the right, open briefcases on their knees, reading a high-lighted excerpt from Borden's book.

Half a dozen B47 bombers were overhauled and redesignated RB47E, to be used as extreme altitude photo-reconnaissance platforms. Without the knowledge or consent of the president, they left contrails high over Russia, well above what was believed to be the effective altitude of anti-aircraft measures of the day.

While we can appreciate LeMay's good intentions, impressive security management and resourcefulness, this unquestionably patriotic but arrogant act fell between insubordination and treasonous provocation.

Be that as it may, photos of military bases confirmed what LeMay and other experts of the day suspected; Russian deployment of offensive hardware, even if not technically superior, far surpassed the US.

Commander Lon Crane, an officer in the Naval Security Group, nudged Lieutenant Commander Ashley Knox. "What kind of grades, did you make in history at Annapolis?" he asked in a raspy whisper.

"Brilliant," Knox replied. "But never mind the history lesson. The good doctor has stated information in writing that would have gotten him lynched a year ago. LeMay still carries a lot of weight in Washington."

Crane smiled as he remembered a late evening at The Sopwith Club and a conversation with several of his Air Force counterparts. They had served with Le May and endured months of terror. The General had a beautiful daughter who considered any base her private hunting preserve. Obliging officers were then caught between lust and LeMay. The sweet young thing yanked their chains mercilessly. If they complained that a proposed date conflicted with duty roster she suggested that she speak to "Daddy" and get it changed. She usually got what she wanted.

Borden's intro was brief, his voice reverberating in the dim room, and he leapt feet first into the crux of the current turmoil. With no allegiance to any political party or intel group, bare facts flew like schrapnel.

Dismissing his introduction with a wave of the hand, Borden launched into a tirade over the current intelligence blunders, starting with the Powers incident. "By the late fifties a second-generation spy plane, now with the knowledge and consent of President Eisenhower, carried a new camera developed by Edwin Herbert Land. Gary Powers carried one of these cameras on his U-2 when he was shot down May first of last year. Ivan's improved technologies proved an unpleasant surprise for heads of the CIA's U-2 program, demonstrating that not all intel can be provided by high altitude photography." Dr. Borden, aware that each group present knew fragments of what he presented also knew that most never knew all the details, never got the full picture. In his classes he used the example of a hawk watching a snake pass through tall grass . . . it could see enough to know its a snake but never saw the entire snake. He also knew his name would emblazen smoldering memos and reports within the hour, licked his fingers and turned a page in his notes.

"After a long series of such encroachments into Russian air space, several of LeMay's planes were lost with full crews, more than matching the losses of KGB infiltrations right here in our own country. These episodes have have kept us teetering on the brink of all-out war for over a decade. Of course, I refer most recently to Rudolph Abel and his all too successful network of boots-on-the-ground agents which we are still dismantling. I offer up this little history lesson because the events I've mentioned are the latest links in a chain connecting us to the current issue I will present today; the latest Russian response to a future burdened with the most potentially disasterous possiblities imaginable.

"The on-going Powers trial is only a minor disaster." Borden paused for effect.

"April seventeenth, nineteen sixty-one, only two weeks ago, we witnessed a major disaster, both militarily and politically: the miserable fiasco called the Bay of Pigs Invasion." Borden's eyes darted nervously about the room at the thirty-four men who sat with pens poised over note pads, breathing now a forgotten function.

"Launched from Tuxpan in eastern Mexico, anti-Communist, anti-Castro Cubans, and friends, launched a massive invasion effort on the south coast of Cuba.

"With the expectation of air support, Cuban patriots rushed onto Playa Larga, code-named Red Beach, and Playa Giron, code-named Blue Beach. There had been perhaps, a modest possibility of success with air cover, but without it, no chance whatsoever," Dr. Borden said through clenched teeth, obviously contemptuous of men in the audience he blamed for the failure through sloppy planning and for failing to convince President Kennedy of the necessity of air support from Guantanamo.

Knox and Crane glanced at each other with raised eyebrows. "Borden is a mad-man stomping through a minefield!" Knox muttered.

"Committed to disavowing involvement, our newly sworn-in President Kennedy signed approval to launch the invasion." Crane could hear career analysts sucking air as Borden put his shiny-new career on the line by placing the blame for the Bay of Pigs squarely where it belonged. "But for reasons no sane person could comprehend, he chose to ignore the persistent arguments from his military advisors and intelligence teams. I think we all know some of those men are in this room even as I speak. President Kennedy refused air support. His reasons were, in part, based on his knowledge that a dozen WWII surplus B26s and B25s were already committed to the mission, supposedly piloted by American-trained Cuban exiles. In reality, American super-patriots flew half of these planes. They were young men from Air National Guard units in Texas, Mississippi and

Alabama. Someone close to Kennedy thought this would be enough.

Tagically, it wasn't. The lack of modern fighters from the Navy base at Guantánamo, and our failure to discover just how large Castro's secret air force had become assured the dismal tragedy that resulted."

The room filled with grumblings and epithets. Borden paused, waiting for the audience to quiet down. He glared at men he felt cared more about their jobs than their country, and with a vicious sweep of his hand turned another page. Chairs rattled and clattered as several men rose and left.

"The current, ill-conceived White House cover-up will crumble, gentlemen," Borden continued in a voice quavering in rage. "It will crumble under the flood of detailed reports poring in from reputable news agencies. Initial accounts were rebuked, deemed as unreliable, content and origins unsubstantiated. International reporting agencies have been painted with a red brush, as communist sympathizers. It won't stick. Several foreign embassies and Bay of Pigs survivors have given accounts to international news agencies with good credentials and a long history of reliability, and they are sharing film and copy with the world."

Aides from the back of the room pushed carts loaded with manila envelopes down the aisle. They counted the occupants in each row and passed out packets of aerial photos.

"This morning, newspapers carried a release from government sources blaming a 'renegade component within the Central Intelligence Agency.' I was informed a few minutes ago that Allen Dulles met with the president yesterday and was asked to step down as head of the CIA."

Thirty voices hummed with the shocking reminder that their exclusive niches were not protected from the vagaries of politics.

"Our concern now is to answer this one question; given that Castro and a communist Cuba will be with us for a while, what does Russia hope to gain by developing closer ties with Cuba?" Dr. Borden paused and peered at his audience.

"Leverage, gentlemen, leverage," he answered. "In Turkey our air bases and Jupiter missile installations array thousands of warheads against every significant Russian target. Cuba can provide the ground for Russia to establish a mirror image of the American nuclear threat and impose a similar level of fear on this country."

Voices rumbled in the darkened room, some expressing doubts that the Russians would dare push their luck that far. Others nodded complete agreement with Dr. Borden's assessment. "There is good reason to believe the Russians are already laying the groundwork to provide nuclear armament to Cuba, and eventually the rest of Central and South America," Borden announced bluntly. "That brings us to today's topic. Last February, a huge barge came through the Panama Canal, another is on its way, and a third is under construction in Japan."

An hour later, Lon Crane stared blankly into his opened leather briefcase at the close of the session. *The aerial recon photos could be wrong,* he thought. *The inspectors signed off on the first barge as a floating miniature refinery. The Cubans might have discovered oil reserves and negotiated for a cracking plant. From the air, one twelve hundred barrel tank can look a lot like another.*

The other members of the briefing session stood and conversed in low tones. Nervous hands shuffled copies of reports and eight by ten glossies of high altitude views of a Russian naval base on the Kamchatka Peninsula where the barge had been outfitted with the tanks and machinery it required. There were also photos of four Cuban harbors, including the harbor of Mariel, just outside Havana.

Dr. Borden perspired heavily in the center of a small group of analysts who physically towered over him, but he stood his ground on the report's accuracy and the intelligence supporting it. Crane heard him loudly rebuff arguments against the report being outragously inconsistent with current political views. Borden shook his fist in the air in frustration. "I'm not a politician and neither are you. This is hard intelligence and the politicians will just have to deal with it. I pity the idiot who puts his neck on the line by trying to twist this into something less or different than it is!"

It's much too early to hit the panic button, Lon Crane thought to himself, and closed the lid to his briefcase. *Then why do I have this knot in the pit of my stomach?*

Commander Ashley Knox walked beside Crane as they approached "the coal mine" at Langley later that afternoon. Knox and Crane were Navy Intelligence's liaison with the CIA, and best friends. "What are the Dutch doing, getting mixed up with the goddamned Russians and Cubans? They're NATO members, f'Chris'sakes! It doesn't make sense!" Knox objected as they passed through the first security checkpoint.

"There's no solid evidence they are," Crane fired back. "This new barge may be carrying papers from New Zealand, for all we know. Forged papers are nothing new in this game. And the Japanese will work for anyone who flashes a bankroll. That doesn't mean they're doing any more than chasing a profit. Hell, next time, maybe the Russians will have a barge built at the Electric Boat Works at Groton, Connecticut."

"What does all this have to do with Cuba?" Knox pressed. "They haven't developed much beyond sugar cane, bananas, and cigars. But if they've found oil, why shouldn't they refine their own gasoline?"

"Be careful what you eat, even if it's served up on a silver plate. You're far too eager to buy the obvious, Ash," Crane warned. "Nobody wants this to be a false alarm more than I do, but until we know better, we have to assume the barge is what the big boys think it is; a miniaturized rocket fuel plant."

"There's no way we'd let the Cubans develop an offensive missile system. The Monroe Doctrine . . . ." An armed guard at the second security station interrupted the conversation to check the photos on the clearance tags hanging from their pocket flaps.

"It doesn't apply," Crane interrupted. "Cuba is a recognized Western Hemisphere nation. If we could prove the Russians are colonizing Cuba, or exerting significant influence, or some form of coercion, that's another matter."

"But this pair of barges," Knox objected. "They could be anything; Borden said so himself."

"What if they're not *just anything*," Crane asked. "The Watane Kai Shipyard in Yokohama is building a third barge right now, again for a fictitious Dutch client. I'll bet your paycheck it will make a trip to the Petropavlovsk Naval Base, just like the first two."

"Borden says," Knox persisted, "the Russians know about our fly-overs, and this second barge is playing a cat-and-mouse game, something their predecessor didn't bother about. Why? If the first barge made it through with papers for a refinery, why wouldn't it still work?"

"That alone justifies a certain level of suspicion," Crane said, "and where the hell do they expect to hide something that big?"

They paused at the third and last checkpoint. "Fly-overs of Cuba confirmed that the first barge, which had papers sending it to the Dutch Antilles, never arrived there. We now know it, and that has made us suspicious. And they know we'll inspect the second barge more closely. What did you do to miss this?"

"I had a nature call. That bozo from the Defense Mapping Agency tried to take my seat. Remember?"

"Oh yes. The guy with the Jersey accent," Crane recalled. "Well, instead, the barge's cargo was deposited ashore in Cuba, and the barge itself became a floating warehouse in Kingston, Jamaica. It's still there. The tanks removed from the barge look similar to tanks at installations in central Russia already known to be a rocket fuel plant. Check Borden's photos."

"They think this because of the high altitude photos of storage tanks? How can they be sure?" Knox asked.

"That's the problem; they're not sure. The placement of pipes, valves, and pump stations strongly suggest it is. The photos and Borden's team of analysts made the big boys nervous," Crane said, smiling. "They're still smarting over an embarrassingly poor intel performance in Cuba. Did you catch what he said about Cuba as a distribution center?"

"Damned straight!" Commander Knox snapped. "We're supposed to find some way to absolutely confirm these suspicions . . . or disprove them."

"If it is a rocket fuel plant," Crane said, "we could also determine the kind of rocket fuel it's intended to produce. That would tell us what kind of missile, and that tells us warhead capability, range, and potential targets."

Commander Knox shrugged. "This is either a case of horrific paranoia or a declaration of war. But which?"

"Turning Cuba into a distribution center for Russian-made missiles and warheads would directly threaten two thirds of the US. I agree. That sounds like a declaration of war," Crane said. "If they're installed at the southern end of Argentina or Chile, already struggling with their own Red factions, they could also close the Drake Passage and the Strait of Magellan. Cuban missiles could control Caribbean approaches to the Panama Canal. All sea routes for surface vessels could be closed. South America would be a wedge between our Atlantic and Pacific fleets. A handful of Russian subs between Australia and Indonesia and between Australia and Antarctica would deny passage between the Indian Ocean and the Pacific. We'd be boxed in. You're right, Ash. We would never stand for that."

They paused to scan the last two pages of the report that outlined assignments for the men who attended the briefing session. "We're at bat on this end," Crane said. "We've pulled an old-timer out of retirement for this one. Right now, he's bringing his brother's body back from Europe. Wilson Donahue says he needs something to occupy his time."

CHAPTER THREE

He must needs go whom the devil doth drive.
John Heywood

In the sultry early morning of June 13, 1961, on the west coast of Panama, in the center of Golfo de San Miguel, my raft, Gosling Two, lagged behind the other ten-man Zodiacs. Half an hour earlier, we had departed from the intersection of the line of demarcation, the line that marks the entrance into the gulf and Pollux Intercept, our primary navigation reference line arbitrarily drawn from our camp to the center of the demarcation line. Captain Abbott had ordered us to run nav exercises and monitor radio communications from the *guias*, our guides on loan from the Panamanian navy and natives to our area of operations.

We returned to Base T an hour after dawn. Our group of eight hard-asses, listed as "independent contractors" in DC, was greeted by the usual grumblings of Buryl Gates, our ninth member, a surly demolitions specialist who had been assigned radio watch for the night. We found breakfast waiting for us. The mess tent was squared away, the coffee was strong and hot and the powdered eggs weren't scorched. Someone even made biscuits. Woods, Collins and Nash, three of the old duffers in the photo team, hovered about like schoolboys, waiting for one of us to tell them they were great cooks. Bishop broke first. Whether a sincere act of decency or an attempt to just keep the peace, I could only guess, but in fact didn't much care. Of course, we were glad for a good meal, and the geezers did seem to want to please us now. I caught myself wondering what changed their attitudes.

"Please pass those wonderful biscuits, Mr. Nash," I said.

From my corner of the the mess table, I watched Loomer re-establish himself as an authority instead of a den mother. Dr. Roche was easily his greatest challenge.

"I don't want to talk to you, Donny. And keep away from me with that ax handle," Roche grumbled.

"It's the handle of a pick, Bernie, much heavier than an axe handle." Loomer pressed Roche against the wall of rations that divided the mess area from the living quarters of Captain Abbott, our commander, and Rubio Williams, second in command. Loomer held the balk of hickory threateningly in his right hand. "This is in the area of contract, Bernie, and you don't have to talk to me, but like it or not, you will *listen* to me." Loomer picked up Roche's left elbow and roughly directed him to the empty palapa for a brief, private conversation. When they returned to the mess tent for their food trays, Loomer wore a cordial smile, but Roche presented a scowl, and seethed with anger and defiance.

Seeing Loomer knock Roche into Gosling One the night before demonstrated to the others something was wrong. This didn't fit with Woods' account of the mission or our role as chauffeurs. And Dr. Loomer had his hackles up over another stupid remark by Nash. By the time Loomer reamed them out and explained the mission again, they were very upset.

"This is far riskier than . . . er . . . what you presented to us at Alamo . . . Alamogordo, Donny," Woods whined.

Again Dr. Donald Loomer told his photographic team about the nine of us and our training and what we were doing out on the water at night. They were shocked. "Bernie actually . . . er . . . struck one of them," Woods stammered.

"Compañeros coming in," Bishop shouted, pointing at the lone battered aluminum fishing boat, trailing a plume of white exhaust. "Looks like Jorge and Pello."

We gathered at the beach to meet them. Rubio rushed them to the mess tent. Being possessed of a curious nature, I tagged along.

Pello ambled up from the beach and threw the nav board down on table number one, took a grass stem from his teeth and stabbed an oily finger at the chart. "Aqui!"

Larry Abbott shook his head. "That can't be. We wouldn't take a canoe in there, let alone something the size of the Galveston warehouse district."

We were briefed later and had the same reaction as Larry. Rio Sucio was a bad choice. Way too shallow. They would surely ground out at low tide. Why would they take the barge in there?" I guessed at the only possible answer; navigation error. They had probably tried to find their way into the maze of islands in the mouth of the Cucunati River but missed by turning one channel too soon, and wound up in the shallow, exposed, dead-end Rio Sucio estuary.

The error was very bad luck for them, but exceptionally good luck for us. This meant there was a possibility that the Angels, a Cuban security force four miles to the east, couldn't provide security. Moving a large group through forest and swamp could take days, even in broad daylight. They would have to move the barge, maybe tonight, more likely tomorrow night, depending on tide fall. This was the chance we'd hoped for, a shot at the barge without its Cuban escorts.

To the west, another estuary of an unnamed stream arched northwest, and then swept northeast, forming a beaver-tail peninsula to the west of Rio Sucio. We never entered this branch because it was too shallow and narrow for the barge, but it might provide access to a staging area for us.

We loaded the *compañero's* boat with all the rations and water it could carry, as well as machetes and axes. They were told to rejoin Roberto and Juan, move into the unnamed bay's head and clear a campsite. We would follow in a few hours.

Intending to rest, the eight of us who spent the previous night swatting mosquitoes also hoped for an early rain to wash away sweat and insect repellent which now felt sticky and smelled rancid. Maybe that was just us. The air was hot and still and rain seemed only a breath away.

The late morning was too hot to rest. Moving about the camp, we now carried weapons openly. We dragged ammo boxes out of trunks marked "survey equipment," and filled extra clips and slipped them into throw-away bandoleers. Field packs bulged with fatigue pants and rag-top boots. No sandals in the boonies.

Larry labored over codebooks until four long messages filled the note pad while I did a final check on the telephone switchboard. I made several trips in and out of the com-tent while loading the phones and boards. That's when I overheard Rubio decoding the replies to our messages.

Rubio closed the notebook and leaped to his feet, waving a paper with the one word reply from Gander. "Go!" he shouted at Larry.

Eddy Rush, Bishop and Nelson peeled the bright Pan-American Highway decals off the plywood consoles of the rafts and quickly painted dark matte gray over the high-gloss varnish. They taped boot socks over the running lights to cover the chrome, and removed the plexiglass windshields.

Keener and Bennett checked batteries, loaded an extra fuel tank and an extra fuel hose for all four rafts, and this time, there were life jackets for everyone.

Our rain came on time that afternoon, lighter and of shorter duration than usual, but it was enough. The smell was gone from our fatigue shirts, even though they were still wet. They'd be sweat-soaked within an hour anyway.

The mosquitoes swarmed as the light faded.

Our evening's entertainment began at nineteen thirty hours when dotty Mr. Woods asked Larry a question that stopped him in his tracks. "When . . . er . . . will you come back for us?"

"We won't have to come back for you," Larry answered. "You're going with us."

"Oh, no. We're not er…combat…er . . . photographers," Woods insisted in a strained voice. "We're only here to shoot photos of the barge when you have possession of it. You . . . er . . . come get us then."

"Time constraints won't permit that as an option, Mr. Woods," Larry told him. In his louder voice, he shouted commands to the men in the mess tent.

"Okay, Dr. Loomer, round them up. Bishop, Donlin, Gates, Nelson! Load their gear. Loomer and Nash are in Gosling One, Roche is in Gosling Two, Woods is in Gosling Three and Collins in Four."

"Gates, you're in Gosling Three. Bring your toys and the ANGRC-9." Larry barked, checking his watch. For the first time, Base T would be totally abandoned. It was an hour and a half to low tide, and only a half an hour of daylight left.

Nelson, Bishop and I tried to explain to the photographers that we didn't have room for aluminum trunks in the rafts. They needed to collect their gear in soft bags. "Pretend you're tourist and hang cameras around your necks," I told them. "Running in the boats would get crowded, rough, and wet. Things could happen hard and fast."

"All the more reason for the protective cases," they argued.

"The fuckin' foot lockers ain't going," Gates roared. "You have three fuckin' minutes to figure out what you need and carry it to the rafts or I'll kick your sagging asses."

In three minutes, they determined who would take what equipment without duplication, film and flash as needed, wrapped them in towels and stuffed them carefully into waterproof equipment bags. The Kodak Commandos reluctantly started for the rafts.

We kept the rafts afloat because we didn't want to ever strand out on the falling tide which could be over forty feet at times. They had to always be available at an instant's notice. I carried Dr. Roche's cameras to the my raft, Gosling Two, its bow tied to the endless mooring line. I carefully set them in the bow, high and dry on our ration boxes, deep under the spray hood, and spread a GI poncho over them.

As I waded back to the beach, Mr. Collins hurried toward the rafts, cradling a large, heavy, blanket-wrapped instrument. It was clumsy and difficult to handle because of an ungainly mounting bracket that dangled nearly to his knees. Bennett, returning from loading Woods' equipment, offered to assist Mr. Collins. An expression of panicked indecision twisted Collins' face as he stopped suddenly and turned away. "No! You don't have the slightest idea of what I'm carrying!" When he reached the water's edge, he stopped again, his face clearly displaying his thoughts. *Who is more physically fit? Who is most accustomed to the beach and movements of the rafts? Who is least likely to dump a twenty thousand dollar camera in the drink?*

As he surrendered the awkward burden to Bennett, the blanket fell away. Pale gray letters across the side of a complex camera read "Victor Hasselblad AB." Bennett placed the camera in Gosling Four, probably wondering why all the fuss.

Threatened with grounding on the falling tide, the loaded rafts were hauled out to bob on the mooring line, the props raised out of the shallow water. They were a little stern-heavy, especially Gosling Four with the extra burden of the ANGRC-9, the camp's long-range radio. I had just started my second trip for Gosling Two when Roche and Collins politely re-stated their request.

The Poplin Pirates still wanted us to carry them out to the rafts! Dr. Loomer had pronounced these geezers fit, but Eddy and I agreed they could be winded by a game of croquet. And if they were even close to being fit, they should damned well be able to get themselves into the rafts.

In Washington, people jumped through hoops for these men. We felt no such obligation. It was more than their egos could stand. Roche and Collins exploded at Eddy and me. On my third trip out to the rafts, already burdened by the nav board, four ammo belts and the BAR, they again insisted we carry them.

"Hell no!" I shouted at Roche and Collins.

Roche trudged beside me as I continued my walk to the mooring line. "Donlin, you don't look much like a paid killer," he jeered.

"You don't look much like an asshole, but there you go."

"Watch your lip, you fucking third-rate grunt. You're talking to your superior," Roche screamed in my face.

Too much! Something snapped inside my head. I dropped everything but the BAR. "You think I need your lip, you son of a bitch?" I shouted in his face. "You wanna show me what you've got, you whining prick!" He grabbed at my weapon and I slammed him in the chest with the rifle butt, hard, and it knocked him off his feet. He snatched at my weapon to keep from falling, and went down, gasping for breath, the BAR across his stomach.

Sprawled on his back in the muddy sand near the water's edge, he struggled against the weight of the weapon. I took a step toward him and he thought I intended to kick the shit out of him. The thought had definitely crossed my mind.

"You idiot!" Roche shouted. "You broke my ribs! I'll sue your ass!" As I extended my hand, he extended his, thinking I was offering to help him up. I slapped his hand away, picked up the BAR and cleared sand out of the flash-hider.

"You moron! Get away from me. I can't go anywhere. My ribs are cracked."

Loomer helped Roche to his feet and tried to determine the extent of his injuries. Larry and Rubio started on me.

"You were set up," Rubio explained in whispers. "He doesn't want to go and you gave him an out, Donlin. Donahue may have to order a med-evac to get him out of here." Bent and holding his ribs, Roche moaned and whimpered.

"No, he won't. Roche isn't hurt," I said. "Did you see the way he reached for my hand and wanted me to help him up? Nobody with broken ribs wants to get up like that. He's faking it." I slung the BAR, picked the rest of my dropped gear, and wadded out to the raft.

Larry and Rubio looked at each other, nodded and turned to Roche. "Sorry, Dr. Roche." Larry sighed apologetically as he drew his .45 automatic. "We can't leave any wounded behind. We can at least give you a decent burial. Get the shovels, Eddy."

Stunned by the unexpected acceptance of his complaint, and terrified by Larry's grotesque sense of humor, Roche turned white and his mouth fell open. "Wait! Maybe I'm just bruised a bit!"

"You wouldn't deprive me of the pleasure of dumping your ass in a hole, would you?" Larry asked, with a slight smile that could easily have been a grimace. "Get in the boat! Everybody! Get in the boats!"

Sharks and stingrays? No. Again, the duffers balked at wading through the mud and dirty water because they didn't want to get their clothes wet or their sneakers muddy. "I'll go with you," Nash said, "but could you please just get me into the raft dry?"

The rafts could have been pulled up on the beach in just a few seconds, and with much less effort than it would have taken to carry the photographers, but now principle was involved. They still tried to call the shots, and still tried to degrade us to subservient roles. Besides, we were already wet and muddy; why should they stay dry?

Bishop and I were fed up. Keener and Eddy were close behind. We looked at Larry. He gave an affirmative nod.

The others were over the side in knee deep water before I could untangle myself from the bow line. We howled with laughter as the photographers scurried up the beach, spattering each other with water, sand and mud. Certain that we had no intention of carrying them, they scattered like chickens.

But the very mud they wanted to avoid hampered their escape. "Leave him alone! Roche is mine!" I shouted. Roche knew I would half-drown him before he got anywhere near the raft.

"I'm going, I'm going! Keep away from me, Donlin!" Roche shrieked. He dashed around me and threw himself headlong for the raft.

Loomer waded past him, holding his pick handle over his head, a drum major for a very muddy, very chaotic parade. Bishop, stripped to the waist, had Nash and Collins by the collars of their custom tailored jump suits, pushing them through the sand and water. Keener and Gates cornered Woods and drove him into Gosling Three like the dull, stubborn old goat he was. He was so upset he could only howl his objections. "Donny, I . . . er . . . must protest . . . er . . . this abuse. This is . . . aahhh . . . inexcusable!" he stammered.

"Everyone accounted for?" Larry asked, lighting a cig he had mooched from Bishop. Each raft responded in the affirmative. We poled out to deeper water, untied the bow lines, lowered the props, and fired off the outboards. "Course two-three-three. Gosling Two takes the lead, Three and Four are flankers and I'll tag along. Run at fifteen knots, and listen for the whistle to change course."

Some of us were more enthusiastic about the state of affairs than others. For the first time, Base T was unmanned. For the first time, we all wore life jackets. And for the first time, Gates, with his caps, fuses, timers, det cord and a hundred and fifty pounds of C-3, joined us.

The range lights glowed brightly, but the rest of the camp was completely dark, and all four Goslings slipped along nearly invisible except for the scarlet loom of the compass. We kept one another in sight by the pale blue streak of bioluminescence trailing in the wake of each raft.

I steered while Keener argued with Roche about how to don his life jacket. "Dr. Roche, would you like me to help you with that?" I asked in my most polite voice.

"No! Stay away from me. Both of you. I can manage by myself," he shot back.

All of us knew it's nearly impossible to put on a life vest in the water, but somehow didn't much care if Roche knew. We left him alone in the dark with his complex puzzel of straps and buckles.

Ordered to keep off the radios, we ran close enough to hear Larry's brass whistle. We would then cut the engines to idle and listen for voice commands. Twelve minutes out on Pollux Intercept, Larry blew two blasts and I cut the throttle.

There were fourteen men bobbing in a tight circle. Gosling Three slipped past me on the left and I saw Gates seated on the starboard side on the transom, his right hand looped into the lifeline and his left with a death grip on the steering cable. Leaning toward the console, his face was a bizarre red mask with an expression of stark, paralyzing terror.

This had been the leverage Larry and Rubio used on him. Do your job, stay out of trouble and we won't put you in the boats. But even though he did his job, he still kept the camp in a constant turmoil, still provoked fights and pulled only half the extra duty as the rest of us. His future with Larry was axed. In quiet resignation, terrified beyond description, he tried to resist his horror of water, to overcome, deny, and suppress.

Futile. Everybody's options run out sooner or later, and now Gates' own kennel of saltwater demons were chewing him over.

Larry called for the raft-up to see how close Gates was to completely unraveling. Close enough, yet, no one else seemed aware of Gates' condition, or they chose to ignore it because there was nothing they could do about it.

When Gates saw me looking at him, he carefully, slowly, unwound his right hand from the life line and I expected him to flash me the finger as usual, but instead he laid an index finger across his lips, his expression of a plea for my silence. I could scarcely believe a man in such a drastic state could have even climbed into a boat.

After a twenty-five minute run on the new north-northwest course, we stopped again and rafted-up. Larry sighted over the compass toward the northwest. The edge of the forest hung like a strip of torn black velvet tacked across the horizon. The stars in the sky held stoicly in their place, their reflections undulated and fluttered on the backs of a gentle swell.

With a flashlight from his pack, Larry signaled long-short-long-short, Morse code for 'Charlie.' A speck of red light blinked a reply. Short-short-long for 'Uniform.' "That's Pello. We follow him in," Larry said in a low voice. "Get the poles ready. This stretch shoals out halfway to the end."

Then the mosquitoes enveloped us like a fog bank.

CHAPTER FOUR

. . . . and by thy great mercy
defend us from perils and dangers of
this night.
The Book of Common Prayer

The smell of sweat and insect repellent spread over the cluster of boats. Roche winced as he anointed his sunburned pate. Gosling Two barely stayed out of Gosling One's exhaust stream as we crawled toward a pinpoint of red light and threaded our way through the narrowing channel.

Two of our boats could not have passed. Branches and lianas closed in, low-hanging, grasping, tearing at our faces, and snaring baseball caps.

I put my glasses in the pocket of my fatigue shirt and stuffed my ball cap into the console locker. The low rumblings of our engines sounded like a deep growl from the jungle itself.

Rapid flashes of red light appeared a few yards ahead, signaling us to turn off engines and lift the props out of the mud. Keener picked up the pole and thrust it into the black ooze under the raft. The smell of decaying vegetation fouled the air and the mosquito escort doubled.

The pole rattled in the overhead branches each time Keener reset it. We inched slowly forward, our progress severely impeded by the same skegs that improved high-speed maneuverability. Unexpectedly, the jungle disappeared from our right side, giving way to a steep dune, high as a house and covered with saw grass and an occasional stunted palm.

The raft sighed through the muck of mud and algae. Three more shoves and we slipped to the right and nosed in beside Larry's raft.

The *compañeros'* boats stretched their full length on shore, resting on a bed of sand and seashells, probably an ancient Embera Choco midden.

We ran long lines up the rise and tied off to the stumps of trees cut many years ago. The dark silhouettes of the *compañeros* stood out against pale, thin, moonlit clouds. They looked down at us as we struggled to unload the passengers and equipment.

I had no knowledge of their military rank, but, by whatever power, for whatever reason, Roberto had emerged as the undisputed leader of the *compañeros*. The four men were our guides on loan from the Panamanian navy, and one-time inhabitants of our hunting ground. Pello, Juan and Jorge hesitated even to follow Rubio's orders without a word or nod from Roberto.

At last, all four descended to help and Roberto reported to Larry that he had scouted and found the tug and barge. In his four-hour venture along the shore of the Rio Sucio he saw no one on our broad and swampy peninsula.

Our assembly area lay inside a dense thicket of scrub cedars and pines. A six-foot circle of hearthstones gave evidence that someone else had once been established here.

The caked ashes were flat and dark, the residue of a long abandoned Embera Choco farmstead. While Roberto scouted, the other three *guias* had cleared the area of saw grass and brush. Our camp spanned a saddle in a ridge that paralleled the sluggish stream that brought us here. A single lantern hung on a stake near the center of a thirty-foot circle. The dim light couldn't be seen past the next ridge forty yards away.

We made several trips between the boats and the encampment. Weapons first, then communication equipment, rations, cameras, and jerry cans of water. Everything lay in a more or less organized manner around the edge of the clearing. We considered ourselves in a hot area, therefore weapons remained within arms reach. Each of us sorted and cleaned as best we could. Tent panels and ponchos covered radios, telephones and cameras, regarded as our most valuable and sensitive equipment.

After a few comical attempts at getting into their hammocks, the photographers stopped complaining, smeared on more insect repellent, and went to sleep. Larry posted two sentries: one at the boats and one at the top of the second ridge, both with PRC-6s. He and Rubio set up the ANGRC-9 we had dragged from the boats and into camp. We then rigged an antenna and set up the hand-crank transmitting generator.

I started for my own hammock when Larry pointed to the telephones and three rolls of WD-1 wire. "Run this tonight. Roberto says we're alone right now. In five or six hours that could change. You, Bishop and Eddy," he said, pointing to a map of the area on the west side of Rio Sucio. "Set up a phone here and lay wire to the other side of our peninsula, say within a quarter mile of the barge, here. From there hook up a phone on each end of a T-line running parallel to the river. End the T-line at two good staging areas. We'll decide which to use when we get there in the morning."

"Okay, Cap. Do I get pack animals for all the equipment?" I asked.

"Sure. That would be Bishop and Rush." He laughed and slapped me on the back. "Maybe you could leave the BAR."

Eddy and Bishop, relying on Roberto's scouting report, reluctantly decided to leave their weapons behind as well. This was a decision we would soon regret, but these were men with more experience and I trusted their judgement. After all, fifty pounds of wire, telephones, switchboard and tools would be enough to carry through a swamp in the middle of the night.

After fastening wire to the base of a tree at the edge of camp, I hung a field phone, wired it up with a lineman's splice and tested the switch board and phone. So far, so good. Two more telephones were packed in waterproofing and stuffed into a backpack.

We strapped on web belts supporting tool kits filled with electricians tape, connectors, wire cutters, strippers and a dozen little odds and ends left by the technicians who last used these bags. We also carried bayonets for split-branch hangars to keep the wire off the ground. We didn't expect the units to be operational for more than forty-eight hours so there was no point in setting posts or burying line.

Eddy and I threaded short pieces of rope through our wire spools and slung them over our shoulders. Bishop, assigned second sentry period, would stay with us only until the first spool ran out. He made a laying bracket from a tree branch and trekked out of camp walking backward, trailing wire. About every twenty paces, we used a bayonet to hack off a branch of cedar or a palm, split it about three inches deep and insert the wire.

"Have fun, boys," Nelson sang out from the deep shadows of a small palm on the crest of the second ridge. He had a perfect view of the open moon-lit savanna sloping to the marsh in the center of the peninsula.

"Try to stay awake, Cupcake. Remember what happened to Pritchard in Rhodesia last year," Eddy fired back.

"I wasn't there, but I heard about it. Served him right, trying to stand sentry duty with a fifth of Johnny Walker Black Label," Nelson replied. "What's he doing now?"

"He works in one of Turm's warehouses in Florida," Bishop said. "He's better off than the two guys who died because he fell asleep. Abbott will never have him back."

"He's damned lucky Larry didn't put a bullet in his head on the spot. No less than he deserved," Eddy growled.

Trailing wire, we backed away from Nelson. Eddy hacked off the end of a branch with his bayonet, split it, and inserted the wire. "Damn!" he cursed in a low voice.

"Cut yourself?" Nelson asked, stealing my question.

"Hell no," Eddy answered. "Worse: there's a splice in this wire, and a black cardboard frapping," he grumbled. "This is used wire, disguised to look like new. God only knows how many more splices."

Under normal circumstances, this was no big deal, but in a hot situation, a very big deal. If there should be a bad splice anywhere in the line, the phones wouldn't work, then someone, probably yours truly, would have to trouble-shoot each splice until the break was found. The only other choice was to cut out each splice and make new ones as we went. "This could turn a two hour project into four or five," I grumbled to Eddy.

Eddy held the light while I cut and stripped the wire. I tied another lineman's splice, two staggered square knots, ends twisted, in the shiny copper strands. I had just started to wrap them with tape when Eddy launched into a blue tirade. Within twenty feet, he'd found another splice. I quickly undid my splice and discarded the twenty feet of wire between. From there on, as we started a splice, we checked the next two hundred feet for more old splices.

By the time we reached the swamp, we had re-spliced three more times. We should have been finished and asleep by then. It would be a long night. To speed things up, we decided to compromise; cut off the electrician's tape and inspect the splice, re-wrapping if it's serviceable, re-splicing if not.

"Good luck," Bishop said as he tossed the first empty spool aside. "See you in a couple of hours. I'll be under Nelson's palm tree when you get back. My turn as sentry."

Stinking water rose to our knees with viscous muck gripping our ankles. Crossing was slow and laborious. Eddy suggested that at the next splice we switch rolls of wire, hoping for fewer splices.

Except for the splices, the wire was allowed to fall into the water because there was little to support it. We gathered small bundles of live reeds and sedge at each patch, and bound the wire to their tops, holding it a foot or so above the water.

A full and white-faced moon hovered in the western sky, bathing the Darien mountaintops in soft light, but seemed reluctant to stain its reflection in the stagnant slurry we traversed.

The marsh took on a sinister character. Water rose above our waists and the reeds and grasses thinned. I knew that leeches are seldom felt when they attach themselves and my imagination shifted to a territory between disgust and panic.

We passed through open areas with floating gardens of water lilies, their blossoms closed as tight as fists. Unseen denizens skimmed, slithered or splattered away. To the left, we heard rhythmic undulations of a heavier body moving in the water and saw ripples march past our chests.

I silently wondered if Roberto had come this way. Keep moving.

When I turned to clear the wire when it snagged under a cluster of lily pads, a frantic gasp startled me.

Eddy was gone!

Circles of disturbed water marked the spot where he had been only a second before. Hair raised on the back of my neck. A roll of wire slowly rose above the surface, streaming green water, algae, and ribbons of dead grass. "nnng, hack! Hole!" Eddy sputtered.

"Splice," I replied, masking my alarm.

"Take care of it on that side unless you think you're man enough to tie one while you tread water," he laughed. "Damn! So much for the waterproof flashlight." He rattled the light and heard the faint whisper of water inside the aluminum case. "It's about as waterproof as my underwear."

"I think I'm man enough to tie one in the dark if I have something solid to stand on," I said.

"Wimp," Eddy chided. "Watch the hole . . . cough . . . . never hit bottom. I swam over here. The tools and wire took me right under," he cautioned.

"How much wire left on that spool?" I asked.

"It's nearly empty. Maybe a hundred feet left," Eddy answered. "Your spool should be more than enough to finish. Pray for fewer splices."

Not waiting to step into the hole, I stretched out into my best sidestroke, holding the spool of wire and backpack as high above the water as I could. Two strokes past Eddy, my feet found the ooze on the bottom and we continued, the water gradually shoaling.

At the water's edge, we made the splice that joined the second spool to the third. Eddy threw the empty spool far out into the swamp. "Damn the son of a bitch who passed that off as new! Usually Heinrich is more careful," Eddy grumbled.

Saw grass made raspy whispers over our wet canvas boots. Sandy ground rose sharply toward another ridge slightly lower than the one west of the swamp where we camped. The Rio Sucio lay a half mile beyond. It was more heavily forested with dense scrub growth under the towering hardwoods that now stood in the light of the moon that nearly kissed the horizon.

When I took my little swim, I must have dunked the spool at least once. Water dripped from the tape around several old splices. At the crest, we rewrapped a splice, working by the light of a waterproof match. Carefully guarding the light of a third match, Eddy bent to help me find a roll of tape I'd dropped and discovered boot prints not our own.

"Roberto's," Eddy grunted. "I have a bad feeling about that guy. He never smiles, never looks you in the eye and he bullies the other three unmercifully. Ouch!" The match had burned his fingertips.

"He stays out of our way and the work gets done," I offered in Roberto's defense. "That's about all any military organization expects, Panamanian or American."

The footprints led along a wide sandy path well cleared of vines and deadfall. We followed it, trailing out our wire. Imitating Bishop's method, Eddy inserted a stick for an axle. The spool rattled and squeaked out a hundred and fifty yards, the longest section without a splice. "I can't believe Roberto had enough time to clear a path like this. The only thing it needs is a light raking and a few dozen Japanese lanterns," Eddy joked.

He held a new match as I finished what we hoped would be the last splice. "I think that makes six new splices and eleven re-wraps," I said.

"I lost count a long time ago," Eddy muttered, splitting another branch with his bayonet to hang the wire. We resumed our easy walk another fifty yards.

Ssssh, POP! crackle!

The noise and the brilliant white light of a parachute flare startled us. The light slashed our faces with the dagger-shaped shadows of palm leaves.

We stared in disbelief. Who'd fired it? And why? By the sound, it came from the far side of the swamp, the way we'd come. It wasn't any of our group; flares were not in our inventory.

"It's those goddamned photographers playing with fireworks!" Eddy snarled. "That's my guess."

High above the swamp, a tiny, errant sun burned on a stainless steel wire leader. Particles of retina-searing white fire drifted over our tracks. It rode a gentle breeze and slowly descended, filling the shadows with a harsh, eerie, surrealistic light.

"Javier? Javier?" A strange voice shouted from the shadows beside the trail. Two figures tumbled from hammocks, dark figures with dark hair. Like us, they tried to comprehend a grotesque world etched in Prussian blue and blinding white light.

"Donlin, you get the one on the right!" Eddy shouted at me as he threw himself on the Cuban sentry to the left. I stood there, a roll of electrician's tape in one hand, and a pair of wire cutters in the other. "Get him!" Eddy roared as my man, shielding his eyes from the flare, stumbled toward an M-1 carbine propped against a tree.

I could hear the heavy blows Eddy slammed into the other sentry, but I was frozen. If the other sentry reached that carbine . . . . I threw the wire cutters as hard as I could, and they struck him behind his right ear. He recoiled and clutched the side of his face. Again he reached for the carbine and I hit him with a body block Coach Rowden would have been proud of. We went to the ground, but he had both hands on the carbine.

Horrible pain exploded in my left shoulder when he slammed me with the rifle butt. I pressed close to him, taking away his room to throw another blow.

I don't remember drawing the bayonet; it was just there, in my right hand. My left hand gripped the lower stock of his weapon, covering the trigger guard. Eddy shouted at me "Don't let him fire a round or we'll be ass-deep in Cubans."

The point of the bayonet had barely pierced the skin of his stomach when he struck me in the face with the front sights of the carbine, gashing my right eyebrow and the bridge of my nose. My glasses rattled away into the undergrowth. He had hurt me much worse than I had hurt him.

I forced myself higher, my chest pressed onto his face, the carbine between us. I struck him again with the bayonet, and again, into the pit of the stomach, but each time he was able to block part of the thrusts with his weapon. At last, the point of the bayonet found its way between his ribs. With all my weight pressed onto the pommel, I felt the blade slide deep into his chest. Furiously kicking, he tried to hit me with the carbine again, and lifted me with the weapon pressed across my throat. He screamed as I twisted the blade and drew it out, moved it an inch higher and drove it down again.

I felt him stiffen and tremble; his breath came in short bubbling gasps. Blood from the cuts on my face ran into both my eyes. In the glow of the dying flare, I could see his grimacing face soften. I smelled black beans sweet cornmeal on his breath. Pink bubbles of saliva and blood formed at the corners of his mouth and glistened in a macabre, merciless light. A series of coughs spattered his blood across my face and throat.

His expression changed from anger to despair, from fear to self-pity, to resignation. I pulled the bayonet and wanted to strike him once more, but couldn't. His face contorted as he arched his back, coughing and gasping. He clutched his chest and dropped the carbine, and when he turned from me, I knocked it away.

The world faded to a blotchy, throbbing gray, and I also tumbled to the side. Moments later, when the universe sorted itself into a darkened reality, I found myself kneeling beside the still corpse, trembling, and my breath came in ragged and shallow sobs.

I didn't want to know about him. I didn't want to know he was my age or that he also had two sisters and loving parents. So what if he also had been an altar boy? I couldn't think of him as a patriot in his country in the same way I thought of myself in mine. Hard labor in the cane fields of Cuba, or hard labor in the damned oil fields in Oklahoma, what's the difference? Why him and not me?

Fuck the fortunes of war.

The flare sizzled out somewhere in the swamp we had just crossed. Its light had forever altered my life.

The shadows drew over us once again. I knelt in silence, still and barely breathing. Saturated in blood and sweat, I still felt cold. What had happened? If I moved, would I mercifully tumble out of my hammock, out of my nightmare? Eddy struck a match and showed me that the nightmare was real. "Christ, Donlin! Don't you believe in making a clean kill?"

He reached out to examine the cuts on my face just as the match burned out. In total darkness, Eddy asked, "You okay? He cut you up pretty good."

"He worked me over with the front sights. It's messy but not serious," I told him.

Eddy shuffled about and a beam of light moved across the body a few feet in front of me. "Found a Russian flashlight. Imagine that. This is now our staging area. Wire up a single phone on the tree over there, and then we'll finish up here. These guys didn't know we were around or they never would have bedded down, and we'd be dead men. The good part is that they weren't expecting a relief, either. They wouldn't have risked being caught sleeping."

I felt stiff and didn't want to move, but at last I rose. Eddy's voice sounded hollow and distant as he called me over to his side of the path. My shoulder ached and my head hurt. "Ouch! Careful, Jimmy. You need to put that away," Eddy complained. He dropped the beam of light to my bloody fingers still locked on the bayonet. I had accidentally nicked him.

I was sickened by what I'd done. From a discovered canteen, Eddy helped me wash my face and throat. He prattled away like a school nurse trying to distract a second grader from a skinned knee. He poured water on my hands as I scrubbed them and cleaned the blood off the blade the way any good craftsman cleans his tools.

The light fell across the sentry Eddy had killed. His face was mangled and a length of WD-1 wire still encircled his throat. His kill wasn't all that clean, either.

I stumbled to the edge of the path, fell to my knees, and vomited

CHAPTER FIVE

Nothing is created from nothing.
Lucretius

I sat heavily in the nearly total darkness beside the trail, dizzy and exhausted. I had survived, but why, how did I ever get myself into this situation in the first place?

"Weapons training doesn't really prepare a man for the end result, for the application of the skills you will acquire here," Sergeant Paul cautioned in basic training at Fort Chaffee in July of 1957. "But when it happens, when you have to kill another human being, you will be in an environment so violent and dangerous you will be numbed to it. Your only concern will be to survive, and you will survive only by applying your weapons training, and continuining to apply, and apply, and apply!"

He was a decorated WWII and Korean War veteran, and no doubt spoke from experience. For myself, the world now seemed a deformed, warped reality and I stood in a distant and forlorn expanse of wasteland a million miles from where I thought I belonged, and I wanted that numbness to kick in.

Eddy tugged at me and tried to push me to my feet. "We have to move. The guy who fired that parachute flare may be part of a scouting party. C'mon, Jimmy, we gotta get out of here."

I rose, but my feet felt leaden, and my mind refused to register the events of the past half hour. Eddy's urgings sounded distant, with a curious echo, like a bad long-distance connection, and I fell backward into the events of the previous month, the events that brought me here, to the Pacific coast of Panama, to Golfo de San Miguel.

* * * *

Mrs. Paulson, resident supervisor of Thatcher Hall banged on my door at 6:15 a.m., mid-May 1961. "Jimmy Donlin, you have an important phone call at the desk. Please hurry. We don't want to tie up the office phone too long."

I didn't want to tie up the phone at all. On the other hand, why would I have an important phone call? I was finishing up my freshman year at Central State College in Edmond, Oklahoma and the only thing that could justify an important phone call for me was my mother's heart condition.

Suddenly overwhelmed by panic, I raced to the phone.

I was relieved to hear Lt. Larry Abbott's overly congenial and slurred voice. My panic faded, replaced by a guarded curiosity. Was our unit being activated? The first thing he did was correct me. "I was promoted to captain four months ago, Cowboy, just before they loaned me out to some D.C. boys," he said. "We need to get our heads together for a little pow-wow. Something big is coming down the track, and I thought of you. Come see me at the Holiday Inn at fourteen hundred hours exactly. I'm in room two-sixteen. I'll buy you lunch."

"It'll have to be dinner. I work at the Rainbow Bakery this afternoon until seven . . . nineteen hundred hours. Also, I don't have a car."

"Whatever," he snapped in a rushed voice. "Gotta go. Call me at eleven and we'll work out the little details. I'll be back in town by then." I heard a woman laugh hysterically, then a click and dial tone.

I sat in my ten o'clock English 101 class. My nostrils flared at the aroma of coffee that drifted from jocks who strolled past the open door, fresh from the student union. Some assholes have no sympathy for the dead and dying. The classroom clock above the chalkboard said fifteen minutes until eleven and I fidgeted in my desk, legs and brain numb from inactivity. The class dragged, even on good days, and this was not a good day. Amusement, curiosity and anxiety played tag inside my head, thankfully trampling the hell out of my usual boredom, presently generated by instructions for writing a formal term paper.

Larry Abbott and I became good friends in our Army Reserve unit, but the tone of his voice brought a tingling sensation to the back of my neck and put me on edge. Something was up. It wasn't another goddamned poker game this time. Losing his brand new Thunderbird swore him off poker for good. That's what he said when we parted company at the Greyhound Bus Station in Leesville, Louisiana and there was as much sincerity in his eyes and voice as I'd ever known of him. This was bigger. It took a lot to excite Larry Abbott: good liquor, bad women or big money. I didn't know what any of them had to do with me.

I scribbled notes on bibliography and footnotes, but my mind wandered back to this morning's rushed phone call. Ruminating over the hurried, almost frantic, demand that we meet later this evening, I nervously tapped an annoying rhythm with my pencil and caught nasty glares from the instructor and her aide. Why would Captain Abbott drive a hundred and twenty miles to see me? I was still in the Reserves, but not his unit. He had been second officer of my old unit, the 409th Special Forces, USAR.

Op. cit, loc. cit., idem., ibid. Explained and noted in semi-legible script. And buy a copy of *A Manual for Writers* by Kate Turabian at the bookstore.

At five minutes till, I started packing up. The aide seemed annoyed and the instructor glared at me as if I had just passed gas in church.

Tough.

The week I turned seventeen, early in my senior year of high school, I joined the Army Reserve. This was completely contrary to the traditions of the varsity football team and all the FFA boys. For generations all the town's young men had joined the National Guard, Oklahoma's Forty-fifth Infantry Division, the famous Thunderbirds.

During that first year, I went through the usual series of exams and aptitude tests then began several interesting training programs including interpretation of aerial recon photos, only because it was already being taught and they were short of bodies. Out of high school, I did my six months active duty, evenly divided between basic training, advanced infantry and an intense, abbreviated, down-and-dirty eight week session in more aerial photo interpretation, communications, and reconnaissance. When I went back to Tulsa, I was reassigned to my old unit, the Three Seventy-seventh Infantry Regiment, Headquarters, Headquarters Company, recon platoon.

I considered joining the Regular Army for a full hitch, but issues at home needed resolving first, the biggest of these was a college education, which held the possibility of a career as an officer if I decided to go back to Regular Army. After a few months of floundering around, filling out endless applications for jobs that paid little or that, at the age of eighteen, I was obviously unqualified for, I got a job as a roustabout with an oil well repair company. When the Reserves reorganized, I volunteered for a newly formed company, the 409th Special Forces. The following summer I went through jump school at Fort Benning, Georgia.

We spent as much time on the firing range and jumping as an active duty company. Some weekends were spent training in radio and telephone communications. Some of the guys also studied languages. I got demolition school. For seven months I worked in the oil fields during the week and played soldier every other weekend.

In the fall of 1959, I had a shot at going to college. I transferred from the Tulsa Reserves to Oklahoma City. Not a problem. When I left, there were rumors about activating the 409th because of the Cuban problem and some flare up in South East Asia. It was made very clear that if the 409th should be activated, I would be included, no matter where I might be, or to what other Reserve unit I might be attached.

I met Captain Abbott when he was still a lieutenant, second in command of the 409th, under Major Herndon. Our friendship really formed in August of 1960, while doing low level jumps at Camp Polk, Louisiana. I didn't mind the jumps but I hated the swamps, especially the snakes.

I must have been staring off into space. The redhead two aisles over thought I was ogling her. The snub seemed excessive, to the point of being laughably juvenile. I had little interest in dating this gorgeous girl, knowing her present companion was a theater arts major. What the hell would we talk about?

When the bell rang, the others packed their books and papers. I abandoned everything at my desk and rushed to the pay phone in the hall. I called Captain Abbott at the Holiday Inn and confirmed time and place. He mentioned something about an interesting summer job, and I desperately needed an interesting summer job, one that paid enough money to see me through my sophmore year.

It was typical May weather. A cool, sweet spring was quickly slipping into a hot and humid summer. In the evening, Captain Abbott picked me up after work at the Rainbow Bakery. He seemed embarrassed about the car, but said he didn't want to attract attention. In a Plain-Jane slate blue Oldsmobile, he wouldn't.

The captain seemed more reserved and distant than his true nature could tolerate. His handshake was too firm and too long. His smile projected an unexpected screen, a falseness, with eyes that didn't fit smiles unless he was a six-pack ahead. He struggled with his agenda, but couldn't quite find a starting point, that certain sparkling opening remark described in Introduction to Sales Skills 101.

At first, I thought it was because of our friendship, which was in itself unusual because of our age difference. I was ten years younger than the Captain. He was an officer recently out of the Regular Army and I was a Reserve non-com, and more significantly, the greatest difference was my total lack of any real experience. Everything I knew was out of books, classrooms, and field training, and for what his job required, education and friendship were poor criteria.

We had supper at the Corner Cafe. He ordered a New York steak, rare. Still an Okie, I ordered the chicken fried steak, the house specialty. "How old are you, Jimmy, twenty four, twenty five?"

"I'll be twenty two in September." My dark brown hair had started turning gray at the temples at eighteen, and, thanks to jobs that kept me in the sun, my deep tan made me look considerably older.

He squinted and sat quietly, apparently reassessing his decision to see me. Hovering doubts pulled his puffy eyelids together and deepened the wrinkles at the corners of his eyes. "Your 201 file says you've spent a considerable amount of time in training sessions, but it's never been put to real use. Why are you here, wasting your time at Central State College? You could be making beau coup bucks someplace a hell of a lot more interesting than Edmond."

Larry Abbott was gradually resettling into his former self: sober, therefore guarded, but at least genuinely friendly, but worry perched on his shoulder like a pet crow.

He was a little too old to be a rodeo cowboy. That's what he did for a living, if anyone asked. The wiry build, preference for western clothes and cool self-confidence made his claim believable. He maintained a façade that few people breached. Still, we were friends and had been since a certain unpleasantness in a bar in Leesville, Louisiana.

After a dozen beers past prudent behavior and two of the house specialty drinks, something called a Rusty Razor, Captain Abbott was beyond any capacity for acceptable, responsible conversation. He made some unfortunate remark about the comic absurdity of coon-ass Cajuns on Harley Davidsons.

When it became obvious that in his present condition he couldn't handle all four, I accidentally spilled hundred-proof rum over a lit candle lamp. The length of the bar exploded in a mass of blue flames. In the momentary distraction, I was able to get him to his feet and out the door.

I was amazed at our good luck-until I remembered his long visit to the men's room-to find a taxi out front. As we drove away, his new friends scrambled to their bikes only to find that each was missing a link in the drive chain.

Larry Abbott, in a fit of laughter, reached into his shirt pocket and withdrew a bar napkin containing the grease-covered links and pins.

"There has to be more to life than running my ass ragged playing soldier. I could go Regular Army anytime, but it doesn't fit in my plans right now."

Captain Abbott smiled his "you-poor-dumb-son-of-a-bitch" smile and drawled, "I can make you an offer better than Regular Army. Real money, with no hassle, no records, and tax free. Hell, from what you told me, that's better than a year's salary in the oil fields."

"Last I heard we aren't at war and that's what it would take to get me back into active duty. But now you say this has nothing to do with active duty?" Somehow, the idea of active duty was filed away in a different galaxy. I started my Dutch apple pie.

"Ahhhhh, but there it is! We're always at war, one way or another. Most of the people I work for use different dictionaries and atlases. They see the world in a completely different light than John Q. Public. Why does it have to be a US war? Or an open war?" The captain daubed at his shirt, cursing under his breath at a red stain from the injured cow on his plate.

"If you're talking about a merc job, I won't put my citizenship on the line. That's a genuine risk if I carry weapons for another country. And there's no such thing as a mercenary POW."

"Oh, please! You're scaring me!" With another false smile on his face, Captain Abbott mocked such dire concerns. The stain was being stubborn. "Got a good cleaners in this town?" He was dressed in civilian clothes, new, western and cheap. For a few dollars more than the cleaning bill, he could probably buy a new shirt.

"Thanks for dinner, Cap," I said. "Gotta hit the books. I have a paper due in English and a test in American history." As if I thought he gave a damn.

The captain threw his napkin over the remains of his steak, a red stain crept across it, mimmicking the one on his shirt. He waved to the waitress for the check. "Hold on, Cowboy. I've got work for you. Just hear me out." He grimaced with frustration. I decided to listen to whatever he had to say and settled back in my seat.

"Look, Larry, I have a job in the oil fields this summer. It's not much money, but it's at home, free food, no rent, and I walk to work."

"Wait until you've heard all I have to say, but not here. Let me drive you over to your dorm. If you still say no, then no hard feelings. Okay?" The captain dropped a twenty on the table and didn't wait for change.

A soft wind blew the rain into wavering sheets. We dashed out the door and ran for his Oldsmobile. The sweet, cool rain of spring was gone, replaced by the warm rain of full summer, and the air was laden with the smell of dust not yet captured by the huge raindrops.

Bright reflections of neon signs on rain-washed pavement turned Main Street into a shimmering river of colored light. Oblivious to the shower, students packed into convertibles and pickup trucks made their way to the Sonic Drive-in for burgers, fries, and cokes.

Neither of us spoke, and we listened to the news on the radio. President and Mrs. Kennedy were off on a two-day visit to Canada. White protesters of Anniston and Birmingham attacked two busloads of racially mixed Freedom Riders. Rocket scientist hailed the data provided by the sub-orbital space flight of Freedom 7, piloted by Alan Shepard. The announcer shifted to local sports and weather.

The six block drive to Thatcher Hall was dead time. I believe the reason for Larry's silence was difficulty in holding eye contact while driving. More Salesmanship 101.

He parked in the no parking zone in front of Thatcher Hall and reached behind the seat to pull out a battered briefcase. He worked the combination and opened the lid. The briefcase was filled with packs of hundred-dollar bills. He tossed a stack into my lap. "This is just for listening," he said as he extracted a manila folder from the lid and struggled to keep the briefcase between his lap and the steering wheel. "Suppose I could promise you'd never touch a weapon. You just take a short vacation and set up a field telephone system, like the one at Camp Polk, and fly home with six thousand dollars in your pocket. Would you be interested?"

"Keep talking," I said. College was over for me for a year, while I lived at home and saved money for another semester or two. At this rate, a BA would take about eight years. Money talks, even sings. Six thousand dollars was an opera.

"What I'm about to tell you will involve you legally, even if you decline the offer. How do I know you can keep your mouth shut?" He knew he could trust me, or he'd never have driven down from Tulsa. This was a subtle ploy to edge me into an affirmative frame of mind. More Salesmanship 101. I really began to resent his fumble-ass efforts to manipulate me.

"Then don't tell me anything," I snapped, and tossed the money back to him. "Good night, Cap," I said and unlatched the door and threw him a sloppy salute as I set my feet on the curb. He still wasn't squaring away.

"Wait one, Cowboy. Hear me out."

I'd never known him to be anything but straight forward. I pulled my feet back inside and closed the door.

"I'll listen but lay it out fast and simple." Even clumsy and obvious, this new approach made me nervous. Whatever it was, it wasn't big, it was monumental.

"The US government is our client. The specific organization will, for the time being, remain unidentified." He tossed the money back into my lap and pulled two papers from the manila envelope. "You'll need to sign one of these papers tonight. One accepts the offer, the other rejects it. There are certain legal restrictions with each. I suggest you sign the acceptance contract first, then listen to the offer. If you don't like it, then I'll tear it up, and you'll sign the other. Which ever you choose, this will take about three minutes."

"Say what you have to say and then I'll sign one of them. Take five minutes if you like."

Larry Abbott smiled and put away the declining paper. He turned on the dome light so I could read the proposal. It said that I had accepted employment with the Pan-American Highway Development Corporation as an equipment and materials transportation management technician. Some sort of truck ape, I supposed. It also said that if I divulged any information, no matter how trivial, about where I would be working or the nature of the work, I could be heavily fined and/or sent to prison. "I'll sign, but if I join you, I want that paper torn up," I said.

"No can do, Cowboy, but when the job's over it will be destroyed along with every other scrap of paper related to our little project. Besides, this is your cover. It explains who you are and what you're doing if any explanations become necessary. Think of it as both a contract and an insurance policy."

It was exactly that. With the promise of perks and a bonus, I signed.

CHAPTER SIX

Till morning fair
Came forth with pilgrim steps,
John Milton

Oklahoma City's Lakewood Hotel was tired and old, on the brink of sleazy. The guests, like the hotel, tended to be a bit frayed. The biggest moneymaking event of the year was in full swing: the annual state Shriner's convention. "You couldn't pay me to go in there, Jimmy." Billy Cook drove me to my meeting with Captain Abbott and friends. "The place is filled with drunk old coots with a bent for practical jokes and throwing up on your shoes." I had elbowed my way through them last year and I knew he was right.

The fourth floor hallway near the back smelled of stale smoke and pine-scented disinfectant. Coarse feminine laughter echoed in the long corridor behind me, near the elevators. At the other end of the hall, half a "WELCOME" sign had been torn off and left on the worn carpet. "COME," the sign now read. Loud country music and more laughter hinted that all the fun at the Lakewood Hotel was behind door 473.

The figures in room 486 were older than I expected, better dressed and better groomed. In faded Levi's and seriously needing a haircut, I felt very much out of place, even though I had all four Jacks from a deck of playing cards stuck in my hip pocket, my informal I.D.

Two small table lamps cast a dim light in opposite corners of the room. Through the window opposite the door I could see flashes of lightening from a distant prairie storm competing with the blinking neon sign over a laundry across the street. Light rain spattered on the grimy windows and settled on the sill in oily pools.

Larry was a dark silhouette hunched over a desk in the corner. With a nod and a gesture to come in, he continued to whisper into the phone. He scribbled notes on a yellow pad that rested unevenly on various portfolios, a US Army file folder, and a sheaf of telegrams. He continued to listen to the receiver, ignoring me completely.

"Who are you?" inquired a tall, slim figure to my right, his entrance marked by a burst of yellow light from the adjoining bedroom. His voice would have been out of place anywhere except a Hilton Head lawn party. It was smooth, a bit high, and richly embroidered with an aristocratic Southern accent.

"I'm James Donlin," I said. "Aren't you expecting me?" The feminine laughter I had assumed was headed for room 473 belled behind me as the door opened. I was brusquely pushed into the center of the room as the door closed, and I heard the faint click of the lock. Older and harder looking party girls stood behind me, shedding their purses and light jackets. Both carried military automatics in holsters held at the small of their backs. That explained their jackets in humid eighty-degree weather.

"We followed him up from the parking lot. There are two other boys in the car. No stops along the way." As the first party girl made her report, she began patting down my back and the other my front. Neither was a bit shy. I didn't mind until they started through my pockets. I just don't like being picked over and I tried to shake their hands away, saying I'd be happy to empty my pockets for them.

There was a sharp rap on the back of my head with something metallic and heavy, and a rough grip threatened to tear the collar off my best shirt. "Now, now," she said, "Don't mess with our little routine. Relax and enjoy it, Honey," she cautioned, and passed her hand across my crotch hard enough that I gasped from both shock and pain.

It was over in less than a minute. The woman behind me turned on another lamp, brighter than the other two, and held out the contents of my pockets for closer examination. Then she presented my belongings to the tall gentleman. "Wallet, comb, pocket knife, change and keys. No weapons, no wires," she said and spread everything out for inspection on a table beside the door. "And a winning poker hand."

A wave of the hand from the tall figure dismissed the two ladies, another gesture indicated that I should shift two cardboard boxes of files and clipboards, and take a seat on the sofa beside Larry's desk. I was startled when Larry Abbott barked "Right!" He slammed down the phone and swung his swivel chair toward me, his face now only a foot from mine. "Donlin, do you speak Spanish?"

"No, sir." Bullshit! He knew I didn't.

"Then you're not invited to this party, Cowboy. See you around," he said and tried to turn back to the phone.

"Wait a minute, Cap!" I shouted at him. I lunged to the desk and spun his chair so we were face to face again. "I've gone through a lot of crap to get this far. On your say, I've quit my job in the oil fields and pre-enrolled for next semester. I'm entitled to more than a goddamned kiss-off!"

"Nobody's entitled to anything! You just don't fit the job description. As for your summer job, you've been paid triple what your oil field job would have paid all summer just to listen to a proposal. Maybe you can still find work and be that much farther ahead. If something comes up, I'll let you know."

The hand on my shoulder was large and manicured. And heavy. I straightened and turned to face the gentleman from the bedroom. He stepped past me and whispered something to Larry. In the dim light of the desk lamp, I could see that the stranger's hair was sandy blonde, fine and thinning on top.

"Jimmy, I've just been informed that as of twenty minutes ago, our Spanish-speaking requirements have been met. You're in, but not speaking Spanish will be a pain in the ass for both of us." He drew a Camel from a pack, started to put it in his mouth but instead crumpled it and threw it into a wastebasket. That explains his foul mood; he's trying to quit again.

His criticism of my linguistic deficiencies seemed to me more than a little hypocritical since I knew he didn't speak Spanish either. What the hell. At least I was in.

I rose and took a couple of steps toward the door, then thought of a few questions. "When should I be ready, Cap? What sort of clothing? How long will I be gone?" I asked in an enthusiastic spirit of the moment. Wrong people. Wrong questions. Wrong time.

The southern gentleman turned to me, tight-jawed, and eyes fierce with anger.

He was politely intercepted by an older, stocky figure who stepped briskly from the bedroom while fumbling with a bundle of yellow notepaper. "Mr. Donlin, my name is Wilson Donahue. This is Mr. Warren. Please excuse his pique. Unexpected difficulties of the past few days have made it impossible to answer your questions. I'm sure you can appreciate that we must reserve such information until we can provide some degree of certainty. Give us a few days."

While Mr. Donahue, stout, gray, balding and in his mid-to-late sixties, shook my hand, Mr. Warren retreated to the bedroom to cool off. He mumbled something about national affairs, rednecks, and high school dropouts.

Whatever was happening, it made Mr. Warren tense. I had a feeling that when Mr. Warren was upset everybody was supposed to tip-toe. When he opened the door, I had a better view of the bed. The room wasn't being used as a bedroom. The deep blue counterpane was covered with legal pads and a half dozen pink file folders, the kind that aren't supposed to leave a secured area. Either these gentlemen were bending the rules or room 486 *was* a secured area.

The better light from the bedroom briefly illuminated a battered, waxed cardboard box beside my sofa. I had overlooked it completely in the deep shadow of the desk. Larry was on the phone again. Mr. Donahue caught the direction of my glance and took me by the elbow. We walked to the sofa beside the desk and we sat down. I had to shuffle a bit to get around the wax-coated container, its label emblazoned with the boast that it contained the finest frozen chickens from Arkansas. The box was actually filled with very old field telephones, two switch panels and a half dozen more-or-less new field radios. They were AN/PRC-6's, short range VHF, line-of- sight and fixed frequencies. Walkie-talkies. They were in much better shape than the telephones.

"Do you read, Mr. Donlin?" Donahue asked.

"Yes, I read. Do these antiques work?" I asked.

Mr. Donahue tossed me a battered and worn field manual. "They have been in, let's say, neglectful and obscure storage. They will be overhauled by a government lab and brought up to perfect condition very soon. Mr. Abbott thinks you have the skills to set up our field communications system. What have you done with telephones?"

"A dozen or so training exercises, several of those in the field," I answered. "Nothing large scale or really long range. And the equipment we used was at least a generation newer than these."

"We know this is one of the most reliable units ever used by the military," Donahue continued. "It's tough, mildew-resistant, has a humidity seal, and Larry tells me the hook-ups are identical to the equipment you've trained on. The age and condition means they've dropped off any materials inventory long ago. They are untraceable. That alone is of considerable value. When you scan the manual, you'll find you can manage any variations from your training."

I wondered if he really believed this crate of obsolete, Korean War vintage junk would ever be reliable. "Abuse and humidity? Over how large an area and how many lines?" I asked.

"No one in our little group has a crystal ball," Mr. Donahue replied, a touch of irritation in his voice. I've got to hold back on the questions. "You'll have to figure this out when you are in your operations area." Donahue turned to speak over his shoulder to Larry who was filling out a day schedule, picking items off his yellow note pads. He lifted the phone as Mr. Donahue spoke. "Captain Abbott, do you have anything for Mr. Donlin?"

"Yes, I do," Larry snapped as he terminated dialing and dropped the receiver back in its cradle. "Cowboy, we're on for this Saturday. You're going to meet some friends of mine. I'll pick you up at zero six hundred hours and I don't do wake-up calls. One more thing. Do not, I repeat, do not write down my name or anyone else's. Nor any appointments, activities, times or place names. By memory only. Is that clear?"

"I understand, Captain. I'll be on the front steps of Thatcher Hall at zero six hundred, Saturday morning."

Larry was wearing his SOB smile again. He turned back to the telephone and Mr. Donahue ushered me to the door. I paused long enough to scoop up my belongings, sort them out and return them to the pockets habit dictated.

"Good evening, Mr. Donlin. I'm sure we'll be seeing a great deal of one another." As we shook hands again, I knew my value to the team was still a question mark as far as Wilson Donahue was concerned.

I had been weighed and found wanting.

CHAPTER SEVEN

A friend should bear
his friend's infirmities.
Shakespeare

Saturday morning was a bust by zero six twenty. Abbott was late. A drizzling rain darkened the walls of the large brick dormitory and rattled down the galvanized drainpipes. The splattering run-off on the cast concrete channel seemed a soothing lullaby, then ran to the street gutter. A peaceful and quiet moment of introspection, spell that 'dozing off,' would have been natural for me if not for my own self-induced chemical poisoning. Goddamn, I hated three-two beer!

My hangover was minor; Larry's was colossal, and he was also thirty-four minutes late. I had seen him this bad only twice before. When he's this burned, his left eye becomes lazy and drifts inward. The expression on his face was one shaped by a crude blending of nausea and pain. He was in one second the little boy who cries for a sympathetic ear and in the next second a wounded bear who will disembowel anyone stupid enough to step within reach. I knew enough to tap dance until I could tell which held the moment.

Several friends and relatives have accused me of having a perverted sense of humor. "Turn left, Larry. I'll buy you breakfast."

He grimaced and rolled his eyes. "Get in, you fucking sadist," Larry said. "Maybe next month, when I'm ready to eat again."

When I opened the door, the handle felt sticky. The interior smelled of a bad accident. The rental agency would charge the Captain dearly for cleaning charges or maybe even replacement of carpet and upholstery. "And keep your remarks to yourself. You know how I get when there's a jump ahead of me. The more advanced notice I have, the more Rebel courage I can soak up."

That was a play on English slang for gin . . . Dutch courage. Larry hated gin, loved bourbon and sour mash; hence, Rebel courage.

There was a strange paradox about Larry Abbott. He was acrophobic. People tried to tactfully direct him to professional help, but being the stubborn type, he was convinced he could "cure" himself. Like most amateur psychologists, he addressed the symptoms and not the problem. What could be more natural for someone afraid of heights than to jump out of airplanes while in an alcoholic stupor? If he had been claustrophobic he would probably have become an alcoholic coalminer.

"Where are we jumping, Cap?'

"No way, Donlin. You'll know when Donahue wants you to know. Not before."

As we left the campus, Larry pulled a pair of nylons off the steering column and let them stream out the window before letting them go. A bra with a cut strap was next. "Last night was a hot interlude in a fog bank, Cowboy."

We drove west. When the rays of the morning sun struck the rain-glazed blacktop, the two-lane country roads seemed ambling pathways of silver. He outlined the morning's protocol as we wound through the low hills west of Edmond. We passed section line after section line, turned south, then west again. The red soil grew pink with the mix of river sand. The prairie was a lush green that hid the red clay almost completely in the cultivated fields of wheat. Elm and cottonwoods lined the sandy banks of the North Canadian River to our left. I estimated we were somewhere northwest of El Reno.

Leaving the blacktop, we bounced and slid over muddy dirt roads with deep ruts cut by vehicles that arrived even earlier. After passing a strip of white engineer's tape fluttering from a fence post we turned onto a field access road, toward the river. We were in a broad, shallow valley.

There wasn't a farmhouse, or barn or a single head of livestock in sight, only two large cultivated fields. This was a secured area and we were on someone's schedule. A lone figure in a jeep, barely visible in the windbreaks, reported our arrival by radio.

The cottonwood and elm gave way to willow and scrub cedar out in the riverbed. Even after the rains, the North Canadian was still little more than a wide, meandering, swath of red clay, sandbars, and water. Water flowed here, stood in clear, shallow pools there, reflecting a broad, blue, clearing sky. Patches of cattails edged the bank on the north side, sumac and persimmon on the south.

Our mud-spattered Oldsmobile turned off the farm road and parked on a rocky flat obscured by a thick and tangled bois d'arc windrow that must have been planted around the turn of the century. It was dense and overgrown, branches entwined to the point of being impassable. Out of sight from the road, we joined two other mud-covered sedans, Wilson Donahue's new, navy blue Cadillac and a not-so-new red Ford pickup.

Larry grumbled something about staying in the car all day and half stepped, half fell out, catching his balance on the car door. I also slipped in the thin coating of red mud that covered this exposed sandstone slab and fell to all fours, cursing Larry for his choice of parking spot. I got up stripping the red slurry off my hands and the knees of my jeans, flicking the excesses in no particular direction. "Hey, watch it, Jimmy! This shit stains!"

"Really? You mean now I own a pair of pink sneakers? Thanks, Larry."

A moderately interesting Saturday morning was ripped open by a long burst of automatic fire, the staccato reverberating in a multiplying echo along the low riverbanks. A covey of quail broke cover near the windbreak.

Four men stood on a sandstone hogback that jutted a little farther out into the river than the point where the vehicles were parked. A six-round burst sent up geysers of sand and water ten yards short of a white painted nail keg across the river.

By the report and rhythm, I could tell they were firing an M3 forty-five caliber sub-machine gun. By the end of WWII, this weapon had established a fair reputation for close quarters combat. It also picked up the nick name "grease gun" because it looked like one. It didn't, unfortunately, have the range or accuracy of the old Thompson, the weapon it was supposed to replace.

Someone in the group saw Larry and me and waved for us to join them. We had taken only a half dozen steps when a seated figure at the pickup stood and strode toward us. It was Mr. Warren and his face was red with anger. "Abbott, you son of a bitch! Where's my wife?"

"How the hell should I know? I don't even know where I am," Larry threw back.

"She was fine at dinner last night. Hadn't had a drop. She went to the ladies room and never came back. Donahue said he sent you to look for her. Just like last time, isn't it? You're two of a kind! Goddamned whiskey-soaked cripples! Where did you leave her?" Mr. Warren demanded through clenched teeth. He was closer now and I could see the veins standing out at his temples.

Captain Abbott never took a step back but he did slow his pace, mostly because of the bad footing. "Don't hand me any of your irate husband crap," he mumbled at Warren. "I'm in no mood for it."

Wilson Donahue had raced around the other side of the pickup and awkwardly stepped in front of Mr. Warren, trying to check what was apparently a scene played before. "Jack, get a grip. You're blowing this thing out of proportion. Jack, damn it, shake it off. Marge is not the priority here!"

"She's not your priority, you mean. She's my wife and . . . ." By this time Warren was close enough to throw a left jab. Slipping in the mud, most of its power was stolen, along with his balance, and the blow only grazed Larry's left cheek. There must have been a little steam in it, enough to knock Larry out of his stupor and self-pity, enough to put him on guard. For an instant, sympathetic understanding flashed in Larry's eyes, but not sympathetic enough to take another punch. His own baseness and disregard for consequences of his choices had once again turned like a serpent and sank its fangs in his ass.

Warren shoved Donahue aside and threw another left at Larry's face. Larry ducked and delivered a sharp left hook into Jack Warren's solar plexus. Warren doubled in pain and his breath left like a brother-in-law when the bar tab arrives. Then Larry precisely delivered right elbow to

Warren's chin that dropped him to his knees. Gasping for air, he let Donahue help him up.

It was over. Righteous indignation evaporated and the real issues came round.

"We need Marge," Donahue growled at Larry. "Senator Kerr is nosing around this reserve. Marge knows people who can shorten the old fart's leash. I sent you to find her. Why couldn't you just bring her back?"

"You had a good idea what would happen when I found her. Same as last time. She had paid someone to stash a fifth of Wild Turkey in the lady's room and invited me to share. The rest of the evening was more or less, like Jack said, pretty much like last time." Captain Abbott turned his back, walked away a few paces and delivered up a string of dry heaves, the result of sudden exertion.

"But you were sober this time. You've always been reliable when you're sober," Jack Warren gasped. "We thought we could count on you."

"Sobriety is such a fleeting thing, like good weather or steady work," Larry spat out between heaves. "Is it Fate's flight of whimsy or are we all just a collection of fumbling, ass-grabbing, sotty misfits? Fuck you, too, Jack. And try not to comment on the obvious. She doesn't hold you or me in very high regard, you know. Jim Beam, Hiram Walker and Jack Daniels are the only men in her life. She wants to crawl into a bottle and you're standing in her way. She wants to beat you to death and I'm just a convinient club. Last night, for a while, I was in that bottle with her. But, hell, I'm just a sloppy, whiney drunk, Jack. She's suicidal."

Donahue walked to the truck and came back with a first aid kit. Mr. Warren spat a little blood from a cut on his lip. "Good morning, Mr. Donlin. Getting acquainted?" Donahue asked in a sarcastic tone while uncorking the peroxide. I grunted a reply and stifled a yawn, trying to convey the idea that all this was old pudding to me.

We fell in together and walked toward the point, stopping at the pickup to replace the first aid kit. "Damn, I hate working with you, Jack," Larry complained, "because you always drag Marge along. She'll ruin you. Two drinks and she'll party with anyone. Someday it will be with the wrong people and she will use the scandal to rip you apart, destroy your career. As for me, you know how I get when there's a jump in front of me." Larry seemed repentant enough, and he was wearing his 'little- boy-with-his-hand-in-the-cookie-jar' expression. It wouldn't play in Tulsa and it didn't play here.

"She was fresh off the lush farm when we came out here," Mr. Warren protested, "and this is a dry state. This was supposed to be our chance to patch things up. You really don't know where she is?" he asked in an almost pleading tone.

"No. The last time I saw her was in the parking lot of the Holiday Inn. She had messed up her dress, and ruined my car, by the way, and bought a waitress uniform from a girl leaving the coffee shop around two o'clock in the morning. Then she got in a truck with the girl and her boyfriend who had waved another fifth of Wild Turkey at us. I was in no shape to stop her. When I had sobered up enough, I drove up to Edmond for Donlin. She'll show up when she's ready. Conversely, we won't find her if she doesn't want to be found." Larry, through another string of dry heaves, couldn't make his voice sound all that consoling.

Jack Warren was a loving, dutiful husband . . . up to a point. Beyond that, sympathy is swallowed by the reality that he had married for money, connections and prestige. This was part of a package deal and Jack Warren had known that long before the wedding ceremony. And as far as Larry

Abbott was concerned, in spite of his moaning and chest beating, Jack Warren stood totally undeserving of any sympathy whatsoever.

Even I felt caught up in this strange blend of domestic chaos, political intrigue, paramilitary subterfuge and whatever the hell we were doing here. Jack Warren and Larry Abbott were not the only ones stuck on this sheet of flypaper.

"As far as your jump is concerned, don't you think it's time to grow up? Get someone else to hold your hand?" Mr. Warren complained. He drifted toward self-righteousness, sounding tired and beaten. Not beaten by Larry Abbott but by a one hundred and ten pound redhead named Marjorie Claire Hamilton Warren. She was the privileged niece of a past president and seven years earlier had helped Jack Warren's career immeasurably. Her relatives and friends filled the triangle . . . THE triangle. Annapolis, Washington and Langley. But now, her drinking and social rampages could easily destroy what she had helped him build. There were whispers that her indiscretions actually strengthened certain associations, whether by personal bonds or blackmail could only be a subject of the wildest irresponsible speculation.

As we neared the base of the long sandstone finger, Larry stepped aside and surrendered to the heaves again.

"You ought to keep her in a cage," he said, catching up.

"She was, in a way," Donahue wheezed, abandoning his stolid bearing for a nearly comical scramble to more secure footing. "We can't keep her there forever. She's no good to us at the lush farm, and she's no good to us when she's drinking. In those rare times when she is available and functional, she is our most valuable asset. She has lunch or plays tennis with people we can't even get on the damned phone. She went to school with the offspring of at least a dozen senators, and they all have cousins or friends who clerk or serve as aides in Congress, and at least two ex-boyfriends in the State Department. The Pentagon is like a frat house to her. Then there are her parents and the country club set. She is our Golden Goose, Larry. So, when she falls off the wagon, we pick her up, dust her off, and put her back on. But your point is well taken. Maybe it's time to pull some duty in a really dry climate. Say . . . Saudi Arabia? Wagon as far as the eye can see. What do you think, Jack?"

"I like the idea of the farm better," Mr. Warren said. "There is no advantage to keeping her sober if we're out of contact with the rest of the world.

"Gut morgen, Heinrich."

"Herr Warren. Good morning Mr. Donahue, Captain Abbott. A beautiful morning. Would you like to join us on the tarp?" A tall, thin gentleman with bushy white hair and sharp features gestured toward the cluster of men assembled on a large water-proof tarpaulin, some standing, some sitting on up-turned ammo boxes, filling the magazines of the weapons they were about to fire.

"She'll be pissed at going back to the farm. But at least she has friends and family to look out for her," Donahue said, sitting lightly on an empty fifty caliber ammo box padded with a folded field jacket.

"No good, Bill. Remember who pulled her off the wagon last time? Her own sister. Before that, her damned snob girlfriend who edits that women's magazine, and before that her old room mate from Brown. Don't you get it? Her friends and family don't support her, they support her drinking." Jack Warren had thought about this for quite a while and had resigned himself to wait for his wife. Every man has a limit to his capacity to forgive, at least that's what he grumbled to Wilson Donahue.

This was an education I'd rather not have. A significant segment of an intelligence entity seemed to be held captive and potentially made dysfunctional by the escapades of a demure and privileged alcoholic socialite.

As I scanned the wares of Sweden, Israel, Italy and West Germany, I wondered if anyone had considered the paradox of Mrs. Warren. Her loving family encouraged her continual self-destructive drinking bouts. Her husband and his associates tried to restore her health but for self-serving motives. What a fucked-up way to live. No wonder she drank.

The Italian nine-millimeter automatic had a nice balance and a grip big enough even for my hand.

"Mr. Donlin, this is Heinrich Turm. He's our supplier of hardware and technical support equipment," Donahue said, as if he were introducing a shoe salesman from Fort Worth.

"Happy to meet you, Mr. Turm," I said, deciding to avoid embarrassing myself by showing off what little German I'd learned in only one semester. The sleeves of his dark blue coveralls were covered with the embroidered patches of more than a dozen European ski resorts. Some were Swiss, some French, one Norwegian, two Austrian, and three from Italy. The most recent one, by the year marked on the lower edge, was large and perfectly stitched on his left breast pocket, from an Andean resort in Chile. He noticed my curiosity about the patches.

"Do you ski, Mr. Donlin?" he asked.

"No, but I'd like to learn some day," I said, "and I'd like to see as much of the world as you obviously have. That's an impressive collection."

"Hopefully, you will see the world under better conditions and for better reasons than most of the traveling I did when I was your age," he replied with only the slightest accent. "But if you travel for skiing, I must recommend my latest discovery. There is a club in Valparaiso that flies you by helicopter to the top of the most spectacular slopes. Then you can ski in new powder for twenty miles. At a pre-arranged field, they pick you up and fly you back to your hotel for a hot bath, dinner, brandy and whatever the evening holds. There is nothing like it in Europe, I can promise." There was a twinkle in his eyes that told anyone who'd care read it, the weapons trade is only his livelihood, not his passion; skiing held that slot.

"Hey, Larry! Did you bring your kit?" Ross Bishop asked. The other three set safeties and shifted their weapons to their lefts as we shook hands. Phil Keener, Pete Nelson and Jack Bennett had all worked with Larry before. 'The kit' turned out to be Larry's fifty caliber ammo box filled with gun smithing tools, lubricants and odds and ends of replacement parts for at least a dozen different weapons.

Someone had fired an M2 carbine and, while checking a loose fitting, dropped a forestock ring pin in the mud. They knew what Herr Turm would say to them; they'd heard it before.

"Perhaps we can talk later, Mr. Donlin. I have been neglectful of my wards of the day." He turned to the others. "Gentlemen, someone has broken one of our toys? You know what Papa Turm does with careless gnomes who don't listen."

In nervous laughter, the group backed away from the wiry old man. "It wasn't me, Hank! It was Bennett, I swear!" a trooper chortled while wiping a black grease smudge from his left hand. They all laughed and pointed at someone with a fresh crew cut, quietly packing clips for the grease gun.

"Hey, Hank! I didn't break nothing! I haven't touched anything but the grease gun. Look at Nelson. He didn't get that graphite on his hands stuffing forty-five rounds! I didn't take anything apart, Hank. Not a damned thing," Bennett protested.

Turm saw that Nelson did indeed have grease on his hands. The clincher was the other three who had now backed away from Nelson, laughing. Nelson wasn't laughing.

"Now, wait, Hank! It was an accident. The pen was loose, so I thought maybe the threads were stripped. I . . . ah! Here it is." Nelson stooped to retrieve the pin at the edge of the ground cloth and nervously wiped away a speck of red mud and replaced the pin in the forestock ring. With a small screwdriver from his shirt pocket he tightened it and presented the weapon to Herr Turm. "The threads *are* stripped," Nelson offered as his defense.

CHAPTER EIGHT

To promise not to do a thing is the surest way in the
world to make a body want to go and do that very thing.
Mark Twain

Heinrich Turm still had the carriage of a man who could
take care of himself. No one in this group had any desire
to tangle with him. I later learned that he had been part of
an elite German parachute unit that had participated in the
German near-disaster on Crete and had later seen action in
Russia.

Because of his linguistic skills and high-level social
connections, the German High Command recruited him
for a specialized intelligence gathering team in Spain.

The end of the war found him sunbathing on the island
of Ibiza and directing friends to secret away confiscated
art treasures, a little Italian bullion and mountains of war
materials.

By the summer of 1947, he had his own office in Berlin,
working for British intelligence. There was something about
the war crime trials, also, but I never heard much more than

innuendo and a little name-dropping. I heard all this on a sweltering day on a muddy beach, somewhere near the end of the earth. I heard it from Heinrich's best friend, Wilson Donahue, the same man who had introduced him to a British intelligence officer, MI5, D Branch, in 1947.

"Enough play, gentlemen. Look at the wares, shoot up the little barrels, make your choices and we shall have a nice lunch," Heinrich groused, gesturing toward a high ridge downstream. For the first time, I noticed the nearly invisible camp nestled against the windrow. Turm and Donahue had pitched two tents about seventy yards away, Turm's the larger because it housed an ANGRC-9 radio, file cabinet and cooking facilities as well as private quarters. The gray-green fabric identified the tents as fairly new NATO equipment, probably of West German or Dutch manufacture. Inside the tents, whose sides were rolled up on three sides, I could see long tables with white table cloths, set with china and silver, even floral table settings and upholstered folding chairs. Another sixty yards downstream, a small generator purred, its slight exhaust drifting into the dense bois d'arc wind break. This was the way to bivouac; all the creature comforts of a three star hotel.

Someone moved in the larger tent, shifting things around on a metal folding table. Behind the cook, I glimpsed a seated woman, back to me, holding an ice pack to the base of her neck under a cascade of flaming red hair done up in a pony tail.

"See anything you like, Cowboy?" Larry asked from behind me, half way to the truck. "I'll keep my promise about you not carrying a weapon, but the others don't have to know and you'll be better off if they don't," he said, just loud enough for me to hear.

I liked that word, PROMISE when Larry said it. It meant something to him. A promise was something to be managed as best one could, for most men. But to Larry Abbott the word was binding in the deepest possible sense, without compromise, without exceptions. It didn't matter with whom such an agreement might be formed, priest, banker, politician, beggar, or lady of the evening; it was his word.

In one of his over-indulgences, I'd heard him rail about someone who claimed his penchant childish. "Fuck Conny Boulger. He thinks I'm still a kid trying to wear a white ten-gallon hat. On the other hand, he has to have a team of lawyers to keep his dealings straight. Nobody will even talk to him without an attorney present. Nobody will socialize with the backstabbing son-of-a-bitch. There are two banks in Dallas whose guards have photos of him and orders not to let him in. Those same two banks will loan me money without collateral, without paper, not even a handshake. Just my word, and I've done it. Over two hundred thousand, all paid back with interest. And Conny Boulger thinks I'm childish. Hell, I've seen used car salesmen throw him off their lots. His uncle owns a Chevrolet dealership in Amarillo, and he wouldn't sell Conny a car unless he had a cashier's check and the paperwork finished before hand, everything locked tighter than a spinster's knees. How can a man live like that? He sees himself as a noble, marauding wolf. Everybody else sees him as some kind of fucking parasite."

I fully understood what he meant about the weapon and keeping his promise. If I'm part of the group, collecting the same pay for the same job, wouldn't they expect me to assume the same risk, including carrying a weapon . . . and using it? His remark had the intended effect. It started me rethinking about how I'd feel if I were one of the others and learned of such a promise. I'd be odd man out. Way out.

Another question pounded at the anvil in my brain. Everyone knows field telephones ain't exactly brain surgery. So why am I here, really?

But mostly the weapons issue grated on me. Painfully. Even if circumstances and events mated perfectly with intent, and the promise was kept, would it make any difference to the rest of the participants? On the other hand, if I gave in and accepted a weapon, I would feel an obligation to use it if the situation got hot. Would I *want* to be unarmed in a hot situation?

"How about the antique?" I asked, pointing toward the bed of the truck and the Browning Automatic Rifle still resting there under a scrap of oily canvas. Larry caught Heinrich's eye and gestured with his thumb toward the pickup. Herr Turm nodded in the affirmative.

I had carried the BAR through advanced infantry training at Fort Ord in fifty-seven. The weapon had been designed to clear out trenches in WWI. It would have been extremely effective, but The Great War ended before it could be put in the hands of our troops. Over the next several decades it went through a series of design improvements, just in time to become a valuable infantry weapon in both Pacific and European theaters.

Larry strained to lift an amo crate of empty magazines and loose rounds. A few minutes of work had the weapon ready to fire. Two of the group were busy with the clips and I broke the weapon down to the configuration I preferred; flash-hider but no bipod.

"It is amazing," Henrich observed. "All this new material available and without fail, Mr. Donahue, your men always choose vintage American military hardware." Mr. Turm made no effort to cover the frustration in his voice.

"It's not so strange," Donahue asserted. "Most of these men trained with this equipment just a few years ago.

Ammunition is still available in huge quantities. There are dozens of variations possible for most of these weapons and skilled armorers around for modifications."

Later, Mr. Donahue and I had a conversation about weapons as a trade commodities, an idea that occupied little space inside my head. "They're still telling jokes in Washington," Donahue said to me, "about how 'farm equipment' for Greece didn't make it to Piraeus but went straight to Haifa. In 1955, two freighters loaded with ammunition for Seoul were never seen again after they cleared port at Cape Town. In 1957, a dozen F-86 Saberjets shipped to Holland turned up in Brazil," Donahue said with amusement in his voice.

I had nothing meaningful to contribute to a prolonged conversation on the matter. Mr. Donahue was called away and I was left in the shade of the pickup waiting for my turn at the white barrels. I thought to myself that at some level of the State Department or National Security Agency or Central Intelligence Agency these events must seem humorous. At the international level, weapons are as much a trade commodity as iron ore, grain or oil. But the ease with which death and suffering could change hands, the seemingly ordinary transactions in weapons and munitions shook me. Did anyone monitor these transactions? In the Korean War, Americans took fire from planes we gave China after WWII. It is unlikely that conscience and common sense could check the dark side of capitalism. Even the dimmest awareness that nothing in the Western Hemisphere is more powerful than profit motive, or cheaper than human life, can generate monumental cynicism.

It struck me that I was, at that instant, a participant in these same horrific transactions, that the services I have agreed to provide are as necessary and tangible as any of the weapons in the truck or the missing cargoes Donahue found so amusing. And the entity I would have expected to monitor weapons sales to questionable states was the same entity that would write my paycheck.

So simple, so easy. It had happened in only three significant choices; the Corner Cafe, the Lakewood Hotel and today. I had become one of "them." I could still change my mind. Dropping out would not change the necessity of the group or its mission. If I dropped out, then someone like me would fill the same job slot. Knowing the mission was justified would make me feel better. I felt sick at my stomach. This wasn't what my parents and Father O'Rourke had intended for little Jimmy Donlin.

As Larry and I walked to the sandstone point, Donahue and Turm argued about recent trends in the design and production of weapons, cost efficiency and how the new generation of arms seem to become more lethal at the same rate they become uglier. It was a truly strange observation, I thought, especially since the BAR on my shoulder could hardly be described as an objet d'art. Yet, he was right. If one considers finely milled steel an aesthetically pleasing expression of the machinist's craft, then the older weapons are beautiful. If the cheaper process of stamping out metal parts and using high-density molded plastics for other parts offends one, then the new weapons, designed to trim production cost, at only a slight loss of efficiency, were truly ugly.

Turm and Donahue fell in behind Larry and me and stood with the men on the rock. "Where'd you dig up that dinosaur?" Bennett asked. Keener and Nelson, adjusting the straps on a pair of the new M14s for shooting from a standing position, laughed as they stepped aside.

"Do you really want to lug that thing around?" Donahue asked.

Bennett suggested that I put the bipod back on, "And maybe some wheels."

"I know this piece. If you have to do any chopping, it's a major ax." I said, loosening the strap and wrapping my left arm into it.

I took a magazine from Larry. I chambered a round and set the selector switch to "s" for a slow rate of fire. This had been one of its first design modifications. Set for 'f' for 'fast rate of fire' it could spew out six hundred rounds a minute. The 's' setting knocked this down to only three hundred and fifty. "What's the target?"

Heinrich stepped forward, sipping from a huge mug of creamed coffee. He stood beside me and waved the mug toward the two small white nail kegs at two hundred and three hundred yards. "We have been scaring the hell out of those for an hour or so. Not much distance for the weapon you have."

"How about that illegal dump a hundred yards beyond the second barrel?" Larry asked. "See that old stove? There is a rusty milk can just to the left. That should be enough of a challenge."

Four hundred yards, but I set the sights for three hundred yards, knowing that without the bipod a BAR will lift a little. No one knew why, just as no one knew why a Garand shoots low if it has a fixed bayonet. I unfolded the hinged butt plate and set it to my shoulder and adjusted to the full weight now supported by my tightly strapped left arm and right shoulder. As I bounced the sights over the target, a sense of familiarity flooded back to eyes and finger tips.

Pressing the safety off, my finger curled to touch the worn steel of the trigger. I bounced the target again and squeezed off a four round burst. The milk can shuddered under a cloud of rust and rolled down the sandy bank, into a reedy pool, and sank.

"Hot damn, Donlin. You've done this before," Nelson snapped over his shoulder. "Let me try a few rounds."

With the safety back on, I took the stock off my shoulder, unwound my left arm from the sling and passed the weapon to Nelson. "I'm going for the first keg," Nelson informed us, and threw his arm into the sling. It was too loose for him and he didn't bother to tighten it. He let off six rounds at the nearest target, the spent brass ringing against an ammo box at Donahue's feet. All rounds missed, throwing up little geysers of water and red mud over and beyond the keg.

"When you change range, you usually readjust the sights, Nelson," Bennett jibed.

"Right. Well, it ain't my baby. It ought to come with a burro. I've forgotten. How much does it weigh loaded?" Nelson asked, passing the weapon back to me.

"A shade over twenty pounds with flash-hider, bipod and full clip," I said as I pressed the safety back on and saw Nelson's face turn red, embarrassed that he hadn't adjusted sights. "As is, about eighteen."

"Try the nearest keg," Donahue urged. "See if you can do better than Nelson."

Larry winked at me. I reset the sights, wrapped the sling about my left elbow, threw the stock to my shoulder and, in a series of short bursts, emptied the magazine at the nearest barrel. Staves, hoops and sand exploded in a geyser of muddy water.

"Now the one at three hundred," Larry said, passing another mag. I inserted the new mag and reset the sights. The second container disintegrated in a confusion of splinters and mud.

"You're right, Bennett. It's not Nelson's cup of tea." Larry looked me in the eye but spoke to Donahue. "What do you think, Bill? This pig might be nice to have along."

"You make decisions in this domain, Larry. This is between you and Donlin."

I understood exactly. My call. The promise now fit like a pair of new shoes, several sizes too small. Tight, very, very tight.

"It seems to have plenty of bore left," I said. "Fairly close pattern. If you think it could be useful, let's take it."

Casual conversation masked a significant change in my tenuous relationship with the group. Selecting the BAR relieved Larry of his promise and I truly became a fully participating member, in for an equal measure of whatever got dished out. For some reason I didn't understand at the time, a feeling of relief swept over me.

"Get serious, Cap. Where we're going, he won't be able to see a fourth that range," Nelson interjected. "And can you imagine carrying that thing through . . ."

"That's enough, Nelson," Larry snapped. "Have you boys made your choices? Remember, everybody carries their own ammo." Larry looked at me. "Except for you," he said, gesturing at me. "You will have help. Bennett, Nelson, Keener. You guys will carry your own ammo plus two belts each of BAR mags. Donlin, you carry four belts. We'll keep these boys close by if anything serious comes up."

The BAR had the nick-name "pig" because of its appetite for ammo in a skirmish. Ten belts, six mags per belt, twenty rounds per mag . . . . that's twelve hundred rounds in about ninety pounds of gear. In an assault, it could all be gone in less than fifteen minutes. "Glad for the help. Exactly where are we go . . ."

"Save the questions." Larry cut me off. "You'll know soon enough."

"What about the BAR, do we ship Greyhound? Does Heinrich tie a ribbon on it? Stamp it 'Air Mail?'"

"We abide by Mr. Turm's rules," Larry snapped at the group, totally ignoring my wise-ass question. "You shoot it, you clean it. The equipment is in the truck. Lunch will be ready by the time you're through." Larry still grimaced at the thought of food.

At the truck, cleaning rods, solvents, cotton flannel patches, oil, lithium grease, and heavy packin grease were set out in metal trays on two folding tables, along with heavy canvas shipping cases. Clean and pack now. Next time we see this hardware, we'll be in the field. "Be generous with the heavy grease, boys. Then stuff and label them with your group number, not your name," Donahue growled at Keener who had already mangled one label and was reaching for a second.

My number was 61-275-26-04-11. Just a number but it breaks down as simply as an automobile tire number. Sixty-one was the year and this was special project two hundred and seventy-five. Twenty-six was a geographic area. Zero-four was the area project manager, odd numbers for military, even numbers for civilian. I was team member eleven. This was to be my personal number for the duration of the project. To keep things simple in the field, this was shortened to 275-11 and would be enough for normal radio, telephone or written communications once we were in place.

I busied myself with cleaning the bore on the BAR and reassembling the bipod while Larry quietly thanked me for accepting a weapon. Was it possible that this was something he was counting on, believing all along I'd cave in and carry a weapon? Anyone in the group could probably string wire and hook up a couple of phones. I knew how to set charges and safety protocols for detonators, but he already had somebody coming in. I could even handle the radios, except for the Spanish requirement. Having the BAR in a fire team could increase firepower by twentyfive percent, but . . . Screw it! I'm in and that's that!

Busy with the minor tasks at hand, my mind wandered, eventually leading me to a humanities class and an overview of Shakespeare. We'd recently read excerpts from Hamlet. There's a line, when he's being ridiculed by friends over his mental state, his frantic distractions over his father's murder and political intrigues. He exploded and assaulted them. "Would'st thou play me like a flute?" he demanded. I suddenly had the feeling that I had just been played like a kazoo.

Larry was the same way about smoking as W.C. Fields about drinking. *"Anyone can quit. I've done it myself a thousand times. Ahhhh, Yes."* Larry bummed a cigarette from Donahue when he came by. As he took a light, he did a double take on the cook tent. Mr. Warren was pacing up and down, waving his arms and shouting in the direction of the redhead with the ice pack.

"Yes, it's Claire," Donahue told Larry. "She crashed at Heinrich's motel last night. Heinrich, Jack, and I were already out here. Hilda brought her out all scrubbed, brushed, coffee-filled and semi-conscious. I didn't know she was here until Hank offered me some of Hilda's coffee about five minutes ago. Jack tagged along and found her on the cot. Jesus, what a row. If I didn't need both of them, so help me . . . ."

"It's a good thing I'm not eating lunch," Larry mumbled. "You'd have to use a club to get me into that tent. Just listen to them. No wonder she drinks." Apparently, Larry quit smoking again, and flicked the unfiltered Camel into the mud.

Keener disassembled the cleaning rods and placed them in a canister. Oily patches were swept into a large paper bag and we passed around a can of hand cleaner. "Hank, are you cooking or is that Hilda?" Keener shouted toward the cleaning tables.

A beautiful brunette in her mid-thirties stepped from the tent and into the sunlight. She did a practiced curtsey, spreading the corners of her apron. She smiled at Keener and held up a large stainless steel spoon with a bright red cherry sauce clinging to it. She turned to present her profile and gave the spoon a long, slow lick. "Oooooh, damn," Keener moaned and jogged off through the mud toward the mess tent.

"Is Hilda Mr. Turm's daughter," I asked Larry.

"She's his wife. When Germany struggled to rebuild itself economically during the Weimar Republic, a lot of citizens, if they had any money at all, left the country. One of Hank's father's business partners wound up in Chile where he married a rancher's daughter. Hilda was their first child. Hank met her on one of his ski trips four years ago."

I could see it in his eyes. Larry and I were thinking the same thing. Two married couples literally in the same tent, yet worlds apart. "Skiing is only her second favorite sport," Larry said. "Her favorite pastime is teasing the hell out of the guys Donahue and I bring out here. She takes particular delight in making Keener sweat. Hank thinks it's funnier than hell up to a point. Keener knows it's a game and shuts it down sooner than Hank would. I think Keener and Hilda are actually friends, if you can see past all the nonsense. Lunch time, Cowboy," Larry said, waving to Hilda. "Maybe I'll have a little coffee."

I could see one other thing about Hilda Turm, something that had escaped the attention of everyone else. She was the only person here who cared about Mrs. Warren and her condition without any motive other than friendship.

After lunch, Donahue and Abbott pored over papers from a briefcase. Keener and Nelson pulled KP.

Hilda helped Mr. Warren get his wife into the car. They departed for Oklahoma City to put Mrs. Warren on a plane for Washington D.C.

Bennett left early on some errand. I helped Heinrich load a few items from the tent, then played solitaire on the tailgate of his truck.

Around three o'clock, Larry and I headed back to Edmond with Keener and Nelson in the back seat. They had come out with Mr. Warren and needed transportation to their motels. Donahue and Bishop followed us to the black top but took a turn to pick up another member at a nearby private airstrip. Some remark about difficulties getting his tools on commercial flights. I later learned they were talking about Buryl Gates, our demolitions specialist, along with several hundred pounds of explosives.

"Keep your duffel by the door, Cowboy. Lightweight clothing, underwear and toothpaste for about three weeks. When we're ready to leave, you might have less than two hours notice."

"Where are we going, Cap?" I asked.

"Panama, Jimmy. You'll love it."

CHAPTER NINE

Of arms and the man I sing.
Virgil

Among men, there is a pecking order that will be established one way or another. Military rank is based on seniority and performance evaluations, but there is always more than that. Such systems impose something dangerously false and artificial in stripes and epaulets and collar devices.

The samurai of sixteenth century Japan had a saying: "When in the company of tigers, be a tiger." I have placed myself in the company of tigers.

Two options stood before me in Thoreauvian simplicity: go, or don't go. If I didn't go, I'd have sixteen hundred dollars in the bank and little to regret. But I'd never know what this was all about, never know if I could have made a worthwhile contribution. I stood on the wrong side of a rite of passage. To a mind still struggling with adolescent idealism, curiosity, and a juvenile need to prove myself, these were important issues. If I did go, I would at least be a fully accepted, participating member of the group. The old samurai proverb didn't say act like a tiger, it said *be* a tiger, not a tag-along technician.

* * * *

We ate supper at an obscure cafe in Clinton, Oklahoma. Stoney's Café apparently had been used as an assembly area before. Larry and several others nodded greetings to cooks and waitresses. "Don't worry about Warren and Donahue. They'll make their own way down south," I overheard Larry remark to a new team member as we slipped into a large corner booth. He smiled at the day's special taped to the menu. "I's Monday! All-you-can-eat catfish, coleslaw, green beans, hush puppies and apple pie. Hot Damn!"

Our waitress pushed another waitress aside to get to our table. Her name tag read LA DONNA. She obviously knew Larry well and giggled when he playfully untied her apron strings. She nodded to Bishop and Keener and called them by their Christian names. "Is there going to be a party over at the Starlight Motel like last time, Larry? If there is, I have to break a date and call a few girl friends," La Donna gushed in a southern accent that seemed to hang in mid-air.

"Not this time, sweetheart. Just a good supper and a sorrowful farewell," Larry gushed back in his best Okie drawl, as rich and heavy as cigar smoke. I knew he had a BS from Kansas State and in the right company, and sober enough, he had no accent at all.

By nine o'clock, the group was complete. Ross Bishop, Phil Keener, Pete Nelson, Jack Bennett, Larry, myself and three men who had been waiting for us in the parking lot when we arrived.

First of the new members, Buryl Gates, had impressed Abbott and Donahue with his talents on more than one occasion, and never botched an assignment. "He can blow the change out of your pocket while you're asleep, and not wake you up," Donahue boasted as we left the camp a few days back. "He used C-3 in ways nobody else had even thought of. Proud of his work, he often left a calling card; his initials blasted into relief in steel plate whenever possible."

The big problem, Larry told me, was that Gates was very hard to get along with. Sour and irritable, he stayed out of everyone's way and demanded to be left alone. He refused to do any job other than his contract and punched out anyone who crowded him. Larry joked that Gates only had two moods; asleep and violent. We weren't expected to take any guff, but on the other hand, it would be best to keep clear as much as possible. And this trip, he would carry his own weight. Larry guaranteed it.

Gates was to be the special project of the second new member, Rubio Williams of San Antonio. Second in command in the field, under Larry. His primary task was communications by radio with Panamanian Armed Forces and area chiefs when operations began. Almost all coms would be by radio. That's why fluent Spanish was required for at least one team member. Two would be better.

I'd assumed Rubio was Tex-Mex but I was wrong. From Buenos Aires, he had served as an Argentine naval officer and later held the rank of first lieutenant in the US Marine Corps. He'd done more sea-time as a Marine than as an Argentine naval officer.

The third new member was an escapee from Fraternity Row. Eddy Rush was recruited because his military background included two years in a prestigious North Carolina military academy and a hitch in the Marines. Eddy was back-up in several areas, including demolitions. That made three of us.

Larry prattled about Panama and having a girlfriend who worked at the yacht club bar at Balboa, and casually asked, "Would any of you birds happen to know something about small boats? Nothing big, now. Just fumble-ass runabouts or work boats, around twenty feet? And how to get around at night?"

It became a reccurring theme throughout dinner. I asked why the interest in boats.

"Donahue wanted me to make these inquiries, but wouldn't say why." Rubio confessed he had no experience with anything smaller than destroyers and even then, not as the operator. Up to now, the only common characteristic among us was that we were all jump qualified, and I wondered how and why boat handling was now required.

Eddy said he knew a little about small boats. Larry smiled and pressed his questions enough to determine that Eddy knew coastal piloting, boat handling, and outboard maintenance and operation. Relaxing as if he had set down an anvil, Larry ordered peach cobbler a-la-mode.

La Donna giggled. "I've got your peach right here, Honey!"

Somehow, Larry and Rubio had a plan to force Gates to subscribe to enough social conventions that people could tolerate working with him. We had no idea what their leverage might be. Leaving Stoney's Café, Gates managed to pick a fight with Bishop before we were half way to the van. Rubio ended it by chopping Gates heavily across the bridge of the nose with the edge of a large plywood clipboard.

"Shit! What was that for, Williams?" Gates roared, cupping his hand under his nosebleed. "This ain't none of your business. I oughta take my duff and hike," he growled, his voice trembling with barely controlled rage. At his massive size and build, he could have taken on Williams and Bishop both, but then he knew Larry would have stepped in. Experience had taught him that was not a fun idea.

"Go ahead and walk. I'll have your replacement in two hours. And in the future, your name will be permanently removed from the job lists. You either shape up or go back to the quarries. And I mean right now!" Rubio had no trace of humor or patience in his voice. I was convinced he meant every word, but had doubts about Gates taking it seriously.

Green as grass, I'd taken a ribbing as soon as I climbed into the van in Edmond. By weight or by volume, I had almost twice the duffel of anyone else. An hour or so after supper, we passed through Burns Flat, a sleepy little collection of cracker-box houses. I was "assisted" by Phil Keener and Rubio in lightening the load. One extra pair of shoes went out the window. "Transistor radio? No. Camera? Ooops! No cameras, Jimmy! Keep the swim trunks, lose the underwear. No hair grease. It'll attract bugs." By the time we turned into Gate Four of Clinton-Sherman Air Force Base, my kit held less than one third of its original contents.

Clinton-Sherman is the Air Force's "Brigadoon" base. Closed for years, it was re-activated in 1954, then closed and re-activated again with rumors of another closing.

Driving along a dark service road, we passed an Air Police jeep, which did an immediate U-turn and raced up behind us. "Hey, Cap, you got an AP on your ass," Nelson sang out from the back bench of the van. Larry began singing "House of Blue Lights" and hit a switch on the dash.

The driver of the Air Police jeep saw a blue light under the rear bumper, made a brief radio transmission, and did another U-turn, resuming his original direction toward Gate Four.

Arriving at an obscure corner of the airfield, we grumbled our way out of the van, sorted out our gear and stumbled after Larry and Rubio. Across broad fields of new-mown grass we could see several ramps, and the distant control tower. Dimly lighted hangars occupied our side. We walked toward a portable Quonset hut housing a guard niche, a long counter and several desks and file cabinets. Inside, two officers and several airmen lounged over Cokes and a radio. Baseball season was in full swing and there was a night game somewhere.

Larry entered and presented an airman with a clipboard, which he in turn passed to the nearest officer. The airman jogged to the van and drove it into the nearest hangar, a blue light still shining under the license plate, our vehicle's initial clearance signal.

The aroma of coffee drifted on the sultry evening air, shifting, disappearing, and then reasserting itself, finally mixing with the sharp smell of new-mown grass and aviation fuel. The figures in the hut, visible through large windows, moved through a much-practiced routine. A major appeared with a mug of coffee, took the clipboard from the captain and shouted something at Larry. Angrily shouting his reply, Larry took two paces forward, pointed to the clipboard and the major's eyebrows lifted and his attitude changed immediately.

Still, we waited half an hour while the major confirmed the coded directives on the clipboard. When the major reappeared, the roster was again passed to the captain. He stepped outside and began calling our names, pointing us toward a line of glaring portable utility lamps with a Hercules C-130 cargo plane waiting at the far end.

There was little activity at twenty-two hundred hours, and none at all at this end of the field except for our group. A half dozen hangars and a row of cinderblock maintenance shops formed a horseshoe. The Hercules slept in the center of these dark buildings, hidden, except for the towering tail fin. The only signs of life within the plane were the dim lights in the cockpit and the cargo bay.

We strung out in a single line as our names were barked. We were expected to quick march for the last hundred yards to the loading ramp extending from the open cargo bay like a rude tongue to lap up a company of miscreants.

My feet became leaden. Something inside me wanted to burrow into the earth and hide; something else wanted to launch me into that plane like an arrow. This is where all but two options faded into the evening air: go or don't go.

"Get a move on, Cowboy, and welcome to the rodeo!" Larry roared and bumped me in the direction of the aluminum cavern that yawned before us, hurling metallic echoes of our footsteps and Larry's coarse urging. The others never looked back. There was no hesitation in their steps, no doubt in their minds, no knot in their guts.

I was last to board. The brightly polished tail fin was covered by the freshly painted words TEXAS AIR NATIONAL GUARD and I wondered what had been painted there twenty-four hours earlier. Department of the Interior? Border Patrol? US Forestry Service? National Fisheries? NSA and CIA kept large fleets of planes farmed out to other services to "shorten inventory." I was fairly certain the patch of polished metal on the fin would have said something other than TEXAS AIR NATIONAL GUARD. Working for an unidentified client felt as intimidating now as it had two weeks earlier.

Whining electric motors startled me. Whirring motors and moaning hydraulic pumps lifted the cargo ramp and I felt consumed, swallowed whole, I was Jonah in the whale. Maybe it was claustrophobia, or maybe nerves. Whatever I had been was being surrendered, shed as a snake sheds its skin. The comfortable, predictable conventions of my life were bitten off by the closing cargo bay door, an umbilical cord to adolescence forever severed.

Warren and Donahue were intermediaries for entities that shaped history. And I was caught up in events in which I had little influence. Any sense of security beyond what our small party could provide by force of arms was stripped away. The members of this group who busied themselves stowing duffel and strapping into aluminum framed seats, for what they considered an acceptable wage, were willing pawns in an enterprise yet ill defined. And something deep in my gut told me that I was totally unprepared for what lay ahead.

If things went wrong, were we expendable? Were we a negotiable asset? A political embarrassment? None of us, with the exception of Larry, knew anything about where we were going or what we would be doing, and keeping his mouth shut was part of his job. Suddenly, it was now obvious to me that he had taken on many assignments like this one.

Two airmen cursed and grunted with the exertion of finishing the tie-downs on a scant cargo of engine parts, four cases of radio batteries and a dozen or so new electric typewriters.

Passengers formed the bulk of the manifest, and not just our unit. One of the crewmen ambled past us, lamenting the heat and humidity. "Screw it. In twenty minutes, you'll be belly-aching about the heaters not working," the other airman replied. They seated themselves forward with two young Canadian naval officers who wore tags from the American Embassy on their lapels.

"Keener! We've got a ready light. Finish the tie-down and grab a seat," Captain Abbott ordered. At the forward end of the open interior, a high bulkhead with a ladder led up to the cockpit. We watched figures silhouetted by panel lights put on headphones and run down checklists, flipping switches and lifting control levers. Engines came to life one at a time, starting with a high-pitched whine that built to a harmonic roar of turbo props and held there. The beast moved.

Starting a slow turn toward the open end of the horseshoe, we gently rocked and bounced. For another five minutes we waited, then aligned with the field markers. We lurched as the brakes released, and raced into linear purpose, into a screaming confirmation that plans do become reality, a vibrating, metallic manifestation of weeks of planning, and the suffocation of waiting. Electrical wiring and hydraulic hoses vibrated against the fuselage frames and skin. When the pilot was satisfied that cause and effect were in balance, the vibrations stopped; only the rush of air remained. The landing gear hydraulics sang a Greek chorus and my final options fluttered downward to swirl among starlings, bats, and fireflies.

Within an hour, my eyes felt sore from rattling in their sockets. We tried to make ourselves as comfortable as possible. The roar passed through a metamorphosis, from being intrusive, to mind eroding, to devouring. By the end of the second hour, several of us fell into a type of sleep, a marbled state of boredom, frustration and exhaustion, a semi-conscious state devoid of rest.

I awoke feeling something was wrong. The noise had diminished to a whisper. "We're over the hump," Eddy said. "We're on a long glide path with the engines at little more than idle. Thought you'd gone deaf, huh?"

Our civilian clothes kept us under the scrutiny of the crew. Military personnel were not allowed to travel on military planes in civies. Obviously, we weren't military and that made our presence a curiosity for the crew and a personal affront to a by-the-book co-pilot. I wore faded Levis, a white knit shirt and a unique pair of white canvass shoes; they had trod the beaches of the Atlantic, the Gulf of Mexico and the Pacific. They also had brick red blotches from the North Canadian River. Maybe not much, but I thought they were something at the time. We all wore work clothes or rough-and-tumble recreational rags.

Everyone but Eddy. He wore an expensive, three-piece business suit. "No big deal," Eddy said, "I have six or seven newer and better than this one." As the only son of a well-established surgeon in Oklahoma City, his family expected him to follow in his father's footsteps. He must have been a major disappointment, having flunked out, or been kicked out, of four colleges in Texas and Oklahoma in the last two years. He bore the title "Black Sheep" as if it should have had a coat of arms. We became great friends.

"Compliments of Mr. Donahue," the crewman said as he passed out cardboard boxes containing cold but substantial breakfasts. Hard-boiled eggs, biscuits, spicy sausage links, two milks, a juice, and a disposable mug for coffee the crewman provided from a pair of large thermos bottles. It was a little past three in the morning and we hadn't eaten since the cafe in Clinton and no one needed instructions.

A letter from Donahue in Larry's box stretched a smile across his face. With the proximity of the other passengers, Larry would not make an announcement but he passed the letter around. The news never raised an eyebrow on anyone except Larry.

No one else had ever seen him drunk before a jump except me. I had never seen him scared of anything except a jump. "You can't negotiate with, or kill gravity," he had lamented. The letter informed him that recent developments made jumping an unlikely option. What developments? And what were our other options? For me, these were questions significant enough to stop a biscuit in mid-swallow, but no other member of our group had the slightest reaction. As low man in the pecking order, I was condemned to blindly follow as best I could.

No one gets through jump school without hearing the stories about the perils of "exiting an aircraft in flight." Inaccurate altimeter readings can jump men below minimum altitude. Anyone who jumped knew the risks of wind shear and tangled shrouds. Mistimed exits put men into mountain walls or high voltage power lines. These general themes make up the bulk of horror stories about jumping, and were well grounded in fact. Larry Abbott and I had seen one of these events, and the gruesome results. Anyone who says they have no fear of jumping is a liar or an idiot. Larry was neither. With the letter back in his hands, he seemed drunk with relief.

The sound of landing gear hydraulics brought a crewman scrambling back to our group. He told us to check our belts, the landing would be a little rough. Eddy passed me a note scribbled on the lid of his breakfast box.

By an estimation of the plane's speed and flight time, he had calculated the location of the landing strip. "Southern Mexico or Guatemala," the note said.

Larry leaned over my shoulder and took the scribble. "Forget it. You aren't supposed to know where you are," Larry growled while ripping the note into confetti. "These guys get pissed off if they think you know more than you're entitled. We're not there yet, and that's all you need to know."

We felt no impact at all in the landing, only a sudden increase in noise and vibration. Props feathered, RPMs fell and the plane slowed and stopped. "We have about an hour," the crewman said. "You have time to visit the snack bar and showers. The day room is closed. Stay out of the ready room."

I was first in and last out of the showers. The snack bar was cleaned out by the time I found it. Two bags of pork rinds and licorice candy had no appeal at six o'clock in the morning. The clerk took pity on me and began restocking a cooler emptied by the vultures who preceded me. He filled it with freshly made egg salad, tuna and roast beef sandwiches from the main locker in the back.

A second glass-fronted cooler received fruit juices, soft drinks and some sort of local meat-filled pastry popular with base personnel. "Be careful. They're muy picante . . . very spicy," the clerk warned. I stuffed a medium paper bag with two soft drinks, an egg salad sandwich and a candy bar. On an impulse, I also bought a cheap camera to replace the one thrown out in Burns Flat, and five rolls of film. I threw forty dollars at the clerk and ran for the plane.

As it turned out, I didn't need to rush. We stood at the edge of the field for forty-five minutes, watching the ground crew truck away tools and turn the C-130, lining it up with the ramp. One of our original crewmen grumbled something about changing a tire on the port side landing gear and we were now nearly an hour behind schedule.

The airstrip was over a mile long, carved out of the tops of a mountain range that ran north and south. Perfectly straight and level, the field was wide enough for two strips. Contrary to our crewman's memory, the ramps were completely finished.

A sprawling building complex and service ramp occupied the last mountaintop, an almost perfectly round and flat excavation at the southern end. The usual hangars, machine shops, barracks, mess halls and tower occupied the same level as the runway. There was also a structure out of place.

On a slightly lower terrace on the west side, sprawled a well kept group of buildings with an architectural style more sophisticated than an air base's utility sheds. Illuminated signs identified a hotel, restaurant, bar and pool. The neon sign at the entrance read, "Iguana Palace." Apparently a rest stop for VIPs.

A distant figure, silhouetted against ramp lights waved illuminated red wands, gesturing toward the C-130. Halfway to the plane, Eddy pointed out the North Star exactly over the far end of the ramp, barely visible in the dawn's first light. It hovered less than half as high as when we first boarded. "Like I said," Eddy whispered, "southern Mexico." Eventually I understood what he meant. The North Star can provide important raw information. The angular distance between the star and a true horizon is the same as north latitude, accurate within half a degree.

We trudged our way toward the plane, along with a new pilot and co-pilot, and resumed our seats. In the dark woodlands on mountaintops beside the field, I could make out electric lights mimicking a heaven overburdened with stars.

Once again, the beast swallowed me.

CHAPTER TEN

. . . . stranger in a strange land.
Exodus 2:22

Numb and exhausted, I dozed again. Eddy woke me, shoving a fist full of money in my face and laughing. "I've been playing poker with Abbott, Gates, Keener and those two Canadian ensigns. We just quit because we're landing." I watched him count over three hundred dollars and stuff it into an inside coat pocket.

The landing was smooth. We broke out our gear and gathered at the cargo bay. Red-eyed and tired, we flinched at the bright sun and gasped when the blast of outside air hit us. It was like stepping into a pizza oven.

Stumbling down the ramp, Eddy shaded his eyes with his left hand. "My God! This is worse than New Orleans! There had better be one of Mama Bennie's quart mint juleps waiting in the wet PX."

Gates, with only the slightest trace of shyness shared his views of the Canal Zone. "Screw this! We'll roast like turkeys in a day. Why don't we just check out of this fuckin' blast furnace and take a first-class bus home! Holy shit, it's hot!"

Nine o'clock and the temperature was already over a hundred with the humidity in the high nineties. Panamanian civilian employees took our bags and escorted us to a nearby hut. We were grateful for the air conditioning unit that growled under an aluminum awning beside the entrance. Our crewmen pushed past us and called out, "This way, gentlemen."

The Quonset hut was long and narrow, manned by Air Force personnel. At the processing counter, a freshly painted sign displayed a sky-blue banner reading "WELCOME TO CRYDER AIR BASE." Done by a deft hand and good eye for design, an elliptical medallion showed a landing C-130 in a wreath of tropical plants and animals and a second banner beneath that read SUPPLY CENTER FOR THE CANAL ZONE. A familiar clipboard appeared and a non-com called our names.

An Air Force officer directed us to a corner in a small mess hall. "Take a coffee break now. In fifteen minutes you will be given chits for a lunch in our mess," he said. "Later, you'll have a briefing on communications, transportation, health and field safety at thirteen hundred. At fifteen thirty hours, trucks in front of this building will take you to temporary quarters. I understand you boys will be doing survey work in the boonies. Well, listen up! From personal experience, know that you don't touch anything you don't have to. Most snakes in Panama are poisonous and all of them are meaner than you."

The captain droned over our names on the clipboard again, annoyed that Captain Abbott was missing. In fifteen minutes, Larry appeared, supporting a heavily perspiring Wilson Donahue who constantly daubed his face with a handkerchief. His face was pale with green bags under his eyes and his balding head was streaked with sweat-soaked gray tendrils. His expensive Brooks Brothers suit was a mess and his saturated shirt clung to his chest.

As employees of the Pan-American Highway Corporation, we would enjoy certain perks and privileges whenever we might be on a military base or in any Canal Zone government installation. We received temporary ID cards, granting us the privilege of getting soused, before lunch, we hoped. Smiling for our photographs and complaining about the ink from the fingerprinting, we knew our "exclusive" membership was indistinguishable from every other individual who tracked through these processing centers.

Technicians in white jackets entered, pushing carts covered with white cloth. In the blink of an eye, five shots apiece left us a little dazed. From the last cart, we were issued canvas kits with "horse pills," medicine for everything from malaria to a variety of local parasites and salt tablets for prevention of sunstroke. Emergency water purification tablets, sun lotion and a dozen bottles of insect repellent filled out the rest of the kit.

A doctor checked Bishop's earache. He complained he got one anytime he flies. Donahue protested when Larry pushed him toward another doctor. It took about two minutes to take Donahue's pulse, temperature, and blood pressure. His pale face and trembling were enough to put him in the hospital as a malaria patient; this was not considered an unusual ailment down here.

In spite of his objections, Donahue got a joy ride in an ambulance. "A little malaria flare up," Larry announced to the group. "He didn't get it here but he can't take the heat anymore. Take the goddamned pills or you could wind up like Donahue, and you never shake it."

In typical military fashion, the morning was 'hurry-up-and-wait.' Our coffee break resumed for another hour. At twelve-thirty hours, we stood in line to sample Air Force food. Salisbury steak, carrots and peas, mashed potatoes and coffee: institutional and bland, but edible. The mess hall was small and noisy. We ate in the Officer's Mess, a cloistered section near the kitchen, out of sight of nearly everyone. The noise drowned much of the conversation. That may have been the idea.

By the time we started dessert, Donahue reappeared, freshly showered and in clean light-weight clothes. He looked better and he didn't tremble but he still wasn't well. "I'll be returning to the hospital right after the briefing. My malaria flare-up has put us a little behind. We're rescheduled for a building nearby. When we finish there, you'll be going to Panama City."

The orientation began on time in a small cinder block building. We sat in folding chairs arranged near a dais with two tables covered with aerial photos, marine charts and survey maps. An Air Force captain, minus nametag, straightened overhead transparencies at the projector. There was also a portable chalkboard and a lectern with light switches. Donahue came in with eight other men. Four were Latinos in uniform, followed by four Anglos in civilian clothes. The youngest, around thirty, was dressed in white coveralls and sported an Elvis Presley haircut, sideburns and all.

An elderly gentleman with thinning gray hair entered. Obviously, a group leader, he wore a white linen suit and a planter's hat. His quick eyes took in every detail of the room and its occupants. The last two were in their late thirties and wore oil-stained blue coveralls, a gold oak leaf showing on the shirt collar of the oldest one. Some of the men took chairs on the low stage, and some behind the tables.

Donahue sat down heavily in the front row, beside Larry, in the only upholstered office chair in the room. He breathed heavily and beads of perspiration glistened on his forehead and ran down his jaws.

Heavy footfalls thumped across the roof and muffled sounds of toolboxes annoyed the assembly on the dais. The temperature of the room felt hotter than when we first entered, easily over a hundred degrees. Donahue, wiping his face and neck with a fresh handkerchief, rose from his chair to ask the Air Force captain a question. The officer, equally hot, restless and impatient, tried to assure him with a whispered answer. "Ten to fifteen minutes, Mr. Donahue. Try to get comfortable. Take off your coat and loosen your tie."

Donahue bristled at being treated like a green tourist, but grudgingly accepted the facts of his condition and the circumstances of our location, and followed the suggestions. As he returned to his upholstered chair, we all felt a refreshing blast of cold air. The clank and rattle of toolboxes and the shuffle of technician's feet across the roof signaled the completion of repairs on the air conditioning unit.

Donahue's shirt and linen suit had developed the same character as his earlier attire. With an effort, he stood and signaled to an Air Police Sergeant at the door. Five men armed with M-14s entered and took positions around the room, the sergeant remaining at the door. We were told to stand as the Sergeant of the Guard read our names off the top sheet of the clipboard. Donahue nodded confirmation for each of us. From the second sheet he checked the laminated identification cards hanging around the necks of the men at the front table. When all were verified, the AP group left to take up stations outside.

Donahue had reseated me closer to the aerial photos on the corner of the table and told me to look through them until the briefing actually began. This put me face-to-face with the Air Force captain conducting security check. The captain signed the third sheet, placed the clipboard on the table and took a seat. While taking a legal pad from a leather briefcase, I caught a glimpse of one of those pink file folders with a heading . . . US Embassy, Secretary of Special Projects. Somebody else bending the rules, or just plain being careless.

Shaking a finger at Captain Abbott, Donahue began his introductions. "Larry, you're taking notes for me. Gentlemen, good afternoon. At last, you get to know as much as we know. This is a secured room. You've been cleared to access this material, but what you are about to hear is to be kept within this group. After the presentation, we'll have time to answer questions. We're also interested in any suggestions you may have at the close of our presentation. That's why Captain Abbott is taking notes for me.

"First, let me introduce our guests. This is Captain Arbiso of the Panamanian Navy," Donahue announced. "He is our liaison with Panamanian intelligence through a mobile radio command center in La Palma, one of our vintage WWII PT boats outfitted with an impressive collection of radio communications and surveillance equipment is stationed there. Captain Arbiso."

"Good afternoon, gentlemen," Arbiso began with the slightest accent and a very formal air. "And welcome to Panama. Mr. Donahue has asked me to explain several important details. We are involved because you will be conducting operations on sovereign Panamanian soil. But we recognize this project is much bigger than our nation could pursue alone. We think radio communications will be monitored by Russian vessels offshore which appear to be fishing boats until you count their antennas. Therefore, any information you gain will be recorded as gathered by Panamanian units conducting field exercises. That information will be instantly relayed to Mr. Donahue's friends at the American Embassy in Panama City by coded signal. To support the cover of Panamanian units in the field, you have at least two radio operators who will conduct all radio communications in Spanish. Frequencies, codebooks and schedules will be provided upon your arrival at camp.

"Here is another reason you need team members who speak Spanish. These three enlisted men," indicating the other uniformed Panamanians seated to his right, "have been selected because they are natives of Panama's west coast and know your operations area very well. Of course, they all speak Spanish, but between them, they also speak two local Indian languages. None of them speak English. This is Juan Chirama, Pello Chunqual, and Roberto Perez. A fourth, Jorge Abrego, is already setting up your camp. Dressed as simple fishermen, they will enhance your cover as a survey team by assuming duties as guides and camp laborers. They shall be your aides . . . *su obreros y guias.*"

Donahue, at last showing signs of relief in the cool air, thanked Arbiso and asked him to remain in the room until the entire presentation was over. "Of course," Arbiso replied, "but the *compañeros* are not needed here. I would like to get them out to camp as soon as possible."

I hadn't realized the room was so dim until the *pescaderos* made their exit into the afternoon's blinding white light.

When our eyes readjusted to the light of the stage, we found that one of the two men in blue coveralls had taken Arbiso's place at the lectern and the other one at the overhead projector. "I'm Major H. R. Mills, USAF, and that is Sergeant Doyle Ramsey at the projector. We run a specialized machine shop here," he said, flipping a switch on the lectern, plunging the room into total darkness. "One of our jobs is to design and build custom equipment for special projects. Sometimes, we just modify existing equipment, as we have for this group."

The overhead projector framed a patch of light and a transparency with a line drawing fluttered onto a sidewall. It showed the top and side views of an unmodified ten man inflatable boat of French manufacture. "We chose a large raft, even though you'll probably never carry more than three or four men. Capacity for technical equipment in protective cases plus the necessity for high speed outboards requires more buoyancy for a larger motor and tankage for extended range. Notice the extension of the side air chambers well behind the transom. This is a standard feature which effectively prevents the stern from 'falling in the hole' dug by the cavitation of a high-speed prop. These boats run flat and fast. The plywood panels forming the rigid sole of each raft create a flat bottom, which plane even at low speeds, even fully loaded. Next, please."

A jumble of confused lines on transparencies passed over the glass top of the projector, at last settling into a recognizable split diagram. One side showed a one-hundred horsepower Johnson outboard with a series of reference numbers indicating several modifications. The other image was a schematic of a cylinder that substituted for the stock cowling of the outboard. "As outlandish as it may look, the entire canister weighs less than twelve pounds and can be removed in about thirty seconds. We made most of it out of fiberglass. Tough stuff, easy to modify, and takes weather. The upper half is a series of water chambers and baffles of welded aluminum glassed to the inside. The unit is mounted with bolts and wing nuts instead of four clasps like the factory production units. Exhaust and cooling water are captured by a manifold and channeled into the baffles where they are vented out the top. The outer casing is high-density sound insulation. Even at full speed, you will detect the raft by the sound of its wash, not its engine noise. Next, please."

The remainder of the slides covered an ingenious method of mounting depth sounders with the transducers fitted inside the raft, in a chamber filled with mineral oil, on the starboard side, next to the battery case. The display was mounted on the steering console, which bolts to the plywood sole between the two inflated thwarts. We also got an introduction on how to use them for navigation purposes with their soundings compared to the updated charts prepared for us by Sergeant Ramsey a week earlier. Apparently, we would see a great deal of Gulfo de San Miguel, Bahia de Panama and the Archipelago de las Perlas.

Major Mills turned the lights back on and Sergeant Ramsey packaged the transparencies. Major Mills took a few questions from Eddy and sat next to Donahue.

The Elvis haircut was a civilian employee of a government agency, which he mumbled beyond all possible recognition. "Bill, Larry. For you boys who don't know me, my name's Herb Donaldson and I am a radio technician. Some people say I'm the best, and I try to keep people thinking that way." His mild brag formed a balance to his self-consciousness. "Hank sent me a batch of telephones to work on. They ain't quite finished but they will be by mornin'. You got six pairs of Prick 6's, er, PRC-6s, all set to the same frequency. As most of you know, there ain't no frequency adjustments on the sixes except in my shop. You got eight PRC-10s, one for each raft, the 'luminum fish boats, one for camp, and one spare. And your ANGRC-9 is in perfect condition. That unit is for camp communication with La Palma and the chopper base up here. Since you boys are well within range of La Palma and transmitting over water, you ain't gonna have no problems if ya' git yer antenna high enough. But if you do, I'm only an hour away.

"Now, Mr. Arbiso said he thinks you might be monitored," Elvis continued. "We are, in fact, being monitored at this time and have been for almost six months. Two Russian trawlers are cruising offshore right now. Ain't had no problems with them jammin' our transmissions but if they do, they get boarded and they know it. So, we just snoop on them and they snoop on us. I s'pect we're both bored as hell. I don't want you juvenile delinquents doin' nothing to make my life excitin'.

"Mr. Donahue asked me to tell you about maintenance schedules on these radios. There ain't none. You scouts is gonna camp out for less than a month. All the batteries and seals is new, so don't go poppin' the back off my equipment. It'll do you just fine. They all got weather covers. Use 'em. Rain is the only thang that'll hurt 'em. Turn 'em on for five minutes onct a day whether you use 'em or not, if you think they might a' got wet. That dries 'em out enough to kill the mold, usually, even if it does run the batteries down a mite. You got battery spares and that's the only reason to open a pack. Don't open nothin' else."

Donaldson, his tortured speech at an end, heaved a sigh of relief. "Any o' you scouts got questions?"

None. Elvis smiled at Abbott and Donahue and let himself out the door. Again, light from a lower sun, reflected from the inner surface of the aluminum painted door, exploded in the room, leaving us blinking and dodging vibrant, geometric ghosts that swarmed our retinas.

"Sergeant Ramsey," Donahue said, "would you please return to the overhead projector? My transparencies are in the manila folder to your right. And now, our quarry. Some sixteen months ago, we were tipped off about a contract for a barge being constructed in a Japanese shipyard. Its size alone made it an unusual project.

"Panel number one in my packet, Sergeant," Donahue said as he stepped away from the lectern. By the light of the projector, he moved to a folding chair to better view the line drawing that settled on the wall.

"Japan is pioneering the idea of building miniaturized floating factories. Fish processing plants take the catch in at one end and off-load crates of canned fish onto lighters at the other end. Timber companies in Brazil had several milling plants built that went up and down the Amazon and its tributaries, producing finished lumber or newsprint that went straight to market.

"Panel number two. We assumed that this would be such a barge, purpose and client unknown. It was interesting to watch the monster develop. Within a week of the paint drying, it was towed into the Pacific, and after a mid-ocean exchange of towing vessels, found a berth in a naval ship yard on the Kamchatka Peninsula. Now, it became more than merely interesting. High altitude photographs showed that some sort of construction continued on the barge and it looked vaguely familiar.

"Five months ago the first barge, similar but slightly smaller than our present quarry, made a canal transit. The manifest, written in perfect English and a copy in Dutch just to make it creditable, listed it as a prefabricated mini-refinery bound for Willemstad. It was inspected and passed by people who know cracking plants when they see them. No one paid much notice. Then we lost track of it. All we know is that it never made it to Curaçao. The barge's tug was Puerto Rican, chartered to a phony company in the Dominican Republic, paid for by a Dutch speaking representative, in advance, in Swiss francs. The barge turned up in Kingston, Jamaica, gutted, being used as a floating warehouse. Then aerial recon turned up dismantled sections of what might be the cargo in a god-forsaken mountain range in eastern Cuba that suddenly has several roads under construction. We blew it. Big time. We're not quite sure what it is, but we're certain it's not a cracking plant. Best guess is that we let a rocket fuel plant through the canal.

"It gets more complicated," Donahue continued. "What kind of fuel for what kind of missile? Our highest-ranking Russian defector, Oleg Penkovski, came out a year ago and even that damned conceited son-of-a-bitch can't tell us what it is. Liquid fuel or solid? Guideline missile or R-14? Both have nuclear capabilities. Range is another matter. Determining what kind of fuel the plant is designed to produce will tell us if Russia is trying to place a large scale, first-strike weapons system on Cuban soil, right at our front door.

"This is where you come in, gentlemen. There is only one concrete limitation. A presidential directive states that we shall not violate the neutrality of the canal. Anything goes on this side of the canal, and it's your baby. If it turns out to be what we think it is and it gets through the canal, the Navy sinks it in the Caribbean, and that could get us in hot water with Cuba or Russia or both. To put it simply, whatever we come up with, we have to make it work, and make it work on the Pacific side."

"Wait a minute, Bill," Larry interrupted. "Are you saying you want us to sink the barge? No problem. Where is it right now?"

"This is not just about sinking the damned barge. We have questions, the barge has answers. First, we determine what it makes. Remember, one of these units is already in Cuba. They may be planning to cook up the world's best cotton candy, set up shop to tan goat hides, or mass-produce Cuban cigars. My money says they're trying to turn all of Central America into an anti-American, nuclear-armed bloc. I don't think we'll let that happen.

"So, if it turns out to be what we think it is, then you take it ." Donahue reached to his left for a pink folder on another chair. Still plagued by malaria, even this slight exertion strained him and he shivered. "And we don't know where it is right now. We lost it four days ago, somewhere down coast. Our analysts think they may be getting cold feet about the canal. Personally, I think they'll show up when they're damned good and ready."

"How are we supposed to tell what this thing makes?" I asked, wiping sweat stains from my glasses with a paper napkin saved from the mess hall.

"That question brings us to our next guest. This is Dr. Donald Glaston Loomer," Donahue said with a nod toward the older gentleman. The ice cream suit stood up. "He has a group of photographic experts who can get the pictures we need and send them to analysts in Washington. You sit and wait for the experts to evaluate and send directions for the next step.

"Dr. Loomer's team has worked for a variety of government agencies. They are the people who designed one of the cameras being used in our newest surveillance aircraft. For this project, we pulled them off a project photographing rocket sled experiments in New Mexico. Your job is to get his men safely into an elevated position in which they will have a clear view at a half mile or less for one hour in good light."

"Mr. Donahue, if I may," Dr. Loomer began. "I've recently learned that an original requisite of this project was that all participants be parachutists. Take a close look at our files. I'm not jump qualified, nor are any of the people who work for me. Also, I'm the second youngest member of my team and I'm sixty-four. Only Bernie Roche is younger and he's fifty-eight. We are not jumping out of an airplane, gentlemen. On to the next option." He paused and made eye contact with Donahue and Abbott, leaving no doubt that his edict was final.

"We can shoot from the rafts while underway," Loomer said, "but not without being seen and not at an angle that will provide a view of the elements of the craft you are most interested in. Their current game of hide-and-seek is perfect for our purposes. Take us in close, Captain Abbott. If the armed forces of Panama discover a suspicious vessel inside territorial waters and not cleared by Panamanian customs, maybe involved with gun-running of drug smuggling, or a plant possibly intended to manufacture war materials, well, who knows what their reaction might be? But our chances for success would be high angle shots in secrecy, maybe from a tree perch. How that could be managed I'll leave up to you."

"Take any excuse, any means to get close enough for usable photos," Donahue added, looking straight at Larry. "Captain Abbott, you and your men are contracted to dispose of the barge if it comes to that," Donahue said, stripping off his tie. "It can't be in the canal or even the approaches to the canal. As previously mentioned, it must be done inside Panamanian waters, with the appearance of an accident, if possible, blatant piracy if not. I don't want to leave it up to the Panamanians. Remember, with the right kind of hardware in Cuba, three fourths of the US could be within range of missiles armed with nuclear warheads.

"Now, who's the team member who knows small boat handling and navigation?" Donahue acknowledged Eddy's raised hand. "You have a nice bonus if you can train at least one operator for each boat and manage the rafts at the camp. When can you start?"

"I'll start right now if I can use those charts and the chalkboard," Eddy offered.

"Sorry, no time," Donahue sighed, wiping perspiration from his throat. "You can start when you get to camp. In the meantime, you have quarters in Panama City while we wait for the fox to break cover. While you're in the hotel, stay packed and don't get separated. These stop-overs typically last about four days, then there'll be a dash for another hiding place closer to the canal. If the barge continues to keep out of sight for three or four days at a time, I'd say you have at least two days in town while the *compañeros* set up camp, then you'll be flown to Base T to try out the rafts and teach your friends boat handling.

"This is where your hunt begins," Donahue continued. "Dr. Loomer and his men will remain in their present accommodations until you're ready for them. Then, they'll be brought in to join you at Base T." Donahue noticed Loomer nervously edging toward another comment and stepped aside.

"I must emphasize," Loomer boomed, "your job is to get us in and out, O-U-T. Whatever is to become of the barge and tug, we are non-participants and insist that we be brought back to our compound before any action is taken. Remember, at sixty-four, I'm the youngest of my team," Loomer droned apologetically. "Two of our team members are sixty-six and the remaining two are over seventy. Most likely, we would only be in your way."

"I'd go along with that," Eddy whispered to me behind the back of his hand. "I wouldn't send this old coot out for pizza."

"Any questions?" Donahue asked as he returned to the lectern.

"I have one," Keener said. "The Canal Zone is filled with military installations with thousands of Marines and Rangers. They have unlimited resources and firepower. Why can't they do this job?"

"Good point," Donahue said, "and one that certainly has not been overlooked. They constitute Plan Zulu, that is, only as a last resort. Naturally, regular forces are intended for deployment in large scale, overt operations. But you know what the Army is like. Those guys can't make an omelette without shelling the hen house. Then there are presidential advisors, the paper trail, news media, congressional reactions, possible UN inquiries, and on and on. We want to remain low profile, if possible, for as long as possible. But if this project turns out to be something your team can't handle, two Marine force-recon companies are on stand-by."

Ross Bishop asked, "Mr. Donahue, you mentioned the barge has already been photographed a hundred times by recon planes. Some of those photos are within my reach right now. Don't these photos give you what you needed?"

"They confirmed that the cargo is similar to the one that made it through last February. They confirm that tankage and plumbing layout in Cuba are similar to installations in the Ural Mountains, just smaller in scale. Weather covers on the barge we're tracking allowed us an outline of tanks but we had no view of the valves, dials and electrical panels we need to see," Donahue announced, leaning on the lectern. "The photos of the naval yard showed enough to convince five members of an eight man analyst group. But, since it's possible we'd find ourselves in open hostilities that could lead to WW III, we must have more and better information."

"What makes you think they'll take the wraps off now?" Nelson asked. "Even if they do go to Cuba, there's a lot of sea time left. And why don't we put our own intelligence people in with canal workers, maybe as a team of safety inspectors?" Nelson brought a nod of approval from several others.

"We considered the safety inspector ploy," Donahue replied, slouching over the podium. If we confirm that it is a rocket fuel plant, it would already be too late to exercise our best options. The Navy would have to take it out on the Caribbean side, which, of course, would initiate open hostilities.

"As for the weather covers, maybe they won't take them off. It has been suggested that a security detachment would have joined them by now. In this climate, some of the tarpaulins would have to come off to provide ventilation to the living quarters we know are built into the barge.

Donahue looked straight at Larry. "One thing I've always liked about the teams Captain Abbott puts together is that they always get the job done without saying 'please' or 'at your convenience.' You boys will take over the barge and rip them off."

"What happens if they change their minds and go back out to sea, away from the canal?" For most of us, it was the first time we'd heard a complete sentence from Gates that didn't include profanity.

Donahue smiled. "We don't care. It gives us more time to counter. Anything that could happen between their hiding place and the canal could also happen in the fifteen thousand-mile voyage around South America, and we'd have a much better opportunity to make it look like an accident. No, they've come this far. They'll go for the canal." He looked at his watch. "Your trucks are outside and you're headed for a steak dinner at my favorite hotel. See you in a few days. Abbott, Rush and Donlin hang back a few minutes. The rest are dismissed." Donahue muttered.

When the others had closed the door, Larry began to climb Donahue's frame. "Now that the others are gone, I want to know who screwed up!" Larry stepped between Donahue and the door, barring any exit before this issue was settled. "This is much bigger than what you presented in April. With nine men in four boats, we can't even come close to covering a body of water the size of Golfo de San Miguel.

And whose stupid idea was the jump? And I don't buy this crap about why regular forces aren't used!" he shouted in Donahue's face.

"That's quite enough, Captain Abbott," Donahue growled, not even slightly perturbed by Abbott's onslaught. "Take a deep breath and calm down. Everybody wearing boots knows your skepticism is justified.

"We've had input from thinktank boys who have never been off the sidewalk. The rest of us knew there would never be a jump. Nevertheless, the project is extremely critical, and it is probably manageable by your group. And if it turns out that it isn't, we have back-up." Donahue pulled a chart and unrolled it on the table. "Golfo de San Miguel is big . . . a big cul-de-sac. Your camp is here," Donahue said, indicating a minute finger of land jutting from a larger peninsula, nearly at the center of the gulf.

"When you find the tug and barge and there are only a few security guards and the usual crew on the tug, your boys can handle them. If it's carrying a larger, heavily armed security force, then another accident will happen to them. Just remember, your first job is getting Loomer's geriatric ward close enough to photograph some valves and dials."

Scarlet-faced, Larry struggled to hold back the remainder of his attack on Wilson Donahue. "As for the jump," Donahue continued, "The D.C. boys think we may still do it. Let's say Loomer's codgers teach three or four of your boys how to use telephoto lenses and we jump them over the barge. If they have a security force on board the barge, the weather wraps would be off, giving us the views we didn't get with high altitude photos. Your boys shoot up a roll apiece, tread water for a while, and the other five pick them up in the rafts. Loomer and friends spend their day sipping Geritol Slings and cranking their Victrolas. We have the shots we need, you go back to Base T and dry out."

Donahue finished with a wink, confirming his confidence in the plan and Loomer's bunch was the same as Larry's.

"I'm not jumping and neither are my men," Larry growled, still red-faced. "Not if they go in the drink. All those boats out there ain't shrimp boats. Scratch that one." Larry asserted.

I wondered what the other boats might be.

"Understood," Donahue sympathized, "and jumping over land is no better. Chances are, their chutes would leave them hanging between the first and second layer of a triple canopy rain forest, and although that's less dangerous than the the waters of the gulf, it's still not really safe."

"We'll come up with something. But nobody jumps in the pool, nobody jumps in the shrubbery," Larry gushed through clinched teeth. "Loomer's bird watchers will get a boat ride and you'll get your photos. I promise," his lowered eyebrows were capstones for a gaze that locked on Donahue's eyes.

Donahue blinked. That was more than he'd expected, with the two words that gave him as much a guarantee from Larry Abbott as any man could give; *I promise.*

"Eddy Rush, I meant what I said about the bonus," Donahue emphasized. "Two thousand extra. Can you teach them to handle the rafts in three days?"

"For two thousand, I can teach them in one day. Everyone will learn piloting, then put the best three in their own boats, I'll take one boat and the rest can rotate as my crew until everyone's up to steering and chart plotting."

"Have you done this before? Do you need any special materials or equipment?" Wilson Donahue beamed, relieved that by chance, Larry had recruited Eddy Rush, an individual who just might be the key in bringing this off.

Eddy returned to the chart of Golfo de San Miguel and studied the water depths around the camp and read a special notation about tide fall. "I will need a full set of charts, hand-held compasses, standard plotting boards, parallel rules and dividers for each boat," Eddy asserted with the authority of someone who knows what they're talking about. "Also a circular calculator for time, speed and distance problems and a stopwatch on each boat. For boat management and ready-rig, I'll need two extra camp lanterns, a mushroom anchor of about a hundred and fifty pounds, four hundred yards of half-inch nylon cable-laid line and two three-inch diameter all-bronze blocks. Also, a white mooring buoy, about twenty inches in diameter. I assume we already have axes and sledge hammers at the camp?" He smiled. "That should do it."

"What? No radar?" Donahue was stunned at the items and did a quick estimate of two thousand dollars.

"That's about right.. All of this is available at the government chandlery near the canal pilot's building. You'll get a price break there," Eddy informed Donahue. "One more thing. I've used inflatables as tenders. Have Sergeant Rumsey send us an electric air pump with hoses and nozzles to fit the air zerks on the inflatables. We don't want to spend all day on those monsters with a foot pump. And ask the sergeant about repair kits."

"Write all this down and I'll get it to Major Mills. How soon do you need all this?"

"Mr. Donahue, how soon do you us operational? How soon do you want to make the rafts secure and instantly accessible?" Eddy knew his place. He let Donahue set his own priorities, even if he was a wise-ass about it.

"Mr. Donlin, I have a pack of aerial recon photos that are anywhere from two days to a week old. We've spent hours on them and never found a clue about where the barge could be hiding. I understand you have a practiced eye. When you get into town, spend a little time on these.

Make me look bad by finding the damned thing. Dates are on the back. Primary coordinates, scale and orientation are marked on the lower right corner of each photo. Enjoy town. Rest now, because there won't be much in the field." Donahue walked us through the door. His ambulance was parked beside our waiting deuce and a half.

CHAPTER ELEVEN

But when she dances in the wind,
and shakes the wings and will not stay,
I puff the prostitute away.
Dryden

Donahue handed the package of recon photos to Larry, threw his coat and tie into the ambulance and climbed in after them. Larry, Eddy and I scrambled up the tailgate ladder into in the truck with Nelson who had loaded our personal gear. Larry told me that Nelson had been left for us because he's subject to motion sickness and the others wanted to keep their socks dry.

The driver had humanely rolled up the canvas cover on the sides of the truck, leaving us sheltered from the sun, but still subject to the discomforts of the ambient temperature and clouds of insects.

We made good time on the highway. That changed when we entered the city. Streams of commercial and military traffic in the middle of Ciudad de Panama limited the truck to second gear. We had spent nearly an hour making a twenty-six mile drive, and thirty minutes on the last four miles.

As we left the Canal Zone, a strong American presence mingled with the Panamanian population. Signs in both Spanish and English advertised everything from tooth paste to legal services. Military supply trucks, American-built busses carrying Panamanian citizens employed by the Canal Company, American businesses on every street and dozens of white faces in any crowd made Panama City seem more like El Paso, Texas.

"Where are we going?" I asked Nelson as we stopped again for a traffic snarl. Nelson smiled and nudged Eddy who slept, using his folded coat as a pillow.

"Donlin wants to know where we're going," Nelson repeated, laughing.

"We should be there by now, I suppose," Eddy shouted over the traffic noise. He checked his watch as he got up from the packing blankets he'd been sleeping on, and craned his neck looking for familiar landmarks. He had been dozing since the detour that took us close to the yacht harbor at Balboa, the only sight so far that caught his interest. "This neighborhood, hummm, could be the Pandora. I've stayed there twice. But I hope it's . . . ."

"Loro Azul!" Eddy and Pete shouted together as the truck turned into a narrow street and stopped at heavy wooden doors set in a high, lichen-covered wall of roughly dressed sandstone.

We dropped from the truck's tailgate as one of the wooden doors opened for us. "Buenos dias, Señor Abbott," a grizzled old man rasped. He smiled a toothless smile and limped heavily as he swung the door wider for our group. The second truck arrived and the gang noisily dropped from the tailgate and embraced the thin, white haired welcoming committee. Larry greeted the elderly Panamanian like a grandfather, and introduced the octogenarian as Pierre Beauchamp, and explained his French name was a result of being born on Martinique. He started working on the canal when it was a French project. The lame old man, dressed in a loose-fitting white shirt and baggy pants, was the patriarch of the family that owned the hotel. "Don't ever play dominoes with this guy; he'll take every cent you've got!" Larry boasted with his arm about the old man's shoulders.

A large, tile paved plaza spread out behind the door. Palm trees edged the plaza, casting agitated shadows across the pavers. Flowering climbers covered the rough surface of the walls and the rusty corrugated iron roof on the hotel's maintenance shops and laundry.

A variety of small shops crowded the south wall, with most of the activity under patched awnings at the front of each *tienda*, in preference to being trapped inside with the heat. Barber shops, curios, shoe shop, leather goods, a small cafe and a clothing store with custom tailoring displayed their goods and services to a mix of locals and hotel guests.

A clinic and a large drugstore filled the entire length of the north side of the plaza. A larger entrance, off the broader street, had a police booth on one side of the gate and a tourist activities kiosk on the other.

We had been delivered to the rear entrance to our hotel. Nothing was visible to indicate which hotel, but Larry, Eddy and Pete Nelson seemed to have been guests here before. Walking through a broad stone arch was a pleasant surprise. An arcade stretched across the rear of the hotel. Its interior length had been recently sprayed with water, with special attention given to the potted palms and scarlet bougainvillea. With the walls still weeping, the evaporation dropped the temperature within its walls by ten degrees. "That old man back there, Jimmy," Larry said over his shoulder, "treat him with respect. He's pushing ninety now. The Canal Company pensioned him off in nineteen-twenty-seven, after an accident took off his left leg at the knee. They gave him a pension of full wages, very generous at the time. Forty-five dollars a month and it has never been adjusted. Donahue tried to help, but no-go.

"He's father-in-law to the owner of this hotel. He tends the door and does odd jobs for his son-in-law and makes a hundred or two a month. He has a nice room on the ground floor of the east side of the hotel so he doesn't have to climb stairs and the hot afternoon sun doesn't get to him. He eats free. Fishes on Saturdays, goes to church with his grandkids on Sundays. Plays dominoes with the cooks till two in the morning. Not so bad when you think about it. But he's a piece of history. Talk to him if you get the chance, and tip him when we leave."

The heavy mahogany doors to the lobby were wide open, their high-gloss varnish mirrored us as we entered. Sunlight never reached the colorful ceramic tile floor. Overhead fans rustled the palms at the entrance and along the wall of yellow louvered panels covering the open windows. The room temperature felt comfortable, if a bit humid.

The long, narrow room was filled with older couples. There was some kind of reunion of American engineers, construction workers, managers, or retired employees. Bent, white-haired men wore pale linen suits and finely woven straw hats with watered silk bands. Their ladies, in cotton pastel prints and wide brimmed straw hats, ambled along with them over the new broad red runner spread the length of the front desk. Some sat in cane chairs in the bar, or in the coffee shop sipping strong black coffee and nibbling *pan dulce*. A few occupied the settees in the lobby, puzzling over Spanish language newspapers, trying to remember the language they had once known so well. Several old men with red-rimmed, watery eyes had come alone. They were the sad ones, their envy of colleagues who still had the sweet companionship of wives painfully obvious..

A tall, gaunt clerk motioned us over. We gave him our names and he passed us our room keys. Abbott, Gates and Williams shared a room. Nelson, Bennett and Keener had a room next to Eddy, Bishop and me. All three rooms were on the third floor on the east side overlooking the plaza.

I started for the room to take a shower but Eddy stopped me.

"Not yet. Let's go back to the plaza," he insisted. At the barbershop, Eddy's instructions in Spanish were followed precisely, and I turned out looking like the fourth member of the Kingston Trio . . . damned short hair! Then the tailor shop. A traditional white cotton Panamanian shirt with small pockets at the breast and large pockets at the waist, a navy blue knit shirt and a maize-colored short sleeve buttoned-down of American manufacture were more than I'd intended to buy. Full-cut beige, linen trousers came next. Then to the leather shop for sandals and a belt. "I think you'll do. You don't look impoverished, at least," Eddy offered as an evaluation on my improved appearance.

By this time, Donahue's promise of a steak dinner became foremost in our minds. Anything we want from the kitchen or bar, he'd said. I looked forward to a shower and clean, new clothes and taking advantage of a foolishly generous offer.

When we arrived back in the room, another suitcase sat on the foot of Eddy's bed. "Had this one sent down to the hotel a week ago and held for me. If we had gone to a different hotel, I'd have sent for it." Somehow, Eddy had known all along where we were going, at least the city and country, if not the exact hotel.

At last, the early evening cooled a little and I took a nap while Eddy showered. Around nineteen-thirty, we locked the room and went downstairs to the restaurant. His Ivy League willow-green corduroy suit had him sweating. He didn't look impoverished, but he didn't look comfortable, either.

Eddy, Bishop, and I sat in the same booth as Rubio Williams and Larry, near a large dance floor and beyond that, a low stage. The rest of our party sat in the next booth. Loro Azul was crowded, loud and smokey. The patrons were a blend of American military, canal employees and tourists with an adventurous bent. All had deep tans, or glowing sunburns, but the main difference separating the military from the other two groups was age.

I opened the conversation with a casual remark that this was a bit distant from the promised paradise. "Stick around," Rubio encouraged. The food that passed our table was generous in portions and the aroma of *pollo al carbon con arroz y camarones en ajo* held our attention until the dishes were placed on another table. I was close enough to paradise to smell it.

"The rafts are ready but not yet in camp," Larry mumbled to Rubio and me as we settled more comfortably into the booth. He leaned on his elbows with his arms crossed. The light reflected off the white tablecloth showed the circles under his eyes. He'd gone far too long without sleep, and the pressure of our project showed on a face that seemed gaunt and strained. "The outboards are at the airfield and will be transported with us. Drinking water is the big concern right now. Either they leave us with four Lister bags or resupply us every other day or so. They think that would draw too much attention so I suggested . . . ."

"Save it, Larry," Rubio interrupted. "Kick back, enjoy your dinner." Larry wore an expression of near exhaustion and needed to rest more than any of us. There was a flash of anger at Rubio's chide, then it faded; he knew Rubio was right.

The five at the next booth were well into their second pitcher of beer by now. The waiter took their order and turned to us. Eddy ordered for me in Spanish. Rubio laughed and ordered, then turned to Eddy and me. "Don't ever order anything in here that includes the word *'grande,'*" Rubio advised. "Not unless you're planning to live on leftovers for a day or two. Do you enjoy a good beer, Jimmy?"

I had never really developed a taste for beer. Left up to me, I'd have ordered coffee, my only vice I could actually blame on the Army. I once asked our mess cook if he ever actually washed the big twenty gallon coffee brewer. "Twice a year," he said. "On Christmas day and the fourth of July."

"Well, Eddy just ordered us a pitcher of Monte Carlo apiece. Enjoy." For a reason I didn't understand, Rubio seemed very amused by this.

Our beer arrived at the same time as the first performers.

A group of rowdy Marines, pardon the redundancy, made a dash for a table at the nearest corner of the stage and pushed it out onto the dance floor to get even closer, only to be rousted and replaced by older canal employees who'd reserved the most favored spot in the house. "Helluva parade, Donlin. You'll see it all this evening. Who's here, tonight, Rubio?" Larry asked, having come in the back way also, and missed the bill in the front entrance.

"Estrella! That's why those Marines wanted the table." The first performers were locals who did excellent impressions of popular American groups. The second was a very talented young man who played classical guitar. Good music, wrong audience. By the middle of his third piece, a soft chanting arose from the back of the club. By the end of his fourth number, it was a roar.

"Estrella! Estrella! Estrella!" The clapping and stomping drowned the efforts of a budding Segovia and he left the stage. I turned to look at the rude factions who stomped and whistled. Everyone had turned in their booths or swung their chairs to face the stage. Near the entrance, I saw two families with children make a dignified but rapid departure. A master of ceremonies begged patience and the Jerry Lee Lewis and Little Richard imitators returned for a brief set.

Two more civilian families left, abandoning the club to shipping clerks, lock operators, pilots, and the young, short-haired, sun-burned grunts, swabbies and jar-heads.

There were a dozen military installations in the Canal Zone. Air Force bases, survival schools, Rangers and Special Forces jungle warfare schools, and Navy supply facilities. Marines, more than all the others, thought they owned the place.

Among them were faces that looked like they had been living on snakes and bugs for a week or two. Beer may have been the first thing they ordered, but pizza, hamburger or steak would have roared from the same breath.

With the clink of pitchers and mugs, a trio of somber faces at my table assured me that I had to drink the beer because the water wasn't safe. I downed the first mug and started to actually like it. Oklahoma permitted only 3.2, which made nice shampoo and beer batter for fish but had a bitter after-taste I didn't like. Years later, I was told the bitter taste was the preservative, necessary because of the low alcohol content. Formaldehyde.

I felt a buzz before I finished the second mug. That was the reason for Rubio's amusement. The alcohol content of Monte Carlo was seven percent, a long way from Oklahoma's Pearl lager! I would be drunk on my ass by the end of the first pitcher and Eddy and Rubio knew it. Eddy nudged me in the ribs. "I hope you're enjoying that beer. It's imported, you know," and laughed, "from way up north in Guatemala."

I laughed with him and turned toward the stage as the mug rose to my lips for another sample . . . and froze. Between me and the stage, resting on the rim of the mug, like the morning sun on the horizon, floated the largest, softest, most beautiful brown eyes I had ever seen. They held the luminous glow of silver spoons dipped in honey. Gracefully curving eyebrows arched above those eyes, the olive skin of her face tamed and softened the harsh light from the stage. Shimmering blue-black hair cascaded down each side of my Monte Carlo. I slowly lowered the glass to gaze upon the face of a Titian Madonna. She blinked and her eyes dissolved the superfluous universe, her long lashes brushed away the broken fragments of rational thinking.

As I lowered the glass, the rest of her face appeared like Venus rising from the foaming crests of the Aegean. High cheekbones, unblemished skin, her full lips modeled the faint, enigmatic smile of a Byzantine icon. She took my breath as first captive and I prayed more would follow. Dimly aware of the fanfare given to Estrella, the stripper that held the whole room in awe, I could not turn from the lovely creature that had just claimed my soul as her own obedient slave.

Wearing a snow-white *pollera,* the traditional Panamanian cotton dress, with a broad band of tiny, bright flowers embroidered across the yoke, she was back-lighted from the stage where a tall, busty and energetic dancer commanded the attention of two hundred men. Through the nearly transparent cloth, my Venus' graceful body stood in astonishing detail. Then her smile broadened. "Buenos noches," she said in fluent lust.

Beer trickled from the corners of my mouth and I think I blew bubbles through my reply. "Buenas noches." Eddy nudged me in the ribs again and handed me my napkin. Rubio, in a very cordial tone crooned a few sentences in Spanish and she answered softly, musically, apart and above the clatter and chaos of flawed and soiled mortals who drooled over Estrella.

"Jimmy, after all your shopping today, do you have thirty dollars on you?" Rubio asked.

Eddy nudged me again. "Yeah," I said. "I have a couple of hundred on me. Why?"

"Well, that's what she costs. Magdalena has just come on the floor this evening and she is now available. For thirty dollars, that is." Rubio was choking, struggling to hold back the laughter that Eddy and Larry let flow like water emptied from a boot. Rubio spoke in the same voice he'd probably use to offer a runny nosed toddler his first ride on a merry-go-round.

I'm sure my mouth was as wide open as my eyes. Even my ears had an erection. There were overwhelming forces within me. They assaulted every caution, every parental warning, every sermon I'd ever heard on the baseness of carnal desire . . . all drowned out by the roaring in my ears. My focus swung like a compass needle, I vibrated like a tuning fork before Magdalena. Somehow, and for reasons I still don't understand, I pulled back.

I was offended by damned near everything: Rubio's tone, Eddy and Larry laughing, thirty dollars, but mostly by the realization that the Venus of my every post-pubescent fantasy was a prostitute.

Stung by my own boyish pride, innocence and idealism, I was in love and she was all mine . . . for thirty dollars. I was stretched between lust and an ill defined, juvenile sense of pride and propriety.

An observant oriental philosopher might have explained my yin and yang were out of balance. My pockets were stuffed with tens and twenties. It wasn't the money as money. What few sexual favors I'd experienced so far had been freely, albeit awkwardly, given. I was damned by my own silly, childish, arrogant pride. Yet in my society of a week ago, there existed a standard measure of manhood: enjoy sex but never, never pay for it.

She stood before me, smiling with an innocence that seemed untouched by the vulgarity of her profession. A blazing incarnation of every lustful dream I could remember, and hundreds to come, she coyly fluttered her lashes and nodded toward the main entrance of the club. There, a set of stairs led to a balcony and a series of rooms that overlooked Via Simon Bolivar. The clientele traffic on the stairs was brisk.

My yin and yang were spinning like a pinwheel.

"Maybe later," I said, startled by my own voice and words that part of me didn't want to say . . . and some parts really didn't want to hear. Even across the language barrier, my strained voice carried not only rejection but apparently insult. Her smile faded, but otherwise she seemed indifferent. Even in the pinched limitations of my unworldliness, I had never intended to offend her. Saying no did not change her occupation or even suggest to her that she should not engage in such commonality. To her, it only meant she had to go to another table for a client.

Making a poised and graceful exit, she offered our table a farewell remark. *"Creo que este guiñeo esta muy verde."* She brought a storm of laughter from Gates, Rubio and Eddy and a table full of locals behind us. Rubio caught his breath well enough to provide a rough translation. Now the non-Spanish speaking members of our group joined in the guffaws.

"She said she thinks this banana is too green," Rubio informed me, bringing a glow to my face a bit rosier than a traffic light. Embarrassment and blurred vision cleared soon enough for me to see her stroll toward the stairs with Pete Nelson's arm around her, and he turned to look back at us and shoot a thumbs up.

For no reason that logic nor any form of intelligent considerations could account for, something tore inside me. She was boyhood's dream, the model of juvenile urges, the ideal woman, the mystic promise, the sacred vessel, and yet she was flawed beyond redemption. A gritty realization slowly formed that this would always be so, and as a participant in the human experience I was not now, nor would I ever be, an individual who could claim the pretentious and arrogant right to expect anything different . . . not better . . . different.

Rubio saw the expression on my face as I watched Nelson walk up the stairs with Magdalena. Compassion was not a quality I'd expected to see in the face of anyone in this collection of barbarians, but it was there on Papa Rubio's, and at least his laughing stopped. After catching a few wisecracks from Eddy and Keener, and a sneer from Gates as he threw a shrimp tail in my direction, the matter was dropped. The waiters arrived with platters of *carne asada y camarones* were set before us, and the episode was not only dropped, but forgotten, at least temporarily.

I ordered another pitcher of Monte Carlo.

Waking around ten the next day, I found Eddy sprawled across his bed fully clothed, reeking of gin slings. After conducting a personal assessment, I found myself in a similar state. Any claim of superiority because I had at least removed my shoes, I supposed could scarcely be justified.

After a shower and lunch, I tried a few hours of playing tourist, by taxi, then on foot, but soon tired of the stultifying heat and humidity. Obviously, the only worthwhile activity would be to nurse another schooner of Monte Carlo in the air-conditioned bar of the hotel. This turned out to be a conclusion reached by the others without the need of spending two hours in the afternoon heat.

The second night in the club was mostly a repeat of the first, except that Magdalena did not approach our table, but nevertheless made several trips up the stairs. Still numbed by finding the girl of my dreams to be a character from a Zola novel, I tried to suppress all outward evidence of the incident's effect on me. A tall, thin trooper with bushy blonde eyebrows and a badly sunburned face escorted her on her last trip up the stairs for the evening. He was drunk but eager to spend his thirty dollars.

Near midnight, my beer developed an odd taste, like Christmas candy. Larry excused himself to make a call. Returning in half an hour, I saw him freeze several booths away and watch us. Fatigue flashed to anger and he charged Eddy, and dragged him from the booth to show him the group members at the next table. "Is this your idea of a joke?" Larry roared at Eddy. "We truck out of here at zero six hundred! Now you get to help me tuck them into bed and roust their sorry asses in the morning!" Larry threw Eddy over the table onto Ross Bishop, who silently slipped onto the floor next to Bennett.

Eddy had been spiking our beer with vodka. When Eddy ran out of vodka, he switched to peppermint schnapps, which explained the Christmas candy taste. Larry, Eddy and I were the only ones still conscious. I was proud of being moderate in all things, and felt obligated to assist. I stood up and stepped over someone sleeping in a horribly contorted position on the floor. "Can I give you a hand, Cap?"

I don't remember anything else until the next morning when someone pushed me into intense sunlight and my head exploded with the stunning, horrendous thunder of the truck's tailgate dropping two feet to my right.

The ride back to Cryder Air Base took about forty-five minutes. Larry and Eddy were the only ones who didn't take a turn hanging over the tailgate. Other vehicles traveling on the *Carretera Interamericana* soon learned to keep their distance while the heat of the day burned away our abuses. (Read that *while the others left a trail of pepermint-scented vomit down the highway.*)

CHAPTER TWELVE

The gray-green stretch of sandy grass,
Infinitely desolate;
A sea of lead, a sky of slate . . .
Arthur Symons

Rubio had to shout over the clatter of the departing quartet of helicopters. "Knock off the grab-ass and get on that equipment. Move it to the mess tent. Pello says this whole area can be under water at high tide and that's only four hours away."

Larry was in one of the tents, stripped to swim trunks, sandals and a baseball cap while he studied a packet of communications from Donahue. Rubio worked from schedules on four clipboards.

"Hey, Donlin! Give me a hand with the rations and jerry cans," Keener shouted from a jumble of equipment and crates on the shoreline beside the skid imprints of the last H-40 to leave. Eddy Rush read the tide-tables and told us it was definitely on the flood.

"No way, Keener." Rubio shouted. "He's setting up the communications tent." He'd still had to roar over the diminishing noise of the choppers that formed an undulating line slithering toward a distant nest across the gulf. Their rotors tore at a hazy, steaming sky, leaving our group abandoned on a peninsula of scrub-covered gravel and sand.

I would rather have helped with the other gear. At least rations and jerry cans are manageable sized packages. The ANGRC-9 (Army/Navy Ground Radio Communications-model 9) was left on the beach, beneath a deepening gray sky. The *compañeros* helped carry the sixty pound radio, the heaviest com package on the beach, to the tent, only the spare tubes, antennae kit, and hand-cranked transmitting generator would remain for me to manage with no further assistance. It took a dozen seventy yard trips uphill through scorching hot mud and sand.

The next priority had been getting the heavy diesel generator into the shelter of the com tent. It rested exactly where the helicopter crew set it down, eighty yards away on the ridge and fifteen feet below the elevation of the com tent. Rubio and I pushed it two steps up hill over the hot beach, bogged down, dug out and pushed two more steps. In half an hour, Rubio and I were exhausted and the two hundred-eighty pound generator unit sat like the Sphinx.

Two compañeros appeared with log rails and rollers, placed them under the shipping palette and we had the generator in the tent within twenty minutes. Ten minutes more and it was chocked up to the required eighteen inches off the ground. After hoisting a makeshift dipole antenna, Rubio called in his first radio check on time. The ANPRC-6s and 10s (Army/Navy Portable Radio Communications, models 6 and 10) joined Angry 9 in the squad tent. The only other furnishings in our com-center were a small file cabinet for logs and codebooks, a small table and two folding chairs.

From this patch of shade we could see the entire beach and the expanse of the gulf.

We were most grateful that the compañeros completed two jobs we didn't have to tackle. The first was racking the eight fifty-five gallon barrels of gasoline for our boats and two of diesel for the generator. The second was digging the latrine at the edge of the forest. Physical exertion would take a horrible toll on us until we grew accustomed to the heat and humidity, and learned to schedule heavy labor projects for the marginally cooler early mornings.

Our camp at Base T consisted of a string of four squad tents, set up with their skirts lifted to benefit from the occasional breeze. The radio and generator occupied one, two tents held four of us in one tent, and three in the other, and the four compañeros had one to themselves. A larger tent of foreign manufacture stood at the highest ground at the base of the peninsula in the shade of several large palms. Larry and Rubio slung hammocks in this one. Their tent also held the mess and operations areas, partitioned by a wall of various supplies and rations. Sixty yards beyond, at the very edge of the forest a deep narrow trench provided our only sanitation facility.

The remainder of the curving finger of mud, sand, shell and gravel was barren of all vegetation except coarse grasses, a few bushes and a half dozen scrub palms along the spine. According to the tide tables, two thirds of the peninsula would be under water at maximum high tide.

Near the mess/operations tent, we erected three tripods for Lister bags, our only source of fresh water other than our usual afternoon rains. The last equipment to be placed under shelter was the repaired field telephones, switch panels, six rolls of WD-1 telephone wire, and lineman tools.

The compañeros' squad tent sprawled at the exact center of the ridge where it flattened into a broad saddle. They kept their distance from us, but on hot days when the wind was light and blew from the wrong direction, I understood the real reason they kept that distance: the latrine. I wound up sharing a tent with Nelson and Gates.

Pete Nelson and I got along. We had absolutely nothing in common, except a very pronounced dislike of jumping out of aircraft and an interest in historical trivia.

Buryl Gates was a pain in the ass. Sleeping in the same tent with him was to live constantly on the verge of a fistfight. Nelson warned me that Gates would interpret the slightest hint of apprehension as cowardice and weakness and he fed on it. His warped ego delighted in tormenting others, and slashing at anything beyond his elemental understanding. There was little he valued or respected.

The sub-strata of our campsite were composed of some kind of mineral deposit the larger trees could not tolerate. Beyond our camp to the east, though, the largest hardwood trees and mangroves grew right to the water's edge, forming a tangled mass of tall mahogany, palms, mangrove and lianas we rarely penetrated. The compañeros led a few of us into the forest to cut timber for more rails, rollers, piles, and the antenna poles on the morning of the second day. After that, only they ever went in again.

At first, I thought the deep shadows of the forest would provide comfort, but it was on the wrong side for afternoon shade, and it blocked the cool morning breeze from the mountains.

Over the next few days we learned that the rain forest was worse than a false promise of shelter and comfort. To enter its deep shadows was to offer up flesh and blood to denizens from hell. Nights were torment. Pushing aside mosquito netting for air signaled a blood feast. If we closed the netting for protection from insects, we suffocated.

Warning labels made us hesitant to use the insecticide spraying unit and the accompanying chemicals. The bugs were bad but not "potentially lethal if safety precautions are not observed in every detail." The canisters and compressed air sprayers remained in the supply tent. All in all, we'd rather have been back at Loro Azul.

The tide did indeed flood, in every sense of the word. We moved the outboards another thirty feet, gaining two feet of elevation, and placing them above high tide. Flood tide was, however, a blessing in the collection and movement of the rafts.

Even with the rafts deflated and packed in large canvas bags, they were buoyant enough to float. By merely capturing them with nylon line through a D-ring they were secured at the high tide mark. Inflating them three hours later with an electric compressor hooked up to the generator took a little longer than expected. Charged with curiosity, we hurried the process and forgot to insert the heavy plywood panels that formed the sole, then had to deflate them partially to install them. Upon re-inflating, the high air pressure expanded the chambers to full shape and locked the plywood in place. This created a buoyant and immensely stable high-speed vessel for three or four men and equipment. Fully inflated, they were thirty yards from the ebbing tide and water deep enough to float them. They weighed over five hundred pounds but Eddy had no concerns about getting them to the water.

The still crated outboard engines loomed as ominous black silhouettes on the crest, pillars of Baal, and would soon demand sacrifice. I watched them from the shade of the com tent, thirty yards away. Heat waves visibly radiated through the mahogany slats of their shipping crates, and we loathed them in the still, steamy afternoon. We loathed Eddy who claimed to know boats while we worked like galley slaves and he conferred with Larry and Rubio in the shade of the operations tent and drank orange juice over ice cubes.

Following Eddy's instructions, nylon bow lines were secured to each raft, tethering them to stakes beside the outboards. His insanity was blatantly obvious because the boats were already well above the water and were so heavy they couldn't even be carried down the slope, let alone up.

Now that the rafts were inflated, we worked another two hours installing the depth sounders and installed the batteries. Two more hours saw the outboards uncrated and freestanding except for the braces that kept them upright.

The afternoon was white-hot and it burned away our energy and appetite and work became a moment-to-moment unfocused struggle. Long drinks of chemically treated water left a bad taste in our mouths and we looked at the beach through eyes burning with the salt of our own sweat. No matter how hot, the water must be a little cooler and the salt could be rinsed off with a splash of drinking water. There was no concern about wasting water because the *compañeros* assured us it would rain almost every afternoon, some days heavier than others. Leaping over the stack of rough-sawn mahogany crate stock, Keener threw off all his sweat-soaked clothes and raced for the beach, the rest of us at his heels.

Lounging near their scratched and dented aluminum utility boats, smoking and watching the Americanos work themselves into sunstrokes, the *compañeros* spun toward us. Pello flipped away his cigarette and ran to intercept us, with Jorge limping along behind.

"*Alto, alto! Muy peligrosso!*" Jorge shouted, hoping that someone in our group would understand. Pello stood before us, legs apart, arms up with palms out like a traffic cop. We stopped. Pello used his right hand to imitate the waves with the fingers of his left hand inserted vertically and made several passes. "*Tiburon, tiburon!*" he shouted.

This was one of the few Spanish words I knew. The "T" in "Base T" was for *tiburon,* Spanish for shark. The peninsula was an abandoned shark fishermen's camp.

We slowly walked back to the tents, picking up scattered, sandy, stinking, sweat-soaked clothing as we went. For the first time, we noticed lengths of rotted fishing twine, broken hooks of great size, rusty wire leaders, fragments of pottery, bits of charcoal from cooking fires and brown glass from thousands of shattered beer bottles. Jorge's limp was from a cut on his foot the first day on the peninsula. Carelessly working without his sandals, he cut his foot on broken glass.

"*Gracias, amigos,*" Keener shouted to the two fishermen as they returned to their ancient and abused fishing boats. They gave us a casual wave in response, wearing the dismal expressions of annoyed nannies.

All assurances of rain came under suspicion. No rain the first day, and by radio we learned clear skies were predicted for the second. Later that first night, at the day's second high tide, Eddy and I hauled the rafts even higher up the beach and used a minimal amount of our drinking water to wash away the perspiration of our labor.

We needed rain.

In the squad tent, we strung our hammocks between the center post and three of the corner poles. All five posts had been cut from the forest because the issued poles were not sturdy enough to support the weight of three men in hammocks. Under Nelson's direction, the outside end of the bedding was untied and brought to the center post during the day, our bedding and mosquito netting folded inside. This left the tent's interior free of obstruction, providing a shady, airy floor space for a variety of small jobs.

Arriving at the tent after wrestling with the rafts, I noticed someone had already swung my hammock. I'll be damned, I thought. That's very considerate.

I drew back the mosquito netting and slipped out of my sandals. The *compañeros'* camp lantern gave enough light to see that Nelson and Gates were already stretched out, heads toward the corner posts. As I dropped heavily into the hammock, something slammed at my shoulder, then my head. Folds of mosquito netting obscured my view to the right. Snatching up the flashlight that hung from a peg on the center post, I turned the beam toward the far end of my hammock.

Head flattened against its own coils, ready to strike again, a snake of huge proportions, thicker than my forearm, spread across the web of the hammock. Shouting a warning to my tent mates, I opened an entrenching tool to kill it.

The snake dropped to the ground and tried to crawl away. I could see its tail remained at the web of my hammock, pierced and wired to the head ring.

Gates howled with laughter.

Nelson raised his head to see what was going on as the snake struck at my knee. Then the tan, gray and black patches were a blur arching for my arm and I leaped back, bringing more fits of derision from Gates.

"It's a boa. Non-poisonous, but it has a nasty bite," Nelson said. Suddenly, I decided I didn't want to kill it.

At this point, the snake and I were both Gates' victims, and to make this perfect for his grotesque sense of balance, the snake should now become my victim. This I could deny him.

With Nelson's help, I pinned the snake's head to the ground. Nelson snipped the wire that held the snake's tail to my hammock and the boa instantly threw tight coils about my arm.

"Don'cha get lonely? Don'cha need a pet? I know ya don't like girls, but I thought ya might like snakes," Gates managed to blurt out amid guffaws. Rubio Williams stepped into the tent with a camp lantern and washed the interior with glaring yellow light. Hanging up the lantern, he took the snake's head in his left hand and unwrapped the coils from my arm, saying he'd take it to the boonies.

Gates continued to laugh as he stretched and yawned. I drew a bayonet from the tool belt by the entrance, slipped quickly under my bedding and cut the head rope to his hammock, tumbling him to the ground in a tangle of cordage and mosquito netting.

Furious, he tore at the fabric and tried to rise. I slammed the pommel of the bayonet into his ear, bringing a roar of pain and rage. He tried to push himself off the ground with his left hand, shaking the fallen rack against toolboxes and ripping his netting, but he froze when he felt the point of the bayonet under his chin.

I took a fistful of Gates' coarse blonde hair and yanked his face into mine, pushing the point of the blade hard enough that the mosquito netting draped across his chest showed a crimson blotch. He grimaced with pain and anger, nostrils flared and his breath came in moans and gushes. "Have I got your attention, you son of a bitch?"

"Okay, Jimmy," Larry said, slipping between the lantern and the four or five others who appeared to see what was going on. "I'll take it from here." He put a hand on my shoulder, not forcibly restraining me, but urging me to reconsider driving the point home. "I take it you're ready to go home now, Mr. Gates?"

I withdrew the point and pushed his head away.

"Damn it, Larry, it was just a joke," Gates complained, rubbing his right ear. "Nobody got hurt, 'cept me. It was all in fun. There's no reason to get pissed off. I need this job.

Put me in a different tent," he pleaded with an undertone of panic, "or I can sleep with them Pans."

Larry's hands drew me away from the netting-draped thug and reached for the bayonet. I kept it, drawing it away from his extended hand and I remained in a guarded posture. Larry growled at Gates. "We don't need anybody this much. Take your hammock, go sleep in the mess tent. If there's any more crap, you're back up north and permanently off the job list."

Rubio entered, rubbing a bleeding scrape on his arm where the snake finally managed to bite him as he released it.

"I've promised him the same, Larry," Rubio said, opening the first aid kit. "Gates, why is it the only thing you can do right is demolition work?" Rubio asked.

There was no reply. Only quiet resignation that somehow his bad judgment, bad attitude and a rotten sense of humor had boxed him into an uncomfortable corner. Packing his duffel and bedding, Gates grumbled past two men who were ready to end his secondary career and another one who would have been pleased to simply gut him. His brutish antagonism faded and showed features that could have been considered handsome without the constant scowl.

Over the next few days, Gates became more sullen and withdrawn. He grudgingly did his chores and promptly disappeared. Jealously guarding his 'bag of tricks,' he spent his time studying the code manuals. Within two days, he could decode faster than Larry, Rubio or Eddy. And, up to this time, no one knew he spoke Spanish except the *compañeros*.

The morning of the second day found the entire camp operational, except for the boats. They were a good forty yards from water but close enough to the outboards they could be mounted to the transom at the next high tide. One of the outboards had a tripod hovering over it, sturdy six-inch diameter poles, with a block and tackle rattling against the plywood transom. When high tide lapped at the sand under the bow of the raft, it was time to mount the outboard. The block and tackle lifted the black and dark gray monster and swung it out, the skeg drawing a deep furrow in the sand. The rafts surged against their mooring lines. Ross Bishop and Phil Keener loaded fuel tanks and connected the console steering cables and engine controls while knee deep in water.

Nelson and I struggled with installing the tandem batteries in the watertight compartments against the starboard side of the transoms and connecting the electrical leads. Bennett, Eddy and Gates handled the block and tackle as the compañeros 'walked' the tripod to the next three outboards.

Eddy familiarized himself with the tide tables and charts. He found the tide ranges in our area to be more extreme than expected, ten to fifteen meters not being unusual on the Pacific side. For this reason, he radioed Major Mills up at Cryder and requisitioned an extra spool of nylon cordage.

We set the heavy mushroom anchor at two hundred yards out, and secured the mooring buoy. A four hundred and twenty yard loop of nylon line ran through two bronze blocks, one shackled into the eye splice that held the mooring buoy. The other block was lashed to a heavy post driven deep into the beach well above the high tide line. To hold the rafts at the ready, Eddy formed a continuous loop through the two blocks with a long splice. At high tide, we had a continuous loop to the mooring buoy.

When the rafts were not in use, they were tied to the loop near the shore. Hauling on the other side of the loop took the rafts, fuel and equipment out to the mooring buoy and deep water where they remained afloat even at low tide.

This kept the boats available for instant use, no matter the state of the tide.

Larry confessed he'd had concerns about needing to make a run with half a ton of raft, outboard, fuel, weapons and equipment stranded on the beach fifty yards from water, or swept off the beach by tidal rips.

While this arrangement kept the boats secure in one sense, another form of security was addressed. While the group relaxed in the shade of their tents, Eddy and Rubio positioned a new stake several yards east of the one that held the mooring loop.

Rubio had talked to the four *compañeros* and they nodded and left the shade of their tent to watch Eddy. He had drawn a line on the chart from our camp across open water at two hundred and thirty three degrees. This line bisected the line of demarcation to Golfo de San Miguel, the line that marks the entrance into the gulf. I don't know why, exactly, but he called it the *"Pollux Intercept."* In geometry a straight line that touches or crosses another straight line is an intercept. The name Pollux had something to do with a little racing sloop he sailed the previous summer on Lake Ponchartrain. Rubio, reading a hand-bearing compass, motioned Eddy to the right and signaled him to drive the stake.

Eddy explained to us later. We would leave and return on this exact bearing of two-three-three- going out and its reciprocal of zero-five-three coming in. Pollux Intercept would not be just a navigation reference line but also a security check. The compass heading from the lantern post beside the compañeros tent out to the one on the beach read two hundred and thirty-three degrees, the same as Pollux Intercept on the chart. The new post was, in fact, the north east end of Pollux Intercept. The reciprocal, or opposite heading is zero-five-three degrees. We must always make our landings on a heading of zero-five-three degrees as a matter of identifying ourselves to the camp sentry. Even our supply choppers were instructed to make the final three-mile approach at the confirmation bearing. Those who approached on any other course would be identified as outsiders and would make their closing in the sights of several weapons.

For night operations, these stakes could be used as a visual range. If we had a raft out at night, a second lantern would be hung on the stake Eddy had just driven at the beach, over fifty yards from the one at the compañero's tent and at least twenty feet lower. We would maneuver the raft until one white light appeared exactly over the other and turn toward them. We would then be on course at zero-five-three degrees and running for the landing area on the beach.

CHAPTER THIRTEEN

By the deep sea, and music in its roar . . .
Byron

The weather forecast was wrong. At sixteen hundred rain drops the size of beer cans hammered us, and for the first time, the millions of insects were silent, at least their noise was drowned out by the roar of the downpour on tent canvas.

The rain gave us an opportunity to wash laundry, shower, shampoo and refill the Lister bags and anything else that would hold water. The rafts became instant bathtubs and washing machines. At the most intense ten minutes, we were beaten down and driven to the tents by a rain so fierce it was painful on our bare, sunburned skin.

Rubio called us into the mess tent as the rain turned to soft drizzle and Eddy began his instruction in piloting. He started with a refresher on latitude and longitude and expanded. One sixtieth of a degree is called a minute and it equals one nautical mile over the surface of the earth. Eddy showed us latitude and tick marks on the sides of the charts where minutes and tenths of minutes could be picked off for the distance scale.

We covered the compass rose, the difference between true and magnetic directions and how to draw out and label a course line. The time-speed-distance problems were unclear at first, especially the function of the number sixty when dealing with minutes of time instead of whole hours. Eventually, it all clicked. With the circular calculator, time-speed-distance problems could be solved in seconds. Piloting was a simple matter of keeping track of course, speed and time.

Compass bearings on buoys or landmarks intersect to confirm a dead reckoning position. In one afternoon we at least grasped the theory.

We took a break from the heat. It was still hot in the shade, just not quite as hot. Eddy worked with Bishop, Keener and Bennett, the three most promising pilots, and threw out a few tricks and short cuts. I overheard terms like "forty-five by ninety," and "running fix." Within the next few days, the rest of us learned these functions as well, in the best classroom of all, out on the water.

Rubio twice stepped between Eddy and Gates, who insisted on calling Eddy 'Ma'am.' In Gates' little mind, only women could assume the role of a teacher. By the end of the session, Eddy had had enough. He laid into Gates.

Well built and eager enough to straighten him out, Eddy threw some vicious blows, but they had little effect on a massive brute like Gate. And Gates was a brawler. Four inches taller and seventy pounds heavier, he absorbed the blows and lifted Eddy off his feet with a roundhouse. Eddy's head snapped back, blood from his left cheek spattered across the nav chart tacked to the briefing board and he sprawled under number two mess table.

Larry spun Gates around, and shot his left hand upward, fingertips spearing the hollow under Gates' larynx. Gasping, his face turned red and distorted in pain. Gates started to lunge for Larry, but remembered the last time he'd tried to take him on, and overcame the impulse. His thoughts were revealed in his expression. "If Larry Abbott fought like other men, I'd kill him." But Larry never fought like other men.

In a calm voice, Larry announced Gates would be taking my place in the boats. Gates' expression changed, his beetled brow furrowed and his eyes widened. A flow of verbal exchanges between Larry and Gates, his voice reduced to a raspy whisper, ended with an apology to Eddy and I was reinstated as a crewman-navigator.

Nelson fired up the kerosene mess stove and served a decent meal, the first we'd had in three days. All other meals had been cardboard-flavored rations, Swedish, I think. We ate chicken soup and canned pot roast with vegetables, the last of the fresh bread, and a wilted salad with mayonnaise and grated cheese for salad dressing.

While we lounged over our dessert of canned peaches and vanilla wafers, Eddy ignored the mouse that curled up under his left eye and explained Pollux Intercept and how to use the range lights. With a flourish of his spoon, he said, "If you do as well on the water as you do sitting on your asses, we won't have any problems," and fished the last peach half out of the can.

The rain passed and brilliant colors streaked the sky in late evening, giving the surface of the bay a glow like back-lighted orange silk. The sun dipped its lower edge into a dense, silver edged cloudbank, the promise of tomorrow's rain. Lines of pelicans skimmed the water, settling in the shallows at the end of our peninsula.

"I think we'd better put our skills to a practical test tomorrow morning, see if this stuff really works," Rubio suggested to Eddy.

"Uh-uh. We go out tonight," Larry interrupted. "Tomorrow, we can do an easy daylight run, take compass bearings and try to do a few running fix problems on the way over, then fill in some blank spaces on the chart before noon. Sergeant Ramsey neglected sector eleven on his chart updating. But tonight, it's all chart, calculator and stopwatch. And if it doesn't work, you'll be late for breakfast."

Larry took a clipboard from his table and read off who went in which boat. "I have our call signs from Donahue. We are 'Operation Goose.' The radio station in La Palma is 'Mother Goose,' the chopper field and com center at Cryder is 'Wild Goose,' Base T is 'Nest,' Donahue is 'Gander,' and the boats are 'Goslings' one, two, three and four." Keener and I were assigned Gosling Two.

"Eight of us go out. Gates, you will stay here to monitor the radio. Right now you can help these men top off two fuel cans for each boat and load nav gear and the PRC-10s. Just enough light left to get us off the beach. Nelson, go fill, light and hang the range lights," Larry barked.

Dishes and utensils were quickly scrubbed in the boiling water of the mess cans, the smell of the strong disinfectant killing any last remnants of appetite. Food was replaced in the bins, and camp made generally tidy by Bishop and Gates when he returned from fueling. His surly demeanor unimproved by the scrap with Larry, his sour tone communicated his resentment of the leverage used against him; whatever it was, it worked. He remained in a vile disposition, but never uttered a complaint.

We heard the call from the beach and raced to help with the boats. Eddy insisted that at night we haul the rafts out to the buoy by hand from inside the rafts before we lowered the props and started engines to prevent fouling the props in the mooring loop and to be sure we were in deep water. Each raft carried spare propellers and tool kits, but replacing a prop in daylight on a workbench was hard enough. No one wanted the job out on the water, especially at night.

We idled at the white buoy. Barely audible, the outboards whispered a bubbling rumble, and blew splatters of dirty water and exhaust out the stack. We coordinated our stopwatches to the exact second. At a nod from Larry, Eddy passed out written instructions to each boat operator, untied the painter and drifted with the engine at idle.

The envelopes gave us courses for a series of timed legs at fifteen knots. That would make the problem easier. One mile every four minutes.

Keener had no more than read the problem than we were rocked heavily as Eddy's boat, Gosling One, rushed out on Pollux Intercept. Following instructions in the packet, Keener and I did the same two minutes later.

Eddy's boat faded into the enfolding night that obliterated land, sky and water, painting all three as a vast, dimensionless black wall as we pounded over his wake.

We steered two-three-three degrees at fifteen knots for sixteen minutes, turned to one-eight-five degrees for eight minutes, then zero-two-three for sixteen minutes. The last remark told us not to change speed, but find our way back to Pollux Intercept and go home. In order to do that, we had to know where we were at the end of the last timed leg. I had done the plot work while Phil steered, his face illuminated by the red glow of the boat compass at the center of the console. He complained how difficult it was to keep on course. The flat bottom provided no 'bite' to help the boat track. All of us soon realized that steering was demanding work.

"On my command, turn to zero-niner-zero . . . . Mark!" I shouted over the grumble of the bow wave. Keener, unfamiliar with the boat, didn't throttle down. The raft made wide, skimming turns, much wider than they should have been. Four minutes later I sang out, "On my command, zero-five-three . . . . Mark!"

We approached the beach five minutes later. The upper light was to the left of vertical. We steered to the right until the top lantern appeared exactly over the lower, then turned toward them. Eddy and Larry were waiting for us with cold beer. Bishop and Rubio, in Gosling Three, silently nudged in beside us.

We heard and smelled Gosling Four before we saw it. Beyond the glow of the lanterns, Bennett cursed Nelson for spraying the inside of their raft with lettuce confetti, chicken soup, peaches, and mayonnaise. Nelson gave an unintelligible reply and blew his nose.

Bennett suggested we draw straws to see who gets Nelson on the next trip. His proposal met an extremely negative response, and Nelson assured everyone that his motion sickness was a temporary affliction, and in a few days he would be past this little problem. Apparently, this was a familiar promise. Bennett came in eleven minutes late because he'd had to steer and plot. Tonight, Nelson was worse than useless.

"A short problem, run over open water with a range at the end was relatively easy and there were mistakes," Eddy acknowledged. "On the other hand, it was a first run. We all returned, in the correct order, and within a few minutes of predicted time. The small errors are a result of sloppy boat handling which can be improved, and tidal currents not factored into tonight's problems." He was smiling, apparently taking some pride in our first attempt at piloting.

Gesturing toward Bennett's boat, Rubio sat on the bow of his boat, took a long draw on his beer, and asked

Eddy, "Did you intentionally put us on a collision course out there?".

"No! There was a possibility of two rafts crossing courses within three minutes of each other," Eddy replied, after draining his bottle of Monte Carlo. "Are you an optimist or a pessimist? Three minutes at fifteen knots is three quarters of a mile. With perfect piloting, that's as close as you should have come. With an error in time or course, or maneuvering, it could get touchy. That's the nature of running these boats. How close did you get?"

"We cut somebody's wake, maybe ten yards behind. I think I heard Nelson and Bennett arguing," Bishop said.

"Nelson, clean up that boat. The rest of you turn in," Larry barked, as disgusted with Nelson's mess as Bennett.

"Rubio and I are cooking in the morning. Then we do some compass work and more timed runs and take soundings in sector eleven. We'll be on the water from zero seven hundred to thirteen hundred. Take sun lotion for your face, wear your long-sleeve fatigue shirts and hats. Eddy will have instruction packets for us in the morning. Make sounding entries directly on the charts and we will update charts at fourteen hundred. Bishop, Keener, take the fuel cans above the high tide mark, behind the stakes. Donlin, turn off the beach lanterns and refill them. Eddy, meet me in my hooch in ten minutes. Bring your notebook."

As I removed the lantern from the hook on the stake, I noticed two figures working to clean up Gosling Four. Nelson and Gates. I was holding their only source of light, so I waited a few minutes. Gates threw buckets of sea- water into the boat, Nelson mopped with his soiled T-shirt and let the battery powered pump remove the water and whatever else may have washed through the strainer. I heard no order given to Gates but here he was, sour but performing. Whatever influence Rubio had over him still worked.

Over the whirring of the bilge pump, Nelson asked Gates a question I couldn't quite hear, but the reply was loud and vehement, at the brink of another fistfight. "What th'fuck d'ya think? Sure it's dull. Going out with you assholes and working arithmetic problems on the water would be dull, too. So what?" The three of us tied the boat to the loop with a camel hitch and sent all the rafts to the white buoy for the night.

Thank God for pancake mix! Watery powdered milk, and scorched powdered eggs didn't pry any eyes open. The metallic whang of canned Donald Duck orange juice is an experience not to be forgotten. But the pancakes were foolproof and the coffee was good and that was enough.

Rubio, Nelson and I got KP duty and Gates cleared the rest of the mess tent and once again pulled radio watch.

We wore what had become our uniform; swim trunks, sandals and baseball caps, in all but the most intensely hot mid-day sun. Everyone except Gates. He wore his sweat-stained "Aunt Jemaima" of a faded blue-gray fabric, the tail of the knot streaming halfway down his back. Fatigue shirts were necessary to protect us from the sun, but we hated them anyway. Always hot, seldom clean and never dry, no one wore a shirt if he didn't have to.

The baseball caps became personal affectations. If you put on your cap and tugged the bill low over your eyes, it was the signal that you were ready to assume your duties. Cap off, or pushed back, you were on your own time. Bishop gave me a worn, bright red St. Louis Cardinals' cap. He had at least a half dozen different lids. A major disadvantage of ball caps was exposed skin on the tops of ears, our daily sacrifice to the sun. A minor disadvantage of baseball caps was losing them when under way at fifteen or twenty knots.

To prevent this, we usually turned the cap backward or jammed them into the steering console locker.

Keener wore a necktie as part of his work uniform. The mess gear included a selection of dishtowels, usually white in the military. One of the towels, however, was an oversized, brilliantly colored floral print with a sky-blue background. We hated it. "It looks like the curtains in my Aunt Madge's bathroom," Bishop sneered. Keener tore it into three strips about six inches wide and four feet long. He wore one around his neck. It made Gosling Two easy to identify at a distance.

As the sun lifted over the forest and began its scorching trek across the gulf, all four rafts bobbed on their bowlines, fueled and ready. Keener and I went through our departure drill as we idled past the mooring buoy. We carried an ANPRC-10 wrapped in rubberized cloth and stowed under the spray hood, ready for scheduled communications. Sector eleven was too far away for the sixes, plus the tens had variable frequencies which gave us boat-to-boat options as well as coms with Base T. The ten shared this space with the spare propeller, small toolbox, puncture repair kit, air foot pump, canteens, and rations. Our sandals, indispensable at the beach but a nuisance in the boats, were strung on a loop in the bow line so they couldn't be washed overboard. Plotting board and nav gear were stuffed into dry bags between the two inflated thwarts, port side of the console, and tied down.

Keener and I wiped sun lotion over faces, hands and thighs, and put on the dreaded dark green fatigue shirts. We played follow-the-leader across the bay, five miles out on Pollux Intercept, and then one-eight-zero degrees to Punta Patino, the southwestern end of sector eleven on the west side of the gulf. Courses were relatively easy to plot because the local variation, the difference between true and magnetic direction, was so small we could usually disregard it for daytime navigation, saving time and reducing the likelihood of serious plotting errors.

Our attempt to gather soundings for area eleven on our chart was disastrous. The scant soundings showed depths of one half to twenty fathoms, deepest along the outer reaches of the bay comprising most of area eleven, and quickly shoaling toward shore.

The water also turned a muddy gray as we entered the bay. Larry was concerned that there were no soundings at all toward the center of the bay or at the entrance of several streams. Breaks in the shoreline gave no indications of what possible hiding place might extend into the depths of a hundred square miles of rain forest. Ignoring Eddy's protest that this project was not only unnecessary but dangerous, Larry insisted we check out sector eleven for ourselves.

Forming an oblique line, we ran parallel courses at ten knots while taking notes of the soundings every forty-five seconds. This would give us water depths each one-eighth of a mile. The light at Punto Barro Colorado marked the northeastern end of the bay and we turned to make our second pass closer inshore.

Gosling Three, with Bishop and Rubio, was the first to run aground. It took another boat to pass a towline and get them back into deep water. Fortunately, the engine was undamaged. After repositioning ourselves to continue the run, with Bishop's boat placed farther to the outside, we resumed our ten knots.

Major Mills and Sergeant Ramsey had modified a British-made knotmeter to bolt onto the transom. It dragged a small impeller between the port tube and the outboard. They said it would be accurate but hard to read. The dial was mounted on the top edge of the transom, port side, next to the motor mount, but it should have been displayed on the steering console, on the side opposite the depth sounder. This was their only botched job. We were not to regard it as accurate under two knots or over twenty-five knots. To put the engine in reverse, the impeller had to be lifted out of the water or the outboard prop would chew it up. This would be unworkable in the close quarters we knew we would encounter over the next few days.

We learned the importance of the raw data the knotmeter provided. Piloting without it could never be any more accurate than our ability to estimate speeds, difficult enough in daylight, but nearly impossible at night. We could never match this instrument's precision, which gave us a true speed to within a tenth of a knot. But at night, someone had to get on their hands and knees with a flashlight to read it!

When Bennett's boat struck, Nelson had been sitting, facing backward, leaning against the after thwart with a note pad and stopwatch, reading the knot meter and listening to Bennett read the depth sounder.

Upon impact, Nelson was thrown in a backward somersault over the bow of the boat, landing in the slime of the tidal flats under four or five inches of murky water. His aerial performance ended with a great splattering of gray-green mud and seawater. With tremendous effort, Bennett, bruised and bleeding from slamming into the console, waded to him, thigh deep in foul smelling ooze.

Gosling Two was closest. We broke our run and turned to try to help. Blood streamed from Bennett's nose, broken when he hit the aluminum frame of the windshield. Fearing we might also strand on the flats, he waved us off.

Bennett reached Nelson, now sitting upright but still chest deep in tidal mud and water, and signaled to us that Nelson was all right. Nelson tried to sort himself out. The impact had knocked the wind out of him and when he drew in his first gasping breath, he choked on mud. By this time, both men were coated with black slime. Nelson wiped his eyes clear and I could see they were filled with panic as he struggled to clear his breathing.

With great effort, they dragged themselves back to the raft only to find their troubles increasing. A broken branch, about the diameter and length of a hammer handle, protruded from an ancient hardwood log embedded in the mud. Held at the break where the flats slope into deeper water, the log presented its spike just below the surface, puncturing an air chamber at the center of the left side.

Equally disastrous, the outboard had kicked up at an odd angle. Examination showed a hopelessly mangled aluminum propeller.

Bennett checked the transom and mounting brackets and found them undamaged. "Get the damned tool box, Pete. We may as well get started now. It looks like the prop struck the end of the log at the same time the branch punctured the air chamber."

Like a snail, Nelson left a trail of ooze the length of the raft to extract the kit and spare prop. Then he stepped out of the raft to slip along the log until he reached the ruined propeller. "God damn, Jack. We may never pull the prop out here with only the (cough!) tools we have. It's mangled all to hell. It looks like an aluminum orchid."

Jack passed him tools to loosen retaining nuts, washers and seals. "May as well try. We're going to be here a while," Bennett said. The distortions caused by the impact forged a grip that would not surrender. Standing with one foot on the log and the other on the transom, Pete labored to remove the large three-bladed propeller.

Nelson shouted when the prop at last broke free of the tapered spindle. "Gooodaaamned fuckin' lump of melted down washing machines! Your mother and father met briefly at a masquerade ball!"

Angry and frustrated, Nelson started to heave the tortured aluminum prop into the mud. "No!" Bennett yelled. "We don't know how we'll swing when the tide comes back. We could slide right over it and get cut up even worse. We'll keep it in the boat until we're over deep water."

They had spent an hour prying off the bent propeller but it only took ten minutes to secure the new one. In the meantime, the tide went out, leaving the boat stranded four hundred yards from, and twenty feet above water.

Nelson showed his true stuff. Being seasick was something beyond his control, but how he handled himself in this episode was not. Sitting on the bow of the raft, he cleaned himself up as best he could, rested, and went back over the side to push and twist the raft until he could extract the branch from the deflated air chamber. Using his drinking water, he cleaned the surface and trimmed the tags around the tear. Bennett pulled and rolled the chamber as close to horizontal as he could, trying to dry the vinyl saturated nylon. The repair kit provided a cleaner-solvent and they finished the patch job in another twenty minutes.

Pete Nelson was exhausted by the time he pulled himself aboard. "Broke it again," Bennett complained, holding a soiled compress over his nose. He had set up the foot pump and began what seemed an endless labor. Half an hour later, Nelson spelled him, bringing the air chamber nearly up to full pressure, more than enough to get back to Base T.

They looked at each other, both of them drained by fatigue, still covered in vile muck and most of their water ration gone. Nelson began to laugh. "Bennett, you're not my first choice to be stranded with in the middle of (cough) nowhere."

"You don't even make my list, shithead!" Bennett said, laughing. He glanced across the gulf and saw the other three rafts standing by, bobbing in the clear, sun-sparkled water a quarter mile to the north. Through binoculars he could make out Larry slowly repeating a gesture: bringing his right hand up to his ear. "Fire up the radio, Pete. Captain Abbott wants to talk to us."

Nelson started to itch from the thin layer of mud that covered him from head to toe, drying and turning a pale gray. Scratching and grumbling, he unwrapped the ANPRC-10, turned it on, dialed in the scheduled frequency and adjusted the squelch. ". . . . ling One to Gosling Four, Gosling One to Gosling Four. Over," crackled through the receiver, the voice not yet recognizable.

"Gosling One this is Gosling Four. Over." Nelson, preoccupied with scratching, tried to hand the mike to Bennett.

"Is number seven hurt? Does he need medical attention? Over?" Captain Abbott asked.

"I need three days at Loro Azul for a bath, steak dinner and R and R. Over."

"Don't we all," Larry sympathized. "This survey project is canceled. Number Ten says in three hours the tide will come roaring in. Put out a line to stay put until the water is deep enough to run the outboard. Otherwise, it will take you higher up on the mud. Out."

Nelson put the radio away and tied a clove hitch to the same hardwood branch that had punctured the raft.

"Do you think that stick will hold us?" Bennett asked.

"If you have doubts, tie it (cough) to something else," Nelson groused, knowing there was nothing else within sight but more mud.

"Maybe your neck." Bennett accepted that choices were limited and both tried to nap in the blazing sun.

A solution to Nelson's mud problem arrived an hour later. The rain fell, in a frustrating drizzle at first, then a cascade, and Bennett tucked the radio into the storage compartment of the console.

Nelson bled black ooze out of his hair and ears, and his shirt changed from pale gray to dark green. As the coating fell from his face, huge red blotches appeared, irritations from some organism in the mud. The raft filled with water. Nelson bathed and washed his clothing while Bennett bailed. The more water in the raft, the longer it would take to float off. He stopped bailing when he realized that in the downpour, the raft filled faster than he could empty. He would wait until the rain stopped.

The sun steamed the broad mud flats through a blistering haze. "Why don't we just use the electric pump to empty the boat?" Nelson asked Bennett, joining his efforts to bail now that the final drizzle waltzed and swayed away to the northeast.

"That might run the batteries down too far. We don't even know if the engine will start. There may have been more damage than just the prop and shear pin. We'll need a margin to trouble-shoot. Just bail, Pete."

Due for a run of good luck, the first came with a jerk, a bounce, and a slow, skidding swing on the bowline. The tide gurgled past them, quickly rising, a foot, two feet, four. The bow of the boat jerked downward, pulling the up-turned forward chambers parallel to the mid-ship chambers. The plywood floors growled. With the tide foaming foul and charcoal gray, the bow took another violent dip. The stern lifted slightly, awkwardly swaying with the heavy outboard tilted up, and Bennett realized they were now in danger of swamping. Nelson dived across the spray hood, drew his bayonet and cut the line that held them to the log.

The raft threw its bow upward and swooped away sideways on the running tide. Bennett lowered the motor and hit the starter, providing a sputtering growl but nothing more.

"Get ready to go over the side! We may already be in water too shallow to run the engine!" he shouted at Nelson. The raft swept toward the forest beyond the mud flats.

Bennett hit the starter again and the outboard roared to life, softening to a whisper as the diluted mud refilled the baffles, throwing its own samples of muck to the tide. The propeller streamed a blackened wake.

"Run for the buoy at Punta Patino. That's the shortest distance to deep water, and I'll start the plot from there," Nelson shouted from the bow, spitting away a fleck of black spray.

Streaking over the water at twenty knots, the remaining rainwater rushed to the transom. The electric pump spewed an arching stream over the port quarter and the muddy water turned clear then stopped when the boat emptied. Flattened out on trim, Bennett and Nelson stripped to 'high-speed uniform,' swim trunks and backward-turned baseball caps. "YeeeeeeeeeHA!" Nelson yelled into the rushing wind, glad to have escaped the misery of sector eleven.

He passed a canteen and a sodden cardboard container of 'waterproof' rations to Bennett. "If only we had real food," he groused to Bennett.

"You whining wimp! Next, I suppose you'll want water skis."

Nelson was constantly on the receiving end of a series of jokes and jibes. When Gosling Four arrived at Base T at eightteen hundred hours, I put aside the recon photos and left the tent to see how well Bennett and Nelson had fared.

There were loud outpourings of sympathetic "oohs" and "aahs" and "poor baby." Bennett was tired and Nelson could have dropped in his tracks. The consoling crowd passed both of them and went to inspect the patch job on the raft.

Numb to our boorish insensitivity, the two casualties of circumstance trudged to their tent and mercifully fell into hammocks. An hour later, Rubio and I brought them dinner, and heard their account. Larry apologized for his stubbornness, especially for not listening to Eddy who had paid more attention to the charts and understood why there were so few soundings in sector eleven. The chart depths were marked at mean low low water, at which time sector eleven is, as we learned, an exposed mud flat, as described in 'NOTE D' on the chart. This has been a learning experience for all of us.

I was amazed that Bennett and Nelson blamed no one for their ordeal. It was simply accepted as a job-related hardship and we all knew there might be more. Cost was limited to an inconvenience to two people, a broken nose for one, one propeller, one raft patch and one stopwatch lost. The watch was already replaced and Bennett and Nelson were discovering new ways and reasons to insult each other.

Larry and Eddy now abandoned all interest in sector eleven. If we couldn't get a raft into any of the streams that emptied into sector eleven, an ocean-going tug and barge couldn't get in either.

CHAPTER FOURTEEN

Give them great meals of beef and
iron and steel, they will eat like wolves
and fight like devils
Shakespeare

That evening, resting after supper, I was half-asleep in Larry's hammock behind the mess tent. I'd finished KP and most of the others were playing poker. I had wanted to listen to the music broadcast from an American station in the Canal Zone and drifted close to sleep.

Larry and Eddy compared figures and charts on the night run we would make in another two hours. At last, with all four problems in envelopes marked for each Gosling, Eddy refilled their coffee cups.

After a few remarks about fuel inventory and what they would like to do with Swedish C-rations, they fell into relaxed banter about their love life back home.

"I don't kid anybody," Larry said. "I'm the original Kissing Bandit, about as monogamous as Grady's goat. Not that I don't love women, it's that I *do* love women," Larry sighed. "Remember La Donna, back at Stoney's Cafe?

She's the female version of me, and we both know it. Settle down? We'd have each other climbing the walls after the first month. What about you, Eddy? Last summer, you said you were going to marry that girl from Louisiana State. What happened?"

"I screwed that up in a major way. I truly loved her. Her dad liked me. He's the one who taught me boat handling and piloting.

"He raced a little thirty foot Sparkman and Stevens sloop on Lake Ponchartrain. She was beautiful. White topsides with teak decks and bright mahogany trunk cabin, coamings and hatches, varnished Sitka spruce mast and boom. She had her name, *"POLLUX,"* in gold leaf across her transom. The old man bought new sails every season. He thought I had a good eye for racing.

"I lived with them all summer, even enrolled for the fall semester at LSU . . . pre-law. That alone pissed off my dad. He still wanted me to follow him into medicine. The wedding was set for December. The future had a definite golden aura.

"Her old man made millions in backing Kerr-McGee off-shore oil exploration and development." Eddy stifled something here . . . . a sob, yawn or chuckle, I couldn't tell.

"But not everything was rosy in Paradise. Cheryl hated her stepmother. It was almost a sibling rivalry, since Bobbi was only six years older.

"The old man caught Bobbi and me in the sail loft of the boathouse. Drove me straight to the airport without saying a word. Never heard from Cheryl or Bobbi again. And LSU wouldn't refund my tuition."

Eddy and Larry howled with laughter. They had their priorities!

"We may be two of a kind, Larry. A week later, my dad got two suitcases with my four Italian made suits, a dozen custom made silk shirts and ties. They were all ripped to shreds, and a box of twelve gauge shotgun shells dumped in, to boot. I understood the message."

"I don't know, Eddy," Larry said. "I've been called a womanizer a lot of times, but I'm not. Ever heard of a woman accused of using men? They do, and can be just as callous about it as any man. People are people. If there's an itch, you can bet there'll be some scratching. The instant that tiny fragment of truth is spoken, somebody wants to get in my face about morality, Christian up-bringing, and the beauty of a physical relationship of a man and woman truly in love, etcetera, etcetera.

"Look at Donlin back there," Larry suggested, waving an arm in my direction. "He had an opportunity to satisfy his every boyhood dream with the most beautiful girl he's ever seen. He threw it away. And why? What would it have meant to Magdalena? Nothing. Or Donlin? By this time, out here in the boonies, nothing more than a nice memory.

"You know, Donlin and I discovered we're both admirers of Mark Twain who once said he never enjoyed himself so much as when he's living down to other people's expectations. Donlin hasn't figured out the real truth of that. He's still trying his damnedest to live up to somebody else's expectations. It'll never make him happy."

You may be right, Cap.

* * * *

Wiping on insect repellent, it seemed odd that we could feel bugs crunching against our skin as we rubbed. The mosquitoes swarmed us at night and waited for us each morning, clinging to or flying near the netting. Dense, wavering clouds of midges, moths, mosquitoes, and gnats, swirled around the camp lanterns that emitted an irresistible yellow-white glow. We were ordered not to keep a dark camp, but to present an air of legitimacy. With the lanterns burning brightly by sundown, luring millions of unwanted six-legged visitors, we could spray a dangerous insecticide each evening or we could endure with the token measure of a repellent. We chose the later.

The reverberating blows of a sledge hammer driving posts into the sandy beach at sunrise of the fifth day seemed odd. Capping the insect repellent, I walked to the landing area where the *compañeros* chopped and hammered with Eddy directing. The completed grid-work platform occupied an area near the beach landing at the mid-point between high and low tide. Crossbars bolted to verticals supported a series of thinner poles, the whole platform sloping toward the gulf. The structure was completed with the early morning tide tumbling over the feet of the *compañeros* as they cleared away their tools.

I spent most of the morning in the shade of the com tent, on the side away from the heat of the generator. The beast provided current for light in the operations tent, a string of a half dozen electric lights, and refrigeration. Occasionally looking up from testing telephones and switch panels, I could observe most camp activities.

It was a pleasant morning. I had a huge mug filled with the first of the coffee and a serving of biscuits with orange marmalade, my favorite. The order of the day was to rest up for another night run, but it was too damned hot to sleep. Better to stay in the shade and watch others work, like Eddy.

When his structure had a foot of water over it, Eddy fired up Gosling One and carefully ran it onto the platform. As the tide rose higher, the raft floated, boxed in by tall vertical poles, and held in place by a tether loosely tied to a center post at the bow.

A little before noon, the tide went out, leaving the raft on the platform, its bottom accessible, suspended four feet above the beach. "How long will it take to install the skegs?" Rubio asked Eddy.

"Two tides a day, four boats . . . two days." Eddy climbed the ladder poles on the side and carefully stepped into the raft. "Let's see if my make-shift dry-dock can handle the weight." The platform creaked and groaned but never wavered.

Walking backward, shaking out loops of an extension cord from the generator, Bennett showed up with a drill and a half-inch butterfly bit. "Shouldn't take more than thirty minutes," Eddy said. "This will improve the rafts' handling characteristics and make piloting more accurate. Pass up the hardware, Jack."

A new mounting bracket for the knotmeter, fabricated from the sides of a salvaged aluminum storage bin, was already screwed into place on the forward edge of the steering console, inside the windshield and opposite the knotmeter. With the tool kit from the bow, Eddy removed the knotmeter from the transom, stored it inside the console locker and straightened up with his head cocked to one side, listening. "Choppers," Eddy said to Rubio. "They're early."

They watched the pair of H-40s turn obliquely south and made the last two miles of their approach on zero-five-three degrees. They settled lightly on the ridge between the *compañero's* tent and ours, swirling dry grass and dust into the air, the rotor wash billowing the tent and shaking the lines.

Donahue was the first one out of the choppers, hunched over, both hands holding his straw hat on his head and squinting through the flying debris.

His color was better and the bags under his eyes were gone. He wore a tan poplin jump suit. With his gray hair in need of cutting and his breast pocket full of pens and a pair of reading glasses, he looked like a college professor on vacation.

Donahue returned our waves and walked down to the beach, relieved to be out of the turbulence of the still spinning rotors. A shirtless crewman followed him out, carrying a battered cardboard box. He lugged his burden past Donahue. Rubio called the crewman over to the raft. Jack Bennett pulled a thirty-inch long four by four out of the container, already cut in a streamlined teardrop with flat sides, pre-drilled and painted, exactly as Eddy described to Major Mills.

Other crewmen unloaded supplies, including two large insulated mess cases. The crewman and I joined his fellows, arriving in time to help Keener and Nelson move the two camp tables into the open area beside the operations/mess tent.

While work continued on Gosling One, Larry and Rubio brought Donahue up to date on the boat handling aspects of our activities. He seemed especially pleased that recon of the gulf was under way as they briskly walked up the beach to the tent, anxious to find shade. Donahue invited Larry, Rubio and me to lunch, leaving Jack Bennett and Eddy Rush drilling holes in the bottom of Gosling One.

We now preferred to have our meals under the shade of a palapa the *compañeros* had built beside the mess tent. The primitive structure was closer to the water and open to breezes. Pole benches around three of the four sides provided a mess area that was cool and comfortable with a good view of the landing area and the northern approaches from seaward. Much of the briefing material was brought out here also, but in the event of rain it was taken back to the tent or covered. The palm thatch roof was neither steep enough, nor thick enough to shed water.

Bishop and two men from the chopper crews set up a chow line on the two mess tables in the shade of the palapa. Keener lit the kerosene heater under the water and disinfectant in the field tanks he'd set behind the second table, just far enough in the open to safely vent the fumes and disperse the heat.

Donahue brought food for twenty men: our group, the compañeros, himself and the chopper crew. Beef, fish, chicken, and shrimp from Loro Azul, with vegetables, rice and fresh baked bread, all steaming hot. The second case was a cooler filled with milk, fresh fruit and a two gallon container of coffee ice cream. We would have elected Donahue the Emperor of Panama.

Larry and Bishop put out mess trays and flatware, but there weren't enough to go around. Several of us decided to 'lounge' until guests ate their fill and cleaned their trays. Keener, Bishop, Nelson and I expected to eat last. Then we remembered our stainless mess kits in our tents, and we joined the feast. I suppose it was the heat, but a moderate lunch and a small bowl of ice cream seemed plenty.

"If only you had Estrella in one of those crates," Keener moaned, jerking his thumb toward the helicopters.

Nelson's voice echoed inside the ice cream cooler as he scooped up his second bowl. "Or Magdalena." I could feel a half dozen eyes turn in my direction. I never flinched.

The whole Magdalena episode seemed distant and foolish. Rising from my shaded seat in a corner of the palapa, I walked out into the mid-day heat to wash my mess kit.

Gates glared at me, then smirked and flipped his last spoonful of ice cream toward me. He missed, the glob sizzled on the vent pipe of the field tank. "He's talking about your girl, Jimmy. Ain'tcha gonna stand up for your girl? Huh?"

The stainless pans and flatware rattled on the hinged handle of my mess kit, my back turned to Gates. The bristle brush nudged off the last clinging bits of rice. "I thought you were my girl, Gates."

A stunned silence gripped all who heard my reply. Even the chopper crews, who didn't know Gates or me, froze.

Keener and Bishop took a step back from the most likely path between Gates and me. It was a good decision.

Flinging his tray wildly aside Gates roared and charged. He leaped over the table between us, and lunged at me. I sidestepped, and threw a mess kit of steaming water and disinfectant in his face. Howling and rubbing his eyes, he grabbed for my fatigue shirt, his right hand cocked to tear my head off. A rushing noise filled my ears, and everything moved in slow motion. An indefinable force welled up in me, and boiled over. Knocking his searching, grasping hand away, I pivoted with a long backstep, snatched up a small breadboard from the nearest table and jammed a corner into the pit of his stomach. Breathless and grimacing, half blinded by the steaming disinfectant, he came on and I slammed the edge of the hardwood slab across his forehead, then a second blow back-handed. Dazed, he went to his knees and reached for a table leg to pull himself up. I was about to hit him with the breadboard again when Larry caught my forearm from behind. "Wait one, Cowboy. We'll need him at some point in the near future. Let's see if Gates is with us on this."

By now I couldn't have cared less. If I still had some juvenile ideas about women, it was nobody's concern but mine. And I was tired of being ridden about it, especially by Gates. "He's all yours, Cap. I'm going to the latrine." As I turned away, Keener and Bishop took another quick two-step backward, this time to make way for me.

Also a good idea.

Cooling down half way to the trench, I became aware that my right hand still gripped the breadboard by its handle, like a meat cleaver, and I tossed it in the general direction of the palapa.

When I returned to the palapa, I fished my mess kit from the bottom of the tank. Gates was moaning, stretched out in Larry's hammock, and Rubio was pouring cool water into his red eyes. There was a large bump over his left eyebrow and another at his right temple.

Jack Bennett and Eddy Rush trudged up from the beach, late for lunch. "What? Why didn't someone call us? And what's the matter with Gates?" Eddy asked, filling his tray with the last of the shrimp.

"No way would you believe it," Keener said, laughing.

"That's right," Nelson added. "Don't let Donlin's beanpole build and poker chip glasses fool you. He has a black belt in bread board." There were chuckles around the shade. Even Rubio laughed, spilling water across his patient's bare chest. Gates, apparently feeling the humor was at his expense, tried to rise, but Rubio simply lifted the edge of the hammock, dumping Gates back into the pocket. He moaned again and put a hand to his forehead.

Was this what it meant to be a tiger? To be prepared to answer violence with violence? To meet mindless insult with mindless brutality? Maybe I was too tired and hot, out of my element and out of my mind.

No, this was exactly what being a tiger meant. Gates' constant, vicious hazing scarred everyone. His harangues, insults and bullying were endless. Fatigue, heat and harassment brought me to a point at which anger and violence were natural responses. Right, wrong, other options, and consequences were not even the faintest of considerations. Keener and Bishop had seen it in my eyes, had known what Larry Abbott knew; if I had struck that third blow, I would have killed Gates, and I moved up in the pecking order.

CHAPTER FIFTEEN

Which men go armed to seek . . .
Archibald McLeish

About fifteen hundred, Donahue walked toward the one remaining helicopter, the other two already specks on the northern horizon. He passed a small map case to Larry, exchanging a few words through puffs of smoke and shook hands. Later events disclosed this packet to be an updated radio code for our group.

Donahue took me aside and apologized for the time he thought I'd wasted looking for the barge in the recon photos. "Larry has our most recent set of photos," Donahue said. "Yesterday Dino Brugioni called me. He's head of the National Photographic Interpretation Center. They located the barge about three miles farther south than the southernmost photo in the envelope I gave you. It's anchored in a small bay, partly covered with rusty corrugated iron, thatch, potted palms and stacks of bananas, it looked like a wharf and warehouse from the air.

"A dozen fishing boats and canoes tied up to it made the impression very convincing. We only spotted it because someone followed procedure to the letter and compared the photo to one taken of the same area two months ago. We want to know why they're waiting, and patience is not my strong suit," he confessed. "We may have to send you men in there to find out."

Donahue, Larry and Rubio discussed the matter further and agreed that, in spite of Donahue's impatience, we would play a waiting game. If they wanted to take the barge through the locks, their last chance to modify or disassemble the significant components, it must be done soon, and Golfo de San Miguel held dozens of hiding places where they could do it.

Charted channels with lighted buoys marked the entrance to the gulf and pointed the way to a confusion of forest-shrouded waterways beyond. This was their best option, and after that, a run due north to the canal, probably with telltale valves and circuit panels taking a different route at a different time.

At this point, we believed we had the advantage. Inside the gulf, dozens of long, narrow bays and channels with water deep enough to float the barge extended far beyond the range of curious eyes except for a few small fishing boats. We waited at Base T, between the entrance to the gulf and most of those potential hiding places.

On the morning of the seventh day, we prepared to reconnoiter the first of five bays north of Base T. Like fingers of a withered, arthritic hand, they fanned out from northwest to northeast. Larry and Rubio decided to take a systematic approach and start with the largest inlet, and the one nearest the entrance, the Rio Congo.

Burdened with three fuel tanks and rocking to a light northwesterly swell, the plywood floor panels of the rafts groaned and creaked as their edges rubbed together. For the first time, we carried weapons. Racked horizontally on the starboard side of the console and under oiled canvas, they were out of sight but accessible.

The four *compañeros* left before first light in one aluminum boat. They were assigned to act as "*guias*" or scouts. It was their choice to carry no weapons or radios, relying instead on their fishing equipment and ragged clothing to convince any hostile eyes they were but humble local pescaderos. We would rendezvous four miles north of Isla Josefa.

I was still sleepy after helping repair the original patch on Gosling Four, falling into my hammock at zero-two-hundred hours. At zero-six-hundred, we apparently needed further confirmation that Captain Abbott could possibly be the worst cook in the western hemisphere.

After breakfast, I secured our gear and rations in Gosling Two and took full advantage of a brief period of idleness to sleep another twenty minutes, curled up in the bow of the boat, with our goddamned Swedish C-rations as my pillow.

Keener fired off the engine and swung our bow toward Gosling One, already a hundred yards out on Pollux Intercept. Ross Bishop and Rubio Williams raced past us, waving their radio receiver at Eddy and Larry. A minute later, still fumbling with his receiver, Larry stood up, bracing himself on the console, and made a circular motion with his right hand over his head. Assemble here.

The scheduled situation report on the ANGRC-9 delayed Rubio's departure. Mother Goose, our Panamanian station in La Palma, relayed coded information from a US Naval Intelligence monitoring station and it took a while to work out. There had been a short exchange of radio transmissions northeast of Base T, in Spanish but not Panamanian.

The transmitting groups called themselves "Angel One," "Saint" and "Sugar." One of the names seemed to have significance to Rubio. Triangulation with a team of land-based directional units placed the transmission twenty miles from Base T, close enough to put us on our guard. Who they were and what possible connection they had with the barge could only be a matter of a wild guess . . . or maybe not so wild. Now a sense of urgency and caution reshaped every aspect of our activities.

Rubio claimed the Angels were Cuban insurgents, their confirmed recent activities placed them in the highlands of Bolivia. The core of their unit had been trained by European mercenaries, mostly ex-Foreign Legionaries, under the noses of Batista's corrupt police and military.

The Angels became an elite force, specializing in advance support of Castro's revolutionaries. According to the reports of Cuban loyalist forces, their mission had been to win over local populations and the elimination of opposition, by any means necessary. They were an equivalent of our own Special Forces. Their reputation in combat was outstanding.

"Cap, there are only nine of us. How many of them?" Keener asked, wedging Gosling Two back into the nervous conversation. Gosling Four brought Bennett and Nelson up to our port side, curious about our delay.

"Hell if I know," Larry admitted. "Our guys counted three transmitters, not the men around them. If they came in from the Caribbean side, they'd have to cross dozens of banana and coffee plantations, the Darien Range, then wade chin deep in swamp to get where the Navy Intel boys say they are. Not damned likely. And the Navy says they're on the Cucunati River. If I had a project like that, I'd slip in by boat at night, over a period of weeks, and bring a small mountain of supplies. Unlike us, they wouldn't have the advantage of resupply by air. The bad news is, there could be hundreds of men waiting for the barge by this time."

"That would account for the barge's delays. Their security force and technicians were not in place," Rubio suggested. "They still intend to remove all the pieces that would give away the game, and send the rest through as a partially completed cracking plant, just like the one last February, with no evidence to the contrary."

"And the components they remove would be under guard until another arrangement for transporting them can be found," Larry agreed. "Donahue's guess was right. They'll be headed our way, but won't go to the south side of the bay. There's too much activity around La Palma, and the southern bays are too exposed and shallow, like sector eleven." Larry murmured, almost to himself.

"There is one," Keener offered, "but they would pass right by Base T. If the barge has a draft under six feet, they could make it in."

"Not likely they'd go for that," Larry replied. "And I'd bet our bar tab at Loro Azul they know we're here. Anyway, why settle for one bay on the south side, where they could easily get boxed in? I'd go for the north side with mazes of islands and open-ended channels with dozens of possible anchorages. And just as many hiding places for a security force."

"What about aerial recon?" I asked Larry. "They can't hide from that again. What can they gain if they know we're here and dismantle the plant anyway?"

"They'd be more worried about Panamanian gunboats boxing them in at this point. They can cover anything that can be seen from the air, besides they can't be boarded from an L-19," Larry answered.

"As for dismantling, they have a shot at finishing what they started," Rubio remarked. "They're betting we won't make a move without hard evidence to swing world opinion in favor of the US. That's why we need those photographs. The actual valves and control panels would be even better."

"We continue today's patrol exactly as planned," Larry ordered. "We'll run at our normal cruising speed in column, spaced at fifty yards. Donlin, I want a mag in your BAR, a round chambered, safety on, but out of sight. No radios. Hand signals only."

Larry's systematic approach to familiarize our group with the estuaries to the north seemed a good idea. And if local Indians could be contacted, they might provide information about strangers in their territory.

Rubio had called the Indians by the name Cucunati, but that actually referred to their locale, the watershed of the Cucunati River and its estuaries, one of the easternmost bays on the north side of the gulf. Two groups of indigenous people occupied this section of the Darien rain forest: the Emberas and Embera Chocos. In recent decades, their farming activities brought them out to other bays on the north side of Golfo de San Miguel, including the hillsides to the west of the Rio Congo.

Columns of smoke to the north confirmed Embera Chocos were clearing new fields. They lived by small-scale slash-and-burn agriculture and subsistence fishing and hunting. Nothing on record indicated they had ever been hostile, but they shied away from contact with outsiders. Occasional visits from the Catholic mission in La Palma during the dry season, along with medical aid from a variety of church and international humanitarian organizations kept their small population healthy.

* * * *

Adding the skegs to the rafts vastly improved performance. A little forward of center, they provided a much-needed lateral resistance, and a fulcrum to help the raft make tighter high-speed turns. So tight, in fact, hand lines had to be strung to give passengers an even chance of staying in the boat. The rafts' tendency to sideslip was reduced by two-thirds. A center hole in the skeg also relocated the aperture for the knotmeter impeller and placed the read-out in front of the helmsman where it belonged.

In addition, Eddy installed a combination light stanchion and flagstaff at the transom of each raft, flying the American flag over the Panamanian. On each side of the console, he placed a bright decal of the Pan-American Highway Corporation logo. Up forward, running lights, green to starboard and red to port, brought us up to regulation, all courtesy of Eddy Rush and Wilson Donahue, and Bennett, who did the wiring.

The gulf was as smooth as glass, reflecting streaks of clouds, vivid orange and lavender, fading remnants of dawn. We stayed on Pollux Intercept for eight miles, and turned northwest behind Isla Iguana, keeping well inshore to clear its reef. Altering course to north-northwest, toward the brushy pinnacles of Isla Josefa, we expected to meet the *compañeros* four miles beyond. Making our approach to Isla Josefa at low speed, we scanned the coast of the long, low peninsula that formed the northern side of the entrance to Golfo de San Miguel. We tried to carefully time this leg for high tide to avoid another grounding. We missed. The tide had turned an hour before we approached the rocky outcroppings and the depth sounders flashed bright, erratic, double and triple bounce signals.

Gosling One turned sharply to starboard, stirring up a track of black mud. We followed suit, but once in deep water, ran parallel with the coast again, and entered the Rio Congo's long and narrow bay. The *compañeros* were nowhere in sight.

The estuary was no more than half a mile across and lined with a mass of tangled mangroves at the water's edge, no taller than a man's head. Beyond, an uneven mix of towering hardwoods, dense groves of pines, and broken skeletons of a once grander forest promised a difficult passage to anyone traveling inland on foot. A scrub-covered ridge hunched its back behind the dense jungle to the west. To the east, we saw a mirror image of the woods toward the west stretching across distant slopes above the flood elevations.

Our rafts cut silvery, undulating, herringbone patterns across the brackish water. Faint whispers of our wash breaking in the exposed roots of ten thousand mangroves slipped along with us. At the far end of the estuary, a soft Caribbean wind slipped over the Darien slopes and spilled onto the gulf, spreading cat's paws on the mirror-like surface of the Rio Congo.

In these first stirrings of the morning breeze, the smell of wood smoke visited and departed. We edged the eastern side. The water broadened and the jungle thinned, revealing blazing slopes above the eastern shore. Sheets of pale, blue-gray smoke lazily climbed the sultry air.

In an unexpected break in the forest wall, a freshly built camp of ten low palapas stood on a gently sloping sand beach. Nearby, a trickle of fresh water flashed over a rock ledge into the salt-fouled water of the estuary. Among the narrow dugout canoes, we saw the *compañeros'* two aluminum boats. By the time we reached the camp, the only figures in sight were Roberto, Jorge, Pello and Juan.

The men of the camp tended the fires, clearing this season's secondary farm plots half a mile away. At our approach, the women had gathered the children and quickly, quietly disappeared into nearby woods, leaving cooking fires untended, fish still flapping in baskets, and laundry dropped at water's edge.

The four guides strode through the camp, dragging half a dozen poles to the beach. Twelve feet long, straight and debarked, they would be used to push the rafts over shallow water with the engines turned off and props raised to minimize draft. One was provided for each raft and both of the fishing boats.

After making a run as far up the bay as the barge could likely go, the *compañeros* had stopped at the village on their return trip. Jorge was Embera Choco and his ability to speak the language soon put the Indians at ease.

The *compañeros* learned this extended family group had hunted and fished its way out of the Cucunati a month earlier and had had no contact with anyone from home waters. An hour before we arrived at the village, they had shared rations and cigarettes with the clan's patriarch and made inquiries about strangers. Jorge said the old man, barefooted and shirtless, but wearing a brand new pair of Levi's, smiled a toothless smile, drew deeply on a Camel and blew a cloud of smoke. Jorge shrugged. "He said that we are the only strangers in his land."

CHAPTER SIXTEEN

Darwinian Man, though well behaved,
At best is only a monkey shaved.
William Schwenck Gilbert

"Yu, yu, yu, wuh, wuh, wuh, WUH, WUH, WUH, WUH, WUH, wuh, wuh, wuh, wuh, yooooouuuuueee, WUH, WUH, WUH!"

Nelson and I stormed out of our tent, squinting into almost total darkness, swearing we would kill the prankster who woke us at zero-four-hundred. "By God, there'd better be a reason!" Pete snarled.

The only lights in camp were the lantern at the *compañero's* tent to our left and the glare of a single bare electric light at the mess tent to our right. Three figures sat at table number one, their backs to us, facing Rubio and Larry, all pondering the intricate waterways on an operations chart.

"You've noticed we have company this morning," Rubio said, bemused, instantly repeating his remark in Spanish as we stumbled into the light.

Jorge, Pello and Juan turned their laughing faces toward us. Pello pointed to the nearest section of the forest, high in the trees. Jorge imitated our wake-up call and broke up in laughter. He spoke to Rubio, jerking his thumb at me.

"He asked if you recognized your mother's voice," Rubio translated, smiling.

"Yes, I did. She said she has warm feelings for you, Jorge," I jibed back.

Rubio translated, bringing a flurry of laughter from the *compañeros.* "Parrots, insects, toucans and tree frogs. Now we have a dozen black howler monkeys sounding reveille."

Nelson yawned and stretched. "Donlin, break out your BAR. We'll reset their alarm clock."

"Now, now," Rubio humorously cautioned. "They're house guests. Larry chased one off the palapa roof just before you guys came in. Brassy little bastards."

"Not so little," Larry added with a laugh. "Not if you measure him by his voice." Another long string of barks and shrieks echoed out of the forest.

Eddy appeared with a tray of cups and a stainless pitcher of coffee. "Two more cups, Guys?"

Yu, yu, yu YU, WUH, WUH, WUH, WUH,yiiieeeeoooou! Ooo! Ooo! Ooo! The silhouettes of the howlers crowded the nearest branches, curious about the aroma of coffee and our activities.

The *compañeros* smiled at Nelson and me and stirred several spoonfuls of sugar into their coffee. Juan threw in two more for good measure. "They're scouting again, this time farther to the east," Larry informed us, "all the way to the Cucunati." He didn't like our team fragmented but he thought it necessary. The *guias* were to look for signs of Angels and any conditions or hazards not indicated on the charts. Or anything that looked liked preparations for the barge; excavations, clearings, dredging, or new navigation markers.

"When do we go out?" I asked him.

"We don't. Donahue will be here by ten-hundred hours."

Gates entered the tent from the direction of the latrine. He must have been right under the monkeys. Muttering and cursing, he glared at us. He was also annoyed at having his sleep cut short, but Gates didn't seem to focus his anger. Mad is mad and everybody gets an equal share. He fell into his hammock, turned away from the glare of the bulb over the table, and was soon snoring.

Roberto's voice rang out in rapid fire Spanish. "Breakfast," Rubio translated. He rolled up the chart and handed it to Pello. "Eggs, bacon, fried bananas, a sweet cornmeal mush, Donald Duck orange juice and more coffee. Or you can wait for Larry to whip up something."

"We'll take our chances with Roberto," Nelson said. "No hard feelings, Cap?"

Feigning a near mortal injury to his pride in culinary achievements, Larry whined, "If that's the way you feel about it, I'll never cook for you again."

Nelson laughed and shot me a thumbs-up. The pungent aroma of fried bananas spilled over the chest-high wall of ration boxes that divided the kitchen area from operations. Picking up stainless trays, the others paraded past the camp stove.

The morning coffee was stronger than usual and the jolt of caffeine nullified my hunger, at least for the moment. I stepped outside the tent and leaned against a corner post of the palapa. To the east, thin gray clouds half-heartedly attempted to suppress an irresistible dawning of another white-hot day. For now, the air was still and almost cool. A pair of black fins sliced through the water to my left, barely fifteen feet out.

The wisps of clouds turned pink and orange then faded away. I could see black silhouettes in the trees, some nibbling on leaves and bark, some exploring the limits of the branches, using their tails as safety lines seventy feet above the ground. Satisfied with the dawn they had barked into existence, the monkeys drew the sun higher with still more shrieks and barks.

I joined the others at breakfast. Rubio talked quietly with the *compañeros* and walked them to their boat. As we cleared away the table, Rubio returned and sat to finish his coffee. "They don't like Swedish C-rations any more than we do," he said, smiling.

"They're better than starving," Eddy said, "but only just."

We finished checking air pressure in Gosling Four's patched air chamber, sometime around 09:30, and turned toward the chatter of distant rotor blades. Very low, a single chopper approached on the correct bearing. At the center of the sand spit, beyond the compañero's tent, the H-40 lightly kissed the tops of the salt grass and spun one hundred eighty degrees to face the sea. The engine sighed and the rotor blades fluttered to a stop. Donahue bounded out, his face stubbled and pale with dark circles under his eyes again, and rushed to the mess tent.

Rubio handed him a mug of coffee and brought him to number one table. Ignoring all pleasantries, Donahue began. "I didn't think the news could wait. We know they're monitoring our transmissions, so the radio is out for this intel report." He took a deep draw of coffee and settled back in the folding chair. "So far, we've read everything right. The barge is located and the original tug has turned up at Punta Arenas in Costa Rica, undergoing repairs to its prop and rudder bearings. There must have been some serious miscalculations in slipping the barge in shallow water down coast. Day before yesterday, another ocean-going tug made a canal transit from Puerto Rico and went straight to sea, without a tow, and turned south. We think he's going after the barge."

"He could be going after a freighter broken down in the sea lanes." Larry offered.

"We checked. No assistance requested by anyone. It cost a fortune to run diesels on a sea-going tug. He's not just cruising. Furthermore, our Navy Intelligence people have heard more chatter between Angels, Saint and Sugar. They're not in the same place they were two days ago. Angels have not moved at all." Donahue asked for water and fumbled in his shirt pocket for a bottle of pills.

Rubio, showing unusual signs of impatience, in a tone just short of a demand, asked, "Where are they now? Any idea how many?"

Donahue chased the pills with several gulps of Donald Duck orange juice, and contorted his face, at first enraged we would give him a drink so nasty, fading to apologetic that he had provided no better for us. "They're eight miles north-northeast, apparently settled in, but we have no idea how many."

Eddy and I stared at Donahue, then we read the thoughts on each other's faces. We could be face-to-face with Saint and Sugar by raft in a half-hour run around the bulging end of the peninsula. That's too goddamned close!

"I realize I may have gotten you boys in over your head. Don't forget we have options. At this point, I will ask you to work only as scouts. You might be outnumbered and wouldn't know until it's too late.

"And this brings me to my next concern," Donahue sighed. "Loomer and his photographers will be here soon. You wouldn't believe what it takes to move these guys. Things could start happening fast and it would be better if they could be separated from all their distractions. They like to play tennis in the morning, cards in the afternoon, and drink in the evenings. Keep an eye on them, and don't expose them to anything out here they can't handle. They are tennis club types and a bloody nose would upset them. If they get upset, their very influential friends in D.C. would get pissed at me."

Larry gestured to Rubio to relax, he would draw out of Donahue what they needed to know. "How soon do you expect the barge to move? Do your people still think they'll take cover here in the gulf or make a dash for the canal?"

Donahue looked Larry in the eyes, then Rubio. "I don't have a crystal ball. If the only players on the field were the barge and tug, then I'd say they'll run for the ditch. But we're almost certain the Angels are part of the game. I haven't been able to convince all the analysts, but I'll tell you with as much certainty as I have about anything; the barge is coming in and it intends to disappear in the swamp to the north, with the Angels putting a tight ring of security around it.

"I've been thinking about jumping your men again," Donahue continued. "Before they reach the Angels, while everything is still intact, you cut the tow line and let the barge ground on the mud flats. We're sure the tug sets five or six feet deeper than the barge, which could make it difficult for them to retrieve the barge if it grounds out in the right place. Put Loomer's men aboard with fake salvage papers, take the photos and get them out before the tug can secure another towline. If the photos confirm what we expect, Panamanian forces take over from there."

"We've been over this before," Larry groaned. "You're asking us to jump onto a barge, probably at night, traveling at ten or fifteen knots. Let's suppose we make it, unlikely as that is. What if Angels are already on board? What if we cut the towline and it doesn't ground? The tug could have the towmaster aboard in ten minutes. Sure, we could kill him.

Then the photos confirm it's a refinery, assuming we can get Loomer's crew aboard without an elevator."

"I'm sorry, Larry, that's the best idea I have. You have the latitude to do whatever you think you can pull off as long as you maintain canal neutrality and don't put Loomer's bunch in a hot situation. What do you have in mind?" Donahue held out his cup for a refill.

Larry shrugged and said, "Wing it. We won't be any worse off than we are now. If an opportunity arises, we jump on it. At least we can do recon."

I was happy to hear there would be no jump into water. If the jump gear is consistent with everything else, except the Swedish field rations, an amazing paradox would be perpetuated: intercepting ICBM technology with WWII surplus.

As far as 'other options' went, no one would talk to Donahue about it, but we had our reservations. I held the job slot of someone who had been captured or killed at the Bay of Pigs invasion barely two months earlier. If they couldn't get air support for their operation, what could we really count on?

"When is the earliest they could enter Golfo de San Miguel?" Larry asked.

Donahue half smiled, half grimaced, annoyed that the situation had gotten so far out of control. "Right now," he said, looking in Larry's stunned face. "But . . . . only if they decide to run in daylight, which I doubt. Running under cover of darkness, they could be here tomorrow night, more likely day after tomorrow."

CHAPTER SEVENTEEN

By breaking through the foul and ugly Mists
Of vapors that did seem to strangle him . . .
Shakespeare

By the time Donahue left, we felt anxious and frustrated.
We had hoped for a few more days to familiarize ourselves
with the gulf and now we had only one, maybe two days.
Our *compañeros* were out of reach and the radios they should
have had were in the com tent.

They refused to carry radios because it would give
them away if stopped by hostiles. They were probably right.
The Swedish rations could be accounted for as salvaged or
bartered goods. But American military radios would not be
so easy to explain. Besides, they expected to be back before
midnight. But what if they encountered the barge? There
was no contingency plan. Only their own intelligence and
initiative would tell them to follow the barge. And without
a radio, if they encountered the tug and barge, it could be
six or seven hours before we would know.

To make things worse, we already knew we would make
a night run of our own before midnight. That would mean

we wouldn't know what they found or didn't find for twenty-four hours if Larry left instructions to risk radio coms, and thirty-six hours if he didn't.

In the meantime, we prepared to make a run to the Rio Sucio, which lies between the Rio Congo and the two main channels of the broad and sluggish Cucunati estuary now being scouted by the *compañeros.* We gave all our weapons a protective glaze of heavy oil and stowed them in the rafts. Fuel cans were filled, rations packed and batteries checked.

In the heat of the afternoon we assembled in the mess tent with our plotting boards and charts for a last-minute briefing. Cold bottles of Monte Carlo, a gift from Donahue, weighted down the corners of a collage made from aerial photos. The collection of marginless, glossy black and whites detailed the northern half of Golfo de San Miguel.

Eddy was first to speak. "Take a good look at the notation at the edge of our nav charts."

"The notation that says US Coast and Geodetic Survey?" Nelson asked.

"No, at the top right hand corner," Eddy pointed out.

"It says that the soundings are referenced to the mean low low water. That means we should look at the charts differently. At the entrance to the Cucunati, the depth is only one fathom at mean low water. That's six feet at low tide, and the tug and barge couldn't get through. But at high tide, that same stretch of water could be over forty feet deep. The tug could secure the barge in an area when the tide is on the flood, drop the towline, and get out. They would have at least a ten hour window to disassemble components and be ready to get out on the next high tide. Plenty of time."

"But why would they want to stick the barge up on the mud knowing that only a few hours each day can provide enough water to float it?" Bishop asked.

"For the job they have to do, it doesn't matter if the barge is afloat or bottomed out on the mud," Larry said. "Disassembling the critical elements can be done either way. But the farther up the estuary, the less likely they are to be disturbed by a Panamanian patrol boat. There's no way to hide the barge from aerial recon but they can cover components so they can't be seen from the air. We're guessing they've decided to give up on secrecy and settle for security. If it becomes necessary, they'll invent some kind of navigational problem or structural failure, something that would explain their not being in the approaches to the canal, something that would explain why they've illegally encroached into Panamanian waters. And failing that, somewhere in that jungle are fifty or sixty men with nothing to do except make sure they are not disturbed."

"Lions and tigers and bears! Oh, my!" Nelson gushed in a perfect Judy Garland.

When the chuckling faded, Larry continued. "We don't pick a fight, we pick a position, a photographic vantage point. If we can't do that, we call Gander and he sends down the Marine meat grinders." Apparently, Donahue still had two Force-Recon companies on stand-by.

We made the run to Rio Sucio at twenty knots over glassy water the color of creamed coffee. Gosling One trailed in the diamond formation with Gosling Two at point, flanked by Goslings Three and Four. Weapons were not visible but this was a hot patrol formation. Once in the narrow estuary, any problems would convert the diamond to a skirmish line, with the BAR at the center, covering the entire fire zone.

Fatigue shirts protected our backs on this scorching afternoon. Carelessly, I left mine open and at twenty knots, the lashing tail and stamped brass buttons flailed at my sides and thighs. At the end of our run on Pollux Intercept I'd had enough. Turning my back to the bow, I buttoned the shirt as we wheeled onto a new course line to Rio Sucio. Beyond the transom, beneath the gray haze to the west, I watched the brilliant glow of surf exploding over the mud flats off Punta Brava, just outside Golfo de San Miguel. Salt spray caught the sun like a fragment of white opalescent glass. Violent sea conditions filled the air with such light, and I was grateful for the calm in our corner of the gulf.

Rio Sucio was unproductive. We never went farther than midway up the estuary. The bottom was ideally flat but we could see that broad bands of deep mud would make reaching and boarding the barge very difficult.

"Unlikely," Bishop suggested, "unless they intend to disassemble here and transfer parts to other vessels out in the bay when they run for the canal."

"You mean like those little shrimp boats we passed? Not likely. They could get caught with the gauges and controls they want to secret away," Larry argued. "No, the parts will take a different route, or the same route at a different time and on a different boat, maybe one of those Russian trawlers. We have to get in before anything is removed."

Straight and open to view from deep water, the outer end of Rio Sucio's bay was an unlikely choice. There was no sign of Saint or Sugar, although the mid-point of the estuary was within two miles of their reported transmitting location.

A pair of roughly built fishing boats hauled in small shrimp nets on the break of the flats as we resumed our diamond formation, and set our course back to Pollux Intercept. In the fading glow at the western rim of the world, the lights of a dozen more such craft blinked on randomly across the open waters of the bay.

Two miles from Base T, skimming between the ink-black sea and the star-spattered sky, the diamond formation broke apart, forming a line with Eddy and Larry in Gosling One leading the way. We hit the range on the nose, picking out the lights through clear air. An offshore breeze carried an odd smell, petrochemical and sharp. It grew stronger and absolutely lung searing by the time we stepped on the beach.

The *compañeros* met us at the beach and helped us haul up the rafts. They appeared agitated and angry, all four men trying to speak at once and pointing toward the mess tent. Their eyes watered and they spat and wiped their noses. "Ayeiii, .. su hombre es loco!" was about all I could make out.

Rubio settled on Pello to give an account. He had a black eye and a split, swollen lip but managed to relate an encounter with Gates who became bored with radio watch and took advantage of his entrusted position.

The *compañeros* arrived at camp only half an hour ahead of us, gagged their way through a choking cloud, and caught Gates pilfering their shelter, apparently looking for cigarettes. He had torn open Pello's bag just as the *guias* entered the tent. "Gates was a terror to behold," Rubio translated. "His eyes were wide and weepy, his nose ran and he coughed and drooled. Gates, enraged at the objections to his pilfering, scattered the contents of a canvas bag and attacked Pello. Juan, Roberto and Jorge deflected Gates' onslaught and beat him with clubs and a camp stool until he retreated to the mess tent."

At the sound of a long string of coughing, we turned toward the mess tent to see a hulking figure silhouetted by the glare of the single bare bulb.

The spirituous and acidic air was barely breathable. We were distracted from Gates by a fluttering noise at our feet. The ground under the lanterns by the *compañero's* tent and the one at the beach were covered with the large gray-green moths that usually darted at the camp lights. There were no moths circling the light in the mess tent. The birds that usually roosted in the shrubs behind the mess tent were gone and the hundreds of tree frogs were completely silent.

The entire camp had been sprayed with the dreaded insecticide.

Gates trudged toward us, stripped down to swim trunks, his Aunt Jemima bandanna and sandals. His shoulders slumped, head bowed low and to one side. At first, I thought he showed the submissive posture of a favorite dog caught killing chickens. When he stood within the loom of the lantern we could see his right eye was black and swollen shut, and he favored a shoulder with massive bruises. His upper lip and chin were stained with blood. Scrapes and lumps covered his head, shoulders and back. Grotesque red blotches and streaks compounded those injuries.

Most of his exposed skin had been drenched with the vile mist. "Get back up to the mess tent," Larry ordered. "We have to get you cleaned up. Those are chemical burns. Bishop, fill a bucket with soapy water and break out the number two med pack. And just for the record, Pello and Juan don't smoke."

Nelson took Pello by the arm and led him to the mess tent for a little patching up, too. "Any radio traffic?" Larry asked Gates.

Gates slumped in a folding chair beside table one, with Pello on the other side. "I sent our scheduled sit rep on time, jes' like ya' wrote it." Gates murmured with his head tilted back while Bishop swabbed at several cuts on his cheek. "Later, got two calls from Gander in code. The cabinet is locked or I'd have decoded for you. He made me repeat what he spelled out. Only, *ouch,* gave me four word sets. Mass-aspirin, piano-Grumpy, onion-nylon, and front-zinc."

Five of us began unloading the rafts. Captain Abbott worked to decode the message and Rubio devised a schedule for tomorrow's run. Medicated, Gates fell into an uneasy sleep in Larry's hammock. Larry later complained that there was a better breeze in his corner of the tent, and he spent the night sweltering in Gates' hammock which was slung on the wrong side of the wall of rations and supplies.

Eddy Rush disappeared ten minutes later. I sat comfortably on a camp stool behind the generator, on assigned guard duty, an ammo belt around my waist and the BAR leveled across the whining generator's panel. In the glow of the camp lantern, the four figures at the rafts complained about managing all the gear and weapons while everyone else sacked out early, except Jimmy Donlin, of course.

Two hours later, Rubio took my place and a dark figure left the *compañero's* tent. Eddy stepped into the light, yawned and stumbled to the landing site to check the rafts. We met in the mess tent and sipped the dregs of the day's coffee. "We have guests tomorrow," Eddy whispered into his coffee cup. "That's what Larry got from the code. Loomer's bunch, by boat, fourteen hundred hours."

CHAPTER EIGHTEEN

... the king of artists would be the photographer.
James McNeill Whistler

Dr. Loomer and four of his team of photo technicians arrived by a first-class charter vessel, a converted pilot boat trimmed out in high-gloss white paint and a lot of extra varnished teak and polished chrome. We weren't happy to see them at fourteen hundred, the hottest part of the day. The mud flats prevented their deep draft boat from approaching any closer than two hundred yards. We launched the rafts and ferried them in, along with their technical equipment and a small mountain of personal gear. It was a hot, tedious and exasperating two-hour labor.

There should have been seven old geezers, but the oldest had developed a serious gall bladder problem. A casual assessment of their red noses suggested that a liver problem was more likely. Another team member suffered a debilitating lapse of health somehow vaguely associated with one of their hotel's cocktail waitresses. Both were enjoying drinks on a flight to D.C.

A third member nearly made the next plane when he fell into a burst of unintelligible hysteria over how his equipment was being handled, first by the charter boat crew, then by us.

"Careful, careful! There are lenses in there worth more than your annual salary," a nervous newcomer shouted. Bishop lifted an aluminum trunk the size of a footlocker from the raft.

It wasn't heavy but the mud made for unsteady footing. "What are you doing?" the photographer shouted. Bishop set the protective case on the beach as carefully as a newborn babe. Dr. Roche exploded! Ranting and screaming, he rushed at Bishop. "You idiot! You clumsy oaf!" he shouted and slugged Bishop in the face.

Bishop backhanded him, knocking him on his ass in the mud. Blood trickling from his nose brought threats of criminal charges and lawsuits.

Bald and heavily freckled, Dr. Roche turned red, then purple, as he raged at a safe distance from Bishop. Dr. Loomer and Mr. Nash tried to calm him down. "You can't go around hitting people and not expect a reaction," Dr. Loomer cautioned. Dr. Roche demonstrated highly developed skills at sulking.

Dr. Loomer finally resolved the issue with an undisclosed argument presented to Dr. Roche in private.

Dr. Roche's friend, Mr. Woods, made it a point to let us know our bullying wouldn't work with him. He had dealt with our sort before and had friends in the US Attorney General's office, just in case we gave a damn.

The *compañeros* put up a tent for our guests. We would be cooks and dish washers, as our schedules permitted. But that wasn't enough; they expected us to be their porters and valets. "Our tent isn't right," Mr. Collins protested. "We want to be farther away from that horrible smell."

They wanted their tent at the end of the peninsula, by the little sand beach the tidal rips swept so clean. We couldn't convince them that at high tide, sharks would be swimming under their cots.

"Under their cots, hell!" Eddy laughed. "Over their cots . . . over their tent poles at extreme high tide!"

At first, we thought we were dealing with just a simple misunderstanding, but as the evening progressed, we realized their perception of the mission, their assignment, and our team was comically distorted.

They complained that we had been here for days but had not made the camp habitable. The sanitation facilities were barbaric, they shrieked. Why are the sides of the tent tied up? Where are the showers? No bar? What about laundry services? Is there an infirmary?

Half an hour after an excellent fish dinner, caught and cooked by the *compañeros,* Rubio Williams escorted Mr. Collins to his tent with a very persuasive arm lock. He refused to accept that his bath, in his portable Abercrombie and Fitch canvas bathtub, had used up a third of our fresh water supply.

An hour after sunset, by the light of a kerosene lantern in the newcomer's tent, Rubio explained that we shower when it rains, or we take field baths, caused an outrage among the duffers. Dr. Donald Loomer, a retired naval officer, fully understood the predicament.

"You've grossly . . . er . . . misrepresented this contract, Donny." Woods shouted, waving an accusing finger at Dr. Loomer. "No one should have to endure this. I'll be registering . . . er . . . a complaint with Roger when . . . er . . . we get back."

"There most certainly was no misrepresentation," Dr. Loomer asserted. "I said you'd spend a week in a wilderness area. That didn't mean the grass tennis court at the Mont

Blanc. And here we are, in a wilderness, and you sound like you're ready to quit and go home." Donald Loomer stood up from his aluminum folding cot and turned to face all his charges, determined eyes locked on defiant eyes. "If you insist, you may go home early, tomorrow morning in fact, by air, first class. You could be in Alexandria by breakfast day after tomorrow. Also, you'll be retired before you land. Your offices, workshops and labs will be cleaned out and your cars will be in the motor pool awaiting re-issue by the time you're airborne. If you think I'm bluffing, try me."

"I'll leave you gentlemen to work this out for yourselves," Rubio offered, edging toward an exit.

"No, no. Please stay," Dr. Loomer pleaded. "Those who intend to honor their contract need briefing on camp routine. As you can see, my associates think they're roughing it if they have to use canned cream in their coffee."

Rubio outlined life at Base T and cautioned them away from swimming or venturing into the forest. Mr. Nash even knew a little about the bushmaster and fer-de-lance.

"The rafts are not available for recreational purposes. Stay out of the operations tent except at mess time. You'll be called for meals," Rubio concluded.

"What are your credentials, sir, that place you in a position to give us orders?" Mr. Collins demanded. "We operate under a direct executive authority, and expect associated privileges. We don't take orders, we give them." The tone was insulting and rebellious, possibly a touch racist, and echoed by all but Dr. Loomer.

"Yes, I know about your contract and who signed it," Rubio replied, subduing his impulse to remove Collins' head. "Our team is part of that same contract, bearing the same signatures. We are to locate the barge and take you to it, avoiding or suppressing hostile resistance. I suppose that makes us your bodyguards and chauffeurs, but we are not your cooks, bartenders, barbers, valets or housekeepers."

"I was told there are four, er, er, Panamanians working here. Surely, they can assume some of these..er..camp duties?" Mr. Woods insisted in a slow and gruff stammer through a thin, neatly trimmed white mustache.

"They have contributed as much to our comfort and well-being as is required of them. The remainder of their time is reserved for operations. They don't do laundry, make beds or cut hair. One more thing. When we unloaded your gear, I detected a distinctive clink of bottles. As of now, everybody is on the wagon until we're finished with the mission. Goodnight, gentlemen."

Chalk it up to Argentine speech affectations. Most people would have mislabeled Rubio's tone as friendly, if a bit condescending, but for those who'd known him a while, it was as friendly as the hum of a diamondback. It meant, "Comply or else! This conversation is over!"

Rubio faded into the darkness, striding toward the mess tent. Dr. Roche's voice defiantly boomed, "Drinks are on me, boys!" In less than a minute, and without a sound, Rubio re-entered the tent from the opposite side, tore a fifth of gin from Dr. Roche's hand and poured it over his feet, soaking his velvet house slippers. Fighting off a panicked, fumbling resistance, he repeated the foot-soaking with another bottle of Beefeater's from Dr. Roche's footlocker.

Dr. Roche's face turned scarlet. "Who the hell do you think you are? You won't be able to get a job as a fucking bellboy," he screamed.

Rubio was normally the voice of reason and a model of composure. Yet, faster than the eye could follow, he snatched up Bernie Roche by the lapels of his monogrammed silk lounging pajamas with such force they were both carried into the group gathered behind Roche, their glasses still extended. Ice cubes scattered across the uneven sandy floor. "Okay, okay, okay!" Roche shouted, covering his face with crossed forearms.

"I'll tell you who I am, you little prick!" Rubio roared in Roche's face. "I'm the cannibal who'll have his fork in your neck every time you break step, every time you slow us down or question an order. I'm here to make sure you do your job, and if you don't, I'll send you home with your teeth in your pocket!"

"Excuse me, Mr. Williams, I won't take long," Dr. Loomer interrupted. "Bernie, Mr. Donahue assures me that these men are experts at what they do, also. You should try very hard not to piss them off. Now, do you wish to be on that plane tomorrow?"

With considerable effort, wide-eyed Bernie Roche pushed his chin over Rubio's fist that still gripped his lapels, and pleaded with Dr. Loomer. "Donny, you've known me for eight years. I'm no sluggard. Of course, I'll do my job, but I won't put up with this shit from . . . . Uuunnnnngh!"

Rubio lifted him a little higher. "All right," Bernie Roche conceded. "I..we..will stay out of their way, Donny, if they stay out of ours."

"That'll work for now. Tend to your equipment and be ready to catch a bus on five minutes notice," Rubio dropped Roche back on his feet and turned his attention to a shout from the beach. First call to assemble at the rafts. "I hope you like Swedish food," he said with an odd grin, and jogged for the beach.

"Everyone here's a fucking tough guy," Roche sneered, straightening his royal blue silk pajamas.

Donahue left a folder of papers for Larry and a page from a legal note pad. The yellow sheet gave Larry complete control over operations. The packet outlined a brief contingency report to someone in Virginia, the name blackened out.

It listed a half dozen "best guesses" on where and when the barge would make an appearance. Unfortunately, they were based on old, faulty and incomplete information. The analysts favored the Perlas Archipelago as the most likely stopover. With joint American and Panamanian naval exercises, four resorts, logging operations, fishing and smuggling, the barge could just as easily hide at the yacht club at Balboa. But we were here, giving us an advantage over the analysts and Donahue recognized that. Trusting in Larry's judgment, Donahue stuck his neck a long way out.

Scrawled in red ink, in a labored script that failed to disguise his illness and fatigue, Donahue wrote . . ." C-130 standing by, chutes on board." I would have bet a hundred dollars of my own money the parachutes would be antique, solid panel, gut wrenching T-7s, more WWII surplus. That would be consistent with the theme of this party.

Donahue's outlined plan with all nine of us jumping on the barge and cutting the towline failed to answer several significant concerns. Who brings in the photographers? How do we get off the barge? What if the Angels were already aboard? Obviously, the inflatables still provided the best and most adaptable options.

The last sheet in the packet was a new page for the operations codebook. "Appendix Three: Extraction Methods, Codes and Frequencies. Op. Goose, 26-04, 22 June 1961." The black, three ring binder went back into the cabinet with a thermite grenade taped on top.

CHAPTER NINETEEN

And there the snake throws her enameled skin,
Shakespeare

"No," Larry barked emphatically. "You're in until the job's over. If you don't want radio watch, take Rubio's place in the boat."

"I don't want nothin' to do with them boats," Gates complained. "I heard Loomer said there's a plane for any of them photographers that want out. Put me on it. I ain't doing no good. Eddy Rush ain't got a sense of humor. Donlin can't take a joke and them Pans hate all of us. They'll take any excuse to beat the hell out of anybody. And you ain't done nothing about any of it. I've had enough and you don't need me. Pay me a half share of my contract and get me on that plane."

"I'm betting I will need you before this job is over," Larry said. "You're in for the whole ride, Cowboy. Now, choose radio watch or a boat." He waited for a reply.

Gates hung his head and kicked a lump of wet sand onto the spray hood of Gosling One. "You don't understand,

Larry. Nobody likes me. These guys think the best thing they can do is ignore me. It's been like that ever since we been down here. They either ignore me or pick a fight and I'm tired of it. I just want to go home." At last, he turned back to Larry and looked at him with his one good eye, still not giving the answer Larry wanted.

"Boats it is," Larry snapped. "Rubio, how'd you like a night off?"

"No, no. I'll take radio. But tell them Pans to leave me alone," Gates blurted.

"The *compañeros* are already gone. You'll be all alone for the whole night," Larry assured him. "Except for the photographers. Just stay out of other people's gear and you'll be all right," Larry said, checking his watch; twenty-one hundred.

Gosling One sighed a hollow, echoing whoosh as Eddy lifted the bow and slipped the raft afloat. He turned his cap around and tumbled backward over the spray hood. "I have to go, Gates," Larry insisted, backing toward Eddy and the raft. "Maybe you should stop riding people. They ignore you because that's better than talking to you and getting an earful of threats and insults. If you don't like getting kicked around, then lay off them."

"I ain't done nothing to nobody. Them other guys started it. I was defend . . . ."

"Bullshit! I have to go, Gates. You're staying and you've got radio watch. If it makes you feel any better, your chances of ever working on one of my teams again is thinner than an Irish condom," Larry shouted, swinging a leg into the raft.

Pollux Intercept measured eight nautical miles from our camp to the line of demarcation, a line drawn from the light at Islota Batatilla on the north side of the entrance to the light at Punta Patino on the south side. Everything east of that line was inside the gulf, our primary hunting ground.

We assembled at the intersection of the demarcation line and Pollux Intercept, struggling against the rolling ground swells to keep the rafts together long enough to pick up our radio schedules and four manila envelopes for each boat marked MONTE CARLO, BALBOA, ESTRELLA, and TIBURON.

The station assignments placed the four rafts on the line of demarcation, spaced roughly one mile apart, in deep water to avoid the surf and mud flats. The *compañeros* were assigned the passage from Islota Batatilla northeast to Isla Josefa. If the barge showed, it would have to pass within sight of one of our rafts or the *compañeros*, and this time, they carried radios.

Keener and I took up our assigned position at the south side of the entrance, designated Alpha Station, two miles northwest of Punta Patino. Beneath the heaving swells, the tide filled and nearly emptied the gulf twice a day, and its fierce currents could sweep away lost and insignificant flotsam like Keener and me. Contrary to the forces of nature, then, we were to stay put as best we could. A compass bearing to the light, an estimate of distance off and the depth sounder helped us maintain our position, give or take a hundred yards.

MmmmMMmmidnight brought millions of mosquitoes, and we slipped a little deeper into the gulf. ZzzzzZZzzero-one hundred hours, they buzzed, but abandoned us when we fired off the engine and returned to station. Their in-laws and cousins found us when we arrived back on position. We kept an hourly radio check. By zero-two hundred hours the mosquitoes had learned four-part harmony.

Seated at the console, I pondered whether or not to unbutton my fatigue shirt. Hot on the inside, mosquitoes on the outside. Stupefying heat and humidity and monotony engulfed us. Keener dozed under the spray hood, greasy with repellent.

Mosquitoes.

Snoring.

Zero three hundred radio check. The gravity of the watch was seriously tainted by boredom.

And heat.

And mosquitoes.

Eventually, the sun burned a hole through the eastern mountains and we gladly reassembled at the outer end of Pollux Intercept. After complaining about the sad parties Larry Abbott throws, we formed a line on course zero-five-three, Gosling Four in the lead. We followed at fifty yards, making fifteen knots. I took the helm for a while and broke line slightly to avoid the used Swedish C-rations Nelson surrendered, his face nearly dragging in the bow wave.

When we arrived, we found Base T in chaos. Inside the photographer's tent, Dr. Loomer shouted at Mr. Collins and tried to calm Mr. Woods. Mr. Nash and Dr. Roche were packing. Dense, gray smoke billowed from the mess tent.

Gates sat quietly in the com tent, signing off with Gander. He tilted his head oddly to see from his one good eye. The lids of his right eye were open now, showing the white to be horribly reddened. He busily added to a nearly filled yellow page. His forty-five automatic rested on the table beside the note pad.

Gosling One arrived last. Larry bounded out, leaving Eddy to unload and secure the raft to the mooring line. "Rubio, take my .45 and no matter what I say, don't give it back to me until noon." He rushed up the beach toward the communications tent. "Jimmy, take your BAR and be a sentry for the next hour." Larry shouted over his shoulder.

"I made coffee," Gates offered as Larry approached. Slumping into the camp chair behind him, I inserted a mag and jacked a round into the chamber and set the safety. Gates handed Larry the page of messages and holstered his side arm. "I think I'll turn in now. It's been a pisser of a night." There was a loud shriek from Hasselblad Hall.

"Not just yet, Cowboy. I want a report of what these old geezers have been up to. Start with that scream," Larry demanded.

"That? Woods' been snake bit," Gates stated flatly. "He don't like the latrine so he walked a little ways into the boonies. He was at his ease when something bit him on the left ankle. He saw it; 'bout four feet long and dark brown. He says he's in need of a medical evacuation. Then he got pissed at me 'cause I didn't take on over him. I didn't get excited 'cause I seen there ain't no fang marks so it ain't poison, but he won't believe me."

Nelson ran from the mess tent with a large stew pot streaming a trail of foul smoke and heaved it into the bay. "How do you like your oats?" he yelled at Bennett, laughing.

Larry stormed toward the photographer's tent. This would not be one of his best days in tact and diplomacy. "Get your ass out of bed, Woods. Get dressed, all of you. Damn it, Dr. Loomer, these pathetic old farts are your responsibility. Get 'em squared away or I'll do it for you. Nash, Roche! Don't bother packing. You're not going anywhere. Who's responsible for that stink in the mess tent?"

"Now, see here!" Mr. Collins shouted back at Larry. "Don't take that tone with us! We're not your Indian servants. If you'd been here taking care of your end of the contract, we would have had a pleasant breakfast, I'm sure. But you're late from your night fishing and we had to manage on our own. I had started breakfast when Fred ran into the tent screaming he'd been bitten by a large, venomous snake. I suppose I forgot I had something on the stove and . . ."

"Shut up! Go help clean up your mess. Roche, Nash. Is your equipment ready to use right now?" Larry demanded.

"Well, yes. I suppose it is, really." Mr. Nash answered timidly. "The telephoto lenses . . . ."

"Then go help unload the rafts and refuel. Woods, one more snivel out of you and . . . go help with the rafts," Larry ordered.

Rubio stepped briskly into the shade of the tent as Woods stood up and found himself looking into the face of the man who had told him to stay out of the forest. "I have better work for Mr. Woods," Rubio delivered in edged syllables. "Since you don't like our latrine, you gentlemen shall have one of your own."

Juan and Pello entered with two shovels and a pick for the hard layer just two feet down. "Thank you, gentlemen. Mr. Woods, you've been lucky. Out here, people can't survive on luck. They survive by functioning as part of a team and team members follow orders. For your protection and the protection of others in your team, you and Dr. Loomer are going to dig a latrine right here." At a signal from Rubio, the *compañeros* dropped the tools at their feet with thuds and clangs.

"You can't be serious! We're technicians, not day laborers," Dr. Loomer protested.

"Dr. Loomer, you're a team leader who can't lead because you don't enforce your orders. Mr. Woods, you are a dull old coot who nearly got himself killed because he doesn't color inside the lines. We need both of you here, and functional. Another bone-headed trip like this morning could change that. We'll find a way to get past this little hearing problem. Dig! Right here!"

"Here in the middle of the tent? Live in our own excrement?" Dr. Loomer objected.

"I'm flexible," Rubio proclaimed. "Measure from any tent pole, toward the west, step off twenty paces. Very little brush. Snakes don't like that because they can't take the sun. Make your trench waist deep, wide enough you can stand in it sideways and long enough to lay down in it, straightened out. Get it done by noon or you'll dig another one just like it. You can have all the water you want, but no food until the job's done."

An hour later, Rubio didn't know whether to laugh or cry at their fumbling ineptitude. "I don't normally get into natural history or physics when digging a latrine, but I will make this an exception." Rubio launched into the relationship of slopes and rain water run-off and how the excavated dirt should form a horseshoe, closed at the high end to divert rainwater, and how to lay a covering to prevent flooding out, things most Boy Scouts knew at twelve. Loomer and Woods seemed clueless.

Another half hour passed and the grating sound of the shovels had resumed after a rhythmic thumping of the pick.

Collins, Nash and Roche, fresh from refueling and scrubbing down the rafts, dragged into the mess tent, followed by Keener, Nelson and Bennett. Sweat saturated the clothes of all six men and Roche's bare, bald head displayed a serious sunburn. "Any breakfast yet?" Keener shouted over the wall of ration boxes.

Eddy Rush assured them that scrambled eggs, coffee, pancakes and sausages would be out in another five minutes.

The photographers continued to press an argument about how their pale green, lightweight wash-and-wear jumpsuits were superior to the rag-tag clothing worn by our survey team, further proof of how their seniority, intellectual powers, and influential friends and fashion sense qualified them to be running the whole operation. They were genuinely offended when we laughed in their faces. In our shared opinion, their color-coordinated wardrobe with souvenir Canal Zone patches qualified them to be nothing more than royal pains in our collective asses!

Larry stood up from table number two, the codebook open. "Christ! They've lost the fucking barge again," he growled, his words warped by frustration.

Gates, stretched out in Larry's hammock, lifted his head and asked where it was last seen. "Off Bahia Piña," Larry answered. "That's about thirty miles south of the entrance to the gulf. Maybe we'll get lucky tonight."

CHAPTER TWENTY

Out of the night that covers me,
Black as the Pit from pole to pole,
William Ernest Hendley

I didn't even mind KP. Bishop and I finished about fourteen hundred and trudged off to our tents a little before noon to make our usual preparations for the afternoon rains.

First, we placed our fatigue shirts and dirty swim trunks in a five-gallon bucket with soap flakes. In a smaller bucket, we dropped in toothbrushes, shampoo, a bar of soap and a wash cloth. After placing the bucket in the open near our respective tents, we rolled into our hammocks to nap. The photographers were puzzled beyond all explanation, but mimicked us anyway, except Woods and Loomer who still labored at their digging.

Finished at last, Woods and Loomer sat with their legs dangling over the edge of their new trench, eyeing each other with a seething hatred. Loomer hated Woods because the blisters on his hands were the result of Woods' stupid venture into the undergrowth. Woods hated Loomer because his blisters and his snake bite were the result of Loomer coercing him into taking this assignment in the first place.

With a vindictive bent, they managed to beat the noon deadline but were too exhausted to trek to the mess tent.

They were startled out of their mutual vexation when Larry stood at one end of the new latrine and Rubio at the other. They obviously intended to 'christen' it. Loomer and Woods scrambled unsteadily to their feet as Larry and Rubio urinated into their personal facility. This did not violate its intended use, but it was theirs, they made it and Larry and Rubio seemed unwelcome, vulgar interlopers.

"Four cups of coffee and a glass of OJ. I think I could fill this by myself, Rubio," Larry sighed.

"I know what you mean. Nice job, gentlemen," Rubio remarked, keeping his eyes on the business at hand. "In a day or two, you'll discover you're human, too. Now, strip and set up your buckets and laundry. Have breakfast and rest up."

Mr. Collins walked over from the mess tent with a pair of stainless trays filled with warm leftovers from breakfast. In the shade of their tent, Woods and Loomer ate like lumberjacks.

Half an hour later, Larry and Rubio supervised Woods at the final task of covering the trench with a few pieces of scrap timber and old tent fabric to keep out rainwater. Loomer wearily tapped the butt end of a pick handle on the ground until the head dropped, then placed the handle under his bunk. "Do you need that pick handle, Dr. Loomer?" Rubio asked.

"Yes, I do! I intend to brain anyone who disobeys or even hesitates to carry out any order I may give in the future," Loomer growled, displaying weeping blisters across his palms. Leadership through reason and cajoling was effective in this latitude up to a point. Loomer was past that point.

The rain came late, but it did come, by the bucket. We left our hammocks, stripped off bare-ass naked, and bounded into the cool, dense downpour, scrubbing first ourselves, then our laundry. Gates demonstrated ingenuity by using a large scrap of rusty corrugated iron sheeting as a catchment, filling his bucket three times faster than the others. Not to be outdone, Keener "dipped" two tent poles forming a spout off the front roof panel of our tent, filling our buckets even faster. Keener and Nelson tended the Lister bags, now numbering five. Out on the water, Eddy jumped from boat to boat, starting the outboards and turning on the pumps. By the time the rain passed, we were scrubbed, our laundry was done and the boats cleaned and emptied of rainwater.

The sultry air that trailed the rain left us napping fitfully, tossing and pulling at netting. Worry about the barge braided itself through dreams of food from Loro Azul's kitchen, Estrella, and life in a temperate zone. Tonight could be the night. It could also be another night like the last one: steamy, smothering clouds of mosquitoes and sweeping tidal currents.

Our late afternoon lunch was a sad surrender to vindictive and sadistic Swedish cooks, cooks who bore a spiteful grudge against taste buds and digestion. The photographers offered to cook supper. "We're running out of utensils," Nelson grumbled, annoyed at being chewed out for throwing the pot in the gulf instead of letting Collins spend hours scrubbing it clean. It was too hot to eat, anyway. The rafts were loaded with several days' rations and we considered ourselves on standby without anyone saying a word about it.

By twenty-one hundred, Larry and Rubio agreed that if the barge had not been sighted by now, it would wait for complete darkness to move and would not reach the gulf until after midnight.

"Time for Scandinavian sawdust and cardboard," Larry barked from the com-tent. "Weapons check in the operations tent in one hour,"

Woods and Nash became very agitated when they saw us oiling the weapons. Eddy's oversized gun case didn't raise any eyebrows, nor did the Garands. But when they saw Larry's .45 caliber grease gun and my BAR as we secured them in the rafts, they excitedly called the others. Collins, Woods, Nash and Roche loudly protested being involved in any activity that might include hostilities.

"Woods said you men go fishing at night. You don't need those for fish!" Nash protested.

So Woods was responsible! Apparently he only got every third or fourth word anyone said. He thought we really were a Pan-American Highway survey group, the decals on the rafts' consoles confirming the notion. And he was very confused about our night trips and weapons. But being a sociable type, he never hesitated to offer up guesses and wild speculations as facts. Loomer knew better, but the others would rather listen to Woods. He told much more interesting stories.

"Well, I ... er ... er ... I," Woods stammered, "I thought you gentlemen, I mean it was night and you were on the water so naturally I thought ... er ..."

Roche now understood exactly what was happening. He had listened to Loomer and knew we were not the surveyors and cartographers Woods assumed. "You don't have the barge yet, do you? Donny said we wouldn't even be brought down here until you had the barge. Fucking around here for days and .... you probably don't have a clue where it is, do you?" Roche grumbled. "But you still sent for us? You've really screwed up."

"Such an inconvenience for us all. It really pisses me off how the Russians and Cubans work to their own schedules without even consulting me," Larry growled back at Dr. Roche, countering self-righteous rage with sarcasm.

A ragged metallic scrape echoed from the compañeros ancient boats as they launched off the beach and headed toward the northwest. Clouds of oily exhaust drifted through the lantern light. The rumble of the battered Evenrudes overlapped Roche's criticism of Larry's leadership abilities.

"We don't need any of your sorry excuses!" Roche shouted at Larry above the noise of the *guias'* outboards. "Either you have the barge in your pocket or you don't. If you don't, then we shouldn't even be here!"

Bernie Roche was surprised to hear Dr. Loomer's voice so close behind him. "Get in the boat, Bernie. Now!" Roche started to protest but a sharp nudge in the pit of his stomach with a pick handle distracted him. A second grunt and a backward stumble to the edge of the lantern's light put him knee deep in water with Loomer and a three foot long pick handle still crowding him. "They'll benefit from your expertise, Bernie. Get in the damned boat!"

"Wait, Donny! Now wait! I just want to do my job.. OW!" A tap to the jaw tipped Roche against Gosling One.

"Welcome aboard, Dr. Roche!" Eddy laughed. "Let's go register an objection with the tug captain. He's probably a retired Russian naval officer and I'm sure he'll be almost as sympathetic to your complaints as we are."

Larry tossed a taped bundle of four envelopes into each inflatable and gave a nod to Eddy. Gates hauled on the mooring loop and all four Goslings swung their bows toward the buoy. Twenty yards from shore, the outboards were fired off and bowlines untied. "Donny! I didn't sign on for this! Goddamn you, Donny! Roger will catch an earful when I get back!" Roche, dabbing at a cut lip, trailed a weak chatter through the darkness, blending into the low rumble of our outboards.

"Swim for it, Dr. Roche," Eddy laughed.

"Don't even think about it," Larry countered, and Eddy, still laughing, eased the throttle forward and they slipped from my view.

The trip to our assigned station was slower because the water was rougher than the previous night. Anything over eight knots would have thrown us out of the boat. We confirmed our position by taking bearings on the lighted buoys and settled in for the night, hoping our quarry would show and save us from last night's mind-eroding monotony.

I had cut my wrist on one of the aluminum boats while loading gear ANPRC-10s for the *guias*. Rubio had convinced them they were necessary this trip. In applying insect repellent, the bandage was left uncoated. When we had been on station for ten minutes, the mosquitoes were so thick the bandage looked like a fur bracelet until I greased that up too.

Electrical displays slashed at the distant shoreline toward the southwest. Like a spider, the storm stalked northward on spindly legs of lightning. The still air was even hotter than the night before. I didn't care that Keener only wanted to sleep in the bow; I envied him for his ability to tear off Zs underway. He roused once, swinging his fists, when I took pity on him and anointed the soles of his bare feet, an area neglected in his first coat of bug bane.

Near the entrance to the gulf, we rode six-foot ground swells from the open sea and a chop on top of that. Keeping on station would be harder than last night, but monotony shouldn't be a problem.

The same breeze that carried the cloying smell of low tide on the mud flats brought clouds of winged demons. The insects from the nearby swamp remembered us from last night and invited friends.

Keener snored. I passed the time by constantly refreshing my repellent, taking compass bearings to keep on station, and doing the hourly radio check, leaving the ANPRC-10 on, set to the assigned frequency. After zero-one-hundred sit rep we should be able to catch calls Gates relayed from Base T if anything came up. He had orders to send one of six messages in code to Mother Goose if the barge is ever sighted and Larry would call him to say which message.

Sitting backward at the helm, with my back braced against the steering wheel and throtle, I endured being jerked around by the buffeting waves. Keener babbled in his sleep. At one point, he launched into a long diatribe in German. Ten minutes later he sang a children's song in French. Bishop once told me Keener spoke enough Greek to get himself fed, drunk and laid in whatever order he chose. When English came around again, he cursed his father, his stepmother, his draft board, General Motors and his ex-girl friend in Santa Fe, New Mexico, now married to a CPA.

What could you expect from a former French Legionnaire? Bishop had known Keener for six years and loved him like an older brother . . . when he's sober. "What can a Legionnaire do when he destroys even this last of all refuges for the disenfranchised and desperate," Bishop once asked. Why, sub-contract to the CIA, of course.

Keener was second generation Irish Catholic from Boston and never shared much about the origin of his particular skills, other than to say that he learned most of it in the Marines and the Legion. Larry once told me that Keener was on the top of his list for any contract he'd had in the last three years. His skills in languages were just a convenience. Unfortunately, Spanish was not one of them. Keener's real talents, Larry said, were something no one ever wanted to see up close.

The tide pushed us into the bay again, too close to the mud flats. I started the outboard and turned the bow back toward alpha station, quartering the crests, then slipping over the backs of the large, oncoming swells. When we were once more exactly between the distant light of the buoy at Islota Batatilla and the much closer light at Punta Patino, I turned off the engine and we dropped into the trough of a larger than usual swell.

"Zzzzz crackle . . . . lings, all Goslings, all Goslings. Zero-two-hundred, situation report, by the numbers. This is Gosling One on bravo station. Over."

"Gosling One, Gosling One, this is Gosling Two on alpha station. No activity. Over." I heard Rubio and Bishop report in, and two minutes later Bennett and Nelson.

Familiar routine draped over Gosling Two like a mosquito net. Keener coughed up a bug he'd snored down his throat. The raft quartered itself on each swell. I half dozed in the rhythmic motion, leaning into the swell on the up side, leaning back going down. Perspiration dripped down the back of my neck. It coursed out of my hair, trailed off my cheeks and down both sides of my neck, briefly pooled at the base of my throat and disappeared into the foul oblivion of my saturated fatigue shirt.

Keener snorted up up another bug.

Deeper into the gulf, beyond where the swells slammed into the shelf, the water was calmer and the lights of small fishing boats glided slowly through the black night. Outside the gulf, toward the Perlas, there was only a flat, unreferenced void. The islands were too far away, the line of rainsqualls too dense for lights on the islands to be visible, and the sea was far too rough for small fishing craft.

I tried to get comfortable again, leaned my back against the console and rested for a minute. I thought about dozing off when we fell down the backside of another big roller and bruised my shoulder blade. The same steep wave stuffed Keener into the bow like a frog in a little boy's pocket.

Struggling from under the spray hood, he sat up, rubbing his neck. "What the fuck'd you do?" he grumbled.

"Nothing," I said. "A swell dumped you like an eight ball. It's crowded in there with the tool kit, prop and rations, huh?"

"What time is it?" Keener asked, wiping away the beads of sweat that popped out through the insect repellent.

"Zero two-seventeen," I said. "You thirsty?"

"Yeah, and hungry. How would you like ... um ... notkott och potatis?" Keener asked.

"I'm not hungry, just thirsty . . . . but that one's not bad heated .. DAMN!" I shouted, and threw myself to the port side, straining my eyes against the blackness.

"What is it?" Keener asked excitedly, kicking the rations back under the spray hood.

"I'm not sure. A flash of lightening showed me something west-north-west, something big . . . moving . . . and it has square corners!" I shouted, pointing. Holding our breath, we waited for the next lightening flash. We dropped into the trough of another swell where nothing was visible except the streaked back of the wave bullying its way under us and into the gulf.

As we lifted, lightening flashed again. "Maybe my eyes are playing tricks . . . . there it is!"

The entire tug was visible in profile, this time by a flash of lightening behind us. It dragged a floating city block on a half-mile towline. Even the bright, glossy green stack on the tug was visible, with white bands and a company emblem:

the initials CD inside a circle. They ran at fifteen knots without a single light, not even inside the pilothouse.

The ten was already on and dialed in. Keener snatched up the mike and pressed the key. "Gosling One, Gosling One, this is Gosling Two. Over."

"Gosling Two, this is Gosling One. Affirmative. Radio silence! Out!"

The tug and tow raced toward the northeast. In a matter of minutes it would be well past bravo station. Looking at the chart, I estimated that they would miss bravo station, but charlie and delta stations, because of the changing position of the lightning displays, might not see these monsters until they're right on top of them. Why did Larry want radio silence? We waited.

At Delta station, Nelson entertained himself in the usual manner, hanging over Gosling Four's starboard bow, giving up a late-night snack. A deep throb of diesels and the rush of a gigantic bow wave alerted Bennett. "Nelson, get in the boat and hang on!" He fired off the engine, but before Nelson could drag himself inboard, the raft was swept up and he spilled out over the bow of the boat, into the warm, inky turbulence and into the path of the tug.

The bow wave lifted Gosling Four and threw it forward. The upturned bow refused to bury deep enough to trip. The raft flattened out, diagonal to the tug's bow wave, surfing down the face of the seven-foot wall of water. Nelson was pressed down, rolled over and over until the propeller blades, fortunately not yet in gear, struck him behind the knees and dragged him along.

At last, the bow wave muscled its way under Gosling Four and the raft dropped off the backside. Nelson varied his routine; he pulled himself over the stern and puked *into* the raft. Scrambling over the transom, he was safe, his only injuries a few bruises and a splinter picked up from the screw holes in the plywood transom where the knotmeter had been originally mounted. "Did you say something, Bennett?" he asked.

At alpha station, the passing seconds pounded an anxious cadence inside my head. Minutes dragged by. Five minutes. Ten. "All Goslings, all Goslings, all Goslings. Open the packet marked 'ESTRELLA.' Sit down Roche! Loomer can't . . . click . . . click, Gosling Three, relay to *guias*. Out!"

The *compañeros* were stationed two miles east of Isla Josefa and north of Isla Iguana, rocky mounds, which might block radio signals from Gosling One. Rubio, at delta station, was closer and at a better angle for radio contact.

Our packets were instructions based on four 'best-guess' scenarios Larry, Eddy and Rubio could construct. They told us what to do based on the speed, route and activity of the tug. Middle of the night, no running lights, headed for the north side of the gulf totaled all the real information we had. It was enough. 'Estrella' simply called for us to assemble at the middle of the entrance to the gulf at the intersection of the demarcation line and Pollux Intercept.

We skimmed over the water, running a rollicking course nearly parallel to the swells, taking roller-coaster leaps over the crests and diving into the troughs. Gosling Two barged its way diagonally across the face of the waves, and flung itself down the backs. Unlike the tug and barge, our running lights were on to avoid collision with other Goslings. By the time we reached the deeper water at the mid-channel, the height of the waves sweeping into the gulf diminished and their period increased. I cut the engine but left our lights on.

"Don't you hit me!" Roche shouted, the only sound above the rhythmic whispers of the waves. After a long silence, we heard a calmer voice arguing, "I didn't ask to be out here, Captain Abbott. The idea of retirement sounds better now than it did yesterday." Running lights blinked on a few yards off our port side. Dr. Roche sat with his back to us in the bow of Gosling One, his scowling face washed in the eerie green glow of the starboard running light.

"Not until we tie a bow on this project," Larry answered sternly. "Your options turned to shit when you set foot ashore at Base T," I knew the same was true of me, but unlike Roche, I had accepted the results of my choices.

Another set of lights appeared thirty yards beyond Gosling One, bow on, heading toward us. They nudged Gosling One and all three of us rafted up. Nelson cursed and wrung out his fatigue shirt. "The usual," Bennett offered, not even waiting for the question, and told of their encounter with the tug. "He still has biscuit in his hair. Then a huge bow wave from the tug roughed us up. I went surfing and Nelson went swimming"

"You were that close to the tug?" Larry asked excitedly. "Why didn't you call in?"

"I heard you tell Donlin to keep radio silence," Bennett reminded him. "I had just read instructions in the Estrella pack. I yelled at Nelson to sit upright, we're about to head for Pollux Intercept. I heard the tug but had no idea it was that close, then the bow wave hit us. We never actually saw the tug. It's darker than the inside of an undertaker's watch pocket out there."

"Nelson's lucky you found him. And no life jackets. Fuck the heat. We've got to start wearing them; tonight proves that," Larry ruminated. "How do you know it was the tug and not the barge?"

"I think they were turning, and a long tow cuts the corners," Bennett said. "At first I thought the barge would finish what the tug started, but we never felt more than a ripple from the barge. And I know we were near the tug by the vibration of the diesel engines and prop. You could feel them booming right through the raft. But I'm sure they didn't see us. We didn't have our lights on either, and the helmsman probably had his face in the radar hood and we'd make a pitiful blip. I doubt we'd have shown up on radar at all. The only thing that would have given a blip would be the metal in the outboards and that's so low it gets lost in wave scatter."

"They didn't see us, either," Bishop said, roughly sidling next to Bennett and Nelson. "But we sure got a good look at them! We ran along with the barge for almost a mile."

"It's going to be a challenge," Rubio said, pulling Gosling Three tighter into the cluster by Gosling Two's lifeline. "A twelve foot high steel wall with no visible way to board. We can manage with grappling hooks, but how are we going to get the Kodak Commandos up there?"

"We'll come up with something," Larry answered. "Crank 'em up, Cowboys! I need to be closer to Base T to raise Gates," Larry ordered. "We have messages for him to relay to Mother Goose and Gander."

CHAPTER TWENTY-ONE

Was it for this the wild geese spread
The gray wing upon every tide;
For this that all that blood was shed,
William Butler Yeats

Eddy shook me out of my stupor. What do I do now, coach? I'm in Panama now, I've just killed a man and this wasn't fun anymore.

"You don't have time to think about it, Jimmy. We're neck deep in shit . . . we gotta finish this job and report to Abbott."

The simple job stringing com wire that I'd done a dozen times before in field training would be more than an adventure, I'd thought, and I hadn't even expected to carry a weapon. God in Heaven, what have I gotten myself into? I've just killed a man and the real mission hasn't even started yet.

With my head ringing, I clumsily hung the telephone and wired it up with stiff and trembling fingers. I have to stay functional, can't fall apart here, can't . . . Eddy called me to help drag the bodies of the sentries to a shallow ravine a dozen paces off the path. The digging was easy and we made a decent job of it. We caved in the higher bank and covered the double grave with large rocks from the eroded shelf of earth to keep the soil from washing away any time soon.

Eddy gave the phone a crank and waited. If the phone didn't work we would wire up the other one, but this trip had to give us a good connection with the staging area. Someone answered and Eddy whispered into the mouthpiece. "Check. We've got a live connection. Who fired that flare?" There was a brief pause. "Tell the guys to keep a sharp eye out for us. We're not the only men in the swamp. We're on our way back. See you in half an hour."

Using the flashlight as little as possible, we hid the wire spool and tool bags near the telephone and found my glasses. We bundled the sentries' gear, weighted it with a stone and on the way back, sank it in the deepest part of the swamp. I led the way with a rifle of Russian manufacture, and Eddy followed a few yards behind with the captured carbine, half stumbling as he walked backwards watching the woods at our back.

Exhausted from slogging through the swamp, we paused to catch our breath before starting the uphill walk through the tall grass and undergrowth. We followed the wire across the marsh without using the flashlight even though the moon had almost fallen from its low perch.

At last on dry ground, we sat down to catch our breath. After a few minutes of rest, Eddy flashed a beam to relocate the wire and I glimpsed something metallic to the left. It was the aluminum casing of the parachute flare. American. There was also a set of boot tracks that paralleled the edge of the marsh, crossing our own. The tread pattern matched the ones on the other side of the swamp. Whose were they?

As we passed Bishop, we warned him to keep alert. Like us, he had seen the flare but not the person who fired it.

In camp, Rubio fumbled with the small camp stove, trying to make coffee. He was startled to see Eddy turn Roberto out of his hammock and kick him in the groin. Probably not as startled as Roberto.

Roberto slowly got to his feet and unwisely threw a punch at Eddy, which got him the butt of the carbine in his face. Rubio pulled Eddy away and kept himself between the two. "Eddy, get a grip. What's wrong? Where did you get the carbine? And . . ." he paused as I stepped into the lantern's yellow light. ". . .what the hell happened to Donlin?"

"This son of a bitch nearly got us killed," Eddy shot back through clenched teeth. "Part of it was our own fault for not taking weapons but this bastard said there was no one on the peninsula but us. Wrong! And who the fuck fired off that parachute flare? I'll personally beat in his hollow little head!"

By now the entire camp was up. Our group wanted to know why Eddy was pissed off and why my face was so bloody. The photographers were angry at being roused at zero-three-thirty. Larry, returning from checking on the boats and sentry posts, stormed into the circle and confronted Eddy about the disturbance. "What happened? Did you stumble into a trip wire? I know you're not stupid enough to set off a flare intentionally. You know they saw it at the barge. So much for the element of surprise! And what's this shit with Roberto?" Larry did a double take on me as Bennett daubed at my cuts with hydrogen peroxide. "Donlin, you look like you've been butting heads with a lawnmower."

"You should see the lawnmower, Cap," I said and presented him with the AK47.

Content to let Eddy relate the details of our encounter in the forest, I gratefully accepted a can of rations someone handed me. . . . American C-rations . . . chicken and noodles, my favorite, even cold. It was followed by Rubio popping the tops off the last two Monte Carlos, and God bless him, I don't know how he did it, but they were even frosty cold.

Eddy took a long draw. "It wasn't us, Cap. We didn't set off the flare!" he began. "We thought it was somebody back here."

He skimmed through laying the wire, emphasized the strange tracks on both sides of the marsh, the trail, the flare, and the Cuban sentries, confirming what had only been speculation about the Angels. "The rain this afternoon will erase all traces of the incident," Eddy said.

"Donlin and I did what had to be done. It's tough to take a man out the first time, especially at close quarters. But now we know we can count on Jimmy," he concluded in a casual salute with the bottle of Monte Carlo.

"If I had any doubts about him, he would never have been put on the roster," Larry assured the group. I took the last draw of Monte Carlo and braced myself for the "Attaboys," and "Killer-this" and "Cutter-that," and all the he-man nonsense I expected. It never happened.

Up until that evening, I was the only man in the team who had never killed. Once, Rubio and Bishop kept some sort of running tally, but like Eddy counting splices in the telephone wire, they simply lost track. They must have remembered how it had been for them, and knew what effect the incident would have on me.

"Saddle up!" Larry barked. "Tame 'em and drain 'em! We move out in five minutes. Take one day's rations, one canteen and beau coup ammo. All you get is what you carry. Call in Bishop and Keener. Gates, you stay here with the non-combatants but don't get more than three paces from the telephone. Rubio will call you once on the phone to give you instructions. An hour after that we'll be on the 10." He scribbled something on yellow paper, taped it to a copy of the chart of the peninsula and handed it to Gates who nodded that he understood.

As we prepared to leave, Larry made a cursory attempt to calm Roche who was in a choking rage because only he and Loomer now understood that they and the other photographers were in a truly hot situation. Woods, Collins and Nash had little comprehension of what had just happened and what was about to happen. Woods and Collins were alarmed to hear that someone had been killed, far away they assumed, and were curious why Eddy and I had to string wire in the first place.

"Captain Abbott is worried about them friggin' Russian trawlers off the coast," Gates explained to Collins and Nash. Woods was hopeless. "They could have a monitoring station even inside the gulf. The walkie-talkies are good for half a mile, not enough range for us here since the peninsula is two miles across. If we use the ANPRC-10s, the Russian snoops can hear us. Running the telephones is as close as we can get to safe communications."

Jorge cut and stripped a palm frond staff with his machete and handed it to Eddy. Eddy thanked him and picked up his oversized gun case, plus two ammo belts for my BAR. Captain Abbott, Rubio and I switched from our bright colored baseball caps to OD ragtops. Everyone else covered with olive drab or cammo Aunt Jemimas. They pulled on their long pants and rag boots, filled packs with rations for one day and as much ammo as they dared try to carry.

Filling the canteens was our last task. The tepid water reeked of chemicals. It could at least kill the taste of Swedish rations. We took ten minutes, not five, and got chewed on. It was strangely familiar and comforting.

The team moved in a column, following the wire. Eddy found the deep hole this time by probing with the palm stick. We then shifted to a skirmish line and advanced toward the woods, rounds chambered and safeties off. The dark shadows of the forest could have concealed a thousand men.

Wispy vapors spilled down from the mountains as seven of us spread out in a circle around the telephone, straining to see into the jungle. Rubio and Keener "took a walk." When they returned, they reported the barge a half mile straight ahead, the tug to the right, facing toward the gulf, ready to tow the barge into its originally intended anchorage. There was little activity and no sign of additional sentries on this side of the river.

In a skirmish line again, we crept toward the river. Dawn was a pitiful, gray, a lifeless thing, stillborn in the mountains. It scattered dim patches of light on the forest floor. Fog crept down the slopes like a fox toward a chicken coop, and onto the glass-smooth water of the Rio Sucio, streaming vaporous tendrils through cane, palms and the massive trunks of hardwoods.

Slow and easy. Step and listen. Move eyes in a circular motion; left to right and back again. Trust peripheral vision. Bushmaster. Fer de Lance. Cascabel. Large snakes, among the most lethal on earth: neuro-toxic venom, potentially lethal in less than twenty minutes. No antidote. Aggressive and nocturnal. This was their back yard. Damn it! Think about something else. Anything else. Step and listen. Slow and easy.

Abruptly the forest ended at a white void and I wondered how Rubio and Keener could have seen anything. The sandy earth fell steeply away. I could hear men breathing to my right and left. In the distance, across the water, there was a distinctive hum and the sound of spilling water; the tug's bilge pump.

Men's voices drifted in the morning air, only a few, and scattered. Spanish voices. A wooden spoon tapped the rim of a cooking pot.

Rubio took a fire team of three to the left. Keener took one on the right, leaving me pretty much in the center. Eddy was told to pick a position with good cover and a higher elevation than the rest of us, which he managed within sight of me, about twehty yards to my right. "Move out and pick your spot," Keener said. " Rubio will assign fire zones." With the BAR, I knew my zone would be the entire front of the assault. It was light enough now that I could see that Captain Abbott wasn't with us.

To my left Rubio spaced out firepower for the attack. Amazingly, there seemed to be no indication they'd seen the flare. Along the top of the barge, above the thick, tumbling ground fog, the dark silhouettes of four sentries watched the open end of the estuary near the bow of the tug. Even though the sun effused the east with an edge of white light, few men stirred. With hand signals, Rubio directed us into position. There were seven of us but we would have to lay out the firepower of seventy.

The mangroves at the water's edge were dense but not high enough to shield us from view. Immediately in front of me, a dugout canoe, half filled with water, tugged at the knotted sisal cord securing it to a mangrove root. This was probably how the sentries came to their post beside the path. Maybe they hadn't been there when Roberto scouted.

I'll never understand the workings of my brain. Chalk it up to stress, anxiety or raw fear; this moment held them all. The sisal bowline of the canoe threw my mind into a somersault. I fell out of Panama, vaulted and soared four thousand miles, displaced in an instant, and I was back home. I could see my father in our garden, tending tomato vines supported by wooden stakes and sisal cord, just like the fibers that tethered the canoe to a mangrove root. He carefully coiled the hose after watering the garden. His face was deeply tanned, though his forehead remained white, shaded by his blue and white striped shop cap. His hair was mostly gray now. He would soon leave for work at the small oil field service company, black lunch box in hand, Boss Walloper cotton gloves sticking out of the hip pockets of his overalls.

My youngest sister would be watching him through the kitchen window as she ate breakfast cereal, and my mother would be scolding her for neglecting her household chores. Mom would finish the dishes and start the vacuum, getting ready for ... getting ready ... get ready ... "Get ready!" Rubio whispered at my left. "Donlin! Snap out of it! Get ready."

"How am I supposed to do anything in this fog," I asked Rubio.

"It was clear as a bell twenty minutes ago. It'll be clear again. The sun will burn it away. We don't start until we can see our targets. Eddy takes first shot, then open up. They're all nail kegs, Jimmy," Rubio whispered.

Hardwoods, palms, and random stands of cane overhung the mangroves, and we were sheltered in the deep shadows between them. An ancient mahogany toppled by a seasonal storm sometime within the last year lifted the sand and clay and left a depression nearly four feet deep. I slipped into the pit, scooped out a little debris, deepening the hole. I broke off a couple of roots that jabbed me in the back, and laid the ammo belts out to my right. "Lock and load, Cowboy. These are from Eddy," Keener whispered behind me, tossing two more ammo belts at my feet. "He's to your right. He takes the first shot. Then everybody opens up."

"I've heard," I replied, as I cleared footing for the bipod which I'd decided to leave on.

Nelson lightly stepped into my depression and slapped me on the back. "You were impressive with the pig out on those North Canadian sandbars. Hope you've still got the magic touch." He quietly bounded out, leaving four more ammo belts.

A thousand rounds, I thought to myself. And the nickname 'pig' was deserved for the way a BAR uses up ammo. I hoped it would be enough.

I stretched out of the cavity and strained to look to my right. Eddy took out his weapon, a non-military piece with a thick-walled barrel and fitted with a huge scope. The object lens was at least fifty millimeters. He was equipped as our sniper.

The clearing of a fog bank shouldn't generate anxiety, but in this time and place it did. As I slipped back into the hole, the fog thinned enough to show huge sections of pale blue sky. A light breeze rippled the surface of the bay. I tore off another root, trimmed off the tip of a palm frond and cut down a small clump of grass. Now I could see Eddy clearly as he removed the eye cowl, cleaned the lens, replaced the cowl and inserted a short clip. His motions were sure and practiced. He sighted and adjusted a sand bag support, swung the muzzle up and down the length of the camp, now almost entirely clear of mist. The far shore was only two hundred yards away, the center of the camp another hundred, and clustered mostly in the broad space between the tug and its tow. The last remnants of fog hovered over the water that separated us.

Most of the men in the Angel camp were still sleeping. On the opposite shore behind the tug, I could make out four figures near the water. They slept in awkward positions with no ground cover. Odd.

The temperature rose and the last of the fog lifted. Why was Eddy waiting? Leaning out, I could see him slowly, carefully, pruning branches and vines that interfered with his view.

Perspiration dripped out of the bandage on my forehead and hung on the lower rim of my glasses. I threw off my cap and tore at the gauze. Too white and too tight. The cuts felt ragged and they burned with the salt of my own sweat. My right eyebrow had a lump the size of one of my Aunt Florence's pickled eggs.

Firing from a hole, it seemed best to leave the bipod on. I set the selector switch on fast, safety on, and adjusted my sights for three hundred yards. Start with the men on the beach.

I could barely breathe. My back and shoulders ached with the tension of waiting. Heart pounding, I chambered the first round. Hell, I'll take the first shot!

A figure appeared at the rail of the tug, his uniform shirt hanging open over a white undershirt, insignias bright on his epaulets. Maybe not the commander, but at least an officer. Climbing up on the starboard rail, he held onto the overhead with one hand. As he urinated into the muddy water, the sun shone in a cleared sky and at last Eddy fired.

The officer never knew what hit him.

My opening burst punched mean stitches across the figures on the beach and the mud between them, but strangely, they didn't flinch.

Other men who were already awake went down next. Sentries, cooks and non-coms. Next, I fired at anyone who moved, anything that looked human.

Our location was not immediately apparent to them. Soon, the ones who dared move, found their weapons and returned fire. They crept closer to the tug and barge for cover, major blind spots for us, firing in our general direction when they could.

Rounds whined overhead, clipping leaves that fluttered and spiraled down. In front of our positions, tiny geysers marched in short lines across the water. Bullets sang overhead, pounded the dugout canoe, thumped into my mahogany root ball and kicked up sand beside me. They didn't like my BAR. A round grazed one of the bipod footplates, sending the peeled copper jacket buzzing past my ear.

Our side of the river roared with fire. Framed in my sights, more men went down. Knocked off their feet, rolled on the ground. Broken, torn, bloodied, they fell. Footing became difficult; I stumbled and slipped on half a dozen empty magazines and hundreds of spent cartridges. Within three minutes, my targets consisted of a dozen heads and an occasional muzzle flash.

We took heavy fire from the tug's upper deck and from inside the pilothouse. I sprayed them with three full magazines. Glass shattered and varnished teak splintered. Black smoke belched from the stack as someone tried to start the engines. Emptying my fourth magazine into the tug, I saw two bodies tumble down the interior companionway to the main deck. The rumble of diesels stopped and the engines remained silent, the last streamers of black smoke dissipating in the morning air.

Tug secured.

The uneven ground of the campsite was almost as barren as Base T. Two groups of eight or ten men each ran across this open terrain toward the jungle on the opposite side of the camp, over five hundred yards away. Only three or four had weapons. We were well out of their range so I let them slip into the shelter of the forest and concentrated on the remaining holdouts occupying the top of the barge and a blind spot behind the tug. There may have been more, but these men were the only ones still returning fire.

There was a faint noise, like someone clearing his throat in a long hallway. Gosling One careened around a brushy point on our side of the river, planing at full speed, and ran up on the sandy shore fifty yards in front of the tug. The prop threw a plume of water and black mud as the boat bounced up the beach and stopped abruptly when the skeg took a bite of solid ground.

Larry, covered by Gates and Jorge, leaped from behind the console, firing his grease gun into the group of men taking cover behind the tug. At the stern, three figures rose, holding their hands up. One blind spot taken.

Six Cubans fired from the top of the barge, and Larry tumbled to his left, taking cover near the bow of the tug, bringing four prisoners with him.

The tide was falling and both vessels had grounded on the side next to shore, rolling their topsides toward us. The remaining Cubans found themselves more and more open. The decks of both tug and tow were now almost completely exposed to our fire.

Under the cover of the pilothouse, Gates and Jorge scrambled up a mooring line and over the bow of the tug. They made their way into the galley's companionway. There were two shots and a Cuban stumbled out onto the stern deck. He fell against the towing bits and struggled to stay on his feet. Leaning against the massive cast iron bollards, he raised his hands in surrender, stood a few seconds, then collapsed to the deck.

Jorge burst out onto the upper deck behind the pilothouse. He was driven back inside by a burst of automatic fire from the barge that sent bright red-orange fragments off the balsa life rafts fluttering through the air. A figure rose from the deck of the barge to fire again, a bright rainbow of brass casings lifted from the receiver of his Kalashnikov, only his head and shoulders exposed. As I gathered him into my sights, Eddy blew him over the far side of the barge.

A soiled white flag appeared above the bulwarks of the nearest end of the barge and Rubio called for a cease-fire. Jorge's voice rang out. "Throw your weapons over the side, into the river. If we find anyone armed, all of you will be shot," he warned. They were herded into the open area in front of the barge, fully exposed to our weapons.

From our side of the river, I watched Gates speak into a walkie-talkie. Moments later, a line of vessels rounded the brushy point to the south. It was Roberto, Juan and Pello in their boats, towing Goslings Two, Three and Four, each with wide-eyed and open-mouthed old geezers crouching behind the consoles.

Eddy and I were the last to be ferried across. We found the Cuban prisoners being treated humanely but cautiously after being disarmed. They were allowed to tend to their wounded, collect the dead for burial, cook, eat and drink, even make shelter from the heat, under guard, of course.

Pello was assigned a post on the shady bridge deck of the tug. Eddy complained about the heat of the sun on his corner of the barge and Nelson took a position seventy yards out, standing in the shade of a palm. They would instantly punch holes in anyone who decided to be a problem. Rubio, Bennett and Gates ranged through the barge looking for holdouts. I was assigned as tour guide to five nervous photographers to a safe area where they could ready their equipment for their jobs.

Bishop absolutely despised Cubans. His mannerisms left no doubt that he would take any excuse to kill more of them. I later learned that Hilly Sanders, a former team member, had disappeared in the Bay of Pigs fiasco. He was the man I had replaced and had been Bishop's best friend.

Juan and Gates were assigned the task of clearing out the tug. After heaving six bodies over the gun'l onto shore to be picked by the burial party, they dragged a half-dressed Cuban before Rubio. He had been hiding in the engine room and was in a foul temper, a bit hung over. For a man in his situation, he was extremely belligerent and arrogant.

That wouldn't buy him much here.

From the far end of the barge, Keener called Rubio and Larry. Loomer's boys wouldn't be ready for another twenty minutes so I tagged along. In a distant stand of palm, a small circle had been cleared of saw grass. Three Embera Choco girls cried with fear, naked, and tied spread-eagle to stakes. Jorge spoke to them in Embera Choco. They ranged in age from about eleven to fifteen, the two youngest were sisters and the oldest girl was their cousin. They had been beaten and raped repeatedly, the older one the worse off. Jorge said they'd seen their parents and uncles killed the night before and pointed in the direction of the figures sprawled along the beach, the ones that had received my first rounds.

We retrieved the corpse of a mature female from the water, bloated and mutilated by crabs. She floated under the counter stern of the barge, shot through the head.

Jorge carefully cut the girls loose. They were afraid of us at first. Under their carefully trimmed bangs, their small, nearly oriental eyes were tear-filled and flashed with panic. Keener, Bishop and I covered them in our fatigue shirts and walked them back to the main group. They became upset when they saw the Cuban from the tug, even though his hands were tightly bound behind him.

The youngest became uncontrollably hysterical. Tears traced shinny lines over her dirty face. It was he who'd murdered the adults and ordered the girls tied up for "entertainment." He had personally started with her.

When Rubio confronted the prisoner with the girls' charges, he laughed. Gates translated for me. "They're only worthless Indians. Who cares?"

Jorge swung the muzzle of his carbine onto the Cuban's groin.

Rubio restrained Jorge with a brief sentence. Jorge didn't change his stance in the slightest, but held his fire. "This worthless Indian would like to explain to you that he cares," Rubio proposed, jerking his thumb toward Jorge. Gates translated again. Jorge's back was to me and I couldn't see his face, but I could see the Cuban officer's face. The defiant sneer melted from his face, replaced by tics and trembling jaw muscles.

"Where is your commander? I wish to speak to him," Rubio demanded.

"He's dead," the Cuban replied. "You shot him off the boat while he was taking a piss," Gates translated in a low voice.

I watched Nelson take something from Roberto who had just toured the tug. He hurried up the shore, roughly bullying his way through a burial detail of surly Cubans and presented Rubio a mangled jacket complete with insignia. In the pocket was a wallet containing papers, which identified the prisoner as an army major. "It was stuffed between a fuel tank and a tool locker," Nelson relayed. "Looks like our new friend here. Has he said anything useful?"

"No," Rubio replied, "and I don't expect anything from him. He expects about the same from me. He seems a little worried about Jorge, though."

"If I were a certain Cuban major, I'd be shitting in my pants right about now," Nelson said to Rubio, nodding toward Jorge.

"If he has the slightest idea of what's ahead of him," Rubio agreed. He turned to the major and asked him if he had anything he would like to say to the girls. The major glared at him, tight-jawed. Whether it was proud defiance or fear was not easy to tell, not that it mattered. As I watched, he bit his lower lip hard enough to bleed and his shoulders hunched.

It was fear.

He had good reason to be fearful.

Nelson grasped what was about to happen to the major. He forced the Cuban backward through the midst of the burial detail, to the end of their deepest cut in the earth. Jorge slung his weapon, stepped behind the major and put a foot to the back of his knees, dropping him to a kneeling position at the end of the trench.

The Cuban officer began pleading for his life, his voice quaking and tears streamed down his fear-distorted face. Members of the burial party tried to close around us. Nelson struck two with the butt of his Garand and forced them back. Gates drew his automatic. I stepped a few paces to the side and leveled my BAR. Several heard the faint click as I pressed off the safety. From the barge, Eddy fired a single round, dropping the nearest Cuban into the trench. Game canceled. Rubio ordered them back to their work. They checked their anger instantly. Defiance could obviously be fatal. They backed away, then fell silent and watched when they also realized what was playing out.

"I'm sorry we don't have a priest with us," Rubio said in a soft, cold voice. The insincere tone of the apology paralyzed the major. In a trembling voice, he suddenly pleaded something about the Geneva Conventions. That would not save him. He might have had more time, enough for a formal trial, but the outcome would have been the same. In any case, they probably wouldn't apply. Technically, there was no war, and certainly no young Indian girls would be considered combatants. And if we fit any description at all, it would be that of mercenaries, same as the Cubans. The same international guidelines the major thought might protect him would surely have condemned us.

Rubio may have looked for some small indication of shame or regret. Again, I doubt it would have made a difference. From where I stood, the major seemed choked by fear and self-pity, to the point that if there had been a flicker of regret, it wasn't visible to any of us.

At last, Rubio jerked his thumb sharply across his own throat. In a flash, Jorge repeated the same motion under the major's chin whose screaming protests became a gurgling hiss as he pitched forward, kicking and sliding into the hole. In a few seconds, askew at the bottom of the grave, his thrashing ended beside the Cuban Eddy had shot.

The girls were escorted through the remaining fifteen prisoners but identified only one other as a participant in their torment. He was a bent and grizzled old cook who couldn't have been as old as he appeared. A closer look showed that what seemed wrinkles were actually jagged bands of scar tissue, possibly burns, and the bent posture the result of a mangled leg and foot, a Hero of the Revolution.

Perspiring heavily in the late morning heat, he eyed us with undisguised hatred.

The older girl tried to take Jorge's carbine from him. She shrieked and screamed at the cook, then tore at Jorge when he wouldn't relinquish his weapon. I tried to pull her away and she turned her rage on me. Biting, scratching and kicking, she broke away and started throwing rocks and seashells at the cook. Jorge's blank expression returned as the little girl raved, piecing out what the 'old man' had done to her. The cook made no effort to run or plead. He had seen the major's fate but his eyes burned with more hatred than fear. Scowling at Jorge, he spat at him through rotted teeth.

Jorge shot him in the middle of the forehead and ushered the girls to the rafts.

At first, I felt it was wrong that Jorge killed so easily and in front of these children, but after a little thought on the matter, I understood. These girls had been subjected to extremely cruel mistreatment. Seeing two of their tormentors punished so immediately and severely demonstrated a rudimentary form of justice. They had seen their parents murdered in cold blood. They had been beaten and raped. I doubt they lost much sleep over the Cubans. Another result of the summary executions, we were established as their protectors, not just a new band of abusive captors.

The girls wanted to know about us. Were we going to hurt them? Would we take them away to make them work for us? What has happened to the bodies of their parents? What is to become of them? They were satisfied with our answers except for their last question; we had no idea what would happen to them.

As Bennett tried to clean them up and bandage their ankles and wrists, raw from their fetters, they pleaded with Jorge. "Palma-ma, Palma-ma! Choth-cotla nansh tule pa-aqua. Sapi tomo Padre Ortiz uqu nansh Palma-ma!" The girls wanted to go to an Indian shelter in La Palma operated by Father Phillipe Ortiz. Jorge translated into Spanish and Rubio into English. There was nothing we could tell them. We could be on a chopper in an hour, or camp right here for a week. Far more had been achieved than the original contract called for, and much earlier. No provisions had been made for early extraction. Still, we would do what we could for the girls.

The objective of our mission had been to get within camera range, not take possession, but we did. Almost everything on the barge was intact, give or take a few dozen armor piercing bullet holes. Nothing had been removed; all the gauges, pumps and electrical panels were in tact.

A service port on the shore side swung out and a hinged companionway extended to the riverbank. It was here that Larry nearly killed Roche.

Loomer and Nash sorted out photo equipment. Roche cowered at the beach with Woods and Collins until prisoners, their burial detail completed, were herded into a guarded area and the barge checked out. Then, he whipped himself into an indignant frenzy over the apparent disregard for the safety of the photographers. He launched an attack on Larry with Woods and Collins giving moral support, from a safe distance, of course.

"I can't fucking tell if you're incompetent or just irresponsible by nature! What would have happened to us if you'd lost that firefight? Do you realize what horrific danger you put us in?"

"Sure, but in a worst case scenario, I'd have been killed and wouldn't really give a fuck. A lot like right now," Larry replied, trying to laugh off Roche's tirade. He turned toward Rubio and Gates who were setting up the long-range radio.

"Don't you turn your back on me!" Bernie Roche shouted behind Larry, and grabbed his neck with both hands.

Roche tried to strangle Larry, who raised his left hand over his head and spun to his left. The movement broke Roche's grip and Larry gathered up both of Roche's arms, bringing them face to face. When Roche, both his arms captured by the elbows, looked into Larry's eyes, he knew he'd made a big mistake.

Larry had little to prove to a fifty-eight year old pain in the ass, but this was becoming tiresome. Larry decided not to take advantage of his tormentor, and unwound his grip. Failing to recognize an act of kindness, Roche threw Larry two left jabs in the face! Larry tried to tell him this was not a good idea. Bernie tried to hit him again and Larry unloaded on him, jabbed with his left, first in the face, followed by a right uppercut to the stomach. Roche dropped like a bag of wet sand.

"Now, see here!" Woods shouted, charging Larry, shaking his fists. "You..er..er..you can't..er, that's assault! Criminal! Criminal ... er ... behavior!" Woods would have taken Roche's place, but Collins held him back by the shirt collar, arguing that Bernie Roche needed looking after worse than Larry needed more lip.

The photographers were calm and coherent half an hour after the Roche incident. Curious to see what all the bother had been about, they filed into the barge like they were going to church. "This could take a couple of hours," Dr. Loomer nervously explained to Larry. "Half of the equipment we brought is telephoto and high-speed film. Totally useless this close and in bad light. We may not have enough of the right film for these conditions."

"Do the best you can for now. We may have a couple of days to work on it now," Larry told him.

I disappeared into the monstrous steel box with Dr. Loomer and Mr. Collins right behind, apparently unconcerned that the first sweep of the interior might have missed a Cuban holdout. "Shoot everything inside right now," Loomer said to Collins. Captain Abbott said it'll be an oven in here in half an hour." The metallic echo of his voice rang through the entrails of the barge.

I admit to gawking like a schoolboy. The room did seem an antechamber, did seem like a church, a cavernous steel cloister with heaven's rays streaming through the bullet-pierced hull and deck plates. The long, thin fingers of brilliant white light combed the dark apse and the slightest whisper resounded like a Gregorian chant.

The barge was huge but crudely built. The paint had peeled from the interior bulkheads, exposing bare steel, already caked in thick, flaking rust. Three hundred and forty feet long and seventy feet wide, it would fill a canal lock by itself. We found huge cylindrical tanks secured to the interior floor, their tops pushed through the upper deck, interconnected by a mass of pipes, pumps, electrical wiring, and a bewildering array of valves and gauges, all inside the barge. We could never have seen them if we hadn't taken possession of the barge. There were other tanks on deck, long and narrow, each with a crane to facilitate standing them upright, and a jumble of framing and legs to support tanks and machinery when assembled for production.

The after section held cramped living quarters for maybe a dozen or so, and two offices. The types of pumps and non-corrosive alloys in valves and pumps confirmed that this was a facility for manufacturing solid rocket fuel.

CHAPTER TWENTY-TWO

Remembrance fallen from heaven,
And madness risen from hell;
Algernon Charles Swinburne

Twelve Cuban prisoners buried forty-eight dead. Three of fifteen prisoners were wounded and unable to provide such labor, but two were able to walk, having suffered arm and shoulder wounds. About twenty escaped into the forest. Apparently, all the other filthy participants in the assault on the girls were included among the casualties or escapees. That made eighty-three men and we learned this was but a fourth of the Angels.

One of the prisoners volunteered that the main body of Angels camped only four miles away, divided into three groups that controlled the mouth of the Rio Cucunati where the barge and tug should have been but for a navigational error. I overheard a transmission that the Panamanian Army had just scheduled live ammunition jungle warfare exercise for that area.

What a coincidence.

The girls' parents and two uncles were the last buried. Nelson, Bennett, Bishop and Eddy prepared them in scraps of canvas awning from the tug, allowing the girls to see them for the last time beside the graves, carefully concealing the ragged tears from my BAR. The girls keened and chanted and tried to throw themselves on the bodies, but we restrained them. Extreme tropical heat promotes rapid decomposition. The result is more repugnant than loving relatives should have to endure. We would deny this to the girls.

Keener and I were assigned to go back to the assembly area for the telephones, rations and ammo. The guias were detailed to bring back everything else; all the guias except Jorge, that is. The Indian girls attached themselves to him and couldn't be pried away. Ah, the power of language . . . and kinship.

Our shirts still covered the Indian girls. By the time we got back, Keener and I were suffering from sunburn. We scavenged poles and wire and cut palm fronds to make a small palapa for the radio near the stern of the bullet riddled tugboat. As much as possible, we lingered in its shade.

As we prepared to take our turn at guarding the prisoners, Rubio tore off the radio headset and announced the Cubans would be set free immediately. No provisions for manpower or facilities had been made for guarding or processing, or even feeding prisoners. Nor did the area directors like the idea of having to explain how they had come into possession of Cuban prisoners. If you explain the drum major, you may have to explain the whole goddamned parade, he'd said. All it meant to me was reprieve from the sun and wasting time on guard duty.

And the Panamanians canceled the war games.

Before the release, Rubio addressed them with a one-sentence farewell. "We regret that Cuban blood was spilled over Russian intrigue." Their expressions communicated their uniform sentiment; they would much rather it had been our blood spilled. Gathering up rations and water, they quickly departed, leaving us one prisoner who was so weakened by loss of blood from a leg wound he could not make the march back through the Darien.

Keener and I liked our remaining prisoner, an eighteen-year-old kid. We discovered he spoke English better than we did and also hated our Swedish C-rations.

Rubio and Gates spelled each other on the radio. Over a dozen messages were scribbled across the yellow sheets, bringing order to lives suddenly made formless, totally without value, meaning or direction now that the objective lay secured. We were ordered back to Base T, taking photographers, our one Cuban prisoner and the Indian girls with us.

The photographers were ordered to leave all exposed film in a waterproof container inside the barge. Someone would pick it up. No other evidence of an American presence should be left behind. Be underway in one hour, before the helicopters arrive.

HooooYAH!

After burning C-ration boxes and retrieving telephones and tool bags from the staging area, we loaded all gear into the rafts, breaking down the ANGRC-9 at the last possible minute to make sure no messages were missed. We left the telephone wire strung across the peninsula; our conscience wouldn't allow us to return such mistreated wire to Heinrich Turm. I retrieved the telephone Rubio had used to bring in Gates and the photographers when I went back for the twenty or so spent magazines. We were also ordered to police all spent brass. That didn't happen.

At sixteen hundred hours, we pushed the rafts off the muddy beach in a heavy downpour that was painful on my sunburn.

A line of nine H-40s arrived on time. Seven hovered over the open ground behind the barge. Armed men rappelled fifteen feet to the ground. The other two helicopters landed after the platoon of Marine force-recon set up a perimeter. Four people walked toward the barge but at a distance and in the deluge, they were not recognizable, but I could see that they were not military.

As we reached the mouth of the estuary, an ancient PT boat swept past us, bristling with radio antennas, guns manned and an over-sized Panamanian flag, saturated by rain, struggled in the wind-rush. Under the bridge awning, Panamanian naval officers conversed with two civilians. I believe this tired old boat was "Mother Goose," our mobile com center previously moored at La Palma.

Easing the throttles to fifteen knots, we slipped over the wake of the PT boat, ran a timed leg to Pollux Intercept and headed for Base T. The rain turned cool but the lawn bowlers still complained of heat, hunger, and exhaustion. Muy sympatico, amigos!

There was no rest at Base T. As we set the rafts on the mooring lines, Larry barked out our schedule for the remainder of the day. Set up the ANGRC-9, clean the rafts, change the oil in the generator, weapons check, and scrub the mess tent. All I wanted was a fresh bandage and twenty hours of sleep.

The rain disappeared like a friend who owes money. A blazing sun took its time in passing and my sunburn was hard to live with. I dug a second fatigue shirt out of my duffel bag. The sunburn made it seem too small and the fabric coarse and abrasive. Volunteering to change oil in the generator, I worked in the shade of the com-tent . . . without the shirt.

The photographers sacked out, totally exhausted by lack of sleep, anxiety and the jarring ride back to Base T. A touch of weather kicked up a little chop and our ride home had been rough. They complained about that, too.

Not getting to blow up anything put Gates out of sorts. He should have been glad his water travel was over. Still, he groused and grumbled through his bags and walked into the boonies. A series of muffled explosions scattered flocks of birds over camp and brought Gates back, covered in mud and sand. "Got rid of some bad detonators," he said to Larry in the mess tent, a juvenile grin on his face.

The Indian girls were given a place to rest in the mess tent, but like the photographers, they complained about the smell of the latrine. Within a few hours, Jorge and Pello built them a small palapa on the south side of the point, above high tide, away from both the latrines and they were grateful. Nelson and I slung hammocks between the corner posts and the girls finished building a pole floor three feet above the ground, Embera Choco style.

The next day was spent doing menial chores. I was taking inventory of remaining fuel for the rafts and diesel for the generator when a minor fight broke out between Jorge and Roberto in the mess tent. Roberto objected to Jorge spending so much time mothering the youngsters.

When Rubio interceded, we found that the girls were of Jorge's clan and possibly his second cousins. It meant nothing to Roberto who still insisted that Jorge complete KP chores and help repair a leak in one of the aluminum boats. Jorge became angry. "There is no leak!" he shouted. "This was ridiculous busy work. The girls needed looking after and I'm the one who will do it!" Rubio translated.

Snatching up a roll of wire, his tool belt and machete, Jorge stormed out of the tent and tramped toward the girl's palapa.

Glaring at Jorge, Roberto shook with anger but kept himself under control as long as Rubio, Nelson and I were present.

"Leave him alone, Roberto," Rubio insisted. "Something will be done with the girls as soon as possible. In the meantime, Jorge is right. Someone must look after them and language and kinship gives him a higher niche than the rest of us."

Logic and reason had no application here. Roberto continued to boil, now enraged that Rubio had encroached on what he considered his domain. A few more words were exchanged between Rubio and Roberto, but with little effect. As we left the mess tent, Juan and Pello strolled along with us, casting worried glances over their shoulders. Roberto sulked there, leaning on table one with both fists. We all agreed; he needed cooling off time.

Mother Goose made arrangements to send our eighteen year old Cuban prisoner, chubby Oscar Escobar, home through a liaison at the Guantánamo Bay Naval Base, but he was in no hurry to go home. He had been raised in Jacksonville, Florida and recruited by an uncle in Havana. He may have a problem getting back to Jacksonville.

Oscar turned out to be an excellent cook. The *guias* brought him fish, which he cooked over open coals with pescado salsa de coco, a grated coconut dressing that could have won praises in any restaurant in the world. Fresh bread and some kind of dessert made from the last can of peaches, condensed milk and Bisquick gave us the best lunch we'd had since the Loro Azul fly-in.

Oscar knew why Bishop glared at him, but also knew that nothing he could say would bring Hilly Sanders back or change Bishop's mind. He kept his distance from Bishop and Bishop left him alone.

Just before lunch, I had helped raise and connect a new ANGRC-9 antenna. The web belt and tool bag with bayonet again became part of my uniform of the day. In the heat of late afternoon, still tired and sleepy and full from an excellent lunch, I walked like a zombie and Larry noticed. He told me to sack out a while. I stretched out under the shade of a stunted palm on the crest a few yards from the com-tent. There was a little breeze there and it was outside the traffic area of those more industrious and heat tolerant.

I removed my belt and tool bag. Now stuffed with cleaning rags from working on the generator, it made a perfect pillow.

Cradled in the sweet haven of sleep, I was startled awake when my pillow was roughly yanked from under my head. Jorge had come by, snatched up my web belt, drew the bayonet and tossed the rest back to me. He stormed toward the girls' palapa.

In the com-tent, Gates' forty-five was in its holster, hanging on the back of the folding chair a dozen paces away. I put on my glasses and drew the automatic, chambered a round and ran after Jorge. Something was up.

Halfway to the girl's palapa, I heard a muffled scream, then loud wailing from the smaller girls. I rushed toward their palapa, arriving in time to see Jorge straddle the back of a man on the ground, his trousers around his knees. Jorge wrenched the figure's head back, lifting him by a hand under the chin. I could see the oldest of the girls under him, struggling to free herself.

Reaching deep around his neck with the bayonet, Jorge drew the blade across in a rage, and held him as the girl scrambled away, then let him drop. The figure spun around on all fours, moaning and groveling, and made a feeble lunge at Jorge's legs. Jorge simply sidestepped, pivoted and walked away, forever beyond Roberto's reach.

Within five minutes, the entire camp had gathered. All of Roberto's attempts to separate Jorge from the girls had come to this. I felt little sympathy or remorse for the still figure sprawled at the corner of the small palapa. His dull eyes could not see how the coarse sand absorbed his blood or the tiny ants that even now probed the mysteries of his lips and nostrils.

I dropped the clip out of the .45, ejected the round in the chamber and eased the hammer down. By the time I returned to my palm tree, Jorge had cleaned the bayonet and returned it to its sheath.

In the mess tent that night, Larry announced that Roberto would be listed in his report as a casualty of the firefight for the barge. Any of us would probably have shot the son of a bitch, but because of Jorge's kinship to the girls, it was just as well he had killed him.

Jorge wanted to dump the corpse in the latrine. Request denied. Uncivilized and unsanitary. "Besides, it's less work to dig a grave than a new latrine," Eddie whispered behind his hand.

Next morning, out in the boonies, Jorge, Juan and Pello dug a grave and buried Roberto, leaving the site unmarked. Drawing the short straw, Pello finished the chore of filling in the pit. Working with his head askew, accommodating a black eye attributed to Roberto in a dispute over kitchen duty the day before. Pello patted down the sand and broken sea shells, pissed on the grave, and jogged away to join in dividing up Roberto's belongings.

* * * *

We impatiently waited two days for word of going home. Remember? Home? Better climate, nice people, smaller mosquitoes, and no Swedish cardboard. That place.

The sun was still only an obscure, very distant possibility when Rubio roughly shook me awake. "Gotta get your

BAR, Jimmy! Keep low and quiet. We have a large vessel approaching from the north and on the wrong bearing. Could be hostile. Let's put him in a box, right now."

Keener blew out of the tent first, slinging two bandoleers in one hand, his Garand in the other. As I joined him, we were both dumbfounded by the oversight. On this sand spit there was absolutely no cover and, other than latrines, no trenches had been dug. A survey team would not have needed defensive positions. At this moment, standing in the open, without the slightest depression for cover, the idea deserved rethinking.

"Jimmy, set up behind the generator," Rubio said over his shoulder as he strode toward the other squad tent. "You'll draw as much fire as you put out. Let's get some iron in front of you. Keener, get up on the crest and move as far back as you can and still cover. I'll roust the others to do the same."

We waited, and waited, slapping mosquitoes and sand flies. The faint glow in the east raised the usual sounds of the forest. It was at that hour when the chirps and squeaks of insects and tree frogs were joined by the squawks and whistles of waking birdlife. Deeper in the tangle of green, a troop of howlers sent grunts and shrieks echoing through the camp. The lanterns at the beach drew darting moths to patches of yellow-white light, bright islands in an ocean of dark gray. It's the dawning of another beautiful day in fucking paradise.

Far out on the bay, red and green navigation lights bracketed the bow-on silhouette of a large vessel, unidentifiable in the dim light of early dawn. Its powerful spotlight swept the end of the main peninsula. The vessel slowly turned, a white light at the top of its single mast flickered. A change of course presented us with the red light of the port side and the white stern light. A spotlight found the white mooring buoy and rafts, held a few seconds and went out. The helmsman, obviously unsure of his position, carefully made his way around the broad mud flats.

Gradually the dawn's light increased, and we could make out the broadside silhouette of the Franciscan mission boat from La Palma, here to pick up the Embera Choco girls. Rubio called us back and we secured. He entered the com-tent, and the panel lights of the ANGRC-9 lit up.

We gathered at the beach with fresh coffee to watch the boat proceed slowly westward. Rubio called Mother Goose and suggested they relay to the mission in La Palma to move away from the white bouy because the tide was falling, and drop anchor. We would bring the girls out to them.

A soiled and ragged Panamanian flag fluttered in the developing breeze from the mountains. Figures appeared at the bow and we heard the anchor chain rattle. Thinking this was the boat taking them to Panama City and a flight home, the photographers joined us in a state of excitement, half dressed and dragging hastily packed luggage and camera cases. They were disgusted and sorely disappointed at the prospects of spending another day at ease, enjoying the beach facilities at Campo Tiburon. They grumbled away to the mess tent for their own cup of Oscar's coffee.

Jorge woke the girls and Keener fired off Gosling Two. As the raft hummed away, the girls waved good-bye to the rest of us. White letters on the gray hull proclaimed MISSION de SAN FRANCISCO de LA PALMA along the full length of the paint-sore, gray hull and SERVICIO PARA LOS INDIOS in smaller letters under that. The girls, still wearing our faded fatigue shirts, scrambled up a boarding ladder and fell into the embraces of women they obviously knew. Keener and Jorge returned and sent the raft back out on the mooring line.

Keener trudged his way up the beach shouting at Oscar to start breakfast. He didn't know Oscar had been up an hour and breakfast was waiting. It had been Nelson and Oscar who alerted Rubio to the boat's lights out on the bay.

"The girls were still wearing our fatigue shirts," Keener reported. "The last I saw of them, they were perched on the forward hatch, waving good-bye and eating fried bananas, fish and cornmeal mush off banana palm leaves."

Jorge looked like the loneliest man in the world.

CHAPTER TWENTY-THREE

A man who rides a tiger cannot dismount.
Confucius

Someone should have known better. A high ranking spokesman in the Department of Defense, with more influence than brains, levered a clearance to present a clouded complaint against the USSR at the UN. This tirade seemed vague, but to those in the intelligence community, American or Russian, its meaning was clear enough. This premature attempt at a high profile, self-aggrandizing propaganda blast quickly evolved into a disastrous blunder, generating events as orderly and managable as an average train wreck.

After initial speculations about the purpose of missile fuel production facilities in Cuba, a pro-tem officer ranted about the Monroe Doctrine and sermonized about America's willingness to enforce it. Stupidity, irresponsibility, and an over-riding ambition are always unpredictable and potentially explosive variables.

Whoever authorized this cavalry charge against the Russians gravely jeopardized an already shaky peace. The barge was far from being secure in the neutral waters of the Canal Zone. And this extreme miscalculation would guarantee that the cold war propaganda prize of the decade would become a tiger difficult to dismount.

* * * *

Ruth Hobbs, an overworked file clerk with a bad case of coffee jitters, took a deep breath and placed her hand on the knob of the file room door. The air conditioning was being temperamental again, and certain rooms had been closed off to make the ones occupied by people more comfortable.

Suppressing her resentment that such a decision had been made by her bosses, knowing that she and sixteen other clerks must eventually spend an hour or more a day in that sauna, kept her teetering on the verge of homicide, at least in her daydreams.

Lon Crane, Ruth's immediate supervisor, chalked up her moods to lunar cycles or problems at home. He tolerated the spilled coffee she brought him and files dropped carelessly on his desk. He wasn't the one who had to spend an hour at a time in a second story cubicle with western exposure, no opening windows and no air conditioning. If he had, their solution to the "workplace problem" would have been different. He'd have the air conditioning contractor working as a file clerk.

"Excuse me, Mrs. Hobbs," Lydia crooned. Ruth Hobbs turned the knob and opened the door, allowing Lydia Franks to enter the file room ahead of her. Lydia was the new girl with the security clearance only one grade lower than her own, doing the same job and with eight years less seniority. She had a definite polished air of competence. Her grammar was perfect and untainted by any regional accent. Flawless grooming and carriage gave her a restrained Mamie Van Doren look. She was a package of warm, pink promises and lacey self-confidence. Lydia's cheerful enthusiasm flowed past chauvinism, prejudices, policies and antique dogmas that cling to government work like gravy stains on silk ties.

The smile, the blond hair, large breasts with modestly exposed cleavage presented their own resume. Ruth Hobbs' daydreams of homicide could be broadened.

Miss Franks and Mrs. Hobbs each carried a stack of manila files with color-coded borders and reference numbers neatly printed on their tabs. The folders with the same first four digits would be duplicated and cross-filed under the ID numbers of each of the local area directors. While stapling a recent report from Wilson Donahue, Ruth came across a two-week-old document from Navy Intelligence. The original Nav Intel code number remained and under that was a new number marked in red ink from the Director of Central American Affairs. Under that, a third number referenced her boss, Lon Crane. That's odd, Ruth thought to herself. Both reports mentioned the same area of operations; Golfo de San Miguel on the Pacific side of Panama. Mr. Crane has initialed Wilson Donahue's report but not the Navy Intel report.

Blotting sweat from her forehead with her last tissue, Ruth gathered up the reports. "At least I can escape this suffocating heat for a few more minutes," she mumbled to herself as she brushed past Miss Franks.

She presented the folder to Mr. Crane. "I need your initials beside the file number before I can duplicate and file this," she said.

Lon Crane scanned the single page in the folder and turned white. "But I've never seen this report, Mrs. Hobbs," he said. "Get Commander Knox and Brian Holt in here, and tell them to bring current charts of operations area twenty-six."

Fifteen minutes later, Holt and Knox appeared with a small scale US Coast and Geodetic Survey chart, number 21605, and one large scale British Admiralty chart, number 1929. Mr. Crane was on the phone arguing with another sector head.

"I don't give a damn! The original number is not enough. There's no cover page. This was obviously extracted from a more complete report and I want it all, and I want to authenticate the original sender."

Crane covered the mouthpiece of the phone and lifted his eyes to meet those of Commander Knox. "That's your slice of pizza, Ash. All the time in the world. Take up to an hour. One more thing, hook us up to the nearest monitoring unit in the operations area as soon as possible."

Donahue's communications from Operation Goose and the Navy Intel report mentioned events in the same area but different time periods, bringing the significance of the two crashing together. The information contained in the Navy Intel page clearly indicated Operation Goose was not the short, sweet and simple success the latest report claimed. The barge had had an escort across the Pacific, two submarines, and both were last detected somewhere between Golfo de San Miguel and the Panama Canal.

A pair of subs could make it into Golfo de San Miguel, but only on the surface. The Russian "trawlers" that cruised up and down the coast had always been a worry. They seldom deployed fishing nets and never came into port for resupply, sell fish, or buy ice. With more and taller-than-normal radio transmitting antennae, intelligence knew they monitored American and Panamanian radio signals, making necessary the use of field telephones in the last stages of capturing the barge. Navy Intel knew that one, and possibly both, of those small ships was also a sub-tender.

* * * *

The lights were on late at the Russian Embassy in Georgetown. Gregor Poliakov, Director of Cultural Affairs, wanted to know what the Americans were trying to do. Russian property was in the hands of the Panamanian forces and American cowboys, and must be returned. This could easily provoke an armed response. The Americans are responsible. Poliakov seethed over the outrageous attack on Russian maritime interests, followed by even more outrageous threats in the United Nations. American complaints are groundless. There has been no challenge of their arrogant Monroe Doctrine. Cuba is not our colony, but merely a rustic cousin who asked for help to stem the threat of American imperialism.

An aide knocked at the door to announce an elderly man, thin and bald, with sharp features. The aide placed the visitor's small briefcase on a side table near Poliakov's desk and retreated to the outside office. In polite conversation, Vordal Linkovka pulled Poliakov's thoughts like chess pieces from a board. Pale, heavy eyebrows and keen, gray eyes were consistent with his Latvian mother's lineage. "You think in party platitudes, Mr. Poliakov. Let us be a bit more analytical," Linkovka urged. "We must reject stop-gap measures, we must resist responding to American charges, resist giving credence to their claims. Rather than striking indignant poses and railing against the threats of the Americans, let us try to compile our options, and limit the damage."

"The Americans have our property," Gregor Poliakov insisted. "And they must return it, with apologies for their unwarranted aggression."

"If that doesn't happen, and most assuredly it will not, what would make us just as happy as having it returned?" Linkovka asked. "Or what would make us almost as happy?

And if we don't get that, what would we settle for as an alternative to open hostilities? Consider the possibilities. Otherwise, you, and men like you, will plunge us into the unthinkable, a catastrophe beyond description. Think. There is no time to permit prolonged dialogue between you and insulated bureaucrats in Moscow. You may have to put your career on the line and actually make a decision."

Poliakov didn't like Linkovka. He was clearly an intellectual liberal who thought negotiation and compromise could produce acceptable results, Poliakov thought to himself. *Utter nonsense. He has been in New York four months and suddenly appears in the American sauna called Washington D.C., unannounced,* Gregor thought, still pacing, still scowling, his narrow brow deeply furrowed. *His official papers proclaimed Linkovka a minor bureaucrat from the Ministry of Agriculture. Then I'm a cosmonaut! The problem with the barge has become public and suddenly the highest-ranking man in the Foreign Service, a personal friend of Mikoyan, is at my door! Poliakov swallowed hard but the lump in his throat remained. One misstep and this dried-up old fig will ruin me.*

"You heard the frenzy of innuendo and subtle threats in the UN Secretary General's initial hearing?" Linkovka commented in tones that could have been casual conversation. "It caused a stir with delegates from the Organization of American States. Do you think Costa Rica, Bolivia, Colombia, Honduras and Mexico are anxious to see their backyards become a nuclear battleground for two super-powers? Our mission here is to remove the possibilities of hostilities, to dissolve the anxieties of our friends and possible future allies in the western world."

An elderly woman in a dark gray dress and white apron entered the paneled room with a tray, and placed it on Poliakov's side table.

"The press coverage was modest," Linkovka continued. "The photos are inconclusive. They could be of any barge built for any purpose. Nevertheless, it was picked up by several wire services. News of this volatile situation will not be well received at home." He lifted his glass of sweetened iced tea with lemon. "One of the few American habits I've acquired," he admitted to Poliakov as he sipped from the tall glass.

"There is nothing I can do from here without approval," Poliakov blurted, his voice warped by frustration.

"Do you think doing nothing will garner approval? From whom?" Vordal asked in fatherly tones. "Hand-wringing and excuses will accomplish nothing. Sit down, Gregor, and enjoy your tea."

Poliakov struggled to regain his composure. Beads of sweat formed across his forehead and upper lip. Gregor knew he was the tip of the Russian spear being blunted against an American shield.

"What upsets us about the Americans ruthlessly taking possession of the barge?" Vordal asked in tones not quite so fatherly. "Is it the interference with Russian-Cuban affairs? Is it the loss of our monetary investment? Is it the possible political damage that could result with a disclosure of our intentions, which the Americans now think they can prove?"

"All of these reasons!" Poliakov shouted, his voice quaking with anger. He was fully aware that his superiors in Moscow would be searching for a scapegoat as well as a solution. "And many will blame me for this failure, since much of the past three months' activities were directed from this office. I have been placed in an untenable position!"

Poliakov raged, spilling tea on the chestnut table.

"Come, come, Gregor," Linkovka urged. "The men who planned the barge program are not children. They knew there were risks. They could not possibly blame you. We must focus on what can be salvaged."

Linkovka spent three long hours in the inner office with Poliakov. In the end, a plan was hammered out, a course of action that presented Gregor Poliakov as the man responsible for disarming the problem, the hero of the day, a savior. The solution centered on a basic premise; if the barge doesn't exist, the problem doesn't exist.

"Plan 'A' is a failure," Linkovka asserted. "Russia must now cut its losses and move to other options. The US will certainly not allow rocket and rocket fuel production to be established in Cuba. Perhaps we have the cart before the horse. First install missiles, then manufacturing facilities. Raise the ante. The Americans would perhaps start a conventional war to enforce the Monroe Doctrine, but would they risk a nuclear war? Nikita Khrushchev has assured us they won't. Would they risk a nuclear war knowing that over eighty percent of their country would be within range of a thousand proven solid fuel rockets that cost mere fractions to produce compared to gargantuan, and now unnecessary, ICBMs?

"Besides," Vordal Linkovka continued, "didn't their failure to provide air support for the Bay of Pigs, on the very threshold of their back door, prove they were unwilling to enforce the Monroe Doctrine even by conventional means? If this reasoning is sound, I ask you, Gregor, then how could the barge have been lost to the forces of such indecisive weaklings? The inconsistency is staggering!"

"Inconsistent or not, the barge is in the hands of the Americans," Poliakov grumbled. "Russian property! Pirated by murderous brigands. Gangsters! And don't make so little of the millions of rubles spent in creating the factory and transporting it so far. And how did they manage to snatch it from the Cubans?"

"The barge is certainly lost," Linkovka admitted, "which will make Comrade Kuzevanov very unhappy. This was his pet project from the beginning. And Marshall Molinovski. But it must not be used by Americans to damage Russian prestige and credibility. The photographs will be denied as fakes, of course.

"Witnesses must be subjected to detailed inquiries in an open hearing. They would have to be very inventive to explain how they happened to be aboard Russian property when no legitimate salvage claim existed, and they will certainly be implicated in the murder of six Russian crewmen. In the best interest of all parties, perhaps the barge should just disappear."

And Gregor Poliakov felt like his guts were tied in knots.

CHAPTER TWENTY-FOUR

To see the errors, and wanderings
And mists, and tempests
Lucretius

Donahue was ecstatic. Operation Goose proved far more successful than anyone could have hoped for. In the shelter of the mess tent, its skirts dropped for protection from the storm, he debriefed our team and the homesick photographers. "Joint protests have been filed with the UN and involved embassies," Donahue began. "Dutch and Russian parties claim a floating miniaturized refinery, manufactured in Japan and Russia, was forced to ground out in Panama because the tug had mechanical failure and was forced to seek an anchorage down coast and ran aground. Remember the first tug is in Costa Rica having a new prop installed because it ran aground too? We are very distressed the Dutch are cooperating with the Russians, but that's another matter." he said, taking a sip of coffee. "The Russians have stated, complete lies, of course, that the second tug and our barge developed multiple leaks at faulty weld joints and the tug master feared the tow would be lost in deep water. After grounding the barge in a shallow bay, they were fired on by local bandits and the entire tug crew, Russians, gentlemen, not Cuban or Dutch, was killed except for one officer who managed to escape into the jungle. They want Panama to secure the barge so technicians can repair the splits in the hull plates. Then they want to bring it to Balboa and take it right on through the canal, like nothing's happened."

"Fat chance!" Keener blurted out.

"My sentiments, exactly," Donahue said with a laugh. "But there are people in Washington who want us to return it. It is Russian property, after all. They haven't thought of asking what kind of property, or if that property endangers the US. That's what happens when you overburden a government with attorneys and accountants.

"Actually, the Russians haven't the slightest interest in attempting the canal until they have the disassembled valves and control panels. That's what their technicians really want to do," Donahue continued. "They consistently deny any and all photographic evidence we've ever brought to the UN. They'll stonewall the photos of the barge and without the non-corrosive alloy valves and the control panels; it still might actually pass as a refinery. So instead, we'll take the barge to Balboa ourselves, out of reach of their Cuban friends, who, by the way, have not been located."

"Mr. Donahue," Bishop interrupted, "have you ever been really, really tired? We're tired right now and we want to go home. Aren't we gonna read all this in the newspapers, anyway? Even if we don't, so what? You have what you paid for. I have a girl who gets..ahmmm..impatient..if I'm gone too long."

"Within the next three days," Donahue droned, ignoring Bishop, "we will have filed a second round of protests and can back them up with guided tours of this floating rocket fuel plant," Donahue concluded. His face was almost distorted by a broad smile of satisfaction deepening the wrinkles at the corners of his eyes and the dimples at the corners of his mouth.

"Got it all worked out, huh? That's great," Larry joined in, his impatience bursting through his feeble effort to hide it. "When do we go back to the States?"

A blast of cool air shook the tent and forced its way under the loose flaps. Hard rain rattled on the canvas overhead.

"We'll have a plane for you in three or four days," Donahue assured us. "That's how long it will take to get the replacement tug down here. You guys shot the hell out of the other one. Puerto Rican insurance investigators climbed all over every inch of the damned boat. They were pissed!"

"When do we go back to the States?" Larry asked again.

"It'll probably take a month to repair, but we'll pay for it. Right now, it's a goddamned obstacle. The engines are intact but the fuel tanks couldn't hold enough diesel to get out of Golfo de San Miguel. There were so many bullet holes, the tanks have to be replaced at a shipyard. We'll have two new tugs here early this afternoon: one for the damaged tug and one for the barge. You be ready to leave by then."

"What do fucking tugboats have to do with us? It's a little breezy out, but why can't we get choppers to the air base now?" Bennett asked.

"It's the barge. We're riding shotgun, aren't we?" Larry guessed.

"Part way," Donahue confirmed. "You're a Pan American Highway survey team we're evacuating because of local bandits already reported by the Russians. When you get up coast a bit, the US Navy will take you aboard a real gun boat, a heavy cruiser, I think they said."

263

"Fuck this! We only contracted to get you a clear shot at photographing the barge," Larry argued. "I'd say we've already done a hellava lot more than that. Now you want us to do security?"

"Yes, indeed! You're absolutely right," Donahue agreed through a forced smile, "and I apologize for the delay. On the other hand, you contracted for twenty-one days, and this is only the thirteenth day. I really must insist. Two or three more days and you'll be in Loro Azul for lunch. I'm picking up your bar and restaurant tab again and I guarantee you'll be on the way home within four days."

"This stinks, Bill, and you know it," Larry persisted. "The contract says complete the mission or twenty-one days. This mission is accomplished! Now we want to go home!"

"Damn it, Larry! You know I'm not the one who decides when this mission is over," Donahue shot back. "Neither are you. Besides, there is another reason. Gary Powers is being kicked in the guts in a Russian courtroom. We think we can use this barge to leverage him out of there. Illegal aerial reconnaissance is nothing compared to what the Reds have tried to pull off with that barge.

"Don't think I'm insensitive to how exhausted your men must be. No one could have done what you did. And only one of the *compañeros* as a casualty. But I have to have security, at least until we get it into the approaches to the canal. The best I can do is throw in a bonus for your services. A thousand per man, and you'd still be three or four days short of your original contract."

"When do you want us on the barge?" Larry conceded, straining to be heard over the tent flaps slapping in the wind. Bishop struggled to button them up and got soaked for his trouble.

"Break down everything that doesn't look like a survey team's equipment," Donahue barked. "Load up all weapons, ammunition and radios. Leave anything a survey team would need. Open your cover pack. Scatter a few maps around. Leave a transit," he suggested, waving in the direction of the beach. "Throw out some of the letters in the manila folders. Leave the Lister bags, rations, generator, mess and all regular camp gear. A news team will be here covering the new tug bringing out the barge and your panicked evacuation of camp due to reports of bandit activity. Load the Zodiacs and outboards but keep weapons and radios out of sight. You wouldn't believe the money we have invested in those boats. Board the barge later this evening, outside the gulf, and use the barges crane to hoist the Goslings, outboards and all your gear aboard."

"Do we get extra help? It took four days to set up camp and you want us to strike it in an afternoon," Keener grumbled.

"No help. You're not striking camp, this is an evacuation. Bandits, remember?" Donahue snapped. "This is supposed to look like you're running for your lives. Just take your personal gear," Donahue restated. "Go to the starboard side of the barge at the stern. A crane has been erected and the diesel tank's filled. There's plenty of room for all the gear and we dropped a boarding net to help you get up to the crane."

We stood in the rain to say our farewells to Donahue. Gates rose above his surliness at being denied a safer extraction and joined us at the chopper near the tip of the peninsula now whipped by wind and spray.

A lone chopper bounced and rattled in the gusts, straining against its tie-downs. The H-40's engine sputtered and whined to life as a crewman removed the tethers and boarded. The rotors added to the wind blasts.

Donahue's helicopter shuddered and lurched, then tipped sideways into the wind. It hung over the beach and at last shouldered its way against the wind. As it side-slipped toward the gulf, Oscar Escobar leaned out of the bay tightly gripping a hand rail and waved good-bye, his cherub face a confusion of regret and fear.

The *compañeros* set extra tent lines and tightened the ones already in place. The photographers displayed signs of relief when they heard they would be picked up by boat late the next morning. Air travel under these conditions didn't seem appealing. And the wind was predicted to increase.

We did what we could with Donahue's instructions. The feeble attempt to explain our presence to person or persons unknown seemed a ludicrous waste of time and effort. A few minutes into the project, we abandoned it. The wind would have carried off the notes and maps, and the transit wouldn't stand up in the wind. On to the next chore: loading our gear into the Zodiacs.

The rafts surged and tugged at the lines that held them captive to the beach. We loaded them on the flood tide, slipping them higher and higher as the muddy waters foamed around our knees.

I stacked the last of the spare batteries in front of Gosling Two's steering console and turned to go back for the BAR. Gates stood on the beach, staring at the bay. Golfo de San Miguel was whipped into frothing insanity by the wind, a churning, gray turmoil, streaked with white. Long, jagged lines of wind-driven surf rampaged west to east, exploding into the corner where Base T joined the main peninsula. Gates' white-knuckled, shaking hands gripped the handles of his bags of explosives. His ashen face stared wide-eyed at the sea. I wasn't anxious to go out under these conditions either, but Gates was planted like an oak.

Keener appeared, loaded down with his personal gear. "Holy shit! There must be a hurricane blowing out there on the mud flats!" he shouted over the wind.

Gates dropped his satchels.

"We oughta wa-wait until this f-f-fuckin' storm blows over," Gates proposed.

"You know what they say, Gates. Time, tide and the US government waits for no man . . . or storm." I tried to sound unconcerned, but in reality I felt my stomach twist at the sight of the gulf and wondered what it must be like in the open water beyond the gulf. This time I agreed with Gates.

Gates left his bags on the beach and rushed off to find Larry.

Keener was right about the conditions outside the gulf, but his remarks didn't provide any bracing up for Gates. Half an hour later, Larry came into our tent to chew on Keener for scaring the hell out of Gates who now wanted to be taken off with the photographers the next morning.

"I want to keep the team together and we're riding the barge as a security force," Larry growled in Keener's face. "Loomer's group will go to La Palma on a supply boat, and then board a cargo plane for the Canal Zone when the weather clears. If they miss their hop, they might have to wait at Base T another day or two and get picked up by the same vessel that brought them down.

"Keener, you scared the shit out of Gates, and now he doesn't want to get into the rafts with the rest of us!"

"I don't blame him a bit," Keener said. "He was afraid of water on calm nights. Now, he's got damned good reason to be afraid!"

"Gates is coming with us, and that's that!" Larry shouted in Keener's face. "I keep La Palma as an option, but only if he goes totally to pieces. Right now, I want your goddamned mouth closed around him! Clear?"

Keener puffed up a bit but knew Larry had his own reasons to drag Gates along with us. His hackles were up over being chewed out in front of the rest of us but he'd' get over it.

We said our good-byes to the *guias*, truly friends at our parting. There were regrets about Roberto, but they considered him a trial and an embarrassment. He would not be missed. And they especially appreciated that Larry had protected Jorge with a report that gave a believable cover story of Roberto's death. It didn't occur to me at the time, but that report possibly made all of us accessories to a murder.

Saying farewell to the photographers was a strain. Loomer was at last in full command. Roche had retreated from contact when possible, eating alone and refusing even to drink with his colleagues now that the corks were out. He actually did have two broken ribs from my BAR and a swollen lip from Dr. Loomer's pick handle. He would only talk about the lawsuits he planned to file.

At first, only Larry and Rubio were bold enough to enter their tent. We knew they still chaffed at the undignified manner in which they were forced to board the boats. At last, Nash and Collins came out to see us and wish us well. The rain stopped and all five photographers walked us to our inflatables, peace restored.

The tranquility didn't last long for Roche. "The whole project was screwed up from day one," he fumed. "We should never have been down here until the barge was cleared of Cubans. Then there's the way we've been treated. Insults, physical abuse, endangerment, and no sanitation. I'll sue Roger Ferguson, then Donny Loomer and then you, Mr. Abbott."

"Sorry you feel that way, Dr. Roche. However, I have a question," Larry said. "How will you pursue litigation without violating the security restriction in the contract you signed to get down here in the first place?"

Roche stammered and stormed back to his corner of the tent, his face red with rage. Intimidating civil servants was getting harder and harder.

Plans were modified. The original tug was written off as a major repair project by the claims adjusters, and the plans for a new tug fell through. The original tug must temporarily serve if the barge is to make its scheduled appearance at the Canal Zone. A Panamanian crew installed temporary rubber bladder tanks below deck and new portable radios wired up in the bridge to replace the ones we shot out. The patched hydraulics was their big worry.

At sixteen hundred, we watched the tug through binoculars. It struggled across the bay with its huge tow as tug crewmen shoveled glass shards and ruined gear into the sea. Smoke billowed out of the open engine room hatches. The exhaust manifolds, broken in our attack, were only partly repaired.

The news coverage shot film from the deck of the "Mother Goose" PT boat, the cameraman braced by a man on each side. When the barge lumbered away into the wind and mists, they turned to film us as we hauled ourselves out to the white bouy.

Accurate navigation was supposed to place both barge and rafts at the same place at the same time. Seven degrees, thirty-one minutes north latitude, seventy-eight degrees, forty-four minutes west longitude. This was outside Golfo de San Miguel, where deep ocean currents, upwelling from water over six thousand feet deep, collide with the steep sides of the continental shelf. This location had been a compromise. Ninety degrees off a direct course to the Panama Canal, this was the point at which we would begin a twelve-hour run to join our Navy escort, outside the Archipelago de las Perlas.

We worried about being on the open sea during a near gale. A high level of accuracy in navigation under these conditions couldn't be a realistic expectation, even with the most careful plotting. We could only factor in an allowance for wind and waves and hope for the best.

For the last time, we shoved the rafts off the beach. I didn't feel any affection for this gritty, mosquito-infested gravel bar, yet, living here a week and a half had significantly altered my life. Here, I had made new friends and elbowed room for myself in the midst of adversaries. I discovered that a learning curve can be steeper when your neck is on the line. Through blistering heat and blinding downpours, I'd struggled with self-doubt and boredom, and more than a touch of homesickness. I had tasted fury and terror, and soared with the elation of being alive. All this on a piece of ground that couldn't grow a decent patch of weeds.

No one could be more at home at Base T than Juan, Pello and Jorge. The *compañeros* stayed behind to break the remainder of the surveyor's camp and load it on the supply barge that would come when the storm ended. They would burn or bury any evidence of our occupation of Campo Tiburon. In a month, the bits and scraps we'd left behind would be debris indistinguishable from the rubble left by generations of shark fishermen.

The rafts were heavy and sluggish. At maximum high tide, the water near the beach stretched nearly over the spine and was barely deep enough to float the rafts and much too shallow to lower the propellers. One by one, cursing and struggling against the wind, we hauled out to the mooring buoy to fire off the engines and run out on Pollux Intercept for the last time.

Gosling Two was last to leave. Rain on my glasses made me a poor choice as helmsman. Keener squinted through the spray-streaked windshield we'd re-installed that morning and pushed the throttle to half speed and dodged two of the discarded push-poles from the Goslings that preceded us. Where we were going, out to damned deep water, push-poles wouldn't be needed and I tipped ours overboard.

I coiled the bowline and looked back. The *guias* waved good-bye from shore. One of them stooped to pick something metallic out of the surf. It was the cooking pot in which Collins burned the oatmeal, scrubbed bright by the tumbling surf.

Keener pushed the boat as hard as he could to catch up to the others. Only Gosling Three, with Ross Bishop, Rubio Williams and Buryl Gates was visible in the fading light. We'd planned a raft-up at the end of Pollux Intercept to try to arrive at the barge more or less at the same time.

I marveled at the struggle within Gates. The combination of his irrational fear of water and the present justifiable fear of the sea must have had him terrified. Yet, by bravery or incredible self discipline, he somehow placed himself in a Zodiac. I never saw his face, but his posture was rigid, his hands solidified in a death grip on the cargo straps, and his head had been swallowed by his shoulders.

Gosling Two arrived at the end of Pollux Intercept just as the others, seeing us approaching, formed a line and departed, again leaving us in last place, forty yards behind Gosling Three, much closer than we had been.

The blasting rain and salt spray stung our eyes. I took shelter under the spray hood at the bow of the raft. Pounding southwest, almost dead into the wind, we headed for our rendezvous with the barge.

Outside the shelter of the gulf, the sea became an ominous parade of heaving black walls of water. The Zodiacs handled it well, aside from the drenching. Our course permitted safe quartering of the waves, so we pushed the Zodiac hard, with near stalls on the steep faces of the waves. At almost full power, Keener propelled us into roller-coaster leaps over or through the crests and heart-stopping dives into dark troughs that seemed bottomless.

Too wet and scared to enjoy the thrill, I quit my shelter under the spray hood and focused on Gosling Three's barely visible stern light.

Turning due south brought a brilliant yellow glow into view. The tug was lit up like a La Palma brothel.

Carefully, we approached the tow from the stern. Something was wrong. The tug slowly swung broadside to us and to the wind, then lumbered in our direction. The towline must have broken.

In the distance, a longboat appeared on a crest near the bow of the tug. White oars sent it skittering down the face of a wave like a stiff-legged water beetle. The ship's boat moved away from the tug, downwind and toward us.

The four men looked back when an explosion deep inside the tug carried over the shrieking wind. The tug's lights went out. Billowing thick smoke, the tug quickly listed to port. On a crest, it rolled to its beam-ends, shipping water into the pilothouse and stack. Lightening flashed over its bright green bottom paint as it capsized and sank stern first, leaving the quartet of crewmen alone on building seas.

The wind swung the stern of the barge toward us again, too close to our cluster of rafts. We turned away in the calm of a trough and assessed the problem of climbing the boarding net from a safer distance. Bishop argued with Larry. "What's the point? We're not going anywhere with the tug at the bottom of the sea. Why board now?"

"Two reasons," he shouted at Bishop over the wind. "First, that's what we were ordered to do. Second, being on the barge is safer than the rafts if the sea gets any worse, and it looks like it will. Now . . . who goes up the net first?"

The swells ran at fifteen feet, lifting the barge's stern, and then dropping it with a thunderous crash, soaking us with wind-driven spray.

Nelson was assigned as crane operator. The gear we carried was far too heavy to leave in the rafts when they were slung aboard. The segmented plywood floors could not have supported the weight of gear and crews, but the idea of trying to load cargo nets under these conditions was a frightening prospect.

Bennett put Nelson at the bow of Gosling Four and ran alongside the net. On the crest of a swell, Nelson leaped onto the net and was nearly swept off by the next wave.

Within a few minutes, we heard the crane's diesel rumble and a second cargo net splashed into the sea between Goslings Two and Four. Bennett backed off to let Gosling One off-load the ANGRC-9 and transmitting generator, followed by personal gear, field cases, and code books.

"Now!" Eddy shouted, and then threw the engine into reverse as Larry jumped for the boarding net and scrambled aboard, a PRC-6 hanging on his belt.

Now it was Gosling Three's turn, burdened with personal gear, ammunition and all of Gates' explosives wrapped in canvas cut from the communications tent.

Bishop, like the rest of us, had never handled a boat in these conditions. Even if an operator does everything right, he is still in peril of being swamped or slammed into the side of the barge, or worse: swept under the pounding stern.

It was my fault as much as anyone's. In the rush, I saw too late that Gates had not tied the breast straps of his life vest and the crotch strap hung loosely at his right side, catching under the holster of his .45 automatic. His face was distorted by stark terror. His hands gripped the plywood transom of the inflatable and lashings on the tent. Useless.

Diesel fuel from the scuttled tug now coated every surface of the rafts and our equipment. It streamed from our hair and stung our eyes. Each wave that swept past left us spitting and gagging with it.

There was nothing anyone could do. The timing of the second attempt had been as bad as the first. A steep swell stood the raft on its stern and Gates, almost in slow motion, fell backward out of the boat, slipped through his life vest and didn't come up.

The oil soaked vest bobbed in the momentary shelter under the stern of the barge and tumbled out of sight with the next wave that roared past. The bubbles of Gates' last breath mingled with the swirling water that surged around the starboard quarter and under the barge's transom.

Gates was gone.

CHAPTER TWENTY-FIVE

Still wouldst thou sing, and I have ears in vain-
To thy high requiem . . . .
Keats

We stared in horror as the seconds dragged past with no sign of Gates. There were no tell-tale bubbles, only the breaking crests driving under the rafts. There was no flash of a hand, no frantic gasp or splashing of water to tell us that he was within reach. Keener and Bennett stripped off their life jackets, threw off their caps and kicked off their sandals. They lunged to the side of the raft nearest where Gates had disappeared.

"No!" Rubio shouted. "I won't lose anyone else. Stay in the boats."

I couldn't take my eyes off the spot where Gates went under. I hated him, not just for tormenting me, but for demeaning anyone who came within ear-shot. Still, he was one of us.

"What did you say, Jimmy?" Keener asked.

"Did I say something?"

"Something about Mary. I couldn't understand the rest," he said, his eyes sweeping the water.

"It's been too long. He's not going to make it," shouted a disembodied voice from another raft.

This isn't the way Gates should end, I thought. What about his family? How could we explain? What if I had fallen?

The engines grumbled as we repositioned ourselves farther away from the menacing stern. The barge was our only point of reference; we could now be twenty yards from the spot where Gates actually went under.

In the lee of the barge, the gale softened to a whisper and the sea flattened. The storm held its breath for a few moments, and something inside me melted, swirled, and poured away. I felt transported into Gate's body, I became Gates, I saw what he saw, felt the pain and fear he felt.

I steadied myself against the console and stared into the oil-slicked water. I could only think of Gates; his thoughts filled my head and his terror gripped my soul.

* * * *

Out of the depths have I cried unto Thee, O Lord:
Lord, hear my voice.
Let Thine ears be attentive to the voice of
My supplication.

Vile and imperfect man. Vain and deceitful, full of pride and arrogance, impoverished of mercy and charity. And the Tempest folded over him. Eyes open, limbs frozen in terror, straight and stiff, Gates rolled in the dark, tumultuous brine. Through the foaming crest, lightning flashed fool's gold. The water was warm and insistent and he slipped deeper, feet first, into a bone-chilling thermocline, an up-welling from the ocean floor that came to claim him.

I am the resurrection and the life: he that
believeth in me, although he be dead, shall
live; and every one that liveth and believeth in me,
shall not die forever.
Believeth thou this?"

I've dreamed my end would be so, and I believed it, and
now my nightmares of the sea have summoned up demons
from its depths. My breath is taken in a suffocating kiss,
and I'm locked in an embrace that I cannot shed. I'm a fool
who believed, and am now condemned, in the self-fulfilling
prophecy of my nightmares.

The water tore at his senses. Thundering waves abraded
his every nerve. The booming of the barge hummed in his
bones and lightning flashes danced on the retinas of his wide
open, unblinking eyes. And he slipped deeper, arms above
his head, and fingers splayed.

Hail Mary, full of grace, the Lord is with thee.
Blessed art thou among women, and blessed
is the fruit of thy womb, Jesus. Holy Mary,
Mother of God, pray for us sinners,
now at the hour of our death.
Amen.

Is this the filmy darkness I so dreaded? Is this the
darkness that I dreamed? Am I now dragged beneath the
salt-spumed ether, interred in the womb that bore the
nightmares of my dissolution, the womb that despised me?
Is this the icy amniotic fluid that bears me to oblivion?

Ears shrieked and pinged with the pressure. Sinuses
burned with salt and eyes were pressed deeper into their
sockets.

To Thee, O Lord, we commend the soul of Thy servant,

Buryl Gates, that having

departed from this world he may live with Thee: and whatever his sins he has

committed through the frailty of human nature, do Thou, in Thy most tender mercy,

forgive and wash away.

Through Christ our Lord.

Amen.

Bubbles spiraled upward from the corners of his mouth and nostrils like a broken strand of pearls. His arms slowly closed to his chest. Head bowed, he rolled to his side as if to sleep and the last air in his lungs streamed away.

Darkness wrapped in darkness, the void lay below. A numbing cold bore him downward and out to sea. Downward and away. Downward and beyond our reach, beyond the continental shelf, beyond hope.

In pace requiescat.

CHAPTER TWENTY-SIX

In ruin and confusion hurled . . .
Horace

"He's Commander John Martinson Warren," Ashford Knox announced. "He's presently aboard the monitoring station you asked me to hook up. You can probably talk to him personally as soon as we integrate with the Navy's ultra low frequency transmitters. Hell, I know the guy. We both served on the Boxer in the Pacific in fifty-seven. He tosses his cookies every time he goes to sea, and he's the worst poker player I know."

"Jack was in the embassy in Panama City when this report came across the desk of a naval attaché he knows," Brian 'Sonny' Holt inserted. "I've talked to the attaché. He said Jack Warren went ape-shit, tore out this page and fired off several copies. We got this one and I suppose the area coordinator got the other. It apparently missed the coordinator who had spent some time in the hospital with malaria. He's been released but we don't know if he's caught up on his reading."

Lon Crane rose from his desk and stepped to the table where the charts were taped down. He traced his fingers over the route from Golfo de San Miguel to the Panama Canal. "You mean we have people in the field who don't know there are two Russian subs waiting to ambush them on the way to the ditch?"

"Worse," Commander Knox said. "We've raised this area coordinator, an old-timer named Wilson Donahue. Brian found him at a chopper field coded as Gander. They tried to raise the men in the field, but they've broken camp and their long-range receiver is down. They're headed for the barge and might already be on board. Not only do they not know, there's no way we can warn them." Ash's voice was tinged with concern, for both the men and the project.

Sonny Holt covered the mouthpiece of the phone and cleared his throat for attention. "We have our pet Russian Colonel on the second line. He sounds pissed," he interrupted, handing the receiver to Crane.

* * * *

"Good afternoon, Colonel Penkovski. What do you have for me?" Lon inquired. His forehead furrowed as he endured a tirade that blasted from the receiver. "Sorry. We'll try to make it up to you. Try your account in St. Paul. Maybe they sent it to the wrong bank. Meantime, I'll put a tracer on it.

"They said you have something for us today." Another pause, the tone softened. "Yes, Colonel, anytime you want." Lon gestured for pencil and paper . "I know Mr. Poliakov. We've met on several occasions. Three o'clock this afternoon . . . wait, I'll write it down. We know about the subs. Do they have authorization? Thank you, Colonel. Don't forget to check St. Paul."

Lon Crane had personally ordered a delay on payment for Colonel Oleg Penkovski's last information packet until it checked out. It did. In his gut, he knew this one would, too.

"Gentlemen," Crane said, as he returned the phone to its cradle. "We have a serious problem. The Russian subs have been ordered to sink the barge if it's taken closer to the canal than eight degrees thirty minutes north latitude, along with any US Navy escort and escape if they can." Crane checked the faces of his associates.

They were as astonished as he. "Get Marconetti on the phone and tell him to schedule an emergency briefing with the President. We have a finger-on-the-button situation. Have we got the Navy's on-site monitoring station yet?"

Sonny shook his head, "Negative."

"Christ! Ash, make your phone call and get back here on the double."

* * * *

The rafts kept their distance from the barge, riding in the sheltered water of the downwind side. The tug's crew clumsily labored at the oars of their long boat. At last they joined us and tried to communicate. The captain was Costa Rican and the crew was Panamanian. Not one of them spoke English. We signaled for Rubio and made room for him to maneuver close enough to talk to them.

"The explosion on the tug was no accident," Rubio translated. "They had a radio message to leave the tow line connected and abandon the tug. The captain was last to leave. He had orders by radio to set some kind of timer. They jumped in the boat and rowed like hell."

"Call Larry on a PRC-6. Something's up," I urged. "Have him set up the ANGRC-9 so we can talk to Mother Goose and Gander."

"Good idea," Rubio confirmed, reaching for a PRC-6 under the spray hood. Within half an hour, the nine was set up, sheltered between two tanks on the elevated deck forward of the stern. A temporary antenna stretched to the top of the crane operator's booth. The barge slowly swung its bow toward the wind and we wondered how long this advantageous condition would last.

"The scuttled tug is swinging on the end of its four hundred yard towline," Rubio continued. "Its supposed to drag in the water to keep the barge's bow to the storm and resist drifting."

"Looks like its working," Bennett shouted from Gosling Four. "But what the hell is going on?"

"That's what we have to find out," Rubio agreed.

"They don't need us out here with the damned tug sunk, and there's no taxi in sight."

Nelson fired up the diesel engine on the crane again and brilliant lights burned our eyes. When our eyes adjusted to the glare, we could see the boarding net hanging from the gunwale. The starboard quarter rode a few feet higher with the weight of the tug hanging off the bow. Another wave swept past, still washing over the lower end of the net. Nelson quickly emptied each raft of all but its human burden. As the cargo net thumped onto the deck, Nelson dropped from the operator's cab and worked like a madman. We would be needed on deck to sling each Gosling and its cargo aboard. Then the crew of the first Gosling could help with the next.

When Larry was ready, Nelson jumped on the hand-cranked transmitting generator and tried to raise Gander. We waited while the barge thundered and rumbled. Once again broadside to the seas, it began a slow swing back to bow-on. And we waited. At last, the PRC-6 squealed to life. "Gosling Three, Gosling Three, this is Big Boy. Over,"

Larry's voice streamed from the walkie-talkie, identifying himself by a new code name for our trip to the canal.

We were struck dumb by the news. "Everyone comes aboard, now!" Larry's voice grumbled through the tinny speaker of the six. "Sink all Goslings. Lookouts post to the corners of the barge. Williams and Donlin have jobs below."

I couldn't believe what I had heard. The order made no sense. We had lost a man following orders to save equipment and these boats, and now we sink them. How will we get off the barge? Weapons, explosives, ammunition, records and code books, and personal gear were already aboard, even the spare batteries. That pile of junk isn't worth a man's life. The Goslings weren't either, for that matter.

Goddamn Donahue!

Keener nudged Bennett's boat and told him to get aboard Gosling Two. Bennett drew his bayonet and stabbed each air chamber several times and clamored into our raft. Gosling Four collapsed into a rumpled, gray, shapeless mass. The weight of the outboard drew the transom backwards, tilted and sank, pulling the raft down to hang by air trapped in the tip of the bow chambers. Bennett leaned over the side of our boat to make two more thrusts. Streaming bubbles marked Gosling Four's descent into five or six thousand feet of water.

"What's going on? Eventually, this tub will strand out on some mud flat," Bennett complained. "What will that accomplish?"

Rubio shouted over the wind. "Larry said he'll brief us when we're aboard. Right now, he wants us on the barge. The tug crew stays in their boat."

Eddy brought Gosling One roughly alongside Gosling Two and tossed the bowline to me. "This doesn't feel right," he said. "Talk about burning your bridges. Here goes!" he roared at us, barely louder than the rush of wind. Drawing his bayonet, he imitated Bennett's actions, retrieving his ball cap from the console at the last possible second. The fifteen-gallon fuel can, almost empty and tethered to the outboard by the fuel line, held the raft and engine three feet below the surface, struggling with its burden until Eddy cut it free.

Now the rafts' fuel merged with the dissipating diesel slick.

Keener, at a nod from Rubio as he climbed aboard, put Gosling Two in gear. With the bow pointed toward the boarding net, we surged forward. Keener pressed the bow against the net as one of the swells exploded under us. Drenched and spitting water, Bennett and Rubio leaped onto the net and Keener and I stood by to pick them up if they fell off.

As the next wave lifted Gosling Two within a few feet of the barge's deck, Eddy jumped. The swell passed and Gosling Two took the express elevator into a deep trough. Eddy slipped and plunged into the sea. His bright orange life jacket immediately brought him to the surface between Gosling Two and the barge, in danger of being carried under the stern. He skimmed his ball cap out of the sea as we quickly lifted him aboard to try again. This time, he easily scrambled over the gun'l and onto the deck.

Bishop disconnected the fuel cans in Gosling Three and cast them into the sea. "Some poor bastard shrimp fisherman can use those," he barked over his shoulder, slashed his boat and jumped into Gosling Two.

We had been carried away from the boarding net while Bishop dispatched Gosling Three. "Larry said there's work for you and Rubio, Jimmy. You're next," Keener said and slipped over the crest of a swell, returning us to the barge's stern. Bishop and I jumped onto the net at the same time.

Keener raced fifty yards up the side of the barge and turned, slowly making his way back. He lightly brushed against the rusty plating, timing his approach with the waves. "Piece of cake," he shouted, drew his bayonet as he approached the net. He was in water up to his hips on the rapidly sinking boat when he grabbed the net and the outboard disappeared beneath the sea. The next rushing wall of water lifted both of us as high as the side of the barge, still clinging to the net, and fell away. We dropped, slamming into the steel sides. Stunned, Keener fell back, his left leg tangled in the boarding net. When I reached him, he took my arm and pulled himself upright as another wave broke under us.

We held on. Coughing and sputtering, Keener dragged himself up and over the top and fell heavily on the deck. I managed to roll over the gun'l to fall on top of him.

"Late as usual, Donlin," Larry groused.

My feet were tangled in a huge coil of bright yellow detonation cord.

Then Larry turned his dark mood elsewhere. "Keener," Larry shouted, "get to the highest tank and keep your eyes open for two amber lights, one over the other."

"Over here Jimmy," Rubio called, "and bring Gates' bags." I slung the det cord over a shoulder and struggled with a heavy satchel. "That one's for you; mine's by the hatch. We have orders to sink the barge. Take a look at this drawing," he said, spreading a sheet of rough brown paper as the rain whispered over the deck. He held the beam of his flashlight on an elementary drawing of the barge in profile and indicated where charges should be placed to take the barge under as quickly as possible. The timing of the blasts would be staggered. He planned to blow the stern five minutes after the bow.

"The first charges will take the bow down first. When the second set of charges go off, more water will rush in, of course, but the barge will already be settling deeper at the bow. The blown deck and bottom plates at the stern won't be able to trap any air. She'll go under in less than two minutes after the second detonation," Rubio assured me.

"And this is a good idea, right?" I asked. "The nearest land is twenty miles to the northeast and it's ugly and nasty when you get there. Why is this a good idea?"

The top of a breaking wave swept across the deck and carried the sketch away. "We got an update on the ANGRC-9. The Russians are pissed, Jimmy," Rubio explained. "Somehow, our guys know that in a few hours, maybe less, the Russians will torpedo this barge and all the Navy vessels they can before we take them out. In any case, our prize has us teetering on the brink of World War Three. We'll never get it to the Canal Zone."

"Why not? Donahue thought a lot of the idea a few hours ago. What changed his mind?" I demanded to know.

"There are two subs out there to make sure we don't. At the time, Donahue didn't know about the subs and their orders. The Russians won't let us keep this tub to use against them. If they sink it, we would probably retaliate. The second half of their orders, given in the same paragraph, is to sink all American Navy vessels in the area, and we would certainly retaliate. But if we sink the barge, then they don't have to, and they don't have to sink any of our Navy vessels. Everybody can step back and take a deep breath," he shouted over the wind.

"This is insane," I yelled back at him as another wave broke over the side, sending a cloud of spray arching over the deck. Again we were doused with cold water from the deep, open sea. "Gates is dead, along with nearly fifty Cubans. We could have this goddamned steel outhouse blown from under us any minute and all this makes sense to you, doesn't it, Rubio," I screamed at him, a gust of wind driving the last words back down my throat.

"At this point, it makes more sense than not sinking it. It makes sense because what we've accomplished has made a surprising difference in the world. We proved the Russians intended to distribute nuclear warheads and delivery systems to an unstable Latin American outlaw nation," Rubio answered. "Let's do what we can to survive our contribution," he said, laughing.

"Why is all this so complicated?" I asked. "We did everything that was asked of us and a lot more. Our necks were on the line for this barge and now Donahue wants us to sink it! All I want is to go home."

"If you want things to be simple you should have taken your job in the oil fields. Nothing's ever as simple as you expect. The Russians wanted it, now they don't want it. We wanted it, now we're going to blow it to hell. That's as simple as anybody can make it. Now, are you going to help?"

"I want to hear you admit that it's insane, that's all," I said, straining to be heard over the storm."

"I had the same reaction you did. Again, it's not as insane as not blowing it up," he said, "just ironic."

"So we set off fireworks and take a swim?" I asked.

"The cruiser they promised is behind schedule because of this storm, Rubio said in a lull between gusts. "The Navy is sending a sub to take us off. We're watching for it now."

"In the meantime, set the charges, but we don't set the timers until the sub has boats alongside. Then you set the timer at the bow, then run the length of the barge and set the timer at the stern. Remember, you alone set the timers."

CHAPTER TWENTY-SEVEN

And Jonah was in the belly of the fish . . . .
Jonah 1:17

I removed my life jacket and tied it securely to a handrail on a small deck structure. Rubio shifted the large coil of detonation cord from around my neck to a more secure over-the-shoulder, bandoleer fashion. "You don't have a single cap or detonator on you. That's for your safety," he said, "but after I set my charges, I'll leave one taped to that ladder in the forward hatch where you'll go below. Come back out the same way and the detonator will be there. Insert it into a C-3 potato along with the knotted end of the det cord and push this switch when you see me flash 'Oscar.' The timer for my charges will be on the hatch closest to the net, and you set that one, too. Clear?"

"Oscar; that's dash-dash-dash, right?" This job was for real, the charges bigger than the training packs. Big enough to blow me to hell-and-gone! DAMN! Calm down! Nervous. Of course, dash-dash-dash is 'Oscar.'

FABRIQUE DE GUERRE NATIONAL, BELGIE encircled the dial, inside the clock face. The timing device looked like a large nail or my mother's oven thermometer, except for the teardrop-shaped bulge at the tip, a detonating charge of cyclonite which sets off the "potato" of C-3 and det cord. Cyclonite. Dangerous material, very sensitive to impact. This was not a piece I'd used before.

Almost as if he could read my mind, Rubio tried to reassure me. "It's the most reliable timer in the world, without exception, but don't get careless with it."

I picked up the two large canvas bags, and made my way to the forward end of the barge, staggering and swaying like a drunken oaf across the heaving deck.

It took me fifteen minutes to reach the hatch at the starboard side near the bow. Undogging the hatch took longer than it should have. Gates had inspected the interior while it was still at Rio Sucio. He had been strong and liked trying to intimidate us with senseless displays of strength. This seemed to have been one of those displays. He secured the hatch with far more muscle than needed. I couldn't budge the levers. Sitting on the deck, I kicked them clear and swung the cast iron hatch open with a thunderous crash.

The beam of my flashlight swept the interior as I struggled with the satchel and descended the pipe ladder. The forepeak was an unfathomable madness; bulkheads seemed to flex, jump and tilt. Gratings, catwalks and the miles of tubing clattered and scraped, fighting the strapping and welds that bound them in their places. In an unexpected plunge, the deck dropped from under me, and I fell across the bag, bruising my ribs on blocks of C-3.

As I started to rise, I heard the sloshing of water, yet the deck was dry except for a patch of rainwater under the hatch. This was not the rage of the pounding waves, but a light, rhythmic wash inside the barge, under the bag of explosives and the deck where I sprawled. The beam of light found another hatch, smaller, round and made of welded plate. Lifting the cover, I threw the beam of light into the opening. The barge was double bottomed. The bottom hull plates were awash with rust-stained seawater three feet below. This is where the charges must be placed.

Clipping the flashlight to an overhead I-beam left my hands free. Dropping the det cord on the deck, I tied an overhand knot in one end and embedded it in a double fist-sized lump of C-3 from the bag. This is where the timer-detonator would be inserted. The explosive material, a military grade plastique, had cooled in the dousings and resisted being formed. Leaving enough cord to reach the top hatch, plus three wraps around its raised frame and hinges three times, I tied the det cord to a hatch dog, dropped the remainder of the coil through the lower access port, and followed it down with the bag. Gates obviously never looked down here when he made his inspection.

I don't speak or read Russian, but I knew what they were. The gray cubes with pale blue Cyrillic sent an electrifying chill through me. The barge was already packed with explosives.

Originating somewhere in the interior of the barge, passing through a hole in the transverse framing, a dozen colored wires were bound together with spiraling tape. I could see more bricks as I swept the beam of my light down a longitudinal C-beam. One wire left the bundle and disappeared into the top of a gray cube taped to the recess of the C-beam. The larger bundle of wires made a right angle turn toward the port side of the barge. No doubt, more cubes were packed against the steel framing beyond the circle of my light.

Rigged for electrical detonation, but from what point and by what means would the packages be detonated? There were two possibilities, both bad. The detonating device could be by a radio receiver, and the Russian subs wouldn't even need a torpedo, only the right code on the right radio frequency.

The second possibility was a timer, maybe already ticking. Fear is not our friend; it clouds judgment and makes us clumsy. Still, my discovery tied my gut into knots. Was there enough time to locate and disconnect the radio detonation device, or whatever it may be?

Fuck it! There's no time, I thought to myself. Rubio said our sub would be here any minute. We had to blow the barge as soon as possible. If the Russians sank the barge before we did, they would simply move to phase two and attack our ships, including our taxi to the Canal Zone. Nothing would have been accomplished, and war would be declared within hours. It wouldn't do my disposition any good, either.

The storm boomed with a different voice in this cramped, wet catacomb. The vertical motion of the barge was extreme but slow, lifting high and plunging deep, often with a jolting impact, the shock transmitted directly into every cell of my body, followed by the rush of foul water.

Perspiration flooded my eyes and breathing became difficult. Bad air? Nerves or claustrophobia? It didn't matter which; I had to check it. If I pack up now, it'll only take more time to get someone else down here to do the job. Time we may not have.

I taped det cord and C-3 against the C-beam, opposite and off-set of the Russian charge, which was nearly double the size of everything in Gates' bags. Next, I tied a spur of det cord over to the Russian package. The double charges were staggered to shear beams by blasting in opposite directions at the same instant, tearing out deck and hull plates with them.

Trailing out det cord and dragging Gates' bags, I followed the wires to the next four bundles to rig the same kind of tandem charges. In the confines of this space, shielded by steel plate, and much more concerned with the time element than worries about bullets or shrapnel, I decided the usual dual harness would be a waste of time and material. Anyway, tapping into the Russian charges made better use of my limited det cord.

Soaked to the skin, elbows and knees scraped and cut from crawling over rusted hull plating and raw-edged framing, I made my way to place another four charges in the next section behind the bow. When I had finished, sixteen bricks of C-3 had been placed in tandem with Russian packages. Time to get out!

Favoring an ugly collection of bruises from the storm's buffeting, I retraced my route to the hatch, dragging the last few pounds of C-3 in Gates' bag, back through the steel maze, back to the pipe ladder and hatch..

Drenched a dozen times, the flashlight began to dim and flicker. As I pulled myself through the interior hatch, the light finally quit, surrounding me in a darkness so dense I could taste it. The topside hatch was now a barely visible gray disc that swung above me, occasionally illuminated by flashes of lightning.

Exhausted, nerves strained, I felt for the det cord and satchel, made my way toward the ladder and with trembling hands, started to climb. I found a quilted, waterproof, cloth bag containing the detonator wired to the last tread of the pipe ladder. Carefully placing it in my shirt pocket, I threw the cord and satchel through the opening and climbed onto the deck.

After circling the hatch frame three times with the cord, I reached into the bag to pack more C-3 potatoes a few inches apart. There were five of these, intended to blow the hatch and frame right out of the deck. I reached for what felt like the last package of C-3. It was a half box of Baby Ruth candy bars! Gates had his priorities.

I repositioned the lumps of C-3 around the hatch and inserted the detonator. For the first time in what seemed hours, I stood up and straightened my back. A quick succession of cracks and snaps like popcorn ran the length of my spine. Stiffly, I climbed to the top of a deck structure, holding onto the lip of a ventilator, and threw the satchel and candy bars into the sea. I strained my eyes to see through the rain and spray looking for Rubio's signal.

"It's blacker than my Aunt Evelyn's Buick," a voice complained in the darkness. It was Jack Bennett, standing watch for the mysterious amber lights.

"Our taxi's here, Cowboys!" Larry shouted from the darkness. "Donlin, why didn't you answer Rubio's signal?"

"I just now climbed out of the hole, for one thing. And my light burned out, for another. And I never saw a signal through the rain and spray. Are we ready to start the timer?" I asked.

"Yes," Larry shouted, "then we run for the boarding net. Get in the boat with your duffel. Bennett, throw your rifle over the side and move out! Jimmy, you and I are to be the last men in the last boat. Don't slow me down!"

"Did Rubio tell you about the bonus packages?" I asked Larry who dropped a beam of light on my work. Carefully, I moved the switch that started the minute hand twitching over the face of the timer. "Twenty minutes. Plenty of time."

"The Russian charges? That stuff scares me," Larry confessed, as we struggled toward the stern. "It's unstable and really doesn't like sea water. It absorbs the salt and chemically changes. If it's the old type, it can weep pure nitro, then detonates itself. Primitive stuff! I want to be in Tulsa when this thing blows!"

"Loro Azul, here we come," I hoped, and jogged off toward the stern.

"Twenty-two fourteen. Let's be at the net in five minutes. Think we can make it?" Larry asked, stumbling into me as the barge lifted on a swell.

"Not a chance. Without the storm and with a little light, maybe. I figure eight minutes, at best," I said, drenched again in a breaking crest.

Then I saw the amber lights. They were on the mast behind the con-tower of an ancient Balao class WWII diesel/electric submarine. Its mast bristled with odd-looking antennae. Rolling and pitching, shiny in the rain and lightning, it stood to leeward, three hundred yards off the stern of the barge.

The storm broke heavily on the black con tower, and swept the decks with solid water. One inflatable, with Nelson and Eddy Rush already on board struggled half way to the sub. Then, I glimpsed Keener's rain-soaked necktie streaming in the wind. Two more inflatables with four men each paddled toward the cargo net. "There's our ride," I shouted to Larry, pointing at the first raft as a sailor in one of them reached for the net. He desperately hung on to keep the raft in position, waiting for Larry, Rubio, Bishop, Jack Bennett and me. I didn't want to keep them waiting.

CHAPTER TWENTY-EIGHT

In dim eclipse, disastrous twilight sheds
John Milton

The barge swung broadside to the waves again, wallowing in the deep canyons of black water and staggering with the impact of the waves. Bennett threw himself over the steel cable lifelines and onto the cargo net.

Bennett kept a death grip on the manila lines of the boarding net and braced himself against the surging and pounding. I shouted over the wind as I struggled to put my life jacket back on. "How much time did you give us on this end, Rubio?"

"Same as the other one. Twenty minutes, exactly," he replied.

"Then we have nine minutes between bow and stern charges, and eleven minutes until the bow charges blow," I shouted. "I'd rather have Gosling Two under me! Hope to hell these guys can paddle!"

We threw our duffel into the rafts. The other three swung onto the net while I set the second timer. In the electrical displays, I could clearly see the thin hand sweeping away seconds between this moment and a horrendous explosion that would end a Russian threat and send me home to my mother's cooking. Like Gates and his Baby Ruth candy bars, I had my priorities straight, too.

I followed Bennett, Rubio and Larry, descending faster, passing, urging them to stop dawdling. "What's the hurry?" Bennett asked.

Distracted by a metallic scraping noise, we looked up. As the barge rocked in the swells, the ANGRC-9 slipped across the diesel-slick deck, hung a moment under the lowest lifeline, then broke free, trailing the remnants of the antenna, to plummet into the sea. It missed Jack and Larry by a foot.

"Other than that, we have only a few minutes until the bow charges blow!" Rubio shouted. The sailors in the first inflatable dragged Larry into their raft and motioned us to hurry. We looked at each other as a huge swell heeled the barge to starboard, swinging us out several feet and lifting the rafts to the level of our feet. All three of us let go of the net and slipped into the oily sea beside our rescuers.

The swabbies in the nearest raft dragged me aboard first. I sat up in time to see the muzzle of my BAR slide under the lifelines. Jarred by something behind it, the weapon tumbled off the deck to splash into the heaving madness that surrounded us.

Rubio struggled into my raft, and Bennett dragged himself into Larry's. "Get us out of here," Rubio shouted. Two twelve-volt batteries plunged into the water between the rafts.

The dungaree-clad seamen struck the sea with deep-biting paddle blades and we shot down into a trough toward the sub. "Never mind the sub!" Rubio shouted. "Just get us the hell away! The sub can pick us up after she blows!"

"Sorry, sir. We were ordered to bring you to the Hammerhead," Chief Bo'sun's Mate Haggy barked. "What kind of time margin do we have, sir?"

"As of right now . . ." Rubio said, looking at me; I held up four fingers. "Four minutes, and the sub is too goddamned close to the barge."

"Look," the chief shouted, pointing over the bow. "The Hammerhead's makin' way for us. She'll get us out of here in time. Tipton, pick up the beat."

"You don't understand. It's not just our explosives. There are Russian charges, too, a boxcar load about to go off and we're too damned close," Rubio roared.

At that moment, our overloaded rafts were lined up exactly between the barge and the slow-moving sub. Like the chief, I did not yet comprehend . . . then it struck me. The barge, if the blast severs the towline to the tug now acting as a drag, would be propelled backward by the blast and we and the Hammerhead would be run down!

Looking astern, Rubio saw the barge lift on a swell barely fifty yards behind us. "Chief, take us to port, ahead of your sub. Don't ask why, just do it," Rubio commanded.

"Aye, aye. Forty-five degrees to port," the chief responded. A seaman on the port side complained he was from Iowa and didn't like surfing.

We shot down the faces of a succession of waves, the raft lifting and twisting with the power of the waves and our weight. We gained another forty yards. The sub increased speed and changed course to intercept us, almost out of the danger zone.

Rubio nervously checked his watch. The sub hit us with a search light and picked up speed. The other raft, off to our right and slightly ahead of us, cursed at the course change and increased distance to the sub, drew up to our stern. At last we were no longer lined up behind the barge.

Haggy turned the boats to face into the swells as the sub crept past our starboard side. The bow of the barge exploded with ear-splitting thunder. A tower of flames shot outward and a massive yellow flash blew the sea flat. The force expended itself away from us. Topside and deck plating split away, tearing and peeling back. Large fragments of steel plate moaned overhead, and the water around us hissed with sheared rivets, banding, and broken pipes. The seaman who didn't like surfing tumbled forward, an iron strap embedded in the back of his left shoulder.

Bennett pulled him out of the way, snatched his paddle from the sea and took his place. "Dig in!" he shouted. We turned to see the barge skimming toward us, catapulted by the blast, charging over the back of the last swell. The stern rose higher and higher, its bottom covered in barnacles and streaming sea grass.

The seamen and Bennett lifted us over another crest and we raced down into the trough.

The stern of the barge rose again as it passed us, water streaming from its ragged skirt of seaweed. Its rush spent, the next set of swells slammed directly onto the deck of the barge forward of amidships, sending clouds of spume high into the air.

"Holy shit!" the chief groaned. "What was her cargo?"

The wounded seaman groaned, and tore at the iron strap that protruded from his back. "Pull it out, Haggy! It could punch a hole in the boat," he groaned, and passed out.

"In ten minutes, we get a repeat on the near end. I don't want to be around," Rubio said.

"We have another problem," Bennett yelled at Rubio over the rush of another oncoming wave and the voices of the seamen trying to help the wounded sailor. "We have at least two punctured air chambers. We may have to swim the last fifty yards."

"We can make it to the sub!" the chief shouted, pulling himself off his position and handing his paddle to me. "Dig in! Stretch your guts! We gotta get Bobby to Stitches. We'll be aboard the Hammerhead in three minutes or I start peeling skulls! Now paddle!"

I pulled with the others and we lunged forward, stroke after stroke, stalling at the faces of on-rushing waves, and then waddling over their crests. I heard rhythmic thumps and turned to see Haggy working an air pump to keep one of the chambers inflated. Only a few yards behind Bennett's raft, we paused at a crest to calm the wounded man who had come round again, and I peered through the darkness for the barge, now lost in carbon-black night. In a series of brilliant lightning flashes, I saw it clearly, floating with half its length lifted from the sea.. The waves rushed up the decks, crashing over the tops of tanks, thundering, draping luminous veils of spray over the crane and spilling cascades of water out of the deck's scuppers. The grotesque steel megalith still resisted the power of the sea and the injuries we had done it.

CHAPTER TWENTY-NINE

There's danger on the deep.
Thomas Haynes Bayly

The sub, now past us by a hundred yards, threw its spotlight on the barge again, and swept the sea until we were centered in a bright ellipse. We heard the rumble of diesels and the Hammerhead made sternway to pick us up.

Rubio checked his watch. We still had three minutes until the second explosion. The hull of the sub glided past us, stopping when we were forward of the conning tower and the bow speared the on-rushing waves. The foredeck hatch opened and three of the sub's crew sprang out to pull exhausted men from Larry and Bennett's raft, then mine. Strong hands gently bore the wounded sailor across the deck to lower him down the hatch as the rest of us scrambled up the rust-streaked topsides, dragging our personal gear. Last aboard, Chief Haggy cast the rafts adrift.

Rubio raced to the hatch. When I got below, he stood beside an officer near an intercom to the bridge. "Tell the sonar man to take off his headset. There'll be another explosion any second," he urged.

The charges in the stern of the barge detonated and the entire submarine, the barge much nearer now, shook. The concussion of the blast battered our eardrums. A deep vibration penetrated every chamber, enlivened every surface. Deadly debris rained down the still open hatchway and rattled on the deck. Steel slammed against steel as torn plating boomed against the conning tower. We rolled to starboard and several hundred gallons of seawater poured down the forehatch, sweeping the last three of us off our feet.

The intercom boomed. "Clear the con. Secure the hatches. Pressure in the boat!"

The fore hatch closed behind us and the dogs compressed the watertight seals. "Dive! Dive! Dive!" boomed from the overhead speakers followed by successive horn blasts. The transition from diesel to electric was barely noticeable, but the shift to dive angle was unnerving, compounded by the reaction of still aching eardrums to the increased air pressure. Again, I felt myself in the grip of claustrophobia.

"Bow planes out," a voice boomed from the far end of a long passageway.

As we slipped beneath the tortured sea, the quick motion of the Hammerhead eased, and the uproarious noises of the surface faded and blended with the whine of electric motors and the orderly calls and responses of the crew at their stations. Familiar voices and laughter took the edge off. Somewhere down a corridor, section chiefs sang out damage reports. All secure.

It's over! Our job was done and we were on our way home, at last. In the next fifteen minutes, cuts, bruises, scrapes and sore muscles confirmed our task had not been an easy one, or without costs. Gates' duffel bag topped the pile, and several of us wondered what would become of its contents, and who would write the letter home.

We were escorted down a cramped section of a passageway to rest, out of the way of the sub's crew. Soon, a cloud of steam, the smell of foul clothing and strong soap promised a long denied comfort: a hot shower.

My cousin, Lynn Marie, in a temper tantrum after filing for divorce, once swore that if you undressed men and stood them on their heads, they'd all look the same. Maybe, but the naked guy throwing up in the head is Nelson.

The team members from the first two rafts stepped fresh from the shower to the ship's store, which was opened to provide fresh, dry clothes. Nelson took his time.

Larry, Rubio, Bennett and I were next. Our bags, still weeping seawater, rested in a pile near the showers. The contraptions and fresh water restrictions aside, the hot water was a blessing. Several of us had developed saltwater sores. A corpsman applied ointments, which gave us almost immediate relief.

When we were dressed, a voice on the overhead called us to a debriefing in the officer's mess. "Bring your gear," the voice commanded.

We followed a crewman to a small room painted with many layers of creamy white paint, chipped to bare metal in some places, and great pasty patches and runs of fresh paint in others. The mess was larger than I'd expected, filled with two lockers, a bookshelf, four small tables fitted with rails, and benches, all bolted in place. "The Captain's favorite," the steward informed us, as we pounced on the mugs of coffee and a tray of peanut butter and orange marmalade sandwiches.

The tugboat crew, scrubbed and fed, smiled at us from the farthest table. The tug captain chattered a greeting through a dense mustache and flashed several gold-crowned teeth.

Chief Haggy, who had been with us in the raft, puffed up in the companionway and started to call us to attention. "Belay that, Chief. These are civilian passengers, not Navy personnel," one of the two officers drawled.

"Aye, aye, sir," the chief acknowledged. "Will that be all, sir?"

"Stick around, Chief. Have some coffee with us," Mr. Warren replied.

"Thanks for picking us up, Jack. This could have been a very unpleasant evening, otherwise," Larry said, matching drawl for drawl.

"Our pleasure, Larry. I hear you lost somebody. Who?"

"Gates. I should have been watching him closer," Larry explained. "Pretty damned rough out there. I just didn't . . ."

"It wasn't anybody's fault," Rubio interrupted in Larry's defense. "He took the same risks as the rest of us. We lost him because he couldn't get past his fear of water and he wouldn't follow orders."

"I understand. I'm sorry you didn't get to bring all of them back this time," Mr. Warren sympathized. "I know that has always been important to you.

"But right now, we have to pick your brains about what you've accomplished. Have you heard from Donahue in the last few hours?" Mr. Warren asked.

"Briefly. He told us to sink the barge and abandon all but personal gear. We've been busy since then," Larry replied.

Nelson bolted past Chief Haggy, looking pale and tired. He got a whiff of the peanut butter sandwiches and dashed away again. His second entrance a few minutes later was more composed.

We talked for awhile about taking the barge, about Cubans, the photographers, and recent developments with the Russians. "You were told to drop a hot potato. Personally, I think we should have called their bluff," Mr. Warren asserted.

"They have twenty-four subs off the US Pacific coast right now, from Seattle to Valparaiso," Mr. Warren said. "All of them would be at the bottom of the sea within the first hour of open hostilities. What the hell. Maybe some of our ships would, too. But just like I said in my last report, if this keeps them afloat, why would I care about an over-sized breadbox?"

"There is one final matter," Mr. Warren said. "Our follow-up team reported someone purchased a camera at the Iguana Palace on the way down. That's a violation of your security restrictions. One at a time, send your men down to the chief in that curtained-off area and strip. Dump your personal gear right here on the floor. The rest will remain to confirm that I'm taking only camera and film," Mr. Warren gestured to the far end of the mess.

Nelson went first. Keener elbowed me in the ribs and nodded to his empty coffee cup. I understood. Slipping two rolls of exposed film out of my bag, I dropped them into Keener's cup as he nibbled on a peanut butter sandwich. He covered them with a paper napkin. Keener hated peanut butter.

Chief Haggy motioned for me to step up next. There was nothing to be done about the roll of film still in the camera. The bag was up-ended and the Kodak Brownie clattered across the floor.

"Donlin, is there any more film?" Mr. Warren's tone conveyed a serious level of exasperation. Maybe my defiance of security policy reflected negatively on him. Should I have cared?

My insides tensed. The lie I was about to tell could possibly land me in prison. "I lost a bag of gear when we were still at Base T," I confessed. "Gates said it was the *compañeros*, but I think he took it. Anyway, the only exposed film I have left is what's in the camera. Do you still want me to strip?" I asked.

The affirmative response was barely out of Mr. Warren's mouth. I kicked off my new sneakers and pulled off the white T-shirt. I'd started for the far end of the room, unbuckling my web belt, when the second officer finally spoke. "That won't be necessary. We have the camera and film," Captain Hightower said through a cloud of cigarette smoke.

A Marine sergeant presented himself to the seated officer. "Mr. Gardner's compliments, Sir. You're needed on the bridge. Now, sir."

I put my shoes and shirt back on, and returned to my seat beside Keener. As Captain Hightower rose, Keener dropped the napkin with the rolls of film into my hand and asked for a refill of coffee.

Lost forever, regretfully, were the only photos of Oscar Escobar cooking, Roche in a rare good mood, the *compañeros* and Oscar Escobar playing soccer, Rubio, Eddy and Larry playing tag football against Keener, Nelson, Bishop, and Bennett and one close-up shot of another visiting troop of howler monkeys. Also lost, I believe, were the only two photos of Gates ever taken when he wasn't giving the photographer the finger: asleep in both frames. The rest was unexposed film.

In an instant, all hell broke loose! Alarms sounded general quarters. The lights went out for a few seconds and came back on, red and dimmed. Sleepy-eyed crewmen rushed to their stations with shirttails flapping and unlaced shoes thumping on the steel deck. The galley erupted with the clatter of cooking pots being secured and stoves being turned off.

Chief Haggy told us to stay put as he bolted aft. Mr. Warren slipped into the booth with Keener, Rubio and me. Rubio nodded at Warren. "In case of attack, you guard the coffee?"

"In the last twelve years," Jack Warren replied, "I've done my sea time, but this is my first trip on a sub. I'm here as liaison for Naval Intelligence. Take a look at my shirt. Do you see any dolphins there?" he asked, tapping his chest with a thumb. "Hell, no! At this point, I'm a passenger, just like the rest of you."

An ensign entered and saluted. "Mr. Warren, I'm instructed to report to you from the bridge. May we speak?" His nametag said TAYLOR.

"Permission granted to speak freely here. These are the men who took the barge in the first place. What's the situation?" he asked.

"There are blips on the sonar, sir. Two subs, not ours and they're closing. Range is nine thousand yards. Captain Hightower said you predicted an encounter, sir?"

"Thank you, Ensign Taylor. Keep me informed," Mr. Warren snapped back. "Damn, but I hate being right sometimes. Gotta go to the bridge."

We heard loud commands down the passageway. The whine of the electric motors rose to a higher pitch and the boat lunged forward. The room tilted, then swerved, and I spilled my coffee. Pressure built in my ears. Leveling out, we swerved again, in the opposite direction. From the distant bridge, I heard Ensign Taylor's tense voice sing out, "Still closing, sir."

"I thought they wanted the barge sunk," I said to Rubio and Mr. Warren.

"My God," Warren blurted, and dashed for the bridge. I heard angry voices order him to clear the bridge, but he insisted on speaking to the captain. Again he was ordered from the bridge. A brief scuffling noise progressed down the passageway and two armed Marines roughly shoved Jack Warren into the room.

Rubio stepped between the Marines and Mr. Warren and helped him into our booth. "What the hell was that all about?" Rubio demanded.

"Those fucking subs have no reason to be here, unless . . . . did anyone actually see the barge sink?" Mr. Warren demanded.

Rubio and I looked at each other. "No," we replied in unison. "But we blew the hell out of both bow and stern. There must have been half a ton of explosives," I said.

"She's floating on her tanks, isn't she?" Rubio interrupted.

"That's my guess. We have to confirm, otherwise our captain's now confronted by two Russian subs that might just be trying to finish your job and then take us out," Warren grumbled.

"This had better be good, Jack," Captain Hightower blurted as he swung into the room. "You don't waltz onto a bridge for a conversation when we're at general quarters."

"I know that," Jack Warren said. "Don't stand down on my account. I've just learned that the barge might still be afloat. Can you bounce a sonar signal and see if it's still on the surface? I'd bet that's their target, not the Hammerhead."

The captain glared at Commander Warren. "You don't get to shoot craps with my boat. But we will bounce a signal." The captain departed for the bridge.

Mr. Warren lifted a cover at the end of the table and extracted an ashtray. It was a large ceramic dish with a bright emblem of an eagle, anchor and lettering encircling the emblem with gold rope edging. "US NAVY CRIMINAL INVESTIGATION DEPARTMENT."

"That's the current game at the embassies and most Navy offices, jenking they call it, petty theft of items with departmental emblems. The farther away from your own department the better," Mr. Warren explained. An elaborate item for burning rubbish, I thought. Larry and Mr. Warren smoked and waited with two Marines posted at the narrow companionway.

Captain Hightower burst into the mess. "My exec has the con for two minutes. Did you place any charges to break the tanks?".

"Negative," Rubio admitted. "We strapped our packages to blow out the barge's plating at the bow and stern. But the tanks had open access ports. They should have filled by now."

"They haven't," Captain Hightower interjected. "The ping was as clear as a church bell. The damned thing is wallowing on the surface.

"Good news about the other subs, though. I put us on a course away from the barge and ninety degrees off Ivan's course," Captain Hightower said. "They didn't change course. That means you were right, Jack; they're interested in the barge and not the Hammerhead, at least for now. By the way, the goddamned smoking lamp is not lit"

Jack warren grimaced at his breach of regs and snubbed out his Camel. "At least not yet. If I remember correctly, you said we're not armed well enough to take on two Russian subs," Commander Warren said, dropping his butt into the objet d'art. "This is a discrete radio monitoring vessel, a Big Ear, eavesdropping on those Russian trawlers, mostly. We have tons of radio gear, four language specialists, and two experts on Russian submarine tactics, but we're short on ordnance?"

"As of directives dated June of nineteen-sixty, even we have to be armed," Hightower said. "Half the crew wants to take on the Russians right now. The intel group thinks they're insane. I know they're nuts."

"Why? The Navy doesn't hand out boats to pussies. Sub commanders are supposed to be real tigers." Larry said, stamping out his Camel.

"Think of me as a de-clawed tiger. We're not at war, for one thing," the captain said. "Not yet, and I want to keep it that way. As for armament, it's a joke! We carry only six WWII type torpedoes; slow, short range, low power, and not very accurate. But installing modern weapons with guidance systems on the Hammerhead would have cost more than building a new sub. Twenty years ago, submarines were hard for another sub to hit." Captain Hightower said with a grimace. "That's where you'll find most congressional thinking, twenty years behind. The Russians have this boat out-gunned in number and sophistication of weapons."

"Then let's not do anything rash," Mr. Warren drawled.

"Not a chance!" Captain Hightower laughed. "Carrier based ASW hunter-killers will be on scene within two hours. If the Russians start something, they'll finish it."

CHAPTER THIRTY

Delays have dangerous ends.
Shakespeare

Fresh from her brief morning coffee break, Ruth Hobbs enunciated into her intercom, "Comrade Poliakov has been routed through on line three, Mr. Crane." Too much of her time was spent screening calls. Lydia Franks would manage them while she and Mr. Crane sat in a briefing room with the big boys in one hour and thirty-three minutes.

"Mr. Poliakov, I hope you have good news, because if you don't, then I have really bad news," Lon Crane blurted into the mouthpiece.

Gregor Poliakov seethed into the receiver. "I haven't called to listen to crude threats. If this is your way of managing serious communications between our governments, then I have nothing to convey to you." He waited for the clumsy apology he wanted to hear. He heard only faint static and the rhythmic pulsing of blood racing through the capillaries in the soft tissue of his own ears. Once again he must deal with the frustrating American obstinacy he had learned to despise.

"You seem to have confused my office and staff with the protocol section of the State Department, Mr. Poliakov. Did you not understand what I said?" Lon Crane asserted. "You have subs inside Panamanian waters, deployed in an offensive array against one of our subs. Now you want to talk about my manners? Be sure to include that in your next communiqué to Moscow," Crane drawled into the mouthpiece.

"I have called," Poliakov insisted in a voice distant and impersonal, "to inform you that your submarine is not the object of our exercise, and suggest you so inform your submarine commander. Our vessels are there to dispose of a certain Russian property. There is no reason for alarm. When the matter is concluded, our submarines can send their reports and the matter is closed, unless they are fired upon!"

"Not even close!" Lon Crane argued, suppressing an urge to shout into the receiver. "Our activities have been within the territorial waters of a nation under treaty with the US, and with that ally's consent and participation. You have entered territorial waters without prior consent and have placed warships in an attack posture. You expect this to be ignored? Your subs have the entire Pacific Fleet on Red Alert."

"Choose your next step very carefully," Poliakov warned. "Your inflexibility has brought both of us to the brink of disaster. All for the sake of . . . what did your man in the field call it? . . . 'an over-sized bread-box,' I believe. Make sure your words and actions can justify the results."

"The very same applies to you, Mr. Poliakov," Crane threw back. "No more phone calls. You play your hand and we'll play ours. As I understand, the barge and its cargo no longer exist. You have two hours to get your subs outside Panamanian waters or we'll sink 'em!"

The buzz of the dial tone roared in Poliakov's ear, a monotone dirge, a dirge for a deceased career.

Crane tore through the folders on his desk looking for the last communication from Golfo de San Miguel. He had just read it a few minutes earlier. In Jack Warren's concluding paragraph, he found the line ... "a lot of trouble for an over-sized bread-box." Less than two hours old and the Russians were quoting from his Navy Intel reports! Did they now have the technology to unscramble the Navy's ultra-low frequency radio transmissions? Did they have access to codes and schedules? Worst of all was the possibility that someone from his office ... No! That was not possible.

When he talked to Ashley Knox about the route of Warren's report Knox turned white. "It's worse even than you think! I just got a call from the boys at National Security Group. The Russian Embassy just sent Warren's entire report to Moscow."

Lon Crane knew the drill and hit the panic button.

Two hours later Lon Crane arrived at his supervisor's office, and the bloodhounds were waiting.

A three-part coordinated effort to discover the source of the security leak was taken straight from the textbook. Three separate but related messages were devised. The first would be sent by the same relay station as the message Gregor Poliakov had quoted. A second message, similar, but with a few distinctly different phrases would be sent at the same time from the embassy in Panama City, the point of origin of the intercepted report quoted by Poliakov. A third false message would be hand-delivered to Lon Crane's office and placed in his normal loop. The National Security Group would wait to see which of the three versions the Russians relayed. The specific fragment of information in one of the three communiqués would identify the avenue of the leak, narrowing the focus of the counter-intel search.

Certainly Poliakov realized by now he had slipped in quoting Mr. Warren, but the counter-intelligence specialists didn't need another direct quote. With an arsenal of monitoring installations and search techniques, any communications containing a quotation from the "bait" sit-reps would be enough. If Lon Crane was correct and Poliakov was bragging about his access to secured material, an unbelievably stupid mistake, they would know within the next twelve hours.

In the last four years, since Lon Crane was promoted from the field and made a coordinator/analyst, there had been no fewer than two hundred similar intrusions into the American intelligence network around the world.

Embassies were favorite targets. Most leaks involved personnel who would sell out their country for less than impressive sums of money. Objectionable lifestyles such as gambling, homosexuality or drug habits made staff members easy targets of blackmail. Other leaks could be associated with tawdry affairs between American Embassy clerks, bored bureaucrats and lesser functionaries that well-tutored Russian field agents found "irresistible." Only a few leaks involved disenchantment with the status quo of the western democracy/capitalism aggregation, or an extreme shift in ideology. All had been discovered by routine "scrubbers," tracers and discrete ferret operations conducted by counter-intelligence monitoring groups.

It was the best of all possible worlds for Crane who considered himself the worst actor in Washington DC. "Go back to your office and act normal," they had told him. How could he act normal, knowing that someone in his office might be a sell-out to the Russians? Fortunately, the tensions generated by the situation in Panama were more than enough to justify his extreme agitation, and he didn't have to act normal, whatever the hell that was.

Lon Crane was in one of his "flash-back" days. He was born and raised near San Angelo, Texas, and people in his office had learned to step lightly when he wore his Stetson, shit-kicking cowboy boots and ribbon tie that had always been acceptable attire in San Angelo. It was considered a costume on the beltway, suitable for TV appearances of senators and representatives who needed to make a splash in the news broadcasts of their home districts, strictly for local consumption.

That didn't cut it with Robert Longstreet Crane. He felt uncomfortable and pretentious if he dressed any other way, his naval officer's uniform being the only exception. In the office, his "Texican" clothes were usually accompanied by a set jaw, a sour disposition, and caffeine-fed jagged nerves.

In his first year as a naval cadet, he'd had a rough time sleeping without the smell of stock pens, and struggled through an exceptionally difficult adjustment to uniforms. His grandfather helped him find middle ground. Steeped in fundemental religion, his grandfather advised "Render unto Caesar those things which art Caesar's." Lon conformed to the Navy's uniforms, structure and policies, but kept in secret reserve his unique, non-conforming self, those things which art Lon Crane's. He learned, eventually, that's how everyone coped.

With elbows on his desk and his chin supported by his fists, he pondered the events in Panama, tried to visualize the face of an old-timer named Donahue. He wondered about the competence and reliability of an aggressive and overly ambitious Naval Intelligence officer named John Warren. And he wondered about the team they had recruited for a high-risk project that suggested, for the first time, the early stages of ulcers his friends promised him would come with this job.

Lydia Franks tapped lightly on his door and entered. She carried a black lacquered tray bearing coffee and graham crackers, Crane's usual late afternoon snack, a habit he'd picked up from the grandfather who had raised him.

She picked up his Stetson from the desk with one hand and placed the tray with the other. Floating across the room, she carefully hung the heavy gray felt hat on the rack beside the oak file cabinet. The slightly rolled broad brim partially obscured an oversized print of Charles M. Russell's "Bronco Busting."

"Good afternoon, Mr. Crane," Miss Frank mouthed in her most formal voice. She'd learned that the slightest familiarity with males would be eagerly interpreted as an expression of personal interest. "Mrs. Hobbs is still on her coffee break, and then she will pick up your hand-carry-only afternoon mail. I promised her I'd fill in until she gets back. Is there anything else I can get for you?"

"No. Close the door on your way out," Crane mumbled, nibbling at his first graham cracker. "Wait! There is one thing. Send Commander Knox in here."

"He's right outside, looking at your maps."

"Charts," he corrected.

"I'm sorry, Sir. They look like maps to me," she said, and slipped out.

Ash Knox ambled through the door, still looking toward the outer office and the pink angora sweater that Lydia Franks filled out so well. She 'brought out his best.' Eyebrows pinched together in a mock expression of deep concern, he said, "When I was a young and ignorant kid, I used to enjoy sea duty. It could never top this place."

"Don't even think about it," Crane offered in a brotherly tone. "When things go sour in your personal life, you don't want to have it in your face all day long at work.

"Have a seat. I've been thinking about the Panama problem. The cruiser won't be at the rendezvous for at least another four hours, right?"

"Roughly four hours," Knox replied. "With this storm in the operations area, it might be as much as seven hours. It's an old boat, twenty-six knots was the best the old girl could do in her last sea test," Knox said defensively. "She's headed to the bone yard for sure, probably within the year. Wait a minute. You're thinking what I'm thinking. If the barge is blown, what the hell happened to Donahue's team?"

"Make the call, Ash. Find out if they're holding a position in the middle of nowhere in those little rafts, or headed for the canal on their own."

Ten minutes later, Commander Knox returned to Lon Crane's office and found him standing behind his desk, bent over a single sheet of paper. "You won't believe this!" Ash blurted. "Donahue and Warren already solved the problem. The team is on the Hammerhead right now, but there's bad news. The barge is not yet on the bottom."

"What? The last report said the barge was blown to bits!" Crane faltered, his voice quaking with exasperation.

Ashley Knox related the guess that the shattered wreckage floated on buoyant, undamaged tanks and showed no signs of sinking. "I don't care if the Russians torpedo the barge. But their orders said sink the barge and all our Navy vessels in the vicinity. Now the barge is still afloat and the Hammerhead is in a stand-off with two Russian subs."

"Do you think the Russians will still follow their orders to the letter, even though we've already tried to sink the barge?" Ash asked.

"Do you think the Russians are in the habit of turning subs over to officers who won't follow orders? This whole project has degraded into a high-level guessing game, but we don't have to guess on that one," Lon Crane moaned.

"The barge has not yet reached the latitude mentioned in their orders, so maybe they won't fire. Or, they haven't fired because it could provoke an attack from the Hammerhead the instant the sonar man picks up a launch. Captain Hightower won't use torpedoes to sink the barge because the Russians would interpret that as an attack on them. Besides, that out-dated boat is almost totally defenseless against an attack from those Russian subs. What a screwed up mess!"

"The Keystone Kops Go to Sea," Crane grumbled. "What sort of air resources are available?"

"Between two carriers due west of the operations area and land-based aircraft, we have enough ordnance to obliterate the entire Las Perlas Archipelago. But the Russians, the Hammerhead, and the barge are too close together. We could send a strike on the barge at night and take out the Hammerhead, too . . . or the Russian subs."

"Put your guys on alert. Go through the under-secretary for authorization but keep security buttoned down as much as possible. If nothing is resolved by noon, we'll designate the barge a bombing target. Meanwhile, if the Russians launch against the Hammerhead, I know the President will authorize a retaliatory strike," Lon sighed. "What about using the Hammerhead's deck gun to sink the barge? The Hammerhead . . ."

"No good," Ash interrupted. "It was removed last year to give her a knot and a half extra speed. There are six torpedoes in the racks and she has a small arms locker. That's all she carries."

* * * *

The red lights of general quarters washed everything in a nightmarish crimson. I had made a brief trip to the head and upon returning, edged my way between the Marine guards posted at the officer's mess. For a moment I had a clear view of the bridge. My eyes strained against the dull, detail-starved glimpse of men exhausted at their stations after four tension-filled hours. No one moved or spoke. Most watched the sonar man, some with prolonged stares, some with quick glances.

SOund Navigation And Ranging . . . SONAR. Pointed straight down, the depth sounders in the rafts had worked the same way, but SONAR units were more powerful and far more sensitive, and they could be aimed horizontally in specific directions. The speed of sound underwater is known. An electronic noise, a "ping," is sent out and the receiver divides the time between the ping and the echo to determine the direction and distance of a bounced signal, providing direction and distance of a target.

"The Russians haven't moved, Sir," Colgate reported to Captain Hightower.

"Sir, I have something!" Near Colgate, at the far end of the same instrument console, sat Redmond. He was twenty-five, pudgy, the result of a fondness for ice cream, and heavily tattooed. His bright red, close-cropped hair seemed to fade away and reappear in the glow of the red lights as he rolled his head and tweaked a series of knobs. But there was something different about Redmond; he was more than a back-up sonar man. Stenciled on the sleeve of his chambray shirt was an odd insignia . . . a lightning rod overlapped by a quill, he was with the National Security Group. His real purpose was to try to identify the Russian subs by prop and machinery "finger-prints" by hydrophones.

He wore a black headset with a spiraling wire connecting him to deadly realities in the external world. He read his screen with the focused, uncanny precision of a piano tuner. Redmond monitored the hydrophones and the screen of his oscilloscope. "I heard one large splash, Sir, then a series of four smaller ones . . . another . . . now another. None of them are in the same place. They seem to be making a straight line between the barge and the Russian subs."

"Shit! Now we can really sweat!" Hightower exploded. "Sub-hunters. They've dropped hydrophone/sonar radio buoys. By now they think they know exactly where everybody is relative to everybody else. I only wish they did."

"Range to Ivan?" Hightower called out.

"Two thousand yards. Slowly closing, sir. Looks like they'll pass behind and above us."

"What's our position, Mr. French?"

"We're closing with the continental shelf," bellowed a figure hovering over the plotting table. "At this depth, course and speed, we'll run aground in eleven minutes, thirty-one seconds."

"Maintain course and speed. On my command, come right ninety degrees."

Hightower eyed his watch, counting off seven minutes, the bridge filled with a cold silence. "Mark! Sing it out, Mr. French."

"Our course is one-one-eight true, running parallel to the continental shelf."

"Ivan's off the screen, sir," Colgate reported. "He might be playing hide-and-seek, hovering over one of the dumping grounds on the slopes of the shelf. He's trying to mask his sonar signature. All kinds of signals down there; old ships that didn't quite make it to the canal, Navy and civilian dump sites. We have to wait for him to give himself away, sir."

"Listen for him," Hightower ordered. "He's afraid of the sub-hunters on the surface. That's the sonar he's hiding from. Mr. French, give me a plot to the barge."

The sub stabilized and hummed with the activities of a well-trained crew. Taylor discretely made a damage report, the result of abnormal maneuvering. A water pipe of questionable integrity broke off the galley hot water heater. The most low-tech unit in the boat fractured and lost two hundred gallons of hot, fresh water. Repairs commenced immediately.

The sharp turn had thrown the Marine on guard at the officer's mess into a bulkhead, breaking his nose and gashing his eyebrow. The medics found him sitting on the floor, daubing at the streaming blood, cursing. "My last good shirt!"

"The barge is at one-six-zero degrees, relative, eight thousand yards," Mr. French read off.

"Give me a confirmation, Colgate."

"Aye, aye, sir. I read one-five-six relative at eight thousand, two hundred yards, sir," Colgate corrected.

"Sir, the barge is on the surface. The storm should have driven it much farther north-west," Billings added from the plot table. "It's only a half mile north of the last confirmed position, sir, slowly drifting toward shallow water"

"There's a deep counter current pulling the sunken tug against the storm. What about the Russian subs?" Hightower demanded of Colgate and Redmonds.

"They've split up, Sir. We still have one trailing us. He's closed to six thousand yards. The other is still off the screen."

"Mr. Billings, Mr. French, plot us a course toward the barge."

"Sir, can't the sub-hunters take out the Russians now that they're more dispersed?" asked Taylor.

"The Navy would like to think so, but you and I know for a fact we haven't made any real advances in anti-submarine warfare since WWII. Their attack on the Russians could just as easily take us out. Crazy Ivan is more predictable than the outcome of an ASW air strike. Let's hope it doesn't come to that," Hightower grumbled low enough for only Taylor, Billings, and French to hear.

"What if we take out the barge? Do you think the Russians would stand down then, sir?" Taylor asked.

"No way of knowing. But if we launch our torpedoes, the Russians could read it as an attack on them and they would launch against us before our torpedoes reached the barge," Hightower replied.

"I have an idea, sir," Taylor said. "Permission to leave the bridge?" Hightower nodded in the affirmative. "Come with me, Chief Haggy," Taylor ordered and dashed to the officer's mess to talk to Larry and Rubio.

Within a few minutes, Haggy returned to the bridge. "We have two volunteers to finish the barge, sir. They think they know which tanks are keeping the barge afloat and where to place charges."

"We don't carry explosives, Haggy. You know that. I've signed every manifest for goods taken aboard and . . ."

"Yes, we do, sir," Haggy insisted. "The Hammerhead's own scuttle charges, sir. They were on my inspection schedule four days ago and they're serviceable. We have dive gear forward in the maintenance locker."

* * * *

Lucky DiMarco, a paissano the size of a baby grand piano, barred Ruth Hobbs from the cafeteria line. "You're going to be a little late for your coffee break today, Mrs. Hobbs," he said in a mock apology.

She turned and tried to retreat the way she had come, but encountered Barton Sims and Paul Gains. They were both familiar faces from staff briefings. She was often assigned the task of taking notes and typing the reports, including input from the two of the three men who now confronted her.

"Bart, do you know this young man? Why is he being rude to me?" Ruth asked, her voice trembling.

Sims looked past Ruth, past DiMarco, and nodded in the affirmative. Two more figures across the room closed on a bald, sharp-featured man with a security clearance card clipped to the lapel of his dark suit. Quickly folding his sports section, he tried to rise. He was roughly seized from both sides and escorted to the foyer to join Mrs. Hobbs.

"All right, Bart, what's this about?" Mrs. Hobbs protested in a voice less tremulous, bordering on defiant. "You work in security. You know me, my clearance is current and as clean as yours. Why are you here with that hard expression on your face?"

Gains took Ruth Hobbs' purse from under her arm and, from a side pocket, withdrew a tiny metal cased camera, pale gray, the size of a pack of gum. A sunbeam from the skylight played on the fifteen-inch chrome chain that swung from a corner, a clever device that gauged the perfect distance for photographing documents.

The sharp-featured man was forced to join the group. Sims took the folded paper and massaged it, then unfolded a few pages until a thick pack of hundred dollar bills stood dull green against the gray newsprint. "This would buy one hellova lunch in here, Mr. Lindsay. Mrs. Hobbs, did you know that Mr. Lindsay has been on our watch list for a year? You, however, are a complete surprise."

Gains jerked his thumb toward the heavy young man with curly black hair. "This is Luciano Di Marco from the Justice Department. You'll spend the afternoon getting acquainted with him," Mr. Gains said.

Rushed along with men holding her elbows, Ruth and Barton Sims bumped into Lon Crane who took all this very badly.

* * * *

The pre-dawn night blazed with stars. Rubio and I scrambled up through the forehatch and the con tower's deck lights suddenly burned them away. Haggy and two crewmen shoved Rubio and me off the foredeck in our tiny inflatable, burdened by satchels of explosives, two waterproof lights and dive gear. Taking up our paddles, we dragged ourselves over the rolling swells.

It took us twenty minutes to reach the barge; it floated vertically with over a hundred feet of mangled plating looming against a streaked morning sky. Now a mass of wreckage with mangled plate and twisted railings and pipes. It stood in grotesque silhouette, the a sun just peering over the eastern rim of the world. Hightower had placed us favorably in relation to wind and current, assuring us the trip would be a quick and easy paddle and we labored toward the brooding hulk. We were still nearly exhausted when we pulled into its long shadow.

"You're an idiot, Jimmy. I could have done this by myself," Rubio grumbled as he tied us to a bent stanchion that held the last fragment of the boarding net. "You could have caught up on your sleep."

"I was bored," I replied. "The devil finds work for idle hands, my grandmother used say. D'you suppose this is it? The devil's work I mean."

"I doubt it. If we bring this off," Rubio said, "nobody gets hurt, no war, and we go home. Only good things happen. Doesn't sound like devil's work to me. Help me on with my tank, will you?"

Our conversation sounded reminiscent of the one we'd had on the barge only the night before, but this was different. This time I was scared, truly scared. A broader array of dangers stood against us, even US forces, and the Russians could send us a torpedo at any second. And even though the storm had stumbled its way across the Comarca de San Blas on its way to assault Jamaica, the sea conditions remained large and confused. We had no way of knowing how long the wrecked vessel could remain afloat. With just the right surge, the right roll, a bulkhead might collapse or a tank fill, sending the mass of rent steel into the abyss with Rubio and me caught inside or tangled in wreckage.

I needed reassurance from Rubio, whose judgment I trusted, who was about to take the same risk I would. My veneer of adolescent invulnerability had evaporated in the past two weeks of tropical heat.

A series of powerful explosions to the northwest startled us enough that we nearly upset the raft. A mere mile away, a line of white plumes erupted from the sea behind a low-flying plane and a pair of choppers hovered with cables in the water.

Another plane with navy markings droned in from the south, banked, and roared toward the barge and us. We held our breath, expecting to see depth charges tumble into the water somewhere near. No bomb bay opened and the P2V-7 Neptune rose to a thousand feet and joined his fellow hunters to the northwest.

At last we could breathe again. The ashen grimace of fear faded from Rubio's face, and I hoped mine, and we returned to the preparations for our dive.

Rubio showed me how to start the pre-set fifteen-minute fuse and where to place the charge to take out the two suspect tanks. "Pull this ring to strike a match and light the fuse. No matter how deep or wet, it will burn. Haggy says we can't waste any time getting to the surface and paddling away."

We rolled over the sides of the raft and sucked at the mouthpieces. The regulator fed us air, the valves opening and closing with a clack. Nodding to each other that the equipment checked out, we fastened on weight belts, wrapped arms around the satchels, and rolled over the side. A cloud of bubbles trailed behind in our descent.

Dawn thrust its dazzling rays through the surface of the sea and washed the mangled deckhouses in fluttering, shifting patches of light. Rubio and I hung on bent rails of the starboard side of the barge, only ten feet down, and we were pushed and shoved by waves left by the of dying gasps of the storm.

The heavy ballast belts took us down faster than I wanted to go, the bundles of explosives, heavy in the rafts, were bouyant enough that they tugged at our elbows. Rubio, face distorted by the pressure at forty feet, appeared a dark gargoyle with bony cheeks and sunken eyes. We tested the dive masks and regulators again. Our single tanks of air would give us thirty minutes to set our packs of explosives and get back to the surface.

We were in a tug of war. The satchels were buoyant, but our belts of lead counter-weights forced us ever deeper. Rubio nodded and gave me a thumbs-up and swung into a jagged maw where a deck hatch used to be, the cover gone along with its coaming, and deck plates curled back like dried corn husks.

I slipped downward, over the shambles of deck structures and twisted ventilators, guided along by sliding down a four-inch pipe, one of the few that still seemed secured by its original bindings, and I passed over a huge hole in the deck, an entire section of deck or possibly a deck structure missing. We had placed no charges here, and so far as I knew, never entered this section of the barge. Then I remembered what Larry had said about how sensitive Russian plastique can be. Sympathetic detonation?

An unspeakable void loomed beneath my feet, the same black, boundless, insatiable monster that devoured Gates. It took me, swallowed me feet-first. The pressure was the grasp of a living thing.

The barge was a jumble of gray planes, variegated and sinister, sections torn and lifted. Cables and tubing swung with the pulsing current, groaning and clanking, maddened in ruination. At sixty feet, I fought the cold currents that tore at the broken plating. Pipes loose from their strapping waved in the surge like canes in a windstorm, rattling and clanging, eerie chimes against my eardrums. Deep rumblings and a soft, rhythmic booming emanated from the interior, and I wondered how Rubio fared.

At around seventy feet the pressure in my ears became unbearable, and a cold upwelling snatched my breath away. The current pressed against the steel remnants of banding and loose cables pointed to the depths as swaying, grinding pipe reached toward the surface. I followed the pipe too far. My foot suddenly jammed between the pipe and a deckhouse.

The vessel lifted on a swell and rotated into the current and I felt the grip tighten. The bones and tendons in my foot flattened and compressed. I could feel tissue separating and I groaned, strained against the pipe, trying to pull it free. Suddenly, the entire barge shuddered and rolled again, and my foot slipped from the steel grip.

With the light from my belt, I threw a beam across the shambles of the deck. The gray silhouettes of the tanks assigned to me were now a few yards above. A school of silvery fingerlings swarmed through the beam and disappeared into a split in the deck plating. Everywhere, streams of tiny bubbles drew dotted lines toward the surface. Two smoky spirals intermingled with the bubbles, probably diesel fuel leaking from a ruptured tank somewhere below. Maybe the scuttled tug still hung on a straining tow line.

With my ears shrieking from the pressure, I struggled with how to reach the tanks. If I let go of the pipe, my counter-weights would only pull me deeper. If I dropped the belt, the buoyant satchel would tow me back to the surface, the job still unfinished.

The solution was obvious, but I was nearly paralyzed by the cold and by the pain in my ears and a fear that edged toward panic. This wasn't my element. The realization that the dive mask's tiny air space and the minute air supply fed to me in short gulps enslaved me, bound me in a claustrophobic stupor far more pervasive than the confines of the sub or the bilges where I planted the first charges in the barge.

With my legs wrapped around the pipe, I pushed the straps of the satchel onto the crook of the arm that held the light. I used my free hand to remove three six-pound lead ingots, dropping two toward another flashing cloud of fingerlings below. The other bar of lead went into the bag of explosives.

Pushing off the pipe, I threw myself at the tanks and caught a handrail on the deckhouse beside the lower tank. Still too heavy, I sacrificed another lead bar. It thumped and banged its way into the abyss.

The eighteen-inch space between the two suspect tanks was now eight feet over my head. I pushed off the deckhouse and shot to the ventilator beside lowest tank and reached for the protruding connections. In a few seconds, the web belts were cinched tightly around the valve stems and the explosives were secured. I drew the fuse and igniter from a side pocket on the satchel and pushed the blast cap into the plastique.

I took the match in my hand and turned my face toward the surface. Where art thou Rubio?

Rubio hung above me. He signaled me to join him at the surface. He made a jerking motion, like starting a lawnmower . . . light the fuse!

I pulled the ignition ring sharply and a yellow flash lit up the deckhouses and tanks, and I began a slow ascent toward the surface. Breathe normally, breathe normally, and exhale slowly and completely, I repeated to myself.

Rubio was in the raft, tank, belt and fins off, his dive light, still on, kicked to the end of the raft. He lifted my tank while I was still in the water, threw in the light, and I climbed aboard. "Did you get all the way to the tank you were supposed to blow?" he asked as he untied the bowline.

"Yes," I said, shaking water from my still aching ears. "I lit off the fuse just before I started up."

"Then our charge will go off about thirty seconds apart, yours first. Let's paddle."

"Which way?" I asked. "Where's the Hammerhead?"

"Paddle down wind. The sub will pick us up no matter where we are. Right now we just need to get as far away as possible."

We pulled with deep and rhythmic strokes. The barge was a symphony of sighs, clangs and groans. Warped by the explosions, and now assailed by the waves of a dying storm, the sounds of its mangled corpse followed us across the sea.

At last Rubio dropped his paddle into the boat and turned to look back. At three hundred yards, we were much closer than I wanted to be. The memory of the first attempts to sink the barge were still fresh, but Rubio insisted that these charges were smaller and under water. "The Hammerhead can pick us up here as easily as anywhere."

The words were no sooner out of his mouth than a muffled explosion lifted a frothing white dome around the wreckage. The barge twisted and swayed and settled deeper in the water. Then the second charge blew. The barge tilted and slipped its jagged stern under the swells and disappeared.

We rested and watched the ASW planes as they made a series of passes over the sea where the barge went down. Suddenly, a dark mass streaked through the water beneath us and was gone, leaving our tiny raft to lift and sideslip, spinning in the turbulent eddies of its wake.

EPILOGUE

... it is a tale
Told by an idiot, full of sound and fury,
Signifying nothing.
Shakespeare

Rubio and I watched a helicopter circle the spot where the barge went down. Its rotors threw up sheets of mists that lifted over the blades to be pulled into the powerful downdraft and blasted back to the sea. The miniature hurricane enveloped the craft and swirled outward, flattening the sea beneath into a trembling, quicksilver bull's eye.

The chopper lowered a teardrop-shaped sonar unit under the surface. A minute later, it rose a hundred feet, hovered, retrieved its drogue and whined westward to join a second hunter.

Barely visible against the still gray west, Bird Dog Two was still engaged in tracking, his drogue cable streaming a rooster tail.

The huge disturbance under our raft had not been a fragment of the barge, but one of the Russian subs making a break for the open sea.

Rubio guessed that the presence of ASW units took the pressure off the Hammerhead. The Russians probably knew from their own sonar that the barge was on its way to the bottom. Now they had no reason to continue the engagement and very good reasons to scramble for an escape route. Running near enough to the surface to be visible to hunter/killer aircraft, the Russian sub sent a clear signal that they have abandoned hostile intentions.

We were not recovered by the Hammerhead. A heavy cruiser wallowed onto the scene, wrapped in a cloud of its own oily smoke. Rubio and I boarded her from our tiny raft.

Within an hour, the rest of our group was also aboard. Keener brought my gear along and made a noble effort to compensate me for the loss of my roll of film. He produced Mr. Warren's prize ashtray that he had stolen from the naval attaché in the American Embassy in Panama City. Keener said Mr. Warren mentioned that the attaché had stolen it from a CID office in Norfolk, Virginia. "Snibbing" or "jenking" souvenirs from various military entities was the current game among Navy personnel.

We made way for the Canal Zone. Upon arrival, we were immediately escorted to Cryder Air Force Base for an attempt at debriefing by State Department bureaucrats. Not one of them really knew who we were or what our mission had been. Since they were not our contract agency, we were obliged to tell these birds absolutely nothing at all.

We felt relieved to learn they were interested solely in reporting on the performance of the photo team and were openly frustrated and confused when they didn't hear what they expected. Eventually, they sorted that out, then discovered they had the wrong files. At this point, I formed an opinion of the State Department that has changed little over the last fifty years.

Things took a serious turn when the grim boys from the CIA took over. We were subjected to a six-hour grilling, one hour as a group and five hours individually. Satisfied that everybody's ass was covered and all pertinent records had either been turned over to them or destroyed in the field, they finally cut us loose.

While Donahue was old-time OSS/CIA, the photographers had been on loan from the Air Force. Frustrated and angry, Wilson Donahue forwarded Larry's verbal report to the State Department, the CIA in Langley, Virginia, and NSA headquarters at Fort Meade, Maryland, since all three had been involved in one way or another. As a result, the photographers found themselves disbanded and retired before their plane landed in DC, including Dr. Loomer. Small loss.

Happy to be out of the boonies, for three days and four nights we were constant inhabitants of Loro Azul's bar. We were clean again, dressed in new clothes, and obviously "fresh from the bush." New and shiny patches of pink skin, edged in tattered "feathers" of sunburned skin, covered each of us. Backs and shoulders were sore to the touch and everything we did seemed a study in slow motion.

On the morning of the second day, one of the bartenders told Larry that the old gatekeeper had died while we were in the boonies. The funeral had been large and well attended. Even executives from the Canal Company and the mayor's office stood among heaps of flowers and hundreds of mourners.

Larry disappeared for over an hour. He told us later that he's spent the time with the family and later with several of the cooks, the old man's best friends and fierce adversaries in thousands of domino games over the last fifty years.

We were in no hurry to leave by the second evening. The waiters and bartenders knew us by our first names and the stage performers dedicated some of their numbers to us when they learned our personal favorites. The rest of the patrons wearied of "Little Egypt" and "Poison Ivy." Our bar tab could have finished my BA and put me through grad school.

Casual banter about military life brought up my nickname from active duty, which re-attached itself to me. I'd learned to like coffee at intel school and I seemed to perpetually have a cup in my hand, earning me the radio call name of "Java."

On the second day, we visited Donahue. He was in the hospital with malaria again, but seemed cheerful enough. His bed was adjusted to a sitting position. Supported by pillows and a small stack of magazines, he assured us the mission was the perfect capstone to a long career, and this time his retirement would be permanent.

Nelson was in the same hospital. When he and Bennett ran aground on the flats, he'd inhaled exceptionally vile slime. The organisms in the mud were ecstatic with the accommodations and climate in his lungs and built a resort. This didn't do much good for Nelson's respiratory functions or disposition. We felt guilty for ignoring him earlier. We thought he had merely been seasick again. He had looked gray and dull-eyed when they took him to sickbay on the cruiser.

Smiling but a bit sluggish, Nelson joined us at Loro Azul on the third night, coughing, popping antibiotics and knocking back. Through the amber haze of Monte Carlo, he started the most vigorous debate ever attempted by the group without prodding by a trained interrogator . . . . who fired the flare the night Eddy and I strung the telephone wire?

Bennett and Keener argued that one of the mentally diminished photographers was playing with a flare he'd brought and accidentally set it off . . . or, not so mentally diminished, set it off intentionally to force us to abort the assault while they were so dangerously close. Besides, there's no way to 'accidentally' set off a parachute flare.

The rest of us argued that even Woods wasn't dull-witted enough nor Roche so vindictive as to be suicidal. I'm sure Roche knew there were several of us who would have killed him with much less provocation.

Ross Bishop alone thought it was Gates, but I never understood how he reached such a conclusion.

Eddy Rush, Larry, Rubio and I believed it to be a third Cuban sentry, a roving scout. We based our theory on the boot prints at both sides of the swamp, which matched the tread pattern on the boots of the forest sentries. Then Bishop reminded us that the Cubans' boots were of American manufacture with the same tread pattern as our own, even two of the photographers, bringing us full circle, back to Woods and Roche. The issue couldn't be resolved with any greater certainty than this. Thin evidence, the others agreed, but the third Cuban scout was the only explanation I would accept.

The return flight to the US was an almost exact reverse of the flight down, except we slept more and Eddy couldn't get up a poker game.

We parted swearing our entire team would get together for Thanksgiving in Las Vegas. It never happened. I was back in school and the others picked up new contracts. They were probably engaged in absorbing the culture of some third-world country whose name they couldn't even pronounce while they blew the hell out of its real estate.

That September, I threw myself a small party. On the third day, I woke up in the TV room of Thatcher Hall, filthy, stinky, and paralyzed with a hangover.

A local TV magazine program, "The Ida Blackburn Show," featured an interview with an Oklahoma City couple who had adopted a child from a Central American orphanage. The little girl had an Embera Choco style haircut.

A couple of friends dragged me off to see a movie: Marlon Brando, Natalie Wood and Karl Malden in "One-Eyed Jacks." I slept through most of it.

When the stupor wore off, I discovered that most of my friends were children: scatter-brained, self-indulgent and spoiled. As the semester wore on, they observed that I had become withdrawn, my sense of humor forever lost. I just wasn't much fun to be around anymore.

For the first few weeks, the redhead in my English class, the one who didn't like me, became permanently and warmly attached to my arm. There were ample benefits. When I began to tighten up the money and developed a budget to make it last, she turned butterfly and flitted away. I was content. Somehow, the way I earned that money didn't fit with how she wanted to spend it.

For reasons unclear at the time, the Dean of Men, who was also a full colonel in the Oklahoma City Army Reserves, knew of my trip "down south," but fortunately not in detail. He had assisted in the personnel scan to locate me for Larry Abbott. He liked his military conflicts straight up, and didn't condone little para-military transgressions. For the next three years he made my life miserable.

* * * *

Shivering on the cold morning of 10 Feburary, 1962 , twenty men, a mix of military, CIA and State Department officials,stood at the American Zone side of the bridge that spanned the Havel river, the border between East and West Germany. Half past eight, four cars ground to a stop at the far end, and dark figures emerged to assemble, a mirror of the ominous group on the American side. A thin and haggard member of the assembly stumbled from a brisk shove to emerge and take a few hesitant steps onto the steel bridge. From the clot of Americans, an older, hard-faced man in a heavy overcoat and felt fedora, separated himself and ambled through the crust of snow to stand facing Francis Gary Powers. They continued their slow walk. Powers looked back at the older man, slight of build, with sharp features and thining gray hair. Powers had just been exchanged for Soviet master spy Rudolph Abel, KGB director of espionage in the US, who had been sentenced to thirty years. American negotiators managed the affair without the leverage of a monstrous, lumbering barge.

In the closing months of the Cold War, in an unprecedented open exchange of information, the Russians disclosed that Powers' U2 had been shot down by an SA-2 missle.

I took Captain Abbott at his word and requested my name be purged from CIA and NSA records. I was satisfied until 1981 when I attended a gun show at the Disneyland Hotel and signed up for a door prize. The raffle ticket asked a lot of unusually detailed questions. Most of them I left blank.

In a few weeks, I began receiving mysterious calls at odd hours. Voices I thought I recognized asked about "a little financial infusion," and asked if I would "enjoy working in a tropical climate." I began to suspect that my name was still on file somewhere, if not with my old employer, then with someone from the old group, curious to know if I might be the same James Donlin they'd known twenty years earlier. Or some idiot was sticking his neck way out recruiting off the raffle cards.

I saw Larry Abbott twice after we returned. The first time was a year after my trip to Panama. He tried to recruit me for a job in the Middle East. My Arabic is no better than my Spanish. I declined.

A year later we met at a political fundraiser, a barbecue on the lawn of a state senator's home in Oklahoma City. A candidate for governor was being honored. I was dating the candidate's niece. Larry tried to recruit me again, this time for a job in Malaysia. It would have been interesting work as a member of a contengent of bodyguards for oil company executives, and for good money. Determined to finish my last year of school, again I said no.

The last I heard, Larry had suffered a serious injury in a car accident on the DC beltway. After recuperating, he bought a motel north of Dallas and settled into semi-retirement.

Over the years, I saw quite a bit of Eddy Rush. I even tried to smooth over a serious rift between Eddy and his father who still had hopes of him going to med school. Not a chance in hell.

Eddy always had money, a flashy car and a girl who looked like last month's centerfold. I envied him. He always had prospects, an angle, an edge. He tried to interest me in some of his projects, but I knew that I'd be letting myself in for serious trouble.

Eddy had become an adrenaline addict. He knew how to make big money, but more important than the money, he needed to be constantly kicking at a snake. He craved high-risk, life-threatening enterprises.

He smuggled diamonds out of South Africa until someone needed the bounty money. Running guns in a couple of banana republics kept the hackles up on the back of his neck and he made more money than anyone could possibly need. Then he tried his hand at smuggling refugees. Then drugs. He had a lot of competition.

It all ended in nineteen eighty-six. Through an odd set of circumstances involving a tattered photo and an unmailed letter addressed to me, the San Diego Police Department asked me to provide a preliminary identification of a body.

It was Eddy.

He had been found in the parking lot of the Chula Vista marina, hands tied behind his back, beaten and shot twice in the back of the head.

The snake won.

The next week was spent in the most heart-rending task of my life. I flew back to Oklahoma with Eddy's casket and tried to console Dr. Rush. Eddy was not just the only son, but the only child of a lonely, bent old man who had worried away his later years over Eddy's life-style. Dr. Rush's eyes revealed what filled his heart. He knew that I too mourned Eddy, but he also blamed me for failing to turn him from his path of certain destruction. In my heart, I felt he was probably right.

Lately, dreams and memories have come into sharp focus. When something in a conversation or a passage in a book hits a trip-wire, forgotten images flash into my head, vivid and real. In the depths of dreaming there are smells of the beach at low tide, diesel oil, the latrine and sweat-soaked fatigue shirts. Wide-awake at breakfast with my family, I've drifted away into the past, my wife's cooking a blessed contrast to the taste of treated water from the Lister bags, the metallic whang of Donald Duck orange juice and Swedish C-rations.

Larry and Rubio credited me with twenty to twenty-five "suppressions" in the attack on the barge and they remain vague shadows framed in the sights of an ancient, murderous weapon. I feel no satisfaction or guilt for knocking them down. Yet, with amazing clarity, I remember the encounter in the forest while laying wire, provoking knee-jerking, teeth-gnashing, sweating dreams in the middle of the night.

I have looked for things in these experiences, things which, in reality, just aren't there. No great truths, no moral lessons, no sense of satisfaction, no glory, no manly pride, no sense of patriotism. Still, they were two weeks that shaped my life, and in some ways, warped it.

We, The Expendable

Funerals are for the living,
I've often heard it said.
Last rites are for the priests,
And oblivion's for the dead.

James Brendan Donlin
St. Jude Hospital
Cardiac ward
Fullerton, California